THE DOOR ON THE SEA

THE DOOR ON THE SEA

Caskey Russell

SOLARIS

First published 2025 by Solaris
an imprint of Rebellion Publishing Ltd,
Riverside House, Osney Mead,
Oxford, OX2 0ES, UK

www.solarisbooks.com

ISBN: 978-1-83786-378-5

10 9 8 7 6 5 4 3 2 1

A CIP catalogue record for this book is available from the
British Library.

Designed & typeset by Rebellion Publishing

Printed in the UK

For my sons
Chet Dylan and Aiden Carl

Dedicated to the Kooyu <u>*Kw*</u>*áan—*
though scattered, not forgotten

CHAPTER 1

LONG AGO, BUT not *looong* ago, in the days of sun and sail before humans hacked down ancient trees, melted ice caps, and sooted sky and land with black smoke, raven got caught.

Salmon.

With raven, it's always salmon. A freshly grilled slab of salmon lay steaming on a table. Of course, the table was inside a house, and the house inside a village, and the village on an island, and the island in an ocean where salmon swam in endless, silver processions.

"I should keep flying," raven thought to himself as he floated by the open door and saw the salmon. "Ignore the smell and keep flying." He was late, you see, for a meeting. Raven flew past the house, but then turned back and circled in the air about the door.

No one appeared.

He flew into the house and landed on the table next to the salmon. "Just a taste," raven said, "and then off to my meeting." He pecked a bite. Delicious. He pecked another bite.

"I deserve the whole thing," raven said aloud. "They can't start the meeting without me." A smirk curled at the back of his beak. "And stupid fatheads must learn not to leave cooked salmon sitting near an open door." He hopped onto the slab of salmon, grabbed it in his claws, and was about to fly off when the door slammed shut. A boy, maybe a man, or a boyish man, from the People of the Sea, stared at raven and smiled.

How to describe the People of the Sea? The have their own name for themselves but we can call them the *Aaní*. They live far away in the north where the earth has crumbled into islands scattered across the sea. If you've never been there, you can see the Aaní homeland in your mind by imagining the ocean washing onto the barnacled rocks and seaweedy shores of an enormous island; above those shores are fields of wild grasses where the Aaní build their villages. Beyond those villages are forests of spruces, cedars, and pines, which grow up the sides of massive mountains. The mountains, of course, are snow-crowned. Now imagine hundreds of such islands strewn across the sea. Greenness on the ocean's blueness.

But you're worried about raven, yes?

Raven flew up to the ceiling, looking for a way out. "No smoke hole?" he yelled. "I hate these modern houses." The Aaní build their homes from trees fallen in the forest or washed up on the beach. They're reluctant to cut down trees, for they know that trees are very much alive. An Aaní house is a bit larger and longer than yours, perhaps, but very comfortable and warm, for there's always a fire in the hearth, which is made of stone and fitted with a metal chimney running up through the roof. Red and black screens and tapestries of animal designs add color and give meaning to an Aaní home, like pictures and paintings give meaning to yours.

But you're still worried about raven, no?

The Aaní boy grabbed a canoe paddle from a paddle rack near the door and smacked raven's less vocal end. "Ouch!" raven cried. A feather flittered down and landed on the table. "That was a tail feather," raven complained. "I need those."

The boy picked up the feather. "I'll keep this."

Raven, of course, can speak all languages human and animal. A few older Aaní can talk to animals. Not dumb animals like the jackass or cow, who don't have much to say, but the smart animals like eagles and wolves, who often have a lot to say. But the Aaní who speak those languages are very old and very few in number.

Raven saw an open cupboard and flew into it. The boy shut the cupboard door.

Raven was in the dark.

"Let me out," raven yelled.

"No."

"I'm raven. I demand you let me out."

"You're *a* raven," the boy replied. "And a thief, too."

"Of course I'm a thief, you dumbass," raven cried. He heard an odd, scratching sound outside the cupboard door. "What are you doing?"

"Tying the cupboard handles together so you can't get out," said the boy.

"Let me out," raven said, "and I promise I'll do whatever you ask." He pushed against the cupboard door with his wing. It didn't open.

"You're a liar," the boy said. "I know you of old." The boy liked that saying. It was a saying storytellers used.

"I can speak every language human and animal," raven said. "I'll eavesdrop on the elk and deer and let you know where they'll be this winter. Good hunting."

"The wolves can tell me that," the boy said.

"You don't speak wolf," raven said.

"How do you know?" the boy asked.

"Because you're a smelly-ass moron who steals tail feathers that don't belong to him," raven yelled. He pushed against the door with his chest but it didn't budge.

The boy stayed silent.

"Do you hear me?" raven yelled louder. "You're a stupid boy who smells like dog crap after skunk-eating time, or skunk crap after dog-eating time, and all the girls hate you, and you have no friends not even a make-believe friend because you are too stupid to know what make-believe is."

The boy kept silent and waited. He would keep raven locked

up for a while to teach him a lesson. Raven hurled himself into the cupboard door but couldn't get out.

"Hey, know what?" raven asked quietly. "You have a fat head. I didn't mention that earlier because I didn't want to hurt your feelings, but your head is very fat. And you have moldy eyes. What a horrid way to go through life. A moldy-eyed fathead. I pity you. Blubberheaded whales pity you, even dumbass animals like bears pity you because of your stupid, fat craphead."

Raven slammed into the door again.

The boy kept silent, trying not to laugh.

"Such a fat head," raven said. "I would think you'd have more brains but with a head full of crapfat there's no room for brains."

The boy couldn't hold it in any longer and laughed aloud.

"Don't you realize who I am?" raven asked. "I'll have you dragged before the Aaní Islands Elders' Council for disrespect and then what would you say to spare your life?"

The boy thought for a second. What would he say? "I'd tell them that we humans don't control our actions. We control only the story we craft afterward." The boy put his ear against the cupboard. He thought he heard a faint chuckle inside.

"All right, what will it take for you to let me out?" raven asked.

The boy didn't answer.

"Okay, okay. Sorry for calling you fathead," raven said. "I didn't mean to call you that. That was an accident. I misspoke."

The boy kept silent.

"Okay. Hear me well, for this is both serious and dangerous," raven said. He was tired of being in darkness. It reminded him of a time very *looong* ago when there was no daylight. And perhaps this boy was different. "If you let me out, I can show you where a Koosh lost its dzanti. That dzanti can be all yours. You'd become the most powerful human."

There was that scratching noise again at the cupboard door,

and then the door opened a crack. One wide eye peered at raven. "I don't believe you."

"Yes, I swear it," raven said. He wanted to peck at the eye, but he was too tired. He'd flown a long way and still had a long way to go.

"No, you're lying, that never happened," the boy said. "A Koosh would never drop a dzanti."

"I'm telling the truth. I saw a Koosh drop its dzanti in a battle at Botson's Bay," raven said. "If you let me go, I promise to take you to it. It's a long way away, of course. A fathead like you could never make it there without getting killed. I stole it—"

"I believe that—"

"I stole it," raven said, ignoring the interruption, "and dropped it in the sea so the Koosh couldn't find it after the battle. They searched and searched for it, but never found it. I'll show you where it is if you let me go."

The Koosh (their full title is Kóoshdaka̱áa, but everybody calls them Koosh) were unlike any living being in the Aaní world. They were unlike any being in *any* world. No doubt in your world you have heard tales of beings so unhuman and horrifying that, even though they may live far away, just hearing about them feels like scaly claws ripping into your stomach from inside; and you banish these creatures to the edges of your mind and try not to think on them, but they lurk in your mind-edges holding knives and calling for your thoughts.

Such were the Koosh to the Aaní.

Every Aaní village was filled with fearsome stories of the Koosh and their treachery. Nobody knew how many there were in the Aaní world, for very few Aaní had seen them; the Koosh lived on an island far to the south. Rumor had it that for many winters there'd been only one until that lone Koosh had helped others enter the world. Aaní legend said the Koosh came from the otherworld, they could speak every language, they could change into any shape animal or human, they had scales instead of skin, and they took the Aaní and other humans captive and stole their souls and minds. Even more horrifying, the Koosh had the *dzanti*—a weapon so dreadful it could call fire from the sky and annihilate villages in an instant.

The boy opened the cupboard door all the way. He wore raven's tail feather behind his ear. "It's a deal. Take me to the dzanti."

Raven flew out and landed on the table. "That's no way to treat anybody, animal or human," raven said. "Can I have a bite of salmon to help gather my wits?"

"You can have a small bite," the boy said.

Raven ripped off a large chunk of the salmon with his beak and swallowed it whole. Ei haaw! Unearthly delicious. "A treasure like the dzanti is surely worth thousands of salmon," raven said. "I'll tell you where the dzanti is if you give me this entire piece of salmon and let me go." Raven rarely tasted such fine salmon. "I promise I'll be back in one moon to take you to the dzanti."

The boy thought for a moment. He could use the time to prepare. "Okay."

Raven grabbed the salmon slab in his claws. "Would you mind opening the door for me?" he asked.

"First, tell me where to find the dzanti," the boy said.

"Open the door and I'll yell it to you as I fly by."

The boy looked at raven and smiled. He opened the door.

Raven shot out of the house, the salmon, still steaming, in his claws. "Laters, fathead," he cawed back at the boy. The boy, still smiling, shut the door. Raven laughed as he took the salmon high up in a tree to eat all of it himself. There would be no sharing with the other birds. Let them lose tail feathers trying to steal their own salmon. Raven peered down at the village. Voices battled inside his head as he ate.

"What a dumb boy," one voice said. "He deserved to lose his salmon."

"He might be dumb," another voice said, "or he might simply be generous."

"Have you ever known any of the Aaní to be *simply generous?*" the first voice replied. "They are a treacherous people. They might give, but they always want something in return."

"You made him a promise," the second voice said, "and now you have to keep it and go again to Botson's Bay. Why in Yéil's name did you make that promise?"

"Because I was trapped," said the first voice, "and because that stupid boy surprised me with that bit about humans crafting a story *after* their actions. Besides, I never keep my promises."

"You never intend to keep your promises when you make them," the second voice said, "but you end up keeping them all the same. How in Yéil's name did you let yourself get trapped?"

"Dláa. Shut up," the first voice replied.

Raven finished eating, stretched his wings, and flew off toward the forest. "A strange boy," he said aloud to the wind. "I never got his name. And why was he smiling?"

CHAPTER 2

RAVEN ARRIVED LATE, heavy-bellied with salmon. The meeting place, known as Shaatleingagi, was a large, wave-shaped clearing made of grasses and a large circle of different-sized stones deep in the forest under the towering shoulders of a mountain known as Shaatlein, not far from the village where raven got caught. Gliding in the winds above the forest, he saw a group of humans waiting for him, sitting on smoothed stones in Shaatleingagi. *A káx yan aydél wé tlátgi*: the Aaní Islands Elders' Council.

Each island in Aaní land had an elder, lifetime-trained, to understand the health of the land and all living things. They met every summer to share their ever-expanding knowledge, but the meeting today was an emergency meeting. In the grasses behind the elders sat their apprentices, men and women of all ages. Every elder in the clearing had an apprentice—except one.

Raven groaned when he saw Íxt, the elder for the island on which they now met. Raven would have preferred to meet with some new leader, someone younger and easier to manipulate than that rancid old man. It had to be Íxt, of course, but raven was still angry with him. After all, it was Íxt's idea that had nearly killed raven. *No surprise Íxt hasn't found an apprentice*, raven thought. *That ancient sack of dog turds has no knowledge to pass on.* He glided over the pine treetops into the wave-shaped clearing and landed on a stone next to Íxt.

15

"Am I late?" raven inquired with faked innocence.

"The sun will be down near the trees before we finish our business here today," Íxt said.

"What is time to me? I am my own time," raven said. "Raven time." He turned from the old man's gaze and looked toward the treetops outside the clearing. Íxt continued to stare at him. Raven flapped a wing dismissively at Íxt's face. "Well? Get started before you die of old age, you decrepit skeleton. I won't interrupt."

Íxt turned to the council. "It's been a moon since we last met and agreed to gather knowledge. We meet today to share that gathered knowledge. Our relatives have traveled far to gather their knowledge and while I am aware that most living beings are not represented here in our council, we cannot wait for the goodwill of all living beings before we commit to action. Inaction could be deadly. I'm afraid I must be blunt and proceed without the usual speeches and long acknowledgments of our ancestors. The gathered knowledge is alarming. Koosh have invaded this world with their death dzanti. They are spreading evil and destroying villages and taking human slaves."

A few of the apprentices gasped. One apprentice, a young Aaní not much older than a boy, murmured aloud, "So they are real? The Koosh?" The young apprentice's elder turned from his stone seat and glared at him. "Forgive me for dishonoring my elder, my clan, and this council," the young man said.

Raven cackled.

"It's quite all right, Chxánk'," Íxt said to the apprentice. "This is an emergency council, and all are welcome to question. But be patient and silent until all the gathered knowledge is presented. Yes, the Koosh are indeed real. Many have now entered our world from the otherworld. And they have brought their dreadful weapons with them."

Chxánk's elder, whose name was Héenjá, spat a dismissive

laugh and said, "Dláa." Aaní elders reserve the word "Dláa" for children when their youthful fears threaten to spread and disrupt the minds of other children, or when an elder is annoyed with the nonsense of youth. No doubt you have elders in your world who dismiss youthful fears in similar fashion. But Íxt was no young man. Íxt was older than Héenjá.

Íxt glared at Héenjá. Héenjá stood up from his stone seat and glared back at Íxt. He wore a woven, conical, cedar-bark hat that formed into a long-beaked hummingbird at its peak. "Dláa, I said. Legends told to frighten children. Mere legend. Has anyone here seen a Koosh?" Héenjá looked around the council. Nobody met his gaze. "Anyone?"

The elders sat silent and lowered their heads. Raven shook with laughter.

"No, Héenjá," Íxt said. "None of us have seen the Koosh with our own eyes, but I know they're real."

"How do you know they're real?" Héenjá asked. He lifted the brim of his hat until the hummingbird's beak pointed skyward. The leather chinstrap tensed under his neck.

Íxt paused and sat silent for a moment. "From our eagle and whale relatives, who have seen the Koosh and have provided us with the knowledge we share here today," he said.

"I respect our animal relatives," Héenjá replied, "but they are prone to mistake."

Raven laughed.

"They are not mistaken on this," Íxt said.

Though neither elder had raised their voice, an uncomfortable tension weighed on the gathering. "Either way, this meeting is pointless," another elder said, breaking the tension. He wore what the Aaní call a 'naaxiin,' a heavy cape made of mountain goat fur dyed in deep hues of yellow and black and woven into intricate Aaní clan designs. Only the most respected elders could wear the naaxiin. "If our eagle and whale relatives are wrong, we gather here in vain, alarmed over nothing. If our eagle and whale relatives are right, we gather here in vain for we can't stand against Koosh and their dzanti." Several elders murmured their agreement. "This meeting is pointless."

Raven screeched with laughter. Héenjá sat back down on his stone seat.

Old Íxt held up his hands. "Please. Elders and apprentices. This is not a meeting to decide a course of action. This is a meeting to share gathered knowledge. We cannot see all the paths that may be open to us. Why give up before we even know the number and terrain of possible paths? Let us share our knowledge, go away and ponder, and then meet to decide which path to travel."

"Yes," said another elder. His hair was matted and covered with white down, which indicated he had access to, and understanding of, the world of eagles. He wore a necklace of eagle talons and spun a carved eagle-head staff in his ancient hands. "Every creature sees the world from different heights." He pointed his staff at raven. "Let us know all those heights before we give in to despair."

"This piece of wisdom from the very same moron who looks as though he eats his own crap," raven said. "You'll forgive me if I don't bow down to your intellect."

"Close your lousy raven beak," Íxt demanded, "or I'll tie it shut."

Raven opened his beak wide and glared in defiance at Íxt.

"Are you going to keep interrupting with your laughter and stupid comments or can we carry on with the meeting?" Íxt asked.

Raven, with his beak still open, pretended to snore.

"Now, tell us, Ch'aak'," Íxt said to the elder with the eagle-head staff, "what knowledge you have gathered."

Ch'aak' stood, lifted his eagle-head staff, and gazed around the clearing. "I was charged to verify the rumor that the Koosh have come in large numbers and fortified Saaw Island.

My eagle relatives inform me the rumor is true. Many Koosh are in our world. Saaw Island is entirely fortified. The Koosh have long been at work in the south while we Aaní have idled here in the north. Ramparts ring much of the island, and a fortress stands behind these walls."

There was silence in the clearing. A few heads hung low.

"How is this possible? It is said that for many winters there has only been one Koosh in our world," the elder wearing the naaxiin said. His name was Jánwu. He looked at Ch'aak'. "I'm afraid your eagle relatives may not understand what they've seen."

"My eagle relatives assure me the Koosh are now numerous in our world," Ch'aak' said. "And we would be fools not to believe them, Jánwu."

Raven laughed. "You're fools regardless of whatever feathered fatbrain you listen to."

Íxt scowled at raven. "Be quiet." He turned to Jánwu. "My informants also tell me Ch'aak' speaks the truth. I believe it has something to do with the dzanti. Somehow the lone Koosh who for so long inhabited Saaw Island has learned how to use the dzanti to usher his evil comrades into this world." Íxt turned to Ch'aak'. "And what of the Koosh prisoners? What of their human slaves?"

"So many they can't be counted. Moving like sand fleas over the island," Ch'aak' said. "Human slaves without number."

"Without number?" Héenjá said. "Come now, Ch'aak'. Everything can be counted. Especially people."

Raven laughed. "Koosh with dzanti and countless human slaves? You're dead. You're all dead." He touched his breast feathers with the tip of his wing. "I'll be fine, of course." He turned to Jánwu. "I may pee on your grave and that fancy cape a time or two in mourning, but I'll be fine."

"Will you please shut up?" Íxt said to raven. "Tell us, Ch'aak', what are the Koosh fortresses made from?"

"Stone, of course, as are the walls," Ch'aak' said. "A huge

stone fortress sits in the center of the island surrounded by a stone-wall maze built, it would appear, to trouble any visitor who attempts to attack the fortress. One river, dark and ominous, runs from the center of the island under a stone wall into the sea. From within their walls on Saaw, the Koosh can outfit massive war parties with their human slaves, and within their fortress they can't be touched." Ch'aak' sat down.

Íxt turned to another elder whose cedar-bark hat had a black-and-red orca design woven into it. "Tell us, Kéet, what knowledge have you gathered about the Koosh canoes?"

Kéet stood and addressed the gathering. "My whale relatives inform me that humans sail these canoes. These canoes are much, much larger than our canoes. And fast, with many sails on one canoe. The Aaní cannot win a sea battle against these canoes."

"What do your whale relatives say of the Koosh?" Íxt asked.

"My relatives have seen no Koosh," Kéet replied. "They assure me that humans sail the large canoes."

"Yet, from their vantage point in the sea, your whale relatives may not be able to see any Koosh aboard these canoes."

"Perhaps," Kéet replied. "But unlikely." He sat back down.

Íxt turned to raven. "Okay. I hesitate to ask, but tell us what you've seen. And cling to the truth. This is no time for your lies, foul bird."

"I was charged to nearly kill myself on the whim of an old fool named Íxt," raven said. "Rumor among smarter birds"—raven turned to Ch'aak'—"and by that, I mean all other birds besides eagles..." Raven turned back to the gathering. "Rumor among smarter birds said a large number of Koosh canoes left their home on Saaw Island and headed to the land of the cannibal giants. So, I was charged by an old bag of chalky turds named Íxt to chase these rumors and determine their truth. I arrived at cannibal giant territory in time to observe the Koosh fighting the cannibal giants in a fierce and frightening battle." Raven nodded his head toward Jánwu. "And contrary to what this cape-wearing dingbat believes, there is indeed more than one Koosh in this world."

"Quit insulting our honored elders," Íxt demanded, "and tell us what you saw. Who won the battle?"

Raven snorted. "Rumor among smarter birds"—raven looked at Héenjá—"and by that, I mean all other birds besides hummingbirds..." Raven turned back to the gathering. "Rumor says the Koosh won and after the battle the remaining giants surrendered. It appears the cannibals are now enslaved to the Koosh, but this is rumor."

"You saw the Koosh?" Héenjá asked raven.

"The what?" raven replied.

"The Koosh, you fatheaded bird."

"You bet. They all wore stupid hummingbird hats."

"Did you see the cannibal giants surrender to the Koosh?" Íxt asked.

Raven flapped his wing at Íxt. "Come again?"

"Did you see the cannibal giants in thrall to the Koosh?" Íxt asked.

"Who's Thrall?" Raven dismissed Íxt with a wing flutter. "I don't know the chap."

"Did you see the cannibal giants become slaves?"

"No," raven said sharply. He didn't like where the question was leading.

"How many Koosh were there?" Íxt asked.

"As I said to this bloated, cape-wearing, half-wit here: more than one," raven said with annoyance in his voice.

Íxt sighed. "How many giants remained after the battle?"

"I don't know," raven replied.

"Surely you counted them," Íxt said.

"Surely I did not," raven replied. "I wasn't charged with counting giants."

"Tell me you counted the number of Koosh canoes."

"I was about to but at that exact moment I forgot how to count," raven said.

"You think giants are slaves to the Koosh, but you don't know for sure. You don't know how many Koosh there are. You don't know how many giants remain or the number of Koosh canoes." Old Íxt exhaled in exasperation. "What in Yéil's name were you doing when all this was taking place?"

"I barely escaped with my life," raven replied, "through the giants' war clubs and spears, venomous mosquitoes everywhere, and the Koosh with their dzanti. Not only have none of you ever seen a Koosh, none of you have seen a dzanti. The Koosh dzanti froze my blood. The legend is true. The dzanti can call fire and flame from mere air. That weapon can call down a destruction unimaginable." Raven closed his eyes and shivered. "I was too frightened to do anything but survive."

Old Íxt looked at raven through narrowed eyes, and raven's feathers ruffled as though rubbed the wrong way. Raven shook to smooth down his feathers. *That fatheaded old turd knows I'm not telling everything*, he thought to himself. "If you don't like my answers then don't send me on stupid missions."

"You know very well what will happen if the Koosh come here," Íxt said to raven. "The living world is in peril. If the Koosh only killed humans, you could go about your selfish life without worry. But the Koosh destroy everything in the sea and on land—the salmon you so desire, all that is living will die." Old Íxt looked around the gathering. "This, my friends, is what we must keep in mind. The Koosh will not only rob every living creature of life, they will steal souls and minds, too. Imagine oceans, streams, and fields all soulless and filled with death."

The word *death* lingered, rolling around the wave-shaped clearing out into the evening. Shadows descended on Shaatleingagi. A chorus of croaking frogs pulsed in the distance. "This is our gathered knowledge. Are there any questions now?" Íxt asked the gathering. A heavy silence had descended onto the clearing. "Shall we close this council, or does anyone wish to speak?"

Raven leaned forward on his stone perch and looked at each elder in turn. "You have nothing to say now, do you, you fancy-dressed buffoons? I *know* you believe me, and respect my knowledge and long-earned wisdom, even though you don't want to. The Koosh are here. And they're coming."

Silence. Not even the apprentices spoke.

Íxt sighed. "Let each of us examine and ponder the knowledge gathered here. Share it with no one. We will meet again, same day and time next moon, and determine what action we shall take." He looked at raven. "No one is to be late."

Raven flapped a wing at Old Íxt's face as he leapt off his perch into flight. He rose only a few feet before he yelped in pain and crashed to the ground. A piece of very thin fishing line was wrapped around his ankle. The other end led into Íxt's hand. Íxt smiled as he waved to the others. "Take hope back home with you or to wherever you are staying and be safe," he said. When the others had left the clearing, Íxt said quietly to raven, "I'm not quite finished with you."

CHAPTER 3

"How long have you had that fishing line there?" raven asked.

"Long before the meeting began," Íxt said.

"You're a cruel, old fathead," raven said, "and you smell of crap. I didn't want to have to mention that, but everyone else is too polite to tell you, which isn't being polite at all. I thought I should be polite and let you know your rotten, old-man buns give off a terrible stink."

Íxt yanked the fishing line, pulling raven's leg out from under him. Raven squawked as he fell over. "I don't want your company any more than you want mine, but I need to know everything you saw," Íxt said.

Raven stood back up on his perch. "I wasn't lying," he said. "I told you what I saw."

"But you didn't tell everything you saw in the land of the cannibal giants. I beg you, tell me all that you saw."

"I told you all," raven replied.

Old Íxt was about to yank the fishing line again, but he decided not to. He thought of raven's weakness, his one, huge, gaping weakness, and decided to use it. "Okay," Íxt said to raven. "I'm willing to make a bargain with you, even though I am concerned about all living things and you're only being selfish. I will instruct one of the Aaní to feed you salmon every day for one moon if you tell me all that you saw. I will make this offer only once, and you know I can tell if you're lying or not revealing everything."

Old Íxt could see he had raven interested. Raven turned his head to and fro, wiped his beak with his wing, but his eyes gave him away. Íxt could see the reflection of baked salmon in those eyes. "I want salmon for a whole season," raven said. "Three moons of salmon."

Old Íxt smiled. *Ah, raven,* he thought, *you are easily fooled.* "Agreed. Now, tell me what you saw."

"And I get to choose which Aaní idiot has to prepare and bring me the salmon," raven said.

Old Íxt thought it a strange request, but he simply said, "Agreed."

"Good. There's a fatheaded little Aaní turd who lives in Naasteidi," raven said. "I don't know his name, but I'll get it for you. He makes the best salmon. I stole a piece today."

"So, we are in agreement," Íxt said. "Tell me what you saw."

Raven took a deep breath. "Everything I said is true, but I left out some truth pieces. I arrived in time to see part of the battle. I was nearly hit with a cannibal giant club and almost speared through, but it was the power of the Koosh dzanti that was terrifying. The air around me exploded. I had a hard time seeing and breathing. The giants' mosquitoes swarmed the Koosh, but the mosquitoes couldn't hurt the Koosh much. The Koosh wear a strange armor that changes colors like the feathers of those stupid snowy owls. The giants ripped trees from the ground and pulled boulders from the earth and hurled them at the Koosh. The Koosh dzanti blasted the trees and boulders to chips and rubble and kept pushing the giants down from their caves in the mountains toward Botson's Bay."

"Their strategy was to force the giants into the bay because the giants can't swim," Íxt said. "How many giants and how many Koosh? How many dzanti did the Koosh have?"

"No more than ten Koosh and I'd guess over five hundred giants, but I don't know how many survived," raven said.

"I saw only three Koosh with dzanti. The rest of the Koosh had powerful crossbows and a seemingly endless supply of bolts. The battle was chaos unlike anything I've seen. With their backs to the bay, the giants lost what little minds they had and fought on in madness. The Koosh used the dzanti and drove most of the giants into the bay where they floundered. The giants that fell into the ocean never resurfaced. Except for one. And that was curious."

"What? What happened?"

"One of the cannibal giants that had fallen in the bay was able to swim or float on the tide and come up behind the ring of Koosh."

"Impossible," Íxt said. "The giants have never learned to swim."

"I am telling you the truth," raven said. Íxt could see in raven's eyes that he was indeed telling the truth. "I saw one resurface and come out of the sea behind the ring of Koosh with a massive boulder. The giant threw his boulder into the line of Koosh who were standing on the rock ledges above the bay. And then it happened."

"What?" Íxt urged.

"The boulder smashed the head of one Koosh and knocked its dzanti loose. The Koosh fell to the ground with its head stoved in. The air around it changed. I can't describe it except the air around the Koosh looked like when you open your eyes underwater. The other Koosh scrambled to its aid and formed a wall around it, but I'm certain it was dead. When the air returned to normal, the dead Koosh was gone. The giants rallied and charged wildly. Attacked from behind by a boulder-throwing, swimming giant, and from the front by that giant's battle-crazed cousins, the remaining Koosh retreated backward off the ledges, but they regrouped and stopped the giants' charge in the forest above the beach at Botson's Bay."

"What of the dzanti?" Old Íxt asked.

"It teetered on the rock ledge above the bay," raven said. "I shot down there, for I was circling above the battle, landed right next to that dzanti and nudged it into the ocean. The shock was unbearable. It knocked me backward. I thought my heart had exploded. I couldn't clear my head to fly. I hopped around on that ledge, probably smoking from the tips of my feathers, trying to avoid a crazy giant swinging his club at me. Mosquitoes swarmed and bit me near to death. I jumped into the ocean to get away and floated, almost dead, until my strength returned and I could fly again. I'm covered with itching bites I can't scratch."

"Surely the Koosh retrieved the dzanti after the battle," Íxt said.

"No," raven said. "I stayed in a tree across from the bay for two days watching and recovering from the mosquito poison. Their retreat drove the Koosh into the woods and away from the place the dzanti had fallen. The battle must have ended when the remaining giants surrendered, but I was too ill to notice. I don't know how many giants lived. I heard rumor from birds that the Koosh rounded up the remaining giants and forced them into slavery, which I assume means the giants must fight for the Koosh."

"What of the dzanti?" Íxt urged.

"After the battle, I saw a group of Koosh searching around the bay for the dzanti, but they couldn't find it in the daylight. At night, the dzanti gave off a faint glow underwater. The Koosh came back to look for it, but it was underneath the ledge of rocks, and quite deep, so I guess they couldn't see its glow. The following day they came back for one last search, and again they couldn't find it, and then I watched them sail out of Botson's Bay in one of their big canoes. The dzanti was still underwater. They left without it."

Old Íxt crossed his arms, leaned back, and drew a deep breath. "Well," he said. "This knowledge changes the flavor of things. Why in Yéil's name did you stay silent about it? Did you plan on retrieving it from the sea after our meeting here?"

"Of course not. I wanted to get rid of it," raven admitted. "I didn't want any of you stupid Aaní getting your fat, crap hands on it."

"Why not? This could be our opportunity to rid our world of the Koosh," Íxt said.

Raven laughed. "You're not thinking of pulling it from the sea yourself, are you? Your ancient, brittle bones could never dive that deep."

"Not me, idiot," Íxt said. "A warrior. Think of what a dzanti could do in the hands of an Aaní warrior."

"Surely one dzanti cannot change what is inevitable."

"I don't know," Íxt replied. "I would like to hope it could, but I don't know." He looked into raven's eyes. "I know you have even less regard for humans than you do for other living beings, but I am need of your knowledge now more than ever. Please be the wise one now, and not the contrary fool you love to pretend to be. Will the Koosh prevail?"

Raven laughed. "Have I ever provided you with knowledge or wisdom before?"

"All you've ever *provided* me is lies and mockery," Íxt replied. "Any knowledge I've gleaned has come from watching how silly you behave. I behave the opposite and people think I'm wise. So please impart to me, just this once, knowledge and wisdom: Will the Koosh prevail over our world?"

Raven cackled. "What makes you think I can impart any knowledge or wisdom now?"

Old Íxt stared into raven's eyes. The two looked at each other for a long time until Íxt raised his eyebrows in surprise. "You don't know?" Raven turned from the old man's gaze. "Even *you* don't know how this will end." Íxt wove his words in astonishment. "I find it both upsetting and intriguing that you don't know. And that's why you're willing to help. You know what the Koosh mean for our world, but you cannot see how this ends."

Raven sneered. "I thought you could see the future."

"One cannot watch the future as one might watch the flight of whales through the ocean," Íxt said. "Seeing the future is like trying to see a far, far distance through heavy fog."

"That's horrid," raven laughed. "Quit trying to sound so wise and poetic. It's embarrassing coming from a skeleton as old and smelly as you. Now, let's discuss my three moons of salmon." He clapped his wings.

"The question in front of me now," Íxt continued, "is do I take time away from convincing Aaní leaders to go to war, and urging our Deikeenaa allies to aid us in battle, to go and look for a dzanti that sits fathoms deep in Botson's Bay?"

"Yes. And a more important question concerns the whens and wheres of my salmon intake," raven said. "I was thinking I could start intaking this evening..."

"Of course, I could send a small war party to retrieve this dzanti," Íxt said, thinking aloud. "A lightning-quick force in a single canoe. They could be there and back in one moon, or two at the most."

"I don't care," raven said. "Let me describe to you what this fatheaded little Aaní turd looks like so you can make sure he has my salmon ready every suppertime for the next three moons."

"You didn't tell anyone else about this lost dzanti, did you?" Íxt asked. He looked directly into raven's eyes.

"Well, not as such," raven said. He turned from Íxt's gaze.

"Whom did you tell?"

Raven looked down at his feet. The fishing line was still tight around his ankle. He scratched a mosquito bite on his breast with his beak and then shook his head.

"Whom did you tell?"

"The same fatheaded Naasteidi Aaní turd who will be preparing my salmon," raven said.

"Why in Yéil's name did you tell him about the dzanti?"

"He trapped me in a cupboard and wouldn't let me out,"

raven said. "I had to promise him something to save my life. He's a vicious warrior who kills for no meaning."

"Describe him to me," Íxt said.

"He smells like bears' buns after hibernation. Dumb as driftwood, but not the smart kind of driftwood. More like that stupid, waterlogged kind of driftwood. I've had better conversations with totem poles. He was drooling and peeing all over himself, but that could describe any Aaní."

"Where does he live?"

"You're not that bright either, are you, you moldy old turd? I told you he lives in Naasteidi."

"What house in the village of Naasteidi?"

"Some stupid house facing the beach with a crappy, carved flicker-bird pole in front and a dumbass eagle pole in back," raven said.

Íxt sighed. The Flicker House. He was certain raven had confronted the grandson of one of his dearest friends. His chest tightened. *Ahhh, Latseen. I'm sorry.* Though his friend had died many winters ago, Íxt often spoke to him in his mind. *I don't know if I can protect your grandson against what is to come. This selfish raven upsets everything, and now he has his claws in your poor grandson. I'm sorry, Latseen.*

Íxt would have to pay a visit to Naasteidi. He took the fishing line off raven's ankle. "I'll talk with that supposed Aaní warrior you ran into today and make arrangements for your salmon," he told raven. "Stay close to Naasteidi. I'll use my bone whistle to call you behind the village on the forest road leading to the mountain path to Yelm on Eastisland. Don't mention a word of the dzanti to anyone else, do you understand?"

"Don't worry," raven said. "That stupid dzanti has given me enough trouble."

"Can I give you a bit of advice?" Íxt asked raven.

"No," raven replied.

"Seeing the future isn't hard. The greatest barrier is you. Remove yourself from your vision and the future's path becomes clearer."

"Horrid. Absolutely horrid," raven said. "My advice to you is twofold. Quit trying to sound spooky and wise, because you're an ass like the rest of us. Full of crap." He held up his wing, puffed out his chest, and opened his beak wide as though about to make a grand proclamation. "Now, heed you well my second piece of advice for it comes with great wisdom," he said, imitating Íxt's deep voice. "You're a moron." Raven shot up into the air, his wingbeats straining hard to get him above the clearing. "Laters, fathead."

CHAPTER 4

ELĀN WORE EIGHTEEN winters on his shoulders and though his childhood had been uneventful, it had at least been enjoyable. But his world had changed as he had grown older, and his life had become unbearable. Every passing winter after age twelve fell upon him with the same depressing blandness until, as he now looked toward his nineteenth winter, he saw only a heavy-throated fog refusing to let go its grip on his future.

Elān lived in the Aaní village of Naasteidi on Samish Island. Samish Island is a large, pinecone-shaped island divided down the middle by snow-peaked mountains. The village of Naasteidi lay on the west side of Samish Island, so Elān and his people were known as Westislanders. Elān was born into the Flicker clan of Naasteidi. Aaní clans are large, extended maternal families who live together in one or two big houses known as clan houses. Elān's clan house, which at one time was full of relatives but now held only Elān and his parents, sat at a prominent place in the village along the beach at Naasteidi. Elān's clan had frayed and unraveled after a score of hard-luck winters ever since his grandfather, the Flicker clan's leader, had died in a faraway land. The war also claimed the lives of many Flicker clan warriors. Without clan relatives, Elān's clan house, the once revered Flicker House, fell into decay and disrepair.

The villagers of Naasteidi didn't hold much hope for Elān reviving the faded greatness of the Flicker clan. In his short life, Elān had excelled at nothing. On the rare occasion that

Naasteidi villagers ever talked of him, they would say, "He's an odd boy, but he is kind. The fall of the Flicker clan isn't his fault. If only oddness and kindness were enough to change fortunes."

But bringing odd kindness to the world was not enough for the Aaní. They valued agitation and action over contemplation and calmness, and valorized those best at fighting and fishing, hunting, swimming, canoe racing, and sailing. They wanted their boys and girls to become warriors. Of course, many Aaní adults would say they hated violence and wanted to see peace in the world, but in stories and songs and ceremonies, the Aaní celebrated violence and war.

Odd boys like Elān went little noticed. He knew how to fish and hunt, he could handle paddle and sail, but he never bested anyone. If he joined a canoe racing crew, he would often be the bailer not a paddler. "Such a quiet, odd boy," people would say as they looked past Elān to the other boys and girls who won awards for fighting, fencing, and archery. At the age of twelve, as you may know, Aaní children went to separate schools, which the Aaní call *Longhouses*. Those destined to become warriors went to live in barracks and attended the Longhouse of War and Diplomacy, as the school for warriors was called. After six winters training in the Longhouse of War and Diplomacy, they would become fully armed warriors; they would travel *Éil'* (the Aaní name for their world) battling foes and protecting Aaní villages, and, if they lived long enough, they'd become clan house leaders.

Those, like Elān, who didn't excel at fighting, became teachers and doctors and builders and carvers and farmers and attended the Longhouse of Service and Trade (as the school for everyone who wasn't to be a warrior was called), where they were enrolled in courses that trained and solidified them into who Aaní society thought they should be, which was usually in the same trade as their parents. There were no dorms or barracks, and students lived at home with their parents, in their clan houses. Skaan, Elān's father, taught reading, writing, and penmanship at Naasteidi's Longhouse of Service and Trade. Elān was fated to become a teacher like his father.

Though he never talked to anyone about it, Elān felt his future was being carved by others, like a totem pole, into sharp-lined stories and form-line patterns. *If I don't take hold of the carving tools,* Elān often thought to himself, *I'll have no control over the story my life and my kwalk will be the last interesting thing that ever happens to me.* A kwalk was a custom throughout Aaní land in which students of both longhouses, after taking final exams, did a twelve-moon stay in another Aaní village far from home. It served as a ceremony marking adulthood and kept up good relations among clans and villages. Elān had only a few moons left before his kwalk. After Elān's kwalk he would return to Naasteidi as his father's teaching apprentice. As Elān saw it, his kwalk was his last chance to recarve his future. *I'll create my own totem pole of life,* he thought to himself, *or burn the pole entire.*

Elān didn't do well in the classroom either. The Longhouse of Service was as boring as life in Naasteidi. Elān often drifted uninspired into his dad's classroom after finishing his own lessons. Elān knew his father was worried about his apathy fog, but Elān was as incapable of reassuring his father that all would be fine since he was incapable of reassuring himself that a fogless future was possible. Beyond feeling incapable, Elān felt little at all. His father would put him to work cleaning writing slates, sharpening quills, and making red and black ink (a mixture of charcoal and blackberries or raspberries). Afterward, his father would force Elān to practice reading and writing in other languages in hopes, Elān knew, languages from far-off places would explode his torpor. The ploy never worked.

Sometimes, though, from the window of his father's

classroom after school, Elān could see young Naasteidi warriors his age training at arms on the beach, or jogging in armor through the surf, or paddling their war canoes in unison out in Naasteidi Bay. Elān dreamed of becoming a warrior. Life's fog lifted when he imagined himself in armor among the warriors, looking at an enemy through the slits of a war helmet. He was jealous of their friendship, their handmade armor, and their hammered, fire-folded swords.

This small dream had smoldered across the years, but often bloomed into flames when Elān imagined himself in a war canoe, in full armor, slamming onto an enemy beach. Elān also knew it was an impossible dream. He couldn't become a warrior now at his age. He would always be a *bookeater*, which is a humiliating term used by the Longhouse of War for those in the Longhouse of Service who spend their lives among books. Though they may not admit it, warriors from the Longhouse of War held the students in the Longhouse of Service, especially bookeaters, in contempt. Elān hated being called a bookeater. As *looong* back as the eldest Aaní elder could remember, no bookeater ever became a warrior, and no warrior ever became a teacher. It never happened.

CHAPTER 5

THE DAY RAVEN stole Elān's salmon, Longhouses of Service and Trade in Aaní villages across Éil' were astir with their annual spring *Atx'aan Hídi*—academic and physical skills competitions—and Naasteidi's Longhouse of Service and Trade was no exception. Elān and his classmates would spend the day in academic and athletic competitions observed by their longhouse teachers, as well as warriors and would-be warriors from the Longhouse of War and Diplomacy, and any villagers who wanted to drop by to watch. Teachers from the Longhouse of Service and Trade judged the academic competitions and bestowed awards for knowledge of Aaní clan history and abilities in songcraft and oral storytelling.

After the academics came the physical skills competitions. Elān dreaded those most of all. The Atx'aan Hídi physical competitions never failed to humiliate him: sword fighting, two-bladed knife fighting, foot and canoe races, and, of course, archery all exposed Elān's weaknesses. He despised the archery competition. Every spring he came dead last. Warriors from the Longhouse of War and Diplomacy judged the physical competitions. Every spring, Elān could feel the warriors' laughter as he loosed his last arrow high over a target a mere twenty paces away. After last spring's Atx'aan Hídi, he had tossed his bow into the Flicker House fireplace.

Maybe I should go to Botson's Bay with raven, Elān wondered as he walked alone from the Flicker House to the Longhouse of Service and Trade for Atx'aan Hídi.

The raven's feather was still wedged behind his ear. His brief encounter with the raven had left him in a state of curious unease. Never had a raven, or any animal, spoken to him. He grabbed the feather and spun it around between his thumb and finger. *It looks like any old raven's feather*, Elān thought to himself. A strange desire came over him and he put the feather's hollow shaft in his mouth and bit down. The feather had an awful, acrid taste. He spit to clear his mouth, wiped his tongue on his shirt, and shoved the feather in his pocket.

If raven's story is true, Elān mused to himself, *Botson's Bay can't be more than a day's journey*. Elān had heard of Botson's Bay, but he didn't know where it was. *The raven promised to take me to the dzanti. I'll sail there in secret with the raven and get it. I'll be the only Aaní to have a dzanti.* He'd heard old stories of raven speaking to humans, and the raven Elān had met was as foulmouthed and rude as the old stories had told. The old stories also said raven was a notorious liar. Elān laughed aloud. *He's lying. There's no dzanti at Botson's Bay.* But Elān was sure the dzanti was real. He'd grown up hearing frightening tales of the Koosh and their dreadful weapon, but he'd never seen a Koosh and had no proof that the dzanti existed. Elān shook his head. *Everyone knows raven is a liar, so why should I believe any of his story is true?*

"Because you're a fathead."

Elān stopped and looked up into the trees around him. It was raven's voice, but raven was nowhere to be seen. Confused, Elān continued along the road toward the longhouse, scanning clan house peaks and chimneys for a glint of black feathers as he went. *Admit it*, Elān said to himself, *the thought that raven returned just now to take you to Botson's Bay filled you with excitement. Admit it.*

"I admit it," Elān said aloud to the small-horizoned world of Naasteidi. "I want raven to take me to Botson's Bay."

"I would never take a fork-headed turd sack like you to Botson's Bay."

Elān stopped and looked around. Again, raven was nowhere. Elān tried to shake loose raven's voice from his head and walked on. Anxiety clenched his stomach as he approached the longhouse in the distance. His classmates walked together toward it in small and large groups. He heard their chatter and laughter. As he aged, Elān had grown accustomed to walking to the longhouse alone. He was his parents' only child and he was used to being the only child in his clan house. He had clan relatives across Naasteidi and Samish, of course, but he had no *ax xoonx'iyán* with whom he could share silence. *My closest friends are my parents*, Elān thought. *I wish I had at least one ax xoonx'iyán my age.*

Elān once had an ax xoonx'iyán, a silence-sharing friend, named Ch'áal', with whom he canoed, fished, hunted, and explored the mountains and ran the forests, but they'd drifted apart over the past few winters. Elān remembered when Ch'áal' told him that he was going to become a warrior, that he was headed into the Longhouse of War and was moving into the same barracks from which his older brother Ch'eet was about to graduate. Elān thought he and Ch'áal' would continue to be silence-sharing friends even in different longhouses, but Ch'áal' stopped visiting the Flicker House after he became a warrior-in-training. A few springs back, after Elān had placed last again in archery, he overheard students from the Longhouse of War teasing Ch'áal' for being friends with Elān. Elān was at his father's classroom window. The warriors-in-training were walking by outside.

"That Flicker clan boy is useless," one of the young warriors said. "He didn't hit a single target."

"Eesháan. What a shame for his parents," another young warrior laughed. "Especially considering who his grandfather was."

"What a shame for the whole Flicker clan. The Failure clan."

All the boys laughed.

"What's he going to do when he's done with his studies?" one boy asked.

"Don't ask me. Ask Ch'áal'. They're best friends."

"I was never friends with that bookeater," Ch'áal' protested. "His parents asked me to hunt and fish with him out of pity. He's worthless and a dishonor to his family…"

The boys strolled out of earshot. Elān's cheeks burned, his heartbeat filled his ears, and his insides tightened as though his ribs were a vise. And then it happened: holes in his vision. Blind spots. Panicked, afraid, he collapsed to the ground and clenched shut his eyes until tears came. In the slow time of the afternoon, laying on the floor of his father's classroom in the longhouse, the blind spots in Elān's vision dissolved into squiggly, flashing lights. When his full sight returned later that afternoon, a massive headache bore into his forehead. And light made him nauseous. He waited until darkness to stumble home. His headache disappeared after two days, but his far vision remained forever out of focus. After losing his silence-sharing friend, the horizon, for Elān, was blurry. Hunting and fishing stopped. Forests and mountains were left unexplored. Ch'áal' faded from his life, and Naasteidi closed upon him in boring sameness.

Elān had almost reached the Longhouse of Service and Trade now. Two large, fine-carved poles painted in red and black stood at either end of the front: a raven pole proclaiming the birth of wisdom and an eagle pole proclaiming the gathering of knowledge. As you may know, the entire Aaní nation is divided into an eagle side and a raven side; every Aaní, no matter what village, is represented by the eagle or the raven. Aaní tradition proclaimed one could only marry the opposite side—eagles only marry ravens and vice versa. The division was also helpful when choosing teams for games or groups for hosting feasts. You wonder how the decision is made, who is eagle and who is raven? As with the gift of life, Aaní identity is a gift from the mother. Elān was gifted into the eagle side of the Aaní Nation as a member of the Flicker clan, which was his mother's clan.

Elān walked between the knowledge and wisdom poles into the Longhouse of Service and Trade. The longhouse was massive: it held a main hall or central gathering place with raised platform seating that could hold almost the entire village of Naasteidi. It contained a dozen classrooms, half a dozen offices, several bathrooms, and two large steam baths. The Aaní, as you know, are fastidious about cleanliness. Every longhouse in every Aaní village has a steam bath.

Elān had signed up for the storytelling competition. He didn't care about the clan history or songcraft competitions. He walked down the longhouse hall into the central gathering place. A small fire burned in the large firepit. Dozens of spectators, eagles on one side and ravens on the other, sat around the hall. Behind a table next to the firepit sat six of the longhouse's teachers: judges of the academic competitions. A group of ten students, the storytelling competitors, stood in a semicircle around the firepit across from the judges. Elān joined them.

One of the judges stood from behind their table. She wore a red-fringed, thick, black blanket over her shoulders. Abalone buttons, tinged greenish blue, formed an eagle on the back of the blanket. The judge addressed the gathering. "Welcome students, welcome relatives from the Longhouse of War and Diplomacy, and welcome all of our eagle and raven relatives from across Naastcidi." She looked along the semicircle of students standing near the firepit. "And welcome competitors. Competitors, when it is your turn, please come forward and select your tokens. You have a minute to craft your story and five minutes to tell the story you craft. The most compelling, best-crafted story shall win. Understood?" The semicircle of students all nodded in assent except Elān.

How can anyone judge one story better than another? Elān thought to himself.

"Then let Atx'aan Hídi begin!" the judge cried. The crowd in the hall hollered in approval. The judge smiled at the line of students and then sat back down. Atop the judges' table sat a bentwood box full of wooden tokens with carved genre images. When their turn came, each competitor would select a genre token and create a story within the drawn genre and then tell the story in front of all the judges and spectators. Elān would go last since he arrived last.

"First competitor, step forward," the judge said.

One by one, Elān's longhouse classmates drew tokens and crafted stories. One or two did well, crafting new stories out of old forms. But most stories followed old familiar patterns: traditional Aaní enemies remained enemies, traditional allies helped Aaní heroes, and in the end the Aaní world was saved and the Aaní way of life reflected from the story to the listeners as the true path of life. Elān watched the audience as they murmured approval or disapproval, smiled or frowned, leaned forward or hunched down in their seats, and an understanding came to him: the audience had the power to shape his classmates' stories. A story is a battle between the audience and the storyteller.

Elān's turn came. He walked to the judges' table and reached into the bentwood box and pulled out a carved wooden token. He drew a long breath and then looked at the carved image: two armored warriors held hands, and in their other hands were swords. Elān had drawn the Hero Twins' Journey genre. As you may know, the Hero Twins is a formulaic genre: twins take a journey in search of a knowledge that will save their people. After many harrowing adventures and escapes, the twins find the necessary knowledge and return home in time to save their clan and nation. Of course, listeners are eager throughout the story to know what knowledge was gathered, but a good storyteller builds the suspense and only at the very end reveals the world-saving knowledge.

Elān looked at his token and laughed. "I'm ready," he told the judges.

"You have a minute to prepare," the judge in the button blanket said.

"I don't need it," Elān replied.

"Then begin."

"My story happens here on Westisland, or Eastisland, or any island in Éil'..." Elān crafted a story about a twin brother and sister traveling through an ocean of dangers to reach the Fire Islands far to the west, where—according to tradition—a special knowledge waited to be gathered. The twins paddled westward day and night and faced three epic battles along the way, Elān told the crowd: a battle of arms and strength against enemy canoes full of archers launching flaming arrows; a battle of magic and skill avoiding cloud-like specters who hovered over the sea and threw real spears before dissipating into nothingness; and a battle of wits and brains outwitting vicious sea-wolf monsters with giant mouths spewing venom, determined to imprison them forever under the waves.

The crowd fell silent, trapped in Elān's word-netting. Elān walked around the firepit feeling the weight of the crowd's suspense, all eyes hungry in expectation. Elān decided to twist the Hero Twins genre upside down. "Before the twins could reach the Fire Islands, a Koosh in a strange canoe, flying through the sky like a thunderbird, sent lightning thrashing down and split the twins' canoe in half, separating the twins."

Many in the crowd moaned at mention of the Koosh.

"Their canoe smashed in two by the Koosh, the twins were flung into the sea," Elān continued. "The brother, weighed down with his heavy clothes, descended to the ocean floor but the sea creatures took pity on him and showed him how to breathe underwater. He was amazed to understand the under-waves world. His heavy clothes became fins and he swam back toward Éil' to tell his people how to breathe underwater." The judges were nodding as they leaned over the table, enmeshed in Elān's storycrafting. "The sister shed her clothes and swam to the shore of the Fire Islands. The birds took pity on her, clothed her in feathers, and taught her how to fly so she could take the knowledge of flight home. The twins couldn't wait to bring their knowledge back home and share it with their people!"

Many in the audience cheered, believing the story to be near the end. The proclaiming of knowledge always signaled the closing of a Hero Twins story. Elān could sense the power his story had on the crowd. They were as anxious for a resolution as raven had been that morning to get out of the cupboard. Elān wasn't finished. "But raven," he sneered, "thought it would be funny to upset the world and trap the brother in the sky and the sister in the sea. The sister fell in her feathers from the sky deep into the ocean. The brother sprang in his heavy fin-clothes up from the sea into the sky. Neither twin could move; they were suspended in sea and sky. Separated forever. Neither twin could leave the world in which they were trapped and neither had the right knowledge for their world."

The longhouse buzzed in suspense and Elān tightened the net. "And raven, my relatives, was as cruel as he was cunning. The twins could see each other, but the other's world appeared upside down. The sea was sky and sky was sea. The twins looked down and up upon each other but couldn't communicate nor connect. In time, the two worlds went to war even though they were all related and each world held a knowledge that could transform the other."

Elān paused as though done with the story. Students and spectators screech-cawed in imitation of ravens' cries, which as you may know is an Aaní sign of appreciation, and yelled "Gunalchéesh!", which as you know is the Aaní word for "thank you." Elān knew he could stop his story now and win the battle, but this was his last Atx'aan Hídi. He needed to be unburdened. He closed with a thought that came to him as a voice from nowhere. "That's the freedom and danger of knowledge," he said, quieting the cawing crowd. "You may discover your most cherished traditions are all wrong."

On those words, the gathering hall fell silent, no longer enmeshed in Elān's story. The eyes grew accusatory. Elān looked at the six judges behind the table. "Our elders and judges may be forced to examine their own close-held beliefs and then have to admit they don't know everything." The judges crinkled their brows, puzzling out Elān's meaning. He looked at his fellow competitors. "And you too, my relatives, may be forced to examine your own close-held beliefs and stories." The students around the firepit looked at each other in confusion. Elān smiled and tossed the Hero Twins token into the fire and delivered his closing line to the entire gathering. "And only then will you have true knowledge; tradition is an empty ear."

CHAPTER 6

ELĀN SKIPPED THE songcrafting and clan history competitions and skulked around his father's classroom in the Longhouse of Service and Trade, flipping through his father's books even though he'd read all of them in his classroom. The presence of books gave Elān a good feeling. He loved being surrounded by them. As the singing and clan history recitations went on to roars of approval in the gathering hall, Elān pulled book after book at random from his father's shelves, read a few pages, inhaled the book's scent as though he were inhaling Aaní history, closed his eyes and smiled as the book's fleeting scent lingered in his nostrils, and then moved on to the next book. Elān was too enraptured reading and inhaling books to hear the academic competitions come to an end and awards being given out.

Elān's reading was interrupted by the voices outside. He peered out the classroom window and saw Ch'áal' and other young Aaní warriors-in-training sitting atop upturned canoes, joking and laughing among themselves as they watched the Longhouse of Service and Trade students take part in the physical competitions. His father came into the classroom to clean writing slates, fill inkpots, and set up the classroom for the next day's lessons. Skaan came to the window and put his arm around his son. A book titled *Haa Kusteeyí*, a biography of famous Aaní warriors, sat open spine-up on Elān's leg. "Not interested in action and adventure?"

"I don't know."

"What competition did you enter?" his father asked. "You have to put your name in for at least one."

"Archery," Elān replied.

"Archery?" his father mused. "You don't always..." He paused. Elān knew he was trying to find the right words. "You don't always find the greatest success in that particular competition."

Elān laughed at his father's awkward words. "Why are physical competitions part of Atx'aan Hídi, Dad?"

"I guess our ancestors of *looong* ago thought all Aaní should know how to defend themselves and their villages, regardless of what longhouse they attend," his father replied. "There's still a world out there where warrior skills are needed."

"Did you ever want to be a warrior?" Elān asked.

"No," Skaan said. "My father was a warrior, you know, and he didn't want that life for me. I've told you that when I turned twelve my father pushed me into the trade and service longhouse and said to the Hits'aati, 'You have two choices: make my son a teacher or make me angry. Now, choose.' The Hits'aati admitted me into the teacher apprentice program that very day without the usual winter's probationary period." Hits'aati is the official Aaní title for the director of a longhouse. "I did well, though, in the Longhouse of Service," Elān's father continued. "I earned my education, and by the time my dad died in Latseen's war against the Yahooni I was through my kwalk and working in this longhouse. Why in Yéil's name do you ask if I ever wanted to be a warrior?"

"I don't know," Elān replied.

Skaan looked at Elān. "Do you want to be a warrior?"

"I don't know."

"Could you kill someone? That's what we ask of our warriors."

"I don't know," Elān said.

"I do know," his father replied. "You never knew your grandfathers, but you should know what haunted them. My dad was haunted by the faces of those he killed in battle. He couldn't sleep through the night. He told me he'd fall asleep for a few hours before the faces of the dead came to him as clear as when they were alive. They couldn't speak; their mouths were sewn shut with bloody thread. The dead stared at him with lifeless yet unforgiving eyes, my father said, and the bodies of their relatives shimmered like smoke behind lifeless, unforgiving faces. He had to stay awake to avoid being haunted." Skaan looked into Elān's eyes. "Even your mom's dad, the great Latseen, was haunted by those he killed in battle. I think the reason Latseen never stayed anywhere long was because he was trying to outpace the stares of the dead." Skaan looked away. "You don't want to be a warrior."

Silence grew in the short distance between Skaan and his son. Both sat at the window, watching the Atx'aan Hídi physical competitions taking place outside. The two-bladed-knife fighting duels were ending and the canoe races were about to begin. Skaan was the first to disturb the silence between them. "You made up a good story this morning. You've always been good at storytelling. Storycraft is well regarded in the Longhouse of Service and Trade. You may become a famous teacher one day." Skaan laughed. "Do you remember when you were eleven or twelve winters, you stole aboard the warriors' canoe as they headed out on maneuvers? You were gone all day before they brought you back. You told me you were captured by Yahooni slave raiders and escaped by tricking them. You jumped overboard, you said, and swam all the way home." Elān smiled at the memory. "You always excelled at asking questions of the truth. Did you prepare a story for all the genres you might draw this morning?"

"No," Elān said. "I drew the twins and made up the story as I went along."

"I thought it was wonderful," his father replied. "Especially the ending."

"Everybody hated the ending," Elān replied.

"Throwing the token in the fire didn't help."

A twinge of shame came over Elān. "I didn't intend to do that. The idea came to me out of nowhere."

"Most people want simple stories with expected endings," Elān's father said. "I think you like stories with unknown journeys and unexpected endings."

Elān laughed. "It's funny because I haven't had any journeys or unexpected twists in my life," he said. "Where do you think I'll go on my kwalk?"

"You know I can't answer that," his father said. "I'm sure our Hits'aati has made arrangements to send you to the village that needs you the most."

"I don't know what I'll be able to do."

"That's up to the village elders," his father replied. "During my kwalk, I did nothing I learned in school. I hauled and chopped wood. I spent my days scouring the beach and forest for fallen trees, chunking them, hauling them back to the village, and chopping them up." His father laughed. "It made me strong, but it also taught me that I preferred making a life for myself inside a classroom."

"You think I'll have to chop and carry wood?" Elān asked.

"You know I don't know," Skaan replied. "A winter does go by quick. It doesn't feel so at your age, but when you get older each winter unwinds quicker than the last. You'll be back here before long and the rest of your life will be right here in this longhouse. But enough with the unknowable. Your mother and I are going out to the Raven's Tail tonight." The Raven's Tail was his father's favorite pub in Naasteidi. "Would you like to go?"

At eighteen, Elān was old enough to drink weak ale, but he'd tried it once or twice and didn't like it much. "I think I'll stay home tonight," he said.

They sat in silence a moment and peered at the competitions outside. The canoe races were nearing an end and the archery competition was about to start. "So, you signed up again for archery?" his father mused. "Both your grandfathers were expert archers. I once saw Latseen hit a target dead center at five hundred paces. As for me, I have a hard time knowing which end of the arrow points forward."

Elān laughed. "That describes me as well."

"Go," Skaan said, "and make me and your grandfathers proud."

"I don't have a bow," Elān replied.

His father nodded to the archery field outside the open window. "You can borrow one from the warriors out there," he said. "Go now."

Elān left the longhouse, walked slow across the Atx'aan Hídi fields, and got in the archery line behind the rest of his classmates. He noticed Ch'áal' sitting on an upturned canoe. They held each other's eyes for a moment before Ch'áal' turned away. He watched his classmates loose three arrows at each of the four targets set twenty, forty, sixty, and eighty paces away. The warrior judges barked out a thirty-second countdown at each target. Elān thought the entire competition pointless. *Why three arrows in thirty seconds?* he thought to himself as he stood waiting his turn, watching his classmates. *You load one arrow right after loosing one. No time to aim or enjoy the shot. What's the point? When will I ever have to notch an arrow before one I just loosed has hit its target?*

Elān stepped to the twenty-pace target firing line without a bow. Ch'áal's brother Ch'eet was on countdown. "Where's your bow?" he asked Elān.

"I don't have one," Elān replied.

"Caraiden," Ch'eet yelled to the aged warrior judging the archery competition. "This one has no bow."

The warrior shook his head. "Let the bookeater use yours," he told Ch'eet.

Ch'eet unslung the bow from his back and handed it to Elān. Elān had never handled a true warrior's bow.

The wood was smooth-worn from long use, not too heavy, and the grip fit his palm and fingers. Ch'eet handed Elān three arrows. The fletching was chomped, but the shafts were trued straight and the flared metal tip sharp. Elān shoved two arrows tip-down in the grass and notched the third arrow.

"Thirty seconds," Ch'eet said. "Ready?"

"Ready," Elān said.

"Thirty, twenty-nine, twenty-eight…" Ch'eet counted.

Elān hefted the bow and pulled the bowstring. The bow felt powerful as it tensed. He aimed just above the top of the target. Even at twenty paces, arrows dropped.

"Twenty-two, twenty-one…"

Elān loosed the arrow. It flew above the top of the target into the field far beyond. He could hear the laughter of the warriors-in-training sitting atop their canoes on the beach. Elān grabbed another arrow and notched it. The warrior's bow was bursting with power, so he didn't pull the bowstring back very far as he hefted the bow for his second shot. He aimed the arrow tip at the lower part of the target.

"Thirteen, twelve, eleven…" Ch'eet counted.

Elān loosed. The arrow flew below the target and buried into the ground just beyond. More laughter from the beach. "Five, four, three…" Elān didn't move to pick up the third arrow. Ch'eet finished his count. "Retrieve your arrows," he told Elān. Elān walked out to the field and retrieved the two arrows that had missed the target. "Move to the next target," Ch'eet said. Elān walked to the firing line for the forty-pace target. He held the bow downward in his left hand and clumped the three arrows together in his right hand. "Are you going to put a couple arrows in the ground at the ready?" Ch'eet asked.

"No," Elān said.

Ch'eet shook his head. "Ready?"

"Ready," Elān said.

"Thirty, twenty-nine, twenty-eight…"

Elān didn't notch. Rather, he clasped all three arrows in his hand, raised them above his head, and threw them at the target. They tumbled haphazardly, landing far short. Ch'eet laughed and stopped counting. "Retrieve your arrows and move to the next target." Elān retrieved the arrows and walked to the sixty-pace target firing line. "Ready?"

Elān nodded and as Ch'eet counted down from thirty, Elān notched all three arrows at once on the bowstring, pulled the bowstring back farther than he thought he could, and launched the arrows into the sky. Ch'eet stopped counting as he watched all three arrows fly far beyond the sixty-pace target. Elān was amazed. He never thought he could shoot three arrows at once that far.

"Retrieve your arrows and move to the next target." Elān ran out into the field and gathered his arrows. He jogged to the firing line of the eighty-pace target. Now he was interested. He shoved two arrows tip-down into the ground and notched the third and peered at the eighty pace target, blurry out in the distance. Ch'eet came to his side.

"You have strength," the young warrior whispered. "More strength than your classmates, as I see it. The bow doesn't tremble when you pull and hold, but your elbow is too low and you're closing your eyes when you release. You'll miss three out of four times. When you pull the bow string back, touch your jawbone with your thumbnail as a reminder to yourself to keep your aiming eye open. Breathe out half a breath, imagine in your mind your arrow hitting the target, then loose and watch the arrow fly into the target. My bow is far more powerful than you're used to. Even at eighty paces you don't have to overcorrect much above the target. Put the tip of the arrow at the top of the target when you aim, and let the bowstring slip, not snap, from your fingertips."

"Stop talking to the bookeater," Caraiden yelled at Ch'eet. "Give him the countdown."

"Ready?" Ch'eet asked Elān.

"Ready."

"Thirty, twenty-nine, twenty-eight..."

Elān hefted the bow and pulled the string back as far as he could. He touched the back of his right jawbone and opened his right eye wide and pointed the tip of the arrow at the top of the target eighty paces away. Exhaling half his breath, aim-eye wide, he loosed. The arrow sang from the bow and thwocked dead center, deep into the target. "Twenty-one, twenty, nineteen..." The second arrow buried into the target next to the first. "Twelve, eleven, ten..." Elān's third arrow twanged from the bow and slammed into the target just above his first two in a nice, tight triangle.

"Yeah, that's it," Ch'eet said.

Elān, trying not to show the elation he felt inside, handed the bow back to Ch'eet. "I've never held a bow like that. Thank you."

"You did well on the last target," Ch'eet said.

"For a bookeater," Elān said.

"For an Aaní," Ch'eet replied. "Go retrieve your arrows."

WHEN ATX'AAN HÍDI was over, after the physical competition winners were awarded, all the students in the Longhouse of Service went with the young warriors-in-training from the Longhouse of War down to the beach to light a bonfire and celebrate with song and games that would last into the night. Elān didn't join his classmates and villagers. He watched them head down toward the beach before he turned and walked back to the Longhouse of Service and Trade. The longhouse was quiet and though the sun had just gone down, candles were already lit in their metal cups along the hallway walls.

Elān walked as quietly as he could past the dining room, the Hits'aati's office, and the large, echoey, central gathering room toward the classrooms at the back. His father's classroom was dark. His father had gone, but the door was unlocked. Elān grabbed his backpack from his father's classroom and walked on down the hall. The other classrooms—the carver's studio and art room, the math room, the drafting and engineering rooms—were all dark too. Elān crept past those rooms until he came to Snaak's classroom. Snaak taught geography, cultures, and languages.

Though the room was dark there was enough dusk light to see by. And Elān knew where to find what he sought. He walked to the back of Snaak's classroom, set down his backpack, and, as quietly as possible, opened a bentwood box holding a large, wooden-spined, hand stitched book full of hand drawn, colored maps of Éil'. Elān flipped to the middle of the book—nobody would notice a map missing from the middle—and ripped out a thick page.

The ripping sounded like raven's squawking and disturbed the empty, quiet classroom.

"Dláa!"

Elān shoved the map into his backpack.

"Elān? Is that you? What in Yéil's name are you doing here?" Snaak stood at the door, holding up a candle against the dark.

"I'm sorry, Snaak," Elān said.

"What are you doing in my classroom, Elān?"

Elān froze. Snaak was every student's favorite teacher. His knowledge of languages, geography, and Aaní custom approached that of an elder, even though Snaak hadn't tasted more than forty winters. Snaak walked into the classroom and lifted the candle. "Elān, what have you done?"

"I'm sorry, Snaak."

"What have you done?"

A voice came to Elān. "I was having one of my episodes of broken vision and headache and needed a dark place to lay down," he told Snaak. "I stumbled in here because my father's classroom was too bright, but I tripped over this box here and knocked out all your beautiful books. I was putting them back, but I picked up that book there by its pages and I think I ripped one of the pages just a tiny bit." Elān closed the upended book from which he'd ripped the map and placed it back in the bentwood. "I'm sorry."

"You're still having those spells?" Snaak̲ asked. His voice softened. "Blindness and headaches?"

"Yes," Elān replied.

"Eesháan. I'll find a cure for you," Snaak̲ said. "I'll ask every Aaní Islands Elders' Council and I'll consult every book until I learn how to cure you, my young Flicker clan friend."

"Gunalchéesh, Snaak̲."

"Head home now." Snaak̲ laughed. "You can't spend your whole life in a Longhouse of Service among moldy books and maps. The whole world of Éil' awaits."

Elān grabbed his pack raced from the longhouse. Lanterns hung on poles lit the village of Naasteidi in a warm amber. Elān wasn't hungry even though it was suppertime and he hadn't eaten all day. He hurried through the village, happy his parents were out for the night. He would try to locate Botson's Bay on the map now stuffed into his backpack. Elān was sure it was a one-night journey at most. Perhaps two nights. He would tell his parents he was going hunting in the mountains. Elān's father would be happy Elān's apathy fog had lifted. Any more than two nights, though, and his parents would be suspicious. Could he sail and paddle for three days straight? For a weapon like the dzanti, Elān was certain he could paddle days without end.

What if the raven never came back as promised? He'd have to go alone.

And if he did get to Botson's Bay alone, how in Yéil's name would he find the dzanti underwater? What if raven was lying?

"Well, hello, young Elān."

Elān turned and saw Jahoon, one half of the Macphee brothers, trundling out the alley near his shop. Brothers

Jahoon and Jumbo Macphee owned the only hunting and fishing supply shop in the village. "Hello, Mr. Macphee," he said.

"You on to the pub this fine evening?" Jahoon asked. His voice was as husky as his body, but there was also a lightness to both voice and body that made Elān believe Jahoon could probably outsprint him in the short distance and outtalk him in the long.

"No," Elān said. "I'm heading home."

"You should be old enough for a bit o' the weak, no?" Jahoon said. "Come along and share a mug, my young cousin."

"I am old enough," Elān said. "But I need to get home. My exams come up in a few moons, and I haven't studied much. My father is at the pub, though."

"Is he indeed?" Jahoon said. "Which one?"

"Raven's Tail."

"Ah, I'm off to Gooch's Dad," Jahoon said. Gooch's Dad, another pub in town, the oldest in Naasteidi and perhaps the oldest on Samish Island, was known more for its food than its brew. "Jumbo heard they have spicy blueberry salmon tonight. He's said he'd wait, but knowing old Jumbo there won't be any salmon left if I don't get to Gooch's Dad straight away. My dear old Jumbo may be blind, but he sure knows how to find his mouth when there's salmon about." Salmon was life for the Aaní. They ate it cooked, raw, smoked, jarred, jugged, pickled, barbecued, for breakfast with porridge, for lunch on pizza, and for supper chunked in seaweed soup. "I may drop into Raven's Tail afterward to chat with your old dad."

"Have a good evening, Mr. Macphee," Elān said.

"And you, young nephew," Jahoon said. "Oh, one more thing. I saw Old Man Íxt rambling through town just now." Jahoon frowned. "I thought he was living somewhere over in Eastisland."

"The last I heard he was," Elān said.

"I know he's friends with your father," Jahoon said.

"With my grandfather," Elān said. "He was friends with my grandfather."

"Ah, yes. Friends with your famous old granddad." There was a fake air of casualness that meant Jahoon was indeed concerned about Íxt's presence. "Funny old man. Did your father mention his coming to Westisland?"

"No. My father didn't say anything."

"An odd old man he is," Jahoon said. "Oh, well. You have a pleasant evening."

"And you too, Mr. Macphee."

CHAPTER 7

As ELAN SAT in his kitchen studying the map splayed before him on the kitchen table, Old Íxt stood outside, watching him through the window. Was it meant to be, Íxt wondered, that, of all people, his dear friend's grandson was now entangled in a net whose ends were held by beings from the otherworld? Was his old friend playing games from the otherworld? It felt to Íxt more than coincidence that Elān should be involved in events unfolding that could save or destroy the human world of Éil'. *Eeshāan, Latseen. I don't know if I can protect your grandson.* Old Íxt slowly opened the door and slipped inside.

"Your ancestors," Íxt said. It was an old Aaní greeting. Originally, it ran, "I honor your ancestors, whose presence I see standing behind you." Such a long greeting was apparently too much for our modern Aaní, and the greeting got whittled away over the ages until it ran simply, "Your ancestors." You don't have to use it with people you see all the time. You use it with strangers and people you don't often meet.

Elān startled and folded the map. "I didn't hear you enter."

"I'm not invisible or dead," Íxt said. "At least, not that I'm aware."

Elān laughed nervously. "Your ancestors. My parents aren't here. They are at Raven's Tail tonight."

"I did not come to talk to them," Íxt said. "I came to talk to you. I heard you had a visitor."

"Oh." Elān became nervous. "Please sit. Can I get you some tea?"

Elān liked Íxt, but always trembled in his presence. Íxt was originally a doctor, but his studies had taken him beyond doctoring. Long ago, he had left Samish Island for ten winters. Away far to the south, Elān had heard, searching for a son that had been kidnapped by the Koosh. He came back much older, wiser, and much, much stranger. He was what the Aaní called an 'over-the-edger,' which was a polite way of saying he was both a little odd and could see things normal Aaní could not. You have such people, no doubt, where you live. Most people hope for, and hopefully plan for, the future, but very few can take a peek over the present time's edge and catch a true glimpse of it.

"A mug of pine needle tea, if you have it," Íxt said. He sat down in a chair next to the door.

"Sure." Elān grabbed a pot, pumped water from the basin into it, and set it on the hearth. They talked a few minutes of pleasantries, as is Aaní custom. You never get straightaway to the purpose of your conversation, you see, for that would be impolite. Old Íxt mentioned the spring weather—a bit dryer than in previous springs—and asked about Elān's parents' health.

"Was he rude?" Íxt asked after the period of politeness was over.

"Who?"

"Your visitor."

"My visitor?"

"Yes, your visitor. Your feathered, foulmouthed visitor."

"Oh, raven," said Elān. "He stole my salmon, so I locked him up for a while."

"Yes, he is a thief if he is anything," said Íxt. "Holler a bit, did he?"

Elān laughed. "He hollered a lot."

Old Íxt gave a deep laugh. "Yéil knows he deserves to be locked up for good. Why did you let him out?"

"I'm sorry?"

"You needn't be sorry yet," Íxt said. "I was wondering why you let him out?"

"I don't know," Elān said. "I guess I felt pity for him."

Old Íxt's eyebrows raised. "You did?"

Elān looked away from Íxt's gaze. He didn't know how to answer. He stood abruptly, fetched the water pan from the hearth and brought it over to the counter. The water was far from boiling. He searched in a cupboard, found and opened a jar containing his mom's pine needle tea—chopped pine needles, mint leaves, dried berries—and poured a bit into the tepid water.

"The laws of water boiling must be different nowadays," Íxt noted.

"It will be ready in a minute or two."

"Odd."

"Excuse me?"

"I thought it odd that you should feel pity for raven after the trouble he gave you."

Elān wondered how much Old Íxt knew. It was obvious he had talked to raven, for how else would Íxt have heard about raven's visit? But surely raven wouldn't have told Old Íxt about the dzanti?

"I felt sorry for raven so I let him out," Elān said. "And I wish I hadn't. He stole my salmon and flew out the door with it before I could smash him with my paddle. Ah, the tea should be ready."

Elān grabbed a metal strainer and poured the tepid tea into a mug and handed it to Old Íxt. "Thank you, my boy," Íxt said. He took a sip. "Anything else happen during raven's visit?"

Elān made a pretending-to-remember face. "Oh, he dropped a feather. I kept it. I put it there on the counter under the cupboard where I trapped him."

Íxt stood from his chair, went to the counter, and picked up the feather. He ran his fingertips over the hollow shaft where Elān had bitten it. "That's odd," Old Íxt said. "Very odd indeed."

The old man finds everything odd, Elān thought.

Íxt set the feather back on the counter and sat down next to Elān. "Is there anything else you want to discuss?" he asked.

Elān froze. His mind reached for something to say. "Can I ask you a question?" Elān said. "It might not be a proper question."

"Those are the best questions," Íxt said.

"Is it true your son was taken by the Koosh many winters ago?"

Old Íxt drew a breath through his nose. He realized then that raven had told him the truth about the Koosh and dzanti for, obviously, the Koosh weighed on Elān's mind. "Yes. The Koosh took my son. It took me ten winters to figure out what happened to him. On a mission for me to the great library at Kugíinaay, he drifted off course. The tides that far south all drift toward Saaw Island. No doubt he was taken as a Koosh slave. I've lost him forever."

Elān sat in silence for a moment after Íxt's words. "That's sad," he said.

Old Íxt smiled. Lines appeared on his forehead. "The thing about sadness is that it only changes shape. It's not as pointy or rough-edged as it once was. It's rounder, less jagged. But the size of the sadness is the same."

"I'm sorry," Elān said.

"Your grandfather Latseen tried to help me get him back."

"I didn't know that."

"He nearly died." Íxt paused. He looked hard at Elān, testing him with his eyes, trying to judge his strength. People in Naasteidi said he was a kind boy, but he couldn't see too well and didn't excel at fighting or sports, and therefore people didn't hope too much for him or from him. But what did these small-minded Westislanders know? What did any Aaní know about a person's worth? The Aaní had already determined who was worthy and who was not long before a person grew up, which blinded them to a person's true worth. Aaní leaders were vain, arrogant warriors, most of whom had never been in a true battle. *Now that the Koosh have come again in large numbers to this world,* Íxt thought, *the Aaní shall be forced to understand who is worthy and who is not.*

This Aaní thought he could see the future, but in looking over the edge he saw only flits of color in an otherwise dark and shadowy vision, and he could rarely understand the flitting images of color when he saw them. He sat in the Flicker House kitchen trying to look into Elán's character and true worth. He closed his eyes, but no flits of color came. He saw nothing. He had only common sense and wisdom to guide his decisions. "Do you want to follow in your grandfather Latseen's path? For that, I fear, is where your path may lead if you persist."

"Persist? I'm not sure what you mean."

"Your grandfather is the only person I know who set foot on and returned from the Koosh island."

"Which island?"

"Please drop the pretense of dull nitwittery." Old Íxt set his mug down on the floor in exasperation. "You know very well what I mean. I extracted from the foulmouthed bird what he told you, and I can see you're contemplating running off and trying to locate a Koosh dzanti by yourself. I fear your search may lead you to the island that nearly took your grandfather's life. He was never the same. I don't know what he witnessed on Saaw Island, but he said he lost part of his soul on that island, and I believe him. Part of him was already dead when he did lose his life a few winters later at the hands of cannibal giants."

Elán quit his faking. "The raven promised he'd show me where a Koosh dropped his dzanti," he said. "At first, I was shocked to hear an animal speak! And then he told some ridiculous tale of a Koosh losing its dzanti. I've always thought the Koosh legend might be true because I'd heard about your son from my father. But I think the part about the Koosh losing a dzanti is a lie. He told me it's on the sea floor of Botson's Bay. I checked out this map to see if I could locate Botson's Bay." Elān held up the map.

"Hmmm." Old Íxt stood and walked to Elān, took the map and spread it over the table. "The raven isn't lying," Old Íxt said, bending down, peering close at the map. "The Koosh are very real, and so are their dzanti." He stood up and folded the map. "And a dzanti does indeed lie on the ocean floor just off the mainland." Íxt handed the map back to Elān. "Return this back to whatever atlas you stole it from. Botson's Bay is not on it. You'll find Botson's Bay only on our military maps."

"It must be far away," Elān said.

"It is. How old are you?"

"Eighteen," Elān said.

"Training to be a warrior, no doubt, like your grandfathers?" Íxt knew Elān was not at the Longhouse of War and Diplomacy.

"I'm nearly done with coursework to become a teacher," Elān said. "But I can hunt and handle a canoe as good as any warrior in the Longhouse of War."

"The best teachers are humble," Íxt said. "You may be longhouse smart, but do you think you're experienced enough to become a true teacher?"

"No." Elān sighed. His shoulders sagged. "I'm not even confident I can teach anyone anything."

"Good," Íxt said.

"And sometimes I'm not sure I even want to be a teacher."

"What would you like to become?"

"I don't know," Elān said. He was too wary of Íxt to reveal his smoldering dream.

"What one thing do you love to do?"

"I guess it would be reading books and storytelling," Elān admitted. "That probably doesn't sound exciting."

"Books are fine," Íxt said. "Sometimes a story is all you need. A story to make you aware of an injustice, to make you remember who you are, and slap you into action. But that's the key. Books have to enfire you to take action against wrongdoings, and I know enfire isn't a word, but it should be, shouldn't it? Do your books ever enfire you to take action?"

"Yes," Elān said.

"Well? Have you ever sailed open ocean with one hand on the tiller and the other hand on the mainsail sheet?"

"Yes," Elān said. "I sailed to Deshu twice last summer to pick up the blacksmith's ore. He gives us free charcoal to make our ink. My father was with me both times, but I piloted the canoe and held the tiller. The second time, I took us around the entirety of Kéet's Island before we came back home."

"Ah. Nothing in the world or in your books can compare to splitting the waves with the bow of your canoe under full sail. Can you read a jishagoon and chart and steer by the stars?"

"Yes," Elān said. All Westislanders could navigate and sail, of course. "I've my own jishagoon and I can read navigation charts." A *jishagoon* is an Aaní nautical navigation instrument that works with the power of the sun, moon, stars and magnetics.

Íxt paused. *Elān is far too young,* he thought to himself, *for a journey to Botson's Bay. And he's a bookeater, not a warrior.* His mind was full of questions, and he shook his head as he thought. Would Elān tell anyone about the dzanti? Would he try to sail to Botson's Bay by himself? If so, wouldn't it be best to send a crew of warriors with him? And if he sent a crew of warriors, should he tell the warriors about the dzanti, or should that secret remain with Elān?

"When are you to take your exams?" Íxt's instinct—and his memory of how he had behaved when he was eighteen—

told him that if he didn't do something, Elān might try to sail alone to Botson's Bay. Raven had lit a spark in the young man, and the young man was too much like his grandfather to not cross the sea in search of adventure.

"In three moons' time," Elān replied. "At the end of the Animals-Give-Birth moon."

"Hmmm." *I'll select a crew of warriors I can trust to protect him, to put Elān's life before theirs*, Old Íxt thought. *Of course, raven will have to go along, for only he knows the exact location of the dzanti. And Yéil knows the trouble that waste of feathers will cause. I'm sorry, Latseen, but I see no other way.*

"It's decided then," Íxt told Elān. "With any luck, you'll be back in time to take those exams."

"What do you mean, back in time to take my exams?" Elān asked.

"Have you ever tried studying while sailing?"

CHAPTER 8

THE ELDERS SAT in the ancient, wave-shaped clearing of Shaatleingagi. A moon had passed since their last meeting. Íxt had proposed his plan: he would send a small force in a lightning-quick war canoe to retrieve the dzanti in hopes of using the weapon against the Koosh. Though he'd kept the villagers in Naasteidi from knowing about it, Íxt had to tell the Aaní Islands Elders' Council about the lost dzanti, but he made the council and their apprentices swear to secrecy. No one outside the Elders' Council could know about it for fear of word spreading to the Koosh.

"So, my friends, we cannot wait. The Koosh will be here soon. Our expedition must leave at once. Latseen's grandson Elān will be in charge. I've secured two Aaní warriors from Naasteidi, one very experienced, and one very green. Chetdyl, a clan leader among wolves and friend to humans, will accompany them as protection against possible Koosh devilry, as will Hoosa, a human black bear relative from S'eek Kwáan. I've arranged for Chetdyl and Hoosa to meet the crew at Quintus Kwáan. They will acquire another warrior, perhaps two, in Yelm. Ch'aak''s eagle relatives will serve as messengers and keep us informed of their progress when possible. Raven here will act as interpreter and guide, for which he will receive a winter's supply of smoked salmon. Are we all agreed?"

Íxt looked around the clearing.

"Agreed," said Ch'aak'.

"Agreed," said Kéet.

"Agreed," said Héenjá, Jánwu, and the other elders.

"Disagreed," raven said.

"Good," Íxt said. "Then we're all agreed. The goal, my friends, is the dzanti—"

"I disagreed," raven interrupted.

"I know," Íxt said. "But both of us know you will end up agreeing to my plans, so let's assume you've already agreed and move on, shall we?"

"You're a rotten old man," raven said. "You already owe me a season of salmon, and now you want me to guide this crazy death canoe with a crew of fatheads who smell worse than a bear's morning buns, and you assume I'll agree? Keep your winter of salmon and go on the trip yourself, you moldy, old skeleton."

Íxt fake-yawned. "Are you quite finished?"

"No," raven said. "When you die, I'm going to remove your bones from your burial house, pee on them, and then use your leg bones to drum a shame song on your stupid, fat skull." Raven held out his wing. "Now I am 'quite finished.'"

"May I speak?" Íxt asked.

"Permission granted." Raven fluttered a wing in Íxt's face.

"For this expedition, the canoe will be provisioned with bentwood boxes of salmon. I will make sure that three of these boxes contain the best smoked sockeye salmon that Naasteidi can produce. These boxes will belong to you alone, and all you have to do is guide the crew to the dzanti once in Botson's Bay. And, when you return, I'll make sure the folks at Naasteidi provide you two seasons of salmon."

"I want five boxes for the voyage," raven said.

"Five boxes it is," Íxt said. "Agreed?"

"Agreed. Any sign of danger and I'll take flight," raven said.

"I expect no more from you," Íxt said.

"Very well," raven said. "I'll go on this stupid journey."

"Very well. When we receive the dzanti," Íxt continued,

"with Yéil's help we will determine how it works and, more importantly, how to use it to our advantage. If we can use it to sink the Koosh canoes at sea, we might be able to save the Aaní and all our relatives—human and animal."

"Describe to me again the crazies going on this stupid journey," raven said.

"You, of course," Íxt replied. "Two Aaní warriors from Naasteidi, one, maybe two, Aaní warriors from the Eastisland village of Yelm, the wolf-warrior Chetdyl, a black bear cousin named Hoosa, and Elán of Naasteidi."

"That fatheaded bookeater whose salmon I stole? The Aaní idiot who still wears diapers and pisses himself?"

"The grandson of a great Aaní warrior," Íxt said, "the only warrior I've known to set foot on the Koosh island and come back alive."

"The only warrior dumb enough to set foot on the Koosh island," raven added. "When do we leave?"

"In three days," Íxt said. "The canoe has been made and will soon be outfitted. You are to remain near the Flicker House at Naasteidi."

Raven screeched a loud, sneering laugh.

"Have you been in contact with Yelm?" Kéet asked.

"No. But Elán will carry a letter from me to the Hits'aati of Yelm's Longhouse of War and Diplomacy. He's a close friend of mine and I do not doubt he will find able warriors to aid us."

"I would wish for more warriors to accompany them," Ch'aak' said.

"What? Only now are you realizing how stupid this is?" asked raven. "All the deer crap you've been eating has made your brain spongy. We won't be in that canoe very long with the danger we are sure to find."

"Your numbers need to be small," Íxt said to raven. "The canoe is small but very fast. You need to outrun trouble, not fight it."

"But if the Koosh canoes are as fast as Kéet's whale relatives have said they are…" Ch'aak' didn't finish the sentence.

"I don't anticipate our crew meeting the Koosh," Íxt replied, "but perhaps the canoe our crew will have can outrun even the Koosh canoe."

"There's only one way to know for sure," Jánwu said.

"Indeed." Íxt looked around the clearing. "Is there any further business here today?" Everyone remained silent. "I must hurry now to the Flicker House at Naasteidi to continue with preparations. It wasn't hard to convince the Hits'aati of Naasteidi's Longhouse of War and Diplomacy to lend me two warriors. Rumors of a Koosh invasion abound in longhouses across Éil'." The Hits'aati of Naasteidi's Longhouse of War and Diplomacy, a one-eyed, ancient warrior named Gutl, had been a friend of Íxt for many years and always respected Íxt's ability to see over the edge.

Íxt shook his head. "I still need to help Elán prepare for the journey and convince Naasteidi's Aankaawu to prepare strongholds in the mountains in case the village needs to retreat. If the Koosh come with their death dzanti, it would be a massacre." An Aankaawu is like the mayor of your town or village. Most every Aaní village across Éil' had a stronghold far from the ocean that villagers could retreat to in times of trouble. Naasteidi's Aankaawu was reluctant to frighten villagers by ordering Naasteidi's mountain stronghold fortified and prepared in case of Koosh invasion. Such a reluctance, to old Íxt's mind, could be deadly. Íxt gazed at everyone in the clearing. "Let's wish our small crew all the luck in this world and beyond." He rose up from his stone and looked at raven. "I must be going. Wait for me near the Flicker House in Naasteidi three days hence and come when I call."

CHAPTER 9

ELĀN HAD SPENT the past moon washed between tides of anxiousness and excitement. Life's fog had lifted and he now saw Naasteidi in the cold, clear light of knowing he'd be leaving soon. He'd kept his upcoming mission secret in the village but had a hard time containing his excitement. He noticed villagers looking at him oddly whenever he spoke. His tone was too thin, and the words came out too quick.

Elān had doubted Íxt could convince his parents to let him go on the journey, but Íxt had convinced them the very night he'd confronted Elān. "The Koosh are in our world in great numbers," Íxt told Skaan and Shaa, Elān's mother. "For some strange reason known only to raven, he has chosen your son to play a part in saving the Aaní and Éil'. I believe it has to do with your father Latseen, Shaa."

"My father?" Shaa asked. "What in Yéil's name has it to do with him? He was killed by the cannibal giants many winters ago—on the mainland!" Íxt was Shaa's father's oldest and closest friend, but she shuddered to think of her son traveling to the same place her father had died.

"I have spent these past several moons gathering information," Íxt had told them. "I've heard from every elder in the Aaní Islands Elders' Council, and the rumors have become more dreadful since the turn of the winter. The Island Yahooni have been entirely defeated and are now prisoners of the Koosh. The Mainland Yahooni have gone into hiding, but surely the Koosh will find them and take them prisoner. Though they bear no love for the Koosh, all Yahooni will enjoy the invasion of Aaní land. They've never forgotten how Latseen defeated them, so they will enjoy and applaud Naasteidi's destruction. The cannibal giants are also defeated and are prisoners of the Koosh. We must take action now."

"My father always trusted you, Íxt," Shaa relented. "I will trust you, but you know how much I've lost when my relatives have traveled to the mainland. Don't lose my son to the mainland too."

THE MORNING AFTER the Aaní Islands Elders' Council, Íxt knocked softly on the kitchen door of the Flicker House where Elān and his parents sat drinking tea. Elān rose and opened the door. Two Aaní warriors—one close to the age of Elān's dad, one a bit older than Elān—stood behind Íxt. They were the same warriors who had judged the archery competition.

"Come in," Elān said to Íxt and the two warriors at the door. The warriors wore light, woven clothes, dyed a faded red and black, of the type the Naasteidi warriors wore during morning exercises. The young warrior had black hair and a youthful smile; the older warrior had thick streaks of gray running through his long, black hair. Scars competed with wrinkles for prominence on his face.

"I believe you know these two," Íxt said.

"Yes," Elān replied. "Hello, Captain Caraiden and Ch'eet. Your ancestors."

"Caraiden," Skaan said. "Come over here." He hugged the old warrior. Caraiden had served with Skaan's father. Caraiden looked surprised and gave only a slight hug in return. "Your ancestors."

"And yours. How have you been, Skaan?" the warrior asked.

"Oh, fine, fine."

"Hello, Shaa. Your ancestors," Caraiden said to Elān's mother.

"And yours," she replied. "How are you?"

"Confused," Caraiden said. He sat down next to Skaan at the kitchen table. "But I've been promised an explanation. Come, Ch'eet, sit down," Caraiden said to the younger warrior. Ch'eet sat down at the kitchen table.

"And you shall have one," Íxt said. He took from a deep coat pocket a map and handed it to Elān. "Take this and spread it on the table."

Elan opened the map and set it on the table. He took a seat next to his mother. Only Íxt remained standing. The map showed all of Éil', including Aaní and Deikeenaa territory, as well as the Island and Mainland Yahooni, and the cannibal giants' lands on the mainland known as K̲usax̲ak̲wáan. The map also showed ocean currents, ocean depths, distances, and estimated paddle and sail times between key military locations.

"That's one of our military maps," Caraiden said. "How did you get that?"

"I liberated it." Íxt smiled. "I've brought you here today, Caraiden and Ch'eet, to prepare you for your journey. I know Gutl informed you some time ago that you would soon be going on a mission for me, but he didn't give you all the information because I didn't give it to him. In short, I need you two to lead young Elān here to Botson's Bay, which is in the land of the cannibal giants." Íxt's finger traced the map from Naasteidi southwesterly to Botson's Bay. "And back, of course."

Everyone sat silent for a moment.

"That's a long journey," Caraiden said.

Elān looked at the old warrior. Caraiden's scarred face showed no emotion, though the lines on his forehead were creased, and his voice sounded doubtful. Elān gazed at Ch'eet. There was a light in the young warrior's eyes.

"You have been to the land of the cannibal giants," Íxt said.

"You know I have," Caraiden replied. "And it's not a place I choose to return to."

"Of course," Íxt replied. "But it's not your choice, I'm afraid."

"Not my choice?"

"That's right. It's not your choice." Íxt straightened up from his hunched posture over the map and glared down at Caraiden.

"You don't know what you speak of, old man," Caraiden barked. "I've been a warrior for as many years as you've seen over the edge. I'm an elder. And if that isn't enough, Gutl owes me a debt from long ago."

"Gutl owes you?"

"Yes," Caraiden said, his voice raised. "Gutl owes me."

"Owes you a debt, you say?" Íxt raised his voice to match Caraiden's. "You dare speak of a debt, Caraiden? In this house? What of the debt you owe Latseen's family? But for that debt, things might now be different with the Koosh."

Shaa protested. "He doesn't owe me..." Íxt held up his hand. Shaa stopped. Elān looked around the table. Every face save Caraiden's and Íxt's appeared confused. Íxt glared at Caraiden, and Caraiden scowled back. A tense silence froze the air in the room.

Caraiden broke the freezing silence and hissed at Íxt, "I'll go, old man, but never speak again of whatever debt you think I owe."

Íxt nodded and smiled. "Good."

Caraiden frowned. "What's our purpose?"

"To guard and protect young Elān," Íxt said.

"I guessed that," Caraiden replied, "but what's our purpose in Botson's Bay?"

"Elān goes there to reconnoiter for me," Íxt replied. "I cannot tell you anything beyond that. You and Ch'eet will guard and protect him on his journey and see he returns home safe."

"Three people? In the land of the cannibal giants?" asked Caraiden. "That small of a crew can't properly handle a war canoe and Elān is no warrior. He's a bookeater."

"The cannibal giants are greatly reduced in number and strength. And you will be joined in your journey by more warriors from Yelm, and by the leader of the wolf clan, and by a black bear human cousin," Íxt said. "And perhaps a bird."

"A bird?" Caraiden asked.

"Just a friendly raven," Íxt said, "in case you need a translator. He won't be any trouble at all. A helpful soul. And I'm providing you with a newly carved, small but fast war canoe from the shop of Old Man Gunyak. A faster canoe has never traveled the whale-road."

Caraiden was about to ask another question, but Íxt held up his hand. "Wait, let me explain to you what has been happening in those faraway lands."

Íxt told Ch'eet and Caraiden the tale you've already heard about the Koosh treachery and evil. Elān watched both warriors as they heard the news. Caraiden's face gave no emotion, but Elān could see Ch'eet was frightened, though he tried to hide it with a serious look.

"Though he may think I'm crazy, Gutl loaned you to me because we're old friends. I assure you I am not crazy. Your journey may aid us in the upcoming war against the Koosh," Íxt told the warriors. "Elān shall be in charge of the expedition, except in an emergency battle situation. Caraiden shall lead the expedition if battle is necessary. But I must stress that you are to outrun trouble at all costs. You shall not engage in battle. Flee from fights and return as quickly as possible."

"I'll go because I gave my word," Caraiden said, "but I don't feel good about this journey."

Íxt looked at Ch'eet. "And you, Ch'eet?" he asked. "How do you feel about such a journey?"

"Fine, Mr. Íxt, absolutely fine," he said. "I've trained a long time for an opportunity like this."

"Very good. So, we must prepare your provisions. The canoe has been selected. Elān will retrieve it this afternoon. Skaan and Shaa have graciously allowed us to use the Flicker House to store our supplies. We will all stay here until the expedition departs in two days. We need to create a list. You will take only the essentials, and even with only essentials the canoe will be packed tight. Elān, would you fetch me a quill and some ink?"

After an hour of consultation, Íxt wrote the following list of supplies:

Provisions
5 large boxes of smoked salmon
5 tiny boxes of smoked salmon
2 large boxes dried berries
1 bentwood cooking box
1 metal lockbox with key (Elān's)
5 large storage skin bags (filled with water)
5 small drinking skin bags (filled with water)
12 fire starters
6 lanterns with extra candles
2 medical kits
3 waterproof seabags for clothes (Elān, Caraiden, Ch'eet)
5 bedrolls and extra blankets
Fishing tackle and dipping net
1 waterproof bag for weapons (with extra sword)
1 waterproof bag for bows (with extra strings)
4 waterproof bags for arrows (with extra points)
2 axes

Spare paddles
Spare rope
Spare sailcloth patching
Sail repair equipment
Weapons and armor oil

"That encompasses everything," Íxt said. He handed the quill back to Elan. "And we must find a way to stow it all. Elān, fetch the canoe."

CHAPTER 10

On the south side of Naasteidi, a massive tree-lined peninsula reached out into the sea. It sheltered the village from the southern winds, which could be quite cold in winter. Along the peninsula sat the Harbor Master's house, official government longhouses, and, at the very end, a military fort topped with a watchtower peeking out toward the sea. The peninsula provided a sheltered harbor for Naasteidi Aaní and made safe beaching for their canoes.

Indeed, you could walk along the peninsula on any given day and see dozens of canoes of all types: ocean-going canoes massive of length and beam-fitted with outrigging and sails capable of taking many warriors throughout Aaní land and beyond; medium fishing canoes with deep, flat bottoms to hold their catch, some with outrigging and sails some not, all with seaweedy nets balled up in their bows; small pleasure canoes made for strolls across the bay in front of the village; and canoes of every other size sat pulled up on the sandy beach along the peninsula and covered with hide or cloth tarps to keep them from drying out and cracking in the sun. The master canoe-builder Old Man Gunyak and his numerous apprentices and carvers made all of Naasteidi's canoes.

An ornately carved and painted miniature canoe in the shape of a killer whale hung from the eaves above the entrance of Old Man Gunyak's shop at the base of the peninsula. The door was open and Elān walked in. The air was dusty but smelled wonderfully of cedar and pine. Tools lined the walls. Two new canoes sat on sawhorses, their reddish-blond wood still rough-hewn and splintery. A staircase off the side of the room led to the second story where Old Man Gunyak lived.

"Hello?" Elān called.

Old Man Gunyak came down the stairs. "Ah, Elān."

"Your ancestors, Mr. Gunyak," Elān said. "I've come to pick up the canoe for Íxt."

"Ah, yes. And yours. Come this way." He led Elān through an attached workshop where massive delimbed tree trunks lay and out through the back on toward the bay. A dozen canoes sat pulled up on the beach, all covered with cloth tarps except for one. "Here it is." The old man pointed to the tarpless canoe. "Old Íxt better appreciate this," he said. "One moon isn't enough time to properly outfit masts and outrigging on a canoe like this. Tell him I should have charged him more for it."

It was small, Elān saw, and narrow. It was painted flat black except for the large figure of an eagle Gunyak had carved on the prow, which was painted dark red—its wings flared back from the centerline along both sides of the body of the canoe. The black paint Gunyak used was of his own making, and he used it on all military craft. It was waterproof and made for very low resistance in the water.

A large main mast shot up from the canoe's center. But there was also something Elān had only seen on larger military canoes: a jib mast near the bow. He and Gunyak walked up to it. The bow and stern were as tall as Elān. The canoe's body was the height of Elān's shoulders. Four thick thwarts flared the sides of the canoe outward. Elān peered into it. The inside was also painted black, and five smooth-sanded seats with indentations for the paddlers' bottoms were fastened into the sides: three seats between the stern and main mast, with the captain's seat at the stern sitting up higher than the rest so as to control the tiller, and two seats between the main mast and jib mast. Between the jib mast and the prow there were metal fittings to store bentwood boxes.

It had double outrigging with netting between the outriggers and paddling slits in the netting along the canoe sides. Stout poles fore and aft fastened each outrigger to hinges on the canoe's body to let the outriggers move up and down in the sea. "It's not large, I'll grant you," Gunyak said, "but it's faster than most anything on the ocean. Ixt said it needed to hold seven people at most, plus provisions, and still be able to fly. It'll be tight, the two people up front won't have seats, but it can hold seven if needs be. There's storage in the outriggers." The outriggers were deep, sharp, and sleek. Elān saw three storage sections—front, middle, and rear—on each outrigger. "Standard tiller. The rudder can be locked up out of the water, of course. The skeg and rudder are narrower and deeper, so it'll cut quite well with much less resistance."

"Has it been on the water?" Elān asked.

"Ah, yes. The boys have taken it out twice," Gunyak said, referring to his apprentices. "They said it flies over the waves when you get both sails unfurled. The sails are made of very light but strong hide with cartilage battens. They'll hold quite a load of wind. That front sail there, the jib, makes the canoe fly. Once it's up, lock its sheet in. No need to fool with it as you would the main, except when you need to tack. The canoe is shallow and doesn't draw much water at all, which means the folks in the back will have to watch their heads with the main boom. Not much clearance for tall folks. Whoever's at the tiller will have to let folks in the back know when to duck, especially if everyone's paddling and not paying attention."

"How do you raise the jib?"

Old Man Gunyak walked toward the front of the canoe. Elān followed. "That halyard there, you see it? Unstrap the sail and haul on that halyard. Once the sail is up, lock the sheet to a cleat and leave it." Metal cleats had been attached along both edges of the canoe, fore and aft of the main mast. The jib sheet could be tied to either side of the mast. "There's one paddle in it you can borrow to get home," Gunyak said. "I assume you'll all have your own paddles."

"Yes," Elān said.

"That's about it," Gunyak said. "Go ahead and jump in."

If you're not familiar with the nautical life, learning the names of all the parts on a sailboat can be more difficult than sailing. Elān grew up nautical and so knew those names well. A mast is the wooden pole that points straight up in the air, which you attach the sail to. The boom is a wooden pole attached near the bottom of the mast to make an L shape. The boom points toward the back of the canoe. The bottom of the sail is attached to the boom. A sheet is not a sail! A sheet is a rope attached to the end of the boom to move it back and forth to catch or spill wind. A halyard is a rope that raises a sail. Battens are stiff pieces of wood or bone that fit into pockets in the sail to keep it taut. The bow is the front of the canoe, the stern is the back, starboard is the right side, and port is the left side. A cleat is a piece of metal that you can attach a rope to. With this knowledge, you now know how to sail.

Elān climbed into the canoe and, with a lot of effort, Gunyak and his workers push-dragged the canoe out into the bay. Old Man Gunyak stood knee deep in the surf holding onto the canoe's stern line. Elān unstrapped the jib sail, grabbed the halyard, and raised the sail. Elān tied the jib sheet around a cleat and walked to the captain's seat in the stern. The wind caught the jib and the canoe began to buck.

"I'm going to let it go," Gunyak said. "You go ahead and take it."

Gunyak let go and the canoe took off, the wind pushing it north, starboard, and shoreward toward the village. Elān grabbed the tiller and pushed it hard away from him to get the bow directly into the wind so he could make ready the mainsail without the canoe being blown out of control by the wind into the jib sail. Once nosed into the wind, the jib sail flapped and the canoe slowed.

Elān was excited. He was all by himself in a military craft normally reserved for warriors. And the canoe was fast with just the jib alone. He yanked up the mainsail. Both main and jib luffed in irons in the wind. Holding the mainsail's sheet in his left hand, Elān grabbed the tiller with his right and pulled it toward him until it was against his back. Both sails stopped flapping and snapped taut as the wind gusted into their pockets, and the canoe flew forward. A burst of adrenaline shot through him as the sails strained and the canoe listed and raced forward. The starboard side outrigger creaked as it slashed deep through the waves.

Determined, he pulled the mainsail sheet tight. The canoe leapt faster across the water; he could hear it sizzle over the waves. He flew past the village up toward the north part of the bay. Elān had never traveled at such a pace. He glanced at the heavy outrigging. It looked to be holding fast, as it should. Beyond the starboard outrigger, the shore went by at an incredible rate.

"Haaw!" Elān yelled. He felt wonderful to be racing across the ocean. He let out the sheet and spilled some wind from the mainsail's pocket, and the canoe slowed slightly. Elān pulled the sheet tight again and the canoe shot forward at an even greater speed. He rode the wind to the far north of the bay, and then let out most of the mainsail sheet until the sail flapped. He cleated the sheet and turned the canoe's stern into the wind. The canoe slowed until it drifted. Elān walked to the bow, untied the jib sheet and lowered the jib sail. He'd bring the canoe in with only the mainsail.

Elān grabbed the paddle and turned the canoe back toward the village. Once turned, he uncleated the mainsail sheet, swung the boom, and pulled back the tiller. The wind caught and shot the canoe onward toward the village. Even with one sail unfurled, the canoe blazed across the ocean. Mainsail sheet and tiller in his hands, Elān could see the roof of his house in the distance. He saw several people gathered outside, but he was too far away to tell who they were. *This is what I've dreamt about*, Elān thought. He'd never sailed this fast. And he was alone with the sea. "In the name of Yéil," he said aloud, "this is wonderful."

The wind blew back his black hair, which was wet from spray splashing over the sides of the canoe. The roof of his house came closer. He saw his mother and father standing with Íxt, Caraiden, and Ch'eet on the beach in front of his house. He pulled the mainsail sheet tight and the canoe sped up. He looked behind him and saw a white foam trail on the sea face. The shore was coming up quickly; he could smell the seaweed on the beach. He pulled the sheet a bit tighter for a final shot of speed, then let the rope out, yanked the tiller, let the sail flap, and pulled the rudder up out of the water. The canoe ran to shore on its own momentum and scraped up onto the beach.

"You had the biggest smile on your face," his father said as he grabbed the canoe and heaved it ashore. "When you went by the first time you had a grin on your face and coming in you were smiling so huge I could see your teeth a long way out."

"Dad, this is the greatest canoe," Elān said. He lowered the mainsail, tied it down, and jumped over the stern of the canoe into the surf. He helped his father pull the canoe up into the dead seaweed, above the shoreline of small, sea-smoothed rocks. They tied it off on a wooden stake in front of their house. Íxt, Caraiden, Ch'eet, and Shaa joined Elān and Skaan walking around the canoe, inspecting the rigging and netting and holds.

"I did not think it would be so small," Caraiden said.

"Speed, Caraiden, is more important," Íxt said. "And I've never seen a swifter canoe."

"All canoes are fast when not loaded," the old warrior replied.

"There's freshwater storage in the outriggers," Skaan said. A middle section in each outrigger had been hollowed out and lined so it could hold water. The lid could be lifted during heavy rains to catch water. Skaan opened the other holds in the outrigger. He sat down on the netting. "On calm days you could lie on this netting or even sleep on it and not get wet," he said. "If there's any chop on the water, though, you'd get soaked." He got into the canoe and felt the sails, which sat tied to the booms. "Íxt," Skaan said, turning to the old man, "I will go in place of my son."

Elān felt his chest tighten.

"I cannot bear to lose my son on this journey," Skaan continued. "I will go in his place."

"I'd be glad to have you," Caraiden said. "I don't mean to upset you, young nephew," he said to Elān, "but your father has more experience. We don't know if we'll come back. I've been on many dangerous journeys. Experience rather than youth is needed."

Elān could feel his face warming. He kept silent, hoping Íxt would say something.

"And I'm sure Shaa would prefer I go instead of Elān," Skaan said.

Íxt sighed. He walked toward Shaa. "What do you say?" he asked her.

Shaa was quiet for a long time. Elān could hear the waves, laughter from the village, and voices from fishermen out in the bay.

"I prefer to keep my son home and safe," Shaa said. Elān's chest felt even tighter. "But I'll let Elān make the decision."

"I'm going," Elān said forcefully. "I need to go."

"It will be okay, Skaan," Íxt said quietly. "Trust your son. He's a capable and curious young man, and he just needs some time on the sea to find confidence in his capability.

He'll be back in no time." He gripped Skaan's shoulder and winked. "You're too old for such a journey, anyway." He turned to Caraiden and Ch'eet. "Go gather your supplies," he said. "The waterproof bags, waterskins, and weapons and armor. Bring them here."

CHAPTER 11

BY EVENING, A mountain of supplies sat in the front room, or 'searoom,' of the Flicker House. It had been many winters since the once great Flicker House had supplied such a journey. The day before their departure was spent loading, unpacking, reloading, re-unpacking, and re-reloading the canoe. The boxes took up the most room, of course. Airtight bentwood boxes. Two were stored in the stern behind Elān's seat, three in the front, and the cooking box under the seat just in front of the main mast. The large skin bags full of water were attached to the netting. Each person stowed his waterproof bag of clothes where he could, and the bags of weapons and armor, along with other equipment, were stowed in the holds of the outriggers. Lastly, they filled the outrigger freshwater holds and secured their lids.

In the Flicker House kitchen, the night before departure, Elān, Caraiden, and Ch'eet studied the military map tacked across the table. Íxt helped outline the route they should take. "From Yelm, head south till you come to the end of Samish and then track a course due west," he said, running his finger across the map. "Keep the Anchor Star directly portside at night, and the bow pointed at the Drifting Star each morning. Keep your jishagoon with you at all times, Elān. Never be without it. The first island you come to, as you know, is Kals'aak. It's a seet and six yaakw distance, about two days at a good paddle throughout the length of the sun, or one and a half if the wind is right."

A *seet* is the average distance a canoe can travel under sail with good wind in ten hours or ten *yaakw*—a yaakw being, of course, how far a canoe can sail in an hour.

"From Kals'aak you can head east to Kéet's Island and the village of Deshu. From Deshu you can choose your route. If you run into trouble, you can make for Shaada."

"Can we stay there?" asked Elān.

"I haven't been there for some winters," Íxt replied, "but the Deikeenaa there are not violent and are still our closest allies, though they'll be suspicious and may raise rumor of your journey. Sleep in your canoe when you can. Stay in the wild if you must get off the ocean, but I would avoid villages. Much risk comes with staying in villages."

Elān nodded a nod too superficial for Íxt's liking, but the old man ignored his misgiving. "The gravest danger will come when you leave friendly seas and venture beyond Latseen's Line."

After Latseen's victory against the invading Yahooni, the Aaní with their Deikeenaa allies drew up a treaty with their defeated enemy. Except for several islands remaining in Yahooni possession close to the mainland in the south, all islands in Aaní and Deikeenaa territory became off-limits to Yahooni. Aaní and Deikeenaa territory was denoted on navigation and military maps by 'Latseen's Line.' Any Yahooni canoe that crossed Latseen's Line into Aaní or Deikeenaa territory was considered hostile and could be fired upon or confiscated. The Aaní and Deikeenaa reserved the right to sail across Latseen's Line and all around the mainland, though over the intervening winters since the treaty it grew more and more perilous to test that right. Most Aaní saw nothing of interest or value on the mainland. A large group of Latseen's warriors remained behind on the mainland after the war to build a fort, known as the Far Out Fort, and a long stone wall, Latseen's Wall, across the interior of the mainland to separate themselves from the defeated Yahooni who had to remain south of the wall. The warriors of the Far Out Fort built a village behind the wall and were constantly battling Yahooni aggression across Latseen's Wall.

"Once you pass Latseen's Line, consider any canoe you encounter to be hostile," Íxt continued. "You will have a decision to make: take down your sails so you will not be seen from afar and paddle—of course, your progress will be much slower, and you will be exhausted—or risk sail and be seen from afar. Whether or not you are pursued, you are sure to be seen if you raise sail, but you will be much swifter and, if need be, have the energy for battle. Elán will make the decision after consultation with Caraiden. Agreed?" Íxt looked at Caraiden, who nodded agreement. "Let us sleep, then. With Yéil's favor, we will all meet here again in a moon or two's time."

Late that night, after everyone else went to bed in the vacant rooms of the Flicker House, Íxt woke Elán. "Once that raven shows you where the dzanti has fallen, have Caraiden, Ch'eet, Hoosa, and Chetdyl stand guard. Chetdyl's nose should keep you safe from the Koosh if they've shape-shifted. If he doesn't detect any Koosh, go ahead and try to retrieve the dzanti. I'm not sure how deep underwater it will be. You might have to fish it out of the sea if you can't dive down to it. Listen. No one has ever held a dzanti. The raven said it knocked him senseless—what in Yéil's name that means I don't know, because I find very little sense in him. If you don't feel comfortable touching it, use rope, or wood, or some other tool to handle it. Once you get the dzanti, keep it in the lockbox. Only you and I have a key. If all is hopeless, unlock the box and try to use it. But I don't think it will come to that. Once you have the dzanti, come straight home. Sail through the night if you have to. Have Caraiden and Ch'eet paddle through the night. They'll grumble, but they're sworn to protect you. Always guard the dzanti. We shall decide what to do with it when you return."

"We should probably give it to our Head Warrior or Hits'aati," Elān said.

"Perhaps. Though there may be other warriors better equipped to use it." Íxt smiled. "How do you feel?"

"Nervous, I guess. A bit scared, too. But also excited. I don't want to let anyone down. I don't want to fail. But this isn't like my studies, or even like reading an adventure in a book. This is real."

"All of us, even warriors, feel that way before a journey," Íxt said. "And your studies? Did you pack your books and writing supplies?"

"I've packed a quill and ink and one book in my clothes bag," Elān said. "I don't know how much studying I'll get done, though."

"Your studies are fine and good. But you can learn a lot by watching the world," Old Íxt said. "Two people can watch the same thing and each learn something different. Think of the salmon. What can you learn from them?"

"What can I learn about them?" the boy asked. "Like what they eat and when they come to the rivers?"

"Not exactly," Old Íxt replied. "What can they teach you?"

"I don't understand."

"What can you learn by observing them? In your mind, see a salmon leaping from a stream. Stop the leap and hold the salmon in your mind. The stillness of salmon. Look at that still salmon from all directions. Now ask yourself to what meaning is the salmon headed? Where are the meanings?"

"I don't understand."

"Why is the salmon leaping?"

"To get upstream," Elān replied.

"Why? Where is the salmon headed?"

"To its birthplace."

"What for?"

"To spawn and create life," Elān replied, "and then die, of course."

"Does the salmon know that? Is it the salmon's own will that pushes it to leap over and over upstream to create life only to die, or does some other will, some other force or instinct, push the salmon through the stream?"

Elān paused in thought. "I don't know."

Íxt smiled. "You should ponder that question. And what you may or may not learn will be different than what other people may or may not learn from our cousin the salmon. You must find your own lesson from the salmon. Be one who searches for meanings in life and not the meaning of life." Íxt patted Elān's hand and left.

Elān couldn't get back to sleep. He lay awake thinking about the next day's voyage, at times nervous, at times excited. He would be at the tiller. Was he ready for that responsibility? He forced himself to ponder Íxt's lesson about salmon and meanings to take his mind off the journey ahead. *What pushes the salmon to struggle against the stream?* he wondered. *Salmon always seem to be full of purpose and intent, so stern and humorless as they leap toward their death. I've never seen a humorous salmon.* He smiled at the thought of salmon joking with one another underwater. *Who knows? Maybe salmon are full of mirth and laughter. I don't know,* he admitted to himself, *and I don't know where to find the meanings either, Old Íxt.*

THE CREW ROSE at dawn, ate a light breakfast of salmon and oatmeal, and gathered at the canoe. Shaa carried a wooden box with her, and Skaan carried a new-carved paddle. "My son," Shaa said. "This is for you." She opened the box and brought out an armored shirt made of thick, overlapping black metal coins sewn onto heavy hide. The faded image of a red flicker tail was painted on the front. The coins had a small hole in the center and strange writing around the outside. From a distance, they looked like black fish scales. Elān had always admired the coin-mail armor on the rare occasions his father removed it from its bentwood box. "This belonged to your grandfather." She handed it to Elān. "The coins came from the Fire Islands far to the west. Your grandfather wore this through many battles across many seas. Go ahead and try it on."

Elān took off his sea coat and put the coin-mail shirt over his undershirt. It was heavy and hung very loosely off his shoulders. Shaa laughed. "Your grandfather was a muscular man," she said. "I'd feel better if you kept this on all the time. A few weeks at sea will help fill your muscles out. This shirt will fit better by the time you return. Keep it as dry as possible, and oil it often."

Elān kept the shirt on and put his sea coat over it. He hugged his mother. His father handed him the new-carved paddle. "Your mother and I had this made for your voyage. It's identical to the one your grandfather Latseen used on his voyages." Elān turned the paddle over in his hands: it was a large, long paddle for ocean voyages. The grip and shaft were sanded smooth and had painted black-and-red rings between the grip and bottom handhold at the throat. A flicker was carved into the top and shoulders of the paddle's blade and the body of the blade was speckled red on white, like a flicker's body. The tip was carved into a flicker's claw. The entire paddle gleamed with a thick coat of waterproofing.

"Gunalchéesh," Elān said. He hugged his father.

"Since you have the honor of leading this expedition," Íxt said to Elān, "you have the honor of naming the canoe."

Such was Westislander tradition. Each time an important expedition set forth on the sea, the captain was allowed the honor of naming the canoe even if the canoe had seen a hundred such voyages. A canoe could have many names during its sea life.

"Have you thought of a name?" Íxt asked.

Elān had. "I name it *Waka*," he said.

"A fine name," Íxt said. "Shaa, do you have the jar?"

Shaa handed Íxt a small jar of herring oil. Íxt took the jar and poured the oil over the bow of the canoe. "Your sea-road begins and ends here." Another Westislander tradition. It would help the canoe find its way home. "Now, board the canoe and I will call the bird," Íxt said. He pulled a bone whistle from his coat pocket and blew three loud shrills. Elān gave his parents one last hug, stepped over the bow of the canoe, and made his way skillfully to the stern. He grabbed his paddle. Caraiden entered with equal skill after Elān and made his way to the middle, in front of the main mast. He took his paddle and laid it across his legs. Ch'eet held on to the bow of the canoe, ready to push off with Skaan's help. They looked at Íxt.

"Are we ready?" Skaan asked Íxt.

"Not quite. We need the bird." He blew again on his bone whistle.

They waited. And waited longer.

Íxt blew his whistle. His anger made the whistle scream.

They waited. Nothing.

The whistle screamed several more times. "One day I will pluck every feather from that bird's body," Íxt said. "We have to wait," he told the crew. They vaulted out of the canoe and walked up to the beach.

Shortly, an eagle came down from his perch high on a cedar beyond the village. He landed on the beach next to Íxt. Elān watched Íxt kneel down and talk to the eagle. He was amazed. Elān heard only short screeches and throaty squawks, but soon Íxt turned to the crew and said, "This is the Eagle clan leader's son. He's been waiting for you to set sail so he can inform his kinsmen. He has no idea where that foul bird has gone off to."

Even though Íxt had told him the Eagle clan would be watching, Elān was comforted to see the eagle. He would have messengers on his journey. He wished he too could talk to the eagle. He promised himself he would learn bird and animal languages—if he lived through this adventure. The eagle gave a few more screeches and then flew off. Elān heard the air being pushed underneath its wings.

THE SUN WAS above the mountains behind Naasteidi before raven flew in. He landed on the top of the main mast, which was shaped like a bird's nest in order to hold a lantern. Raven looked at the scene in the canoe below him. "Where's my salmon?" he asked.

"Caraiden, Ch'eet," Íxt said, "I give you permission to put an arrow through this lazy raven's throat if he doesn't shut up."

Caraiden waded out to one of the outriggers and opened the rear storage hatch. He took from a waterproof bag a bow and string. He then pulled out a waterproof quiver of arrows. "Whether or not the bird is dead or alive, it is a good idea to have a bow within reach. We'll keep this in the canoe."

"Where's my salmon?" raven asked again.

"It's stored in the canoe," Íxt said. "Now, if it fits into your schedule, it is time to depart."

"The only good thing about this death journey is I won't have to see your stupid old slug face, you rotten, moldy skeleton," raven said.

"Are you coming down from there?" Caraiden asked raven, who remained perched on the mast.

"No. I'm staying up here."

Caraiden shook his head. Elān once more stepped into the canoe and made his way to the stern. Caraiden followed after him, bow and quiver in hand, and took his place in front of the main mast. He slung the bow around his body and set the quiver atop a bentwood box. Ch'eet and Skaan pushed the canoe off the beach. Ch'eet waded through the water and then jumped in the bow. The three men grabbed their paddles and reversed the canoe out into the bay.

"I'll see you soon," Elān said to his parents. He turned away so they couldn't see him near tears.

"Your sea-road begins and ends here," his father said.

"Port," Elān said. Ch'eet and Caraiden put their paddles on the starboard side and dug deep into the sea, pulling it toward them. Elān kept his paddle portside and pushed the water away from him. The canoe's bow turned to port and pointed out to the open water. There was a very light breeze coming toward the shore. "We'll paddle past the end of the beach and then see if we can catch the wind," Elān said. Ch'eet and Caraiden kept paddling. Elān used his paddle as a rudder.

The peninsula lay off portside. A few people had gathered by the canoes pulled up along the spit and waved as Elān and the crew went by. Elān unlocked the rudder and pushed it down into place. He set his paddle in the canoe and tried to gauge the wind. It was still slight and moving westward toward shore. "Once we're clear of the peninsula we'll haul the sails," Elān told the crew. The two warriors kept a steady paddle, and the canoe moved slowly through the sea. *We're heavy*, Elān thought. *I wonder if we'll be able to outrun danger?*

They passed the end of the peninsula. "All right," Elān said. "Hoist sails. Ch'eet, untie the jib and lock the sheet to the port cleat. Caraiden, would you untie the main? We will run cross wind till we get south of Samish." The warriors set their paddles down and went to work. Ch'eet untied the jib and hauled on its sheet. Elān steadied the tiller while Caraiden untied the main. Ch'eet tied the jib sheet to the cleat. Caraiden spread the mainsail back along the boom. The wind still blew slight from the west. Elān pushed the tiller out and the sails flapped and caught the breeze. Elān pulled the mainsail sheet tight and the canoe gathered speed.

A sadness captured Elān as he watched Naasteidi disappear.

CHAPTER 12

Around the southwest edge of Samish, the wind blew hard from the west. Elān, catching the wind full in the pockets of the sails, steered within sight of shore. The canoe raced on. The sun was out, reflecting brightly off the sea. A few very white clouds drifted above. The canoe sliced through the waves, leaving a foam trail behind. "*Waka* can fly," Elān yelled to the crew, and for once even Caraiden smiled. It made Elān happy to see the old warrior smile. The canoe sailed much faster loaded than most canoes could sail empty.

An eagle flew high above throughout the journey. At times the eagle would disappear toward shore, and then return to following the canoe. It wasn't long after midday when a second eagle leapt from a treetop perch on shore and flew out to meet the eagle circling the canoe. They circled together for a moment, and then both soared down toward the canoe screeching as they flew past.

Raven still sat atop the mast.

"Is this the meeting place?" Elān yelled up to him. "Is this Quintus Ḵwáan?"

"Don't you speak the eagle language?" raven asked.

"You know I don't. You are the translator."

"Stupid Aaní," raven said. "You Westislanders are the worst. You think only human language is important, you won't teach any other language in your longhouses, and now when you realize it is important to be smart, you want me to translate? The eagle said he could smell your buns' stink way up in the sky."

"Ch'eet, can you see anyone on the beach?" Elān yelled.

"No. We're too far away."

Caraiden lifted the bow, yanked an arrow from the quiver and with incredible quickness fitted it to the string and pointed it at raven. "Tell us what the eagles said," he told raven.

"Put that down," raven screeched.

"Speak," Caraiden yelled. Even Elān jumped at the boom in his voice.

"Yes, yes, this is the meeting place. Go ashore here," raven said, "and put that down."

Caraiden lowered the bow and put the arrow back in the quiver.

"We'll paddle to shore," Elān said. "Take in the sails and keep an eye out for rocks."

The crew was quick to strike the sails down. They took up paddles. In the distance, as they approached, they saw a wolf on the beach. They rowed toward him. They could see he wore armor around his body and head. He was massive, with a chest the size of a tree trunk and paws as large as a bear's. He had dark brown-and-black fur.

The canoe scraped onto the sea-worn beach rocks at Chetdyl's feet.

"Hey, bird," Elān called up to raven. "How about introducing us?"

Raven flapped his wing at Chetdyl and spoke in human. "That's Deer Crap Eater." He pointed his wing at the canoe and spoke in wolf to Chetdyl. "That's Fathead there in the back, Old Man Bellyache in the middle, and up front there"— he pointed his wing at Ch'eet—"is Zero."

Chetdyl narrowed his eyes at raven. "You know I can understand the human language. Those do not sound like the human names Íxt mentioned," he said in wolf.

"Humans give themselves strange nicknames," raven replied.

"Tell them I'm honored to meet them," Chetdyl said.

To Elān and the crew, the wolf language sounded growly and guttural.

"Deer Crap Eater says you all look stupid," raven said to the crew in human, "and that he loves to eat human flesh even more than deer crap, which I find hard to believe."

"Stop," Elan said to raven. "His name is Chetdyl. Tell Chetdyl he's welcome to come aboard. He can sit in front of Ch'eet in the very bow and keep his nose to the wind."

"Fathead loves to eat wolf flesh, so you better sit up front far away from him," raven told Chetdyl in wolf language. "Zero won't eat you because you don't have enough blubber, even though I told him your head was full of blubber."

"Quit being difficult," Chetdyl said to raven. "Tell them I understand human language."

"Deer Crap Eater says he's hungry," raven said to the crew, "and gassy, so you best sit far away."

Elān ignored raven. "Come aboard, Chetdyl," he said to the wolf.

Chetdyl nodded at Ch'eet, who still stood thigh deep in the surf holding the canoe, and then leaped with great skill atop the boxes in the bow. "Good. Now we await Hoosa," Elān said. "Ch'eet, do you want to pull us ashore?"

"I can hold," Ch'eet said.

"Hey, morons," raven said. "I'm going to fly ashore and gather some branches to build a nest up here. Don't send an arrow my way."

"Be quick about it," Elān said. Raven flew off toward the forest and disappeared in the trees. "He's not coming back," Caraiden said. But in a short time, raven returned with cedar branches in his mouth. He landed atop the mast and wove the branches around the little lantern holder. Raven made several more trips and had built a tight-woven green perch by the time Elān saw a man walking on the beach toward the canoe. A group of bears walked beside him.

"Hoosa approaches," Elān called out. He was both excited and apprehensive. He'd heard about the black bear cousins, but could not remember ever meeting one. They were human, of course, but believed themselves to be related to bears. They carried this belief to extremes. They lived in small groups in dens in the forests and protected the bears from hunters or anyone who'd do them harm, especially during hibernation. Neither Eastislanders nor Westislanders intruded on the bear sanctuary, known as S'eek Kwáan, at this southern end of Samish. Hoosa was a black bear cousin. The bears with him were all black bears. Hoosa came close to the canoe and held up his hand. Elān held his hand up in return. He didn't know what else to do.

"Your ancestors. I'm Elān. You must be Hoosa."

Hoosa wore a heavy bearskin coat, pants, and moccasins. His hair was long and tangled in thick coils. He wore a blanket around his shoulders made of skin or hide, clasped at the throat with what looked to be a bear claw. He wore a backpack of similar hide. He turned to a bear next to him. At first Elān thought he was growling, but he quickly realized Hoosa was speaking the bear language. The black bear lowered his head and Hoosa pressed his forehead to the bear's forehead.

He took his backpack off and waded out into the water. "Your ancestors. Where do you want me?" he asked Elān. Elān was surprised he spoke human language so well.

"Right behind the main mast here," Elān replied. "In front of me."

"Can the netting hold me?" he asked Elān, grabbing hold of the net between the canoe and outrigger.

"I think so," Elān said.

Hoosa hoisted himself into the netting and scrabbled over to the canoe. He sat down behind the main mast and shoved his backpack on the floor against the mast.

"That's Caraiden, Ch'eet, and Chetdyl," Elān said, pointing to the crew. Hoosa nodded. "Atop the mast is the bird."

Hoosa looked up at raven and scowled. "I know him."

"I might crap on you since you are sitting right below me, silly little bear man," raven said. "Though, with your hair, nobody could tell if you'd been crapped on or not."

"All right," Elān said to the crew. "Everyone is aboard. As you all may know, we journey to Yelm to pick up one, perhaps two more warriors. There will not be much room in the canoe after Yelm, but we shall manage. I suggest we spend tonight on Doe Island and set off early to make Yelm by tomorrow evening, if the wind is right."

BACK OUT ON the ocean, the wind held easterly and pushed the canoe beyond the southern reaches of Samish. An isthmus on the southeast of Samish known as Point No Point marked a swirl of the winds as the island caused westward winds to collide and rip with winds coming down from the northeast. Elān navigated the swirling winds around Point No Point and drove the canoe northward. Toward suppertime, the green body of Doe Island, a small, heavy-timbered and uninhabited island off Samish, became visible in the distance.

Elān led the boat into Doe Bay on the western side of Doe Island, which had the island's only smooth beach. Outside of Doe Bay, it was ringed with cliffs and boulders. At the mouth of the bay the crew struck down the sails and paddled to shore. Ch'eet jumped into the shallows and pulled the canoe onto the beach. "Tie up," Caraiden said to Ch'eet. "And let's have supper."

"I'll get a fire started," Elān said.

ELĀN HAD A small fire of beach grass burning by the time Caraiden and Ch'eet had tied up the canoe, unloaded bedrolls, and opened the box of smoked salmon. Elān fed cracked driftwood onto the burning grass, and the blaze grew. Ch'eet passed out large, deep-red chunks of smoked salmon. Elān shoved a stick through his salmon to warm it over the fire. Ch'eet gave a piece to Chetdyl who took it in his mouth, set it on the ground, and ate it in small bites.

"Where's my boxes of smoked salmon?" asked raven who was still sitting in his perch on the mast.

"Come eat with us," Elān said.

"Where are my boxes?" raven asked again.

"We have plenty of smoked salmon down here," Ch'eet said.

"I was promised five boxes of smoked salmon," raven said. "If I do not get them I am going to leave, and good luck surviving without me."

Elān went to the canoe and pulled out several small bentwood boxes. "There are five of these boxes all full of salmon. Íxt saw to it himself." Elān held one up and laughed. It was the size of the palm of his hand. "All five are yours."

Raven stared at the box. His beak opened and a thin moan came from him. He jumped up and down in his nest perch atop the mast. "No, no, no. That rotten old chunk of useless turds," he yelled. "That was not the deal! That was not our deal at all!" Raven looked up into the darkening night and yelled, "That was not our deal, old man!"

"According to Íxt, you never specified the size of box," Elān laughed. "Come. As long as you are a member of our crew, you can eat with us." Elān tossed the small boxes back into the canoe and returned to the fire.

Raven continued to hop in anger in his nest. "Rotten, filthy, lying old man. I'm going to kill him. I'm going to kill that rotten, moldy liar."

"Hey, bird," Caraiden said. "Come get a piece of salmon or starve."

Raven jumped off the mast and glided down next to the crew's large bentwood of smoked salmon. "I'll steal your stupid salmon," he said, "but I refuse to eat with you. Now, give me a big piece." Ch'eet reached into the box, brought out a piece of smoked salmon, and handed it to raven. He grabbed it in his claws and flew back up to his perch. Elān could hear him muttering as he ate.

Afterward, as the evening fell, they huddled close to the fire. Though it was late spring, the weather still ran cool at night. Chetdyl tried to talk to the humans—growling in different tones—but he could not make himself understood, and raven was in no mood to translate. When Ch'eet, Caraiden, and Elān spread their bedrolls around the fire, Hoosa stood up. "I prefer to sleep in the woods. I will return at sunrise," he said, and with that, he walked off into the darkness of the forest.

"Should we set a watch?" Elān asked Caraiden.

"We should be fine here on Samish," the old warrior replied. "This wolf will smell any trouble long before we can detect it. Still, I recommend you sleep light."

"Should we set out fishing gear tomorrow?" Elān asked. "We might catch fresh dinner. This side of Samish has those nice king salmon runs this time of winter."

"Yes," Caraiden said. "That's a fine idea. I'll get the fishing tackle. Ch'eet, waterlog the cooking box. And you, Elān, make sure the fire is stoked before you go to bed so we can save a coal or two to take with us in the morning."

CHAPTER 13

Elān woke the next morning to the sound of beach rock crunching underfoot. He opened his eyes and saw Hoosa walking the ocean's rocky edge. The tide had gone out, stranding *Waka*. They would have to be careful with the outrigging in dragging the canoe down to the water. Elān was the last person to wake. Ch'eet and Caraiden had stowed their bedrolls in the canoe and had opened the fresh water hold so Chetdyl could drink.

Elān rose and rolled up his bedroll and stored it in the canoe. He took a handful of smoked salmon from the food box and ate quickly, taking pulls from his water bag as he ate. He put the bag away and walked around the beached canoe, making sure all was well. He didn't see raven in his mast-perch, but when he called up to him, raven's ruffled head looked out over the edge of his nest and, spying Elān, hid back down.

Elān saw the cooking box on the beach and went to it. Ch'eet had waterlogged it by filling it with sea water. Elān tipped it over to spill out the water and then lined the bottom with wet beach sand. He would put in a few coals from last night's fire— if the coals still smoldered. The lid of the box, which had holes in it to allow the air in and the smoke to escape, had a metal grilling rack attached underneath that you could remove from the lid and suspend in the box. While at sea, you could get a fire going in the box and cook your food. The sand kept the fire from burning the bottom of the box, though the waterlogged sides steamed a bit when you cooked.

"I think we're ready," Elān said to Caraiden.

"Very well," Caraiden said. "I attached four fishing lines to the netting at the back of the canoe. Uncoil them when we get out to sea. We'll try metal spoons as lures. If we don't catch anything at the change of tides, we can swap gear."

"Fine," Elān said. "Let's get *Waka* in the water."

The crew heaved the canoe down to the water and paddled it out into the bay. It was a fine, crisp late spring morning. *Waka* slid through the long shadows of Doe Island until it passed the northern end at the same time the sun rose above the islands to the east. The water was calm, without chop or hint of wind. The crew had to paddle. Neither wind nor salmon came throughout the morning.

To the northeast, a few yaakw off Samish, lay Daadzi Island. It marked the midpoint of Samish Island. Elān angled the canoe toward the western edge of Daadzi. Yelm still lay four or five yaakw away. For most the afternoon, Chetdyl lay on a bentwood box in the bow with his head resting between his paws. Every so often he would raise his nose to the wind, look around, and lay his head down again. Elān felt safe having the great wolf with his incredible nose at the prow of *Waka*. As they approached the southern end of Daadzi the wind shifted, coming in from the west. Elān adjusted the mainsail and, as he did, Chetdyl jumped up and stood on the box with his nose high in the air. He turned to the crew and growled. He nosed the wind again, and yelped, obviously speaking in wolf language.

Elān awoke from a daydream and gripped hard the tiller and sheet.

"Trouble," raven said. "The wolf says trouble. Turn around."

"Trouble?" Caraiden asked. "What trouble?"

The wolf growled again in those strange tones.

"He doesn't know," raven said, "but something approaches. Its stench gets stronger. It approaches. We must turn around."

"From which direction does it approach?" Caraiden asked. Chetdyl growled.

"From Daadzi Island," raven said. He looked over the edge of his nest down at Elān. "We must turn around."

"Don't turn around. Stay with the wind. Head northwest toward Samish," Caraiden told Elān. "I see nothing ahead of us between Samish and Daadzi. Whatever it is, it must be approaching from the east side of Daadzi. Make quick for the Samish coast."

"Ch'eet, let the jib out a bit," Elān said. He pushed the tiller away from himself. Ch'eet uncleated the jib sheet and the wind pushed the jib boom out. He then retied the sheet. *Waka* surged. Elān fed out the mainsail sheet, wrapped it once around a cleat, and held the end of the sheet in his hand so he could let out the sail or bring it in according to the direction of the wind. *Waka* was now flying through the sea. Chetdyl balanced on the bentwood box in the bow with his nose still high in the wind. He growled loudly.

"They're coming," raven yelled.

"Paddles," Elān croaked, his voice pinched with fear.

The crew grabbed their paddles and dug into the sea. *Waka* was traveling too fast and the crew had trouble timing their strokes to the pace. At the southern tip of Daadzi, a large canoe with many sails emerged from behind the island, a quarter yaakw away from *Waka*.

"Look at the size of it," Elān said. He'd never seen such a large canoe. Even with his bad eyes he could see it loom on the horizon. He could feel his heart beating, and shivers running from his neck down his back.

The large canoe had two towering masts. Elān counted the sails. Four, three, three. Seven sails in all. He'd never seen a canoe with more than three sails. *How fast is a seven-sail canoe?* he wondered.

"Pay attention," Caraiden commanded. "Hold the sheet tight." The gruff voice brought Elān out of his rumination.

His arms were shaking. He felt dizzy. "Keep full wind in the sails," Caraiden barked. Elān pulled on the sheet until both sails were taut with wind. "Good," Caraiden said. "Now we learn how fast *Waka* is."

The giant canoe turned with the wind and angled toward *Waka*.

"You're all doomed," raven squealed. He shot off his perch into the air and flew for a few moments in tight circles above the canoe. He crapped a soupy string of white poop that landed on the gunwale next to Hoosa and he flew off toward Samish Island, a couple yaakw in the distance.

The large canoe came into *Waka*'s wake. It was coming after them.

Elān held the tiller and mainsail sheet tight as the wind blew *Waka* toward Samish. He focused his vision on a lone, bare peak standing above the forest on the Samish coast. His tiller arm hurt, and he could feel the blisters raised by the hours of paddling. *I can't hold on*, Elān thought to himself. In his mind, he saw himself letting go of the tiller and the canoe lurching wild with the wind. If he let go, the large canoe would easily overtake them from behind. His palm grew sweaty and made the tiller slippery in his hand. He gripped it tighter. A blister burst and stung. It was maddening. He couldn't hang on, and felt tears coming, though he tried hard to keep from crying. He couldn't hold on. His eyes blurred as he stared unblinking at the lone peak in the distance. The tiller pulled against one hand, and the mainsail sheet tore into the other. He couldn't hold.

"Caraiden, can you take the tiller?" Elān pleaded.

"No," the old warrior yelled. "It's too dangerous to switch places now. Hold the tiller and sail sheet and make for Samish."

"They're lighting fire arrows," Ch'eet yelled.

Elān turned to look behind, but Caraiden barked at him. "You're captain. Act like it. We need a warrior now, not a bookeater. Face forward and steer toward Samish. We're out of range of their arrows."

"Arrows incoming," yelled Ch'eet.

"Out of range," Caraiden said to Elān. "Don't falter. Our lives lay in that rope and tiller in your hands."

Tears came to Elān's eyes. He felt the tiller slipping from his blistered, sweaty hand. The rope from the mainsail bit into his hand. The pain was too great. He couldn't hold. "Caraiden, I can't do it," he whimpered.

"Don't let go."

"Caraiden, I can't hold." The mainsail sheet slipped in his palm.

"All arrows missed," Ch'eet yelled.

Tears rolled down Elān's cheeks.

Ch'eet laughed. "Eesháan," he said. "They can't hit us."

Caraiden laughed with Ch'eet. "They can't match our pace." He smiled at Elān. "Now you can look, bookeater."

Elān turned to look at the large canoe behind him. It appeared smaller. "We're outrunning it," he said, half disbelieving.

Caraiden laughed again.

"Haaw!" Elān yelled. "It can't keep up." A warming joy surged through his body. He was wide awake. Suddenly he could hold the tiller and sheet another entire day and night if he had to. The canoe was about a half a yaakw away and receding into the distance.

Waka flew. The outriggers sizzled across the sea. Elān regripped the sheet and tiller. *It's odd*, Elān thought to himself, *how our lives rest on a length of rope and piece of wood.*

"Once you calmed down, you did well," Caraiden said to Elān. "But we won't always be lucky enough to have such a head start. You must learn to be calm and focused the moment danger appears."

Elān nodded and wiped his face with his sleeve. "Chetdyl," he yelled up to the giant wolf. The wolf turned. "Blink your eyes twice if you can understand what I am saying."

The wolf blinked his eyes twice.

"I knew it," Elān said. "Chetdyl, thank you for warning us."

The wolf lowered his head and closed his eyes in acknowledgment.

The *Waka* kept surging northwesterly through the sea, moving so swiftly it felt to the crew as though it rode the air above the waves without the friction of the water. None of them had ever traveled at such a speed. The large canoe continued to recede in *Waka*'s wake for a while, then turned in the other direction and disappeared. "They go the other way," Caraiden said. "Which means they probably weren't Aaní or Deikeenaa, otherwise they'd probably follow us up to Yelm. They must have had a lookout on Daadzi to know we were coming."

"Who do you think it was?" Elān asked.

"I don't know," Caraiden said. "I've never seen such a large canoe, nor have I ever been hunted in my own waters."

Chetdyl growled something in his language.

"I'm sorry but I can't understand," Elān said to the wolf. He heard a screech. An eagle soared high above the canoe. Raven glided below the eagle, heading toward his mast-perch. As he landed, Elān could hear him mumble, "...feather-brained lout. I'll fill his beak with dog crap..." He fluttered into his nest. The eagle flew screeching toward the mast.

"I'll make an omelet with your eggs, dumbass," raven yelled at the eagle as he flew by.

"So nice to have you back, coward," Hoosa yelled up to raven. "I saw what you did before you flew away in fright. I won't forget."

"Shut up," raven said. "Go play pretend bear with your stinking cousins."

"Are you going to fly away at every sign of trouble?" Caraiden asked raven.

"Stop bellyaching," raven said to Caraiden. "Sleepy Old Man Bellyache."

Hoosa looked at Elān. "I hate that bird," he said.

"I need him," Elān said. "He has knowledge I need."

Elān looked up and saw raven squatting on the edge of his nest with his butt hanging out directly above Hoosa. "Watch it, Hoosa," he said. Hoosa looked up, saw the threat, and smacked the mast hard. The vibration made raven lose his balance and fall back into his nest. "I will put an arrow through his ass if he continues to crap on me," Hoosa said.

Raven cawed in laughter.

CHAPTER 14

THE REST OF their journey that day was adventureless. The large canoe didn't reappear nor were any Aaní or Deikeenaa canoes to be seen. The sea was unwalked by craft, and as evening slipped over *Waka* and its crew, they approached the sheltered bay of the village of Yelm. It was dark by the time they entered Yelm Bay, though a three-quarter moon helped light the channel at the entrance. Ch'eet hung a lantern from the jib mast to light up the sea in front of *Waka*. Far off through the bay, the crew could see the lights of the village. The crew took down the sails; they would paddle the rest of the way to Yelm.

It can be dangerous to approach an Aaní village at night from the sea, though the Aaní had ways to make sure friends could approach safely. The Aaní always posted night sentries around their villages to watch for potential night raids from enemies. These sentries, known as the Harbor Master's deputies, were trained warriors and night watch was part of their duties. They reported to the Harbor Master, who was in charge of harbor safety.

As the crew entered Yelm Bay, they noticed signal lights flaring at the outer reaches of the bay; more signal lights flared up along the shore toward the village.

"We've been spotted," Ch'eet said.

It was Aaní tradition for a canoe approaching at night to shoot two fire arrows straight into the air while waiting in the sea in front of the village. The harbor deputies would respond with the steady beat of a box drum—a large, carved wooden or metal drum smacked with a heavy mallet. The canoe crew would then match that beat by hitting their paddles on the sides of the canoe, which, as you might know, echoes loud on the ocean. Sound carries a long distance as it rolls over the sea. The harbor deputies would then send an escort to meet the approaching canoe.

As they neared the village, the crew of *Waka* stopped paddling. "Hold us here, Ch'eet. Ready the fire arrows," Elān said. Caraiden took two arrows from his quiver and laid them across his bow. Elān took the lid from the cook box and unwrapped a coal. He touched a branch to the coal and blew on it until it flamed up. He gave the burning branch to Hoosa. "Light them." Hoosa lit both arrows, and Caraiden shot them straight up through the night, one right after the other.

"Be careful where you are shooting those, Old Man Bellyache," raven yelled down from his perch. "That last one nearly caught my nest on fire."

The crew didn't have to wait long before they heard the box drum. They grabbed their paddles and held them above their laps and beat on the sides of the canoe in time with the shore drum. The sound echoed across the waves and around the forests of Yelm Bay. Elān saw a light dancing at the shore, and watched as the light grew brighter and larger. It came from a lantern held by a warrior stood on the prow of a canoe as it paddled out to meet them. He held the lantern up above his head and strained his eyes through the dark to see *Waka* and its crew.

"State your names and your business."

As captain, it was Elān who would speak at sea. "Elān, Caraiden, and Ch'eet of Naasteidi. Hoosa of the black bear people, and Chetdyl of the wolves. We're all Westislanders."

The warrior held up his lantern and stared at the crew. He nodded as though satisfied with Elān's explanation. "A late hour to be asea for you Westislanders," he said. "What business at Yelm?"

"We meant to be here before sundown, but the wind didn't favor us this morning," Elān said, "and we came across trouble around Daadzi. We're here to meet with Kireti, head of your Longhouse of War and Diplomacy."

"Kireti has told us nothing of this meeting."

"He hasn't been informed of the meeting yet," Elān said. "I have a letter from a dear friend of his. He'll meet with us, I'm sure, after he reads the letter."

"I'll take the letter when we get to shore," the warrior said. "And I would like to hear more about your troubles at Daadzi. Where are you staying this evening?"

"We thought we'd stay at one of the public houses," Elān said. "If they're all full, we'll stay on the canoe."

"The Little Chich has vacancies tonight," the warrior said. "You haven't been here for a few winters, Caraiden. Not since your team lost that close Over-the-Mountain game. I hope your family is well, Elān. Your grandfather is remembered well here in Yelm. Come ashore and we'll get you logged in." The warrior signaled to his crew to turn their canoe around and head to shore. *Waka*'s crew paddled right behind them.

The Harbor Master kept track of all canoes. Yelm citizens could come and go as they pleased; however, if they traveled after dark, or went for a night paddle, they had to inform the Harbor Master. If the canoe didn't return, a search party would be sent. All canoes from other villages had to be logged out and in whenever they took to and returned from sea.

Waka slid onto Yelm's sandy beach next to the escort canoe. Ch'eet vaulted over the side and yanked the canoe ashore. A group of the Harbor Master's deputies holding lanterns, all armed with swords and bows, lined the beach. Caraiden, Hoosa, Chetdyl, and Elān jumped onto the beach and stood with Ch'eet in front of *Waka*. They left their weapons in the canoe since Aaní custom required strangers to be unarmed when visiting villages.

"Have all of you been to Yelm before?" the warrior from the escort canoe asked.

"Many times," said Caraiden.

"Very well," the warrior said. "No need for a long welcoming ceremony. I am Dlan, Harbor Master. I welcome you to Yelm."

He looked at the line of harbor deputies and nodded. A few cleared their throats, and then they sang. The song was called "The Sea-Road," a famous Yelm song with a haunting melody. After the harbor deputies finished singing, Elān and his crew sang their own song, a short sea chant that took its repetitive feel from the motion of a whale's progress through the ocean. After the song was over, Caraiden called out, "Mend the net," and the harbor deputies called back, "We'll mend the net," and both groups—deputies and *Waka* crew together—called out, "and pull it tight around all Aaní."

"Very well," Dlan said after the brief welcome was complete. "Come up off the beach into the Harbor Master's house. We'll get you a warm drink and have a chat."

Hoosa tugged at Elān's sleeve. "The canoe should be guarded, and I prefer to sleep outdoors. I'll sleep in the canoe."

"Fine," Elān said. "Use our bedrolls if you get cold."

"I don't get cold."

The crew left Hoosa at the canoe and followed Dlan up the beach toward a well-lit, carved wooden longhouse. The harbor deputies had shuffled off into the evening to continue their watch. "Keep your shoes on and come on in," Dlan said to the crew. The Harbor Master's house—which wasn't a home, but rather the Harbor Master and his deputies' office—was warmed by a large iron stove in the center. A few desks and couches lined the walls. "There's pine needle tea on the stove there, and mugs over in the corner near the basin. Help yourselves to tea and get warm. I'll get you logged." Dlan sat at one desk and opened a large book. It was the Harbor Master's register. He took a quill from the desk and jotted in the book. Ch'eet, Caraiden, and Elān scooped mugs of tea from the large kettle atop the stove and stood behind Dlan.

"All right," Dlan said. "I know Caraiden and Elān. Who else is aboard?"

"I'm Ch'eet. I'm in the Longhouse of War and Diplomacy at Naasteidi. Caraiden is my mentor-uncle."

Dlan wrote in the book. "Now. Your other crew member. That odd one. The black bear cousin," Dlan said. "What's his name?"

"Hoosa."

"Is he from Samish?"

"Yes," Elān said. "His people live in the forests around S'eek Kwáan."

"We rarely get those folks up this far." Dlan wrote for a while in the register. He looked at Chetdyl, who was stretched out by the stove. "Who's that?" he asked Elān.

"His name is Chetdyl, and I believe he's from Quintus Kwáan."

"That would be wolf territory," Dlan said. He looked at Chetdyl. "He's listening to us."

"Yes," Elān said. "He can understand human language. Have you anyone in Yelm that can speak wolf language?"

"No, no. Of course not," Dlan replied. "They say our elders *looong* ago could speak animal languages. But nobody can nowadays. You could get yourself a raven. Legend says birds can speak any language."

"We've got one already," Elān said.

"You'd be welcome to have him," Caraiden said.

Dlan laughed. "No, thank you," he said. "I'll make a note that you've a raven on board. Does he have a name?"

"We haven't asked and he hasn't told us," Elān said.

Dlan laughed again as he jotted in the register. "Now, Elān," he said, "that's a military canoe out there. You held the tiller. Is this a diplomatic visit, or simply pleasure?"

"Diplomatic," Elān said.

"I don't recall hearing you'd joined the warriors' ranks at the Longhouse of War," Dlan said.

"I haven't," Elān said. "I'm on a mission from Íxt." From inside his sea coat, Elān brought out Íxt's letter. It was addressed to the Hits'aati of Yelm's Longhouse of War and Diplomacy. He handed the letter to Dlan.

Dlan took the letter. "Glad to hear the old man is still alive," he said. "He's been gone for several moons and we worried for him. I'll see this letter delivered tonight and let the Hits'aati know that you'll be lodged at the Little Chich, and I'm sure you'll receive a message from him in the morning."

"Thank you," Elān said.

"How long do you intend to spend in Yelm?"

"We must be off soon. One night, perhaps two at the most."

Dlan jotted in the register. "And the name of your canoe?"

"*Waka.*"

Dlan noted the name in the register. "Now. Tell me of this trouble you had at Daadzi Island."

Elān told Dlan what had happened that afternoon. "You have never seen such a canoe before?" Dlan asked Caraiden.

"Never," the old warrior replied. "And I've traveled far."

"I would think you crazy," Dlan said, "if one of our fishermen hadn't reported seeing a similar canoe a few days ago. Two masts, seven sails. As big as one of the Cone Islands north of Samish, or so the fisherman said."

"Did it chase him?" Caraiden asked.

"No," Dlan said. "But he wasn't under sail. He had a small canoe. He fled back to Samish when he saw it. It's possible the big canoe didn't see him. Could you draw it for me?" Dlan handed Caraiden his quill and Caraiden sketched in the register book a fairly accurate drawing of the giant canoe. "That's as the fisherman described," said Dlan.

"You Eastislanders have an outpost on the eastern side of Daadzi, or you had one. I was stationed there before the Heeni war. What news from the outpost?"

"Nothing. We lost contact a few days ago. We're looking into it. Twenty winters I've been a warrior," Dlan said, "and twenty winters I've watched over Yelm. I've seen wars on land and sea, but in those twenty winters only this mystery canoe has ever unnerved me."

THE ROAD BEHIND the Harbor Master's house led to one of the main roads through Yelm. Unlike Naasteidi, all the roads around Yelm were paved with flagstones—all different shapes and sizes fitted together like a beautiful, multicolored mosaic—including the roads into the forests and along the beaches. In Naasteidi, only the roads within the village had flagstones. The crew stepped onto the smooth, foot-worn stones behind the Harbor Master's house and headed toward the center of the village. It was quiet at this time of night, clear of clouds, with only a fine shower of sea mist in the air. Large lanterns hanging from metal poles lit the village streets. They gave off a warm, yellow glow in the misted night. Chetdyl's claws clacked on the road stones, and muffled laughter and music came from one of the houses as they passed by, but the rest of the village was lulled.

"Do you know the owner of the Little Chich?" Elān asked Caraiden.

"Yes, if he still lives. Keidli's his name. He's a strange old man. Little Chich was his dog, as you probably know. A small black dog with large ears. It's immortal, or so Keidli says. If it's still alive it must be well over thirty winters old."

A note of advice: if you ever stop or call in at the Little Chich, make sure you pronounce the name correctly. It should rhyme with 'each' not 'itch.' Old Man Keidli has been known to turn away folks who pronounce the name of his dear dog incorrectly. "Have you rooms open at the Little Ch*itch*?" they ask. "None. And the kitchen's closed. And the casks are empty," Old Man Keidli replies.

Don't worry, if you do run aground at the Little Chich, a short jog down the road and across the street you'll find the Gooch, whose owner is not so temperamental. The Gooch is the oldest pub in Yelm. Eastislanders say it's the oldest pub on all of Samish. Westislanders claim Gooch's Dad as the oldest pub on Samish. Of course, as you may know, both pubs were called the Gooch at one time until the Aaní began to argue about which pub could claim to be the first and oldest pub on all Samish. The Gooch in Naasteidi then changed its name to Gooch's Dad in hopes of settling the debate, but the name change caused more argument. After the Over-the-Mountain ball games each summer, both teams, Westislanders and Eastislanders, celebrated in either the Gooch or Gooch's Dad, depending on which team won. You can imagine the arguments.

The crew saw a sign of a small, black, big-eared dog below the awning at the front of the pub, swinging in the slight wind. *Little Chich* ran in red letters across the bottom of the sign. Elān put his hand to the door. It felt warm. There would be a fire inside, though the evening wasn't icy. He turned the large, metal doorknob and pushed open the door. Caraiden and Ch'eet entered behind Elān, and Chetdyl walked in last.

The Little Chich wasn't full that evening. Of the twenty or so tables in the main room of the pub, only about four or five were occupied. A wide, well-crafted fireplace sat across from the bar. The bar ran across the main room to the left of the front door. The pub was warm and lit by lanterns on each table and a few hanging from the ceiling.

"Your ancestors," called the man behind the bar.

"And yours," replied Elān.

"Is your wolf safe?" asked Old Man Keidli, who was tending the bar, when he saw the large wolf in armor.

"Yes," Elān said. "His name is Chetdyl. He's a clan leader."

"Sure is big. What can I do for you?"

Elān nodded at Caraiden. "You might not remember me," Caraiden said, "but I stayed here many times over the winters. I'm Caraiden of Naasteidi."

"Nope. Don't remember you."

"Your Harbor Master said we could find rooms here this evening."

"I don't recall owning a Harbor Master." The inhabitants of a nearby table laughed. Elān saw the muscles along Caraiden's jaws flex in frustration.

"I hope your dog is still well," Elān said.

The man shot a look at Elān. "Dog? What dog?"

"Little Chich," Elān said, pronouncing the name correctly.

The man smiled. "He's very well. Good of you to ask." He looked beyond Elān to the fireplace. "Chich," he called. "Little Chich, wake up." Two large ears atop a little black head popped up from a bed near the fireplace. "There's a young man here wants to know you're doing well." A long, skinny black tail wagged in the bed. "Go pet him, if you'd like, young man," Keidli said to Elān. "Of course we have rooms. Take a table and get yourselves warm first. We'll get some food and a mug or two of ale in you and you'll sleep well."

He served the crew a round of ale, and they ordered baked *chaatl* (you probably call it halibut) and herring eggs, for it was herring egg season. At low tide all around Samish, the Aaní planted hemlock branches tied to poles driven into the low tide mud. High tide would flood the branches and herring would spawn on them. Then, after a few high tides, the branches would be gray-white with herring eggs. The

Aaní ate the eggs raw or boiled, and the branches infused the eggs with the piney taste of trees.

After supper, the crew was exhausted. Chetdyl snored lightly by the fire. "The wolf can sleep there tonight," Old Man Keidli said. "You three come with me." He showed the crew to their rooms down the hall. Once in his room, Elān took off his sea coat, coin-mail shirt, and boots, flopped onto the bed, and fell deep asleep face down on the bed cover.

CHAPTER 15

ELĀN WOKE THE next morning still face down on the tucked-in bed cover. The sun came through a window—the curtains still open—and beneath the window sat a small desk. A mirror hung on the wall across from the window. Elān sat up and looked at himself in the mirror. A few days' growth of whiskers darkened his face. His clothes bag with his razor was still in the canoe. He'd been too tired last night to fetch it. He stood and went to the desk. It had a carved wooden pen and stationery in its main drawer, and Elān took out the pen and a sheet of stationery and composed a letter to his parents. He told them of the fun he'd had so far in his journey, and of his first night in Yelm. He didn't mention the escape from the large canoe. No need to worry his parents. He put the letter in an envelope. He'd give the envelope to Old Man Keidli to send out with the post canoe to Naasteidi.

Elan put on his coin-mail shirt and sea coat, slid into his boots, and walked with the letter down the hall into the main room. A few people sat having breakfast, but the pub was quiet. Old Man Keidli sat near the fireplace scratching Little Chich's head. "Morning," he said to Elān.

"Good morning," Elān said. "Am I the first one up?"

The old man laughed. "No, son, your mates have been up for some time. Even the wolf. They breakfasted, paid the reckoning, and left."

"Do you know where they went?"

123

"No idea. You need something to eat? We got some salmon porridge. There's toast with blackberry jam, too."

"A bowl of salmon porridge would be fine, thanks," Elān said. "Would you see this letter delivered for me? It's going to Naasteidi." Elān lifted the letter in his hand.

"Sure. Set it on the counter over there. I'll have it on the next delivery canoe to Naasteidi."

As ELĀN ATE his breakfast, a young man in warrior garb entered the pub. "What do you need Jini?" Old Man Keidli said.

"I'm bringing a message from the Longhouse to some of your lodgers," he said. "A crew from Naasteidi."

"I'm from Naasteidi," Elān said. "My crew and I came in last night."

"What's your name?" the messenger asked.

"Elān. Caraiden and Ch'eet are with me."

"You're the one," the messenger replied. "Hits'aati Kireti will see you presently."

"Fine," said Elān. "I'll round up my crew and head there."

"Do you know where the Longhouse is?"

"Yes."

"I'll tell the Hits'aati you're on your way." The messenger turned and left the pub. Elān took several spoonfuls of his salmon porridge and went to the door.

"Will you be staying another night?" Old Man Keidli asked.

"Sadly, I think not," Elān said. "We appreciate your hospitality." He looked at the small dog still lying in his bed near the fireplace. "Goodbye, Little Chich. I hope to see you again very soon."

ELĀN FOUND CARAIDEN and Ch'eet at the harbor down by the canoe, talking with Hoosa. "Come. We meet with the

Hits'aati." The crew walked through Yelm. The village was alive this morning, full of Eastislanders going to and fro on business. A few muttered "Your ancestors" to the Westislanders as they made their way to the Longhouse, but most hardly noticed the strangers in their village.

Down the main street past the Little Clich and the Gooch, they went left on Nass River Street, the shopping district of Yelm, and through the village to the Longhouse of War and Diplomacy, which was a rather long walk from the harbor. Unlike Naasteidi, where the town hall was the center of the village, the longhouse was the center of Yelm. The longhouse had a large carved front with carved poles at the corners. Two warriors stood at the entrance.

"Your ancestors," Elān said. The guards nodded. "We have a meeting with Hits'aati Kireti."

"Go on in," one guard said.

The crew entered the longhouse. At the front office, a young warrior sat behind a desk. "Your ancestors," he said.

"And yours," Elān said. "We're the crew from Naasteidi. We have a meeting with Hits'aati Kireti."

"I'll get him," the young warrior said. He disappeared down the hall and returned with Dlan and a large, gray-haired, fierce-looking man, who smiled when he saw Caraiden.

"How are you, Caraiden? The letter said two Naasteidi warriors were part of your crew. I'm delighted you are one of the two."

"Thank you. I'm doing fine. And you?"

"I'm doing well," said Kireti. "And you must be Ch'eet, Elān, and Hoosa. Of course, this is Chetdyl."

"Your ancestors," Elān, Ch'eet, and Hoosa said.

"And yours," Kireti replied. "So, Íxt's letter said you are in a great hurry and have use for one or two of my warriors for a trip to Botson's Bay, but he didn't explain why. Typical of the Old Man. I wonder if all Aaní islands' elders are that way? You rarely see them and then they show up unannounced and unexpected, wanting things done right away. What in Yéil's name is happening in Botson's Bay?"

"We don't know," Elān said. "All the old man said is we should go to Botson's Bay and scout the area and report back to him."

"Hmmm. Strange that he'd send you, Elān," Kireti said.

"That's what I thought, too!" Elān replied. "But he was close to my grandfather and he said he wanted me to see Éil'."

"I'll give you one warrior," Kireti replied. "I can spare only one. Something strange and troubling is afoot and I need my warriors here. But I'll give you one of my finest. I heard of the trouble you encountered yesterday near Daadzi Island. Our scouts returned early this morning. Our stockade is demolished, no sign of our warriors or the large canoe. We sent a small fleet to hunt it down. The warrior who I've assigned to your crew was supposed to go with the fleet, and she was upset to be pulled from her warrior ranks to go on your errand to the mainland, so she might not be your most cheerful crew member for a while. Her name is K̲waatk'wa but call her Kwa. She's one of our finest. She's readying her gear and will meet you down at the harbor."

"We appreciate your help," Elān said.

"Bring her back safe within two moons," Kireti replied.

"Take care around Daadzi Island," Dlan said. "We sent a fleet out before morning and they'll be hunting there. Any unmarked canoe will be chased down, and I can't guarantee they'll be gentle. Do you have an Aaní screen with you?"

Elān blew out his breath in exasperation at his own forgetfulness. "No. I forgot." An Aaní screen was a red-and-black flag depicting two birds, Raven and Eagle, facing each other. It was the standard of the Aaní nation. Ocean-going canoes often raised them on their masts when they left their village waters. For some reason, no one in *Waka*'s crew thought to inquire about whether or not a screen was on board. As captain, it was Elān's job to make sure *Waka* had a Aaní screen.

"I can loan you one," Dlan said. He retrieved a small, folded Aaní screen from a drawer in the desk and handed it to Elān. "Fly this if you're spotted by our fleet. That should protect you from harm."

Kwa was waiting for them by *Waka*. She wore highly polished, black metal armor with a red elk horn design on the breastplate. A recurved short bow was slung across her back and a sword hung at her side on a belt. She held a black-and-red war helmet in her hands. Her black hair was pulled back into a short, tight ponytail. She had dark, intense eyes, a narrow face, and wide shoulders that betrayed a warrior's strength with bow and sword. To Elān, she looked a lot older, but, as you know, anybody in their late twenties can appear old to youths of only eighteen winters. Kwa didn't wear more than thirty winters on her shoulders. She was one of Yelm's best warriors and would no doubt become a captain, Hits'aati, and elder one day.

Kwa was talking to raven, who was sitting up in his nest looking down at her. Elān heard raven tell her, "You'll be sitting for seed with us. See, here they come to take you to your death in this leaky canoe. That wolf there devours humans when he can't find any deer crap to eat. His brain is soft, you see, from the deer crap..."

"Your ancestors," Elān said to Kwa.

"Yours. This is the canoe, then?"

"Yes."

"And it comes with the bird?" Kwa inclined her head at raven.

"Unfortunately," Caraiden said.

"I'm Elān. That's Ch'eet, Caraiden, Hoosa, and Chetdyl. We're glad to have you with us."

"Where should I put my gear?" Kwa toed a waterproof bag at her feet. On top of the bag was her paddle.

"Wherever you can find room. It's tight. Chetdyl's up front at the bow. Ch'eet and Caraiden between the jib and main masts. You'll be between Hoosa and me behind the main."

Kwa leaned her paddle against the side of *Waka* and hefted her waterproof bag and crammed it into the bow among the large bentwood boxes. She moved with a quietness and lithe strength Elān had seen in a few elite warriors in Naasteidi. She grabbed her carved paddle and spun it in her hand lengthwise. Standing next to her, Elān saw she was as tall as him. She turned her dark, intense eyes on him and stared straight into his eyes. He turned his gaze away. As you know, as a sign of respect, the Aaní usually don't look another person directly in the eyes unless trying to discern some secret or stress an important point. Elān could feel Kwa's eyes on him.

"You graduated from the Longhouse of War here in Yelm?" Caraiden asked Kwa.

"Yes," she replied. "And have taken my kwalk and have done nine winters of warrior duty already. Kaat' was my mentor-uncle."

Caraiden nodded. "Kaat' and I are friends."

"So, it's not me you should worry about," Kwa said sharply. Kwa pointed at Ch'eet and Elān with her paddle. "These two don't look old enough to have graduated Naasteidi's Longhouse of War."

"And Fathead there isn't even in the Longhouse of War," raven said. "In his village they use him as buoy. His head and ass are full of blubber, you see."

"Is this true?" Kwa asked Elān.

"All true," interrupted raven. "Nothing but fat in this one's ass-head."

"It's true I'm not in the Longhouse of War," Elān replied. "I'm in the Longhouse of Service and Trade, studying to become a teacher of books."

"A bookeater?" Kwa said. "How is it you're the captain of this crew?"

"Íxt put me in charge unless we go into battle—then Caraiden here is in charge."

She turned from Elān to Caraiden. "This is true? You're not the captain of our crew?

"It's true," Caraiden replied. "Stay home if it displeases you."

"What displeases me is my being taken off duty to go on this pointless pleasure cruise to cannibal giant land with a boy captain and an annoying bird."

"Regardless of how you feel about accompanying us," Caraiden said to Kwa, "your Hits'aati has given you an order. As an Aaní warrior you're expected to follow that order, whether you like it or not."

"Then let me state here to this crew and ocean: I don't like my orders," Kwa replied.

Caraiden turned to Elān. "Kwa will obey her orders. Let's put out to sea."

The crew wrestled the heavy-laden canoe down into the harbor bay. Ch'eet stood waist deep, holding on to the netting while the crew loaded in. Elān jumped into the stern of the canoe. Kwa sat directly in front of him. Her carved paddle lay across her legs. She was tall, and she had to duck slightly to miss the swinging boom of the mainsail. Hoosa was much smaller and needn't duck at all.

Elān lifted the screen. "Kireti loaned me an Aaní screen in case we run into the fleet that's out hunting the large canoe." Nobody acknowledged him. He set the screen on the floor behind him. "How did you sleep last night?" he asked Hoosa.

"Ask the stupid bird," Hoosa growled.

Raven poked his head out over his nest atop the mast. "That's no way to speak about the messenger eagle."

"I'm talking about you and what you did last night," Hoosa said.

"What? So I crapped in your hair while you slept. It was late, the night was dark, I couldn't see very well. You've probably crapped in your own hair once or twice by the look of it."

"Bird," Elān called up to raven. "If you keep bothering the crew, I cannot guarantee your safety."

"Ha! You cannot guarantee anyone's safety. Not yours, Turds in his Hair, Old Man Bellyache, Crap Eater, or Young Zero. And now you've added this stupid woman to our crew. Kwa is short for crazy. You all need to worry only about yourselves. This is a journey to certain death. Your death. As for me, I'll enjoy my days as I desire." Raven's head disappeared back into his nest.

"Go ahead, Ch'eet," Elān said. Ch'eet pushed the canoe out toward the bay, pulled himself onto the netting, and scrabbled to his place in the front of *Waka*. "Paddles," he said.

The crew lifted their paddles and thrust them into the sea. The paddles flashed up and dove into the ocean again and again in unison. Elān kept his hand on the tiller and guided them through the channel of Yelm Bay out toward the open water. The crew paddled on in silence out of the channel into the open ocean. Once out of the shelter of the bay, the wind ran from the south, the same wind that had helped them escape the large canoe. Elān had a choice: keep with paddling and exhaust and further exasperate the crew, or unfurl sails and tack back and forth against the wind in a large Z pattern. Their progress would be slow under sails, but the crew could keep their strength. Being unsure what to do, Elān determined to do both. They'd stick to paddles for a while and make toward Daadzi Island, and then unfurl sails. "We'll paddle for two or three yaakw and then raise the sails and tack," Elān said to the crew.

The crew kept digging their paddles into the sea and plowed into the wind along Samish, heading southward and keeping the coast in sight off the starboard side of *Waka*. The skies clouded—a drizzle here and there but no downpouring—but the late morning grew warm. The constant motion of the paddles and rolling waves gave Elān a hypnotic feeling, and he fell to daydreaming and didn't see raven, shortly before lunch, peeking over the edge of his nest at the crew below.

Raven stuck his feathered behind out over the edge of his nest and aimed it directly above Hoosa. He crapped a gloop of grayish poop that landed in the tangled knots of Hoosa's hair. Hoosa brought his hand to his head in reflex. Poop smeared across his palm.

"Gluuchu!" raven yelled.

"Do that again, I'll kill you," Hoosa yelled at raven. He washed his hand in the sea, and then smacked the main mast.

Raven laughed long and loud. Of course, to human ears it was a cackle or a caw, like the screech of ravens near your house when they see you doing something foolish. "Gluuchu" would have been witty if the bird wasn't so irksome. The Aaní played a game called Gluuch which was like your Capture the Flag, except they used balls about the size of your soccer balls instead of flags, and players kicked and passed the ball back to their side of the field (or forest, as the game was often played in the woods) and then kicked the ball into the gluuch—or hole in the ground—from a set distance. A circle was drawn around the gluuch and players had to kick the ball into the hole from beyond that circle. Whenever a player kicked the ball into his side's gluuch, he of course yelled, "Gluuchu!" And the game started over until one team scored five points.

"Gluuchu!" raven yelled again. No doubt you too have friends or enemies who say something twice in hopes of it being funny the second time when it wasn't funny the first. Raven looked from Caraiden to Ch'eet to Elān to Kwa. Nobody laughed or looked at him. "Morons," he said and disappeared back into his nest.

"Stupid bird," Elān said. "Let's raise sail and tack," he told the crew. "And we can eat a bit of food on the way. It'll be a long time before we come to Kals'aak Island with this wind."

"Do you intend to stop for the evening or will we sleep in shifts aboard the canoe?" Kwa asked Elān.

"We'll stop for the night at Kals'aak if we can," Elān said. "If we don't make it that far, we can maybe stop at Doe Island. Let's get the sails up. Pass around the smoked salmon, and watch your head with that boom, Kwa."

The crew hoisted the sails and it was Elān's turn to work. He held the tiller and the mainsail sheet and let the boom swing out portside. He angled *Waka* against the wind and sailed away from Samish. The crew put up their paddles and passed around hunks of smoked salmon. Hoosa protested when Ch'eet offered a piece to raven, but Elān insisted the bird be given some food. Elān tied off the sheet and munched on smoked salmon as he sailed. After a long while, Elān swung the booms starboard and tacked back toward Samish.

Even against the wind, Elān was impressed by *Waka*'s speed. The canoe was at its heaviest—full of food, gear, and crew—and still it sliced quick through the sea. Daadzi Island came into sight off the portside of the canoe as they headed toward Samish. There was no sign of the large canoe or the Aaní fleet hunting it. The wind had died down to a breeze and the seas calmed without chop on the swells. The clouds lightened and the drizzle stopped.

"Caraiden?" Elān asked. Caraiden was resting sideways in the canoe, his back against one side, his feet up on the other. "Can we put in on the north side of Kals'aak in the dark?"

Caraiden thought for a moment. "At Naa Goosh, perhaps, though there are rocks at low tide. I'd only do it at high tide. The other beaches have rocks at high and low tides. I wouldn't risk them in the dark."

Kals'aak was a rocky, cliffy, mountainous island without sheltered harbors, so there was no permanent Aaní settlement there, though the Aaní did have summer fish camps and outdoor longhouse schools on the island. Kals'aak did have several nice beaches. In the winter, though, the winds howled across those beaches.

"We'll make for Naa Goosh," Elān said. "Hopefully we'll arrive before the tide is too low, and with any luck the clouds will roll back and we'll have a bit of moonlight to guide us in."

With the wind still from the south, Elān again tacked away from Samish and cut south of Daadzi Island near the spot they had been chased by the large canoe the previous day. Elān watched Chetdyl for any sign of danger, but the wolf, who was standing atop a box in the bow with his nose to the air, scented no alarm. They sailed past Daadzi and gazed around its east side, but no canoe was at sea.

The tack would take them far eastward, at least four yaakw, and then they'd tack southwest once more and hope to hit the north end of Kals'aak, which lay several yaakw to the south of Daadzi Island. It would be very dark, and very late, before they arrived.

CHAPTER 16

THE EAGLE SCREECHED as it fell through the sky toward *Waka*. Elān would never have believed any animal could travel at such incredible speed if he hadn't seen it. The eagle pulled up just above the stern; Elān could feel the air move beneath his massive wings as he hovered above Elān's head. In his claws, the eagle held a leather pouch, which he dropped with precision into the canoe in front of Elān. He then shot upward, skimming raven's nest as he flew away.

Elān grabbed the leather pouch and opened it. It contained a folded-up letter from Íxt dated from the previous day. Elān read it aloud to the crew.

> *E,*
>
> *Beware! A large Koosh canoe has been spotted off the east coast of Samish, manned by Yahooni captives. How many Koosh are aboard not known. They have destroyed the Yelm fort at Daadzi & have been spotted northeast of Kéet Island. Stick to the southern route. Go well south of Kéet Island before heading west. Flee from Koosh canoe. DO NOT ENGAGE IT. The eagles will be watching your progress as best they can. You can send word through them. You will not find allies east of L's Line so travel at night. May Yéil protect you.*
> *–I*

"Our feelings are confirmed," Caraiden said. "It's a Koosh canoe."

"Perhaps we should call in at the village of Deshu on Kéet's Island tomorrow and find out what news they have," Elān said.

"The letter says we should stay away from Kéet's Island," Caraiden said. "We should heed that advice. Let's make for Kals'aak Island tonight and head far south tomorrow."

"Trust Íxt and Caraiden," Kwa said. "If the Koosh are around Kéet's Island, they'll most likely be near villages."

Elān loved visiting other villages. The thought of sleeping in the wild or asea gave him a feeling of aloneness. But Kwa had a good point. "Okay, we'll put in at Naa Goosh on Kals'aak tonight and head south in the morning."

As night fell, Elān grew worried that he had sailed past Kals'aak. He couldn't see the dial of his jishagoon in the dark, the night sky showed no islands on the ocean's edges, and he didn't want to ask the crew to light lanterns as all the lanterns sat stowed in the outriggers. He hadn't thought ahead to bring them inside the canoe, and he didn't want to show incompetence or uncertainty in front of the crew. The wind ran from the south, and *Waka* was stilling, running the southwesterly tack. The moon glowed behind the broken clouds that filled the night sky, and occasionally it would come out and light up the sea in silver light. Unfortunately, the clouds shrouded the guiding stars. Elān looked again at his jishagoon but it was too dark to read the bearing. He strained to see Kals'aak off the portside, but the horizon was too dark to see the tall, forested mountains of the island. He kept steady his course and resisted his urge to ask for Caraiden and Kwa's help.

"Kals'aak straight ahead," Ch'eet yelled.

"Very well," Elān said. "Ch'eet, can you retrieve the lanterns from the outriggers?" Elān tried to disguise the extreme relief he felt. Ch'eet had a difficult time crawling across the netting to locate the lanterns in the front hold of the starboard outrigging, and he returned to the canoe soaked from the ordeal, but to Ch'eet's credit he didn't complain.

Soon, Kals'aak towered in darkness off *Waka's* bow. No lights or fires lit the island. "Strike the sails," Elān said, "and pick up paddles." The crew took down the sails and secured them to their booms, and then tied down the booms and hefted their paddles. "Hand the lanterns to Caraiden. He can light them," Elān said. He kept his hand tight on the tiller as they approached the island. Without the rustle of wind in canvas, the night was silent except for the slosh of paddles dipping into the sea. If one of the crew knocked the canoe with a paddle, it echoed across the water and off the island.

"I need a lantern," Ch'eet said.

"We'll alert any enemy ashore or at sea with these lanterns," Kwa said.

"We are in our own homeland, Kwa," Caraiden said. "No enemy has stepped on these shores since before Latseen's time."

Caraiden lifted the lid from the cooking box. He took a flint and fire starter from a leather pouch hanging from his waist and cracked a spark into the fire starter. An ember glowed. He put the ember in the cooking box and put tinder atop it and blew it to flame. He then grabbed lantern and candle, lit the candle, and fitted it firmly in the round base inside the lantern. The yellow flame rang brightly in the canoe. He passed the lantern up to Ch'eet, and then lit another lantern for himself. The lanterns had shutters on them that could be opened and closed. Ch'eet took his lantern, opened the shutter full, and climbed up alongside Chetdyl at the bow, holding the lantern up to see what was in front of the canoe. Caraiden hung his lantern from the main mast with its shutter opened halfway and facing portside to shed light around that side of the canoe.

"A lantern at sea is dangerous," Kwa said.

"Seeing where we're going is worth what little actual danger there may be," Caraiden replied.

"Can you see Naa Goosh, Ch'eet?" Elān asked.

"I can see where it's supposed to be," he said. "But it's too dark to see the beach."

"It's too risky," Caraiden said. "We don't have enough moon and the tide is too low. We should sleep on the canoe and sail through the night."

"We can make it," Elān said. "We'll take it slow."

"I'll wait for you on the beach," raven said. "If you make it. Laters, fatheads." He flew off into the darkness.

"The outrigging is too wide for a night landing through the rocks," Kwa said.

Elān was annoyed. "Paddle forward," he commanded the crew.

Kwa, Caraiden, and Hoosa paddled as Elān held the tiller and Ch'eet peered into the sea illuminated by his lantern.

"Rock, portside," Ch'eet called out.

Elān pulled the tiller slightly toward his stomach. "Hold paddles."

The canoe slowed as the crew set their paddles across their knees. Elān saw a large, gnarled, black boulder, still wet with the receding tide, glide past not far from the portside outrigger. "Straight ahead," Ch'eet said.

"Paddle forward," Elān told the crew. "Ch'eet, can you see the beach?"

"No. I can't see much."

"Stop paddling," Elān said.

Waka slid silently through the dark sea. Elān thought he could see several more hull-breaking rocks off to the starboard side of the canoe.

"Rock, dead ahead," Ch'eet yelled.

"Paddle backward," Elān commanded the crew. They dug their paddles into the water backward. Elān saw a rock, barely out of the water, on the portside and shifted the tiller to move the bow starboard.

The canoe bucked and the sickening sound of splintering

wood came from the starboard outrigging below the water line. The scraping sound echoed along the water; Elān could tell by the echo that the shore lay closer than he thought. "Hold us here," he yelled to the crew. "Ch'eet, can you see a way around the rocks?"

"To port slightly," Ch'eet said. "Follow my direction." He pointed with his left arm.

"Paddle forward slow," Elān said. He pushed the tiller and turned the bow to port. The starboard outrigger scraped again. Ch'eet moved his arm to signal dead ahead and Elān followed with the tiller. Elān sweated as he mazed the canoe through the rocks and onto the shore. When they made the beach at Naa Goosh, Ch'eet jumped into the tide with his lantern, set the lantern on the beach, and pulled the canoe up.

As the crew set about getting a fire going and setting up bedrolls, Elān waded into the sea with lantern in hand to check the damage to *Waka*'s outrigging. The rocks had torn a hole in the front hold, filling it with sea water. The hold held waterproof bags of weapons and armor, as well as rope and fishing tackle. It would be impossible to repair the outrigger without getting it out of the sea. In the morning, he'd have to make a temporary repair and have it fixed at Deshu. They had no choice now but to go to Kéet's Island. Elān removed the ropes and tackle and bags and put them in the canoe and went to join the crew on the beach. The fire was going nicely, and the crew was handing around chunks of smoked salmon.

"Sorry for the wreck out there," Elān said to the crew. He looked at Caraiden and Kwa. "I should have listened to you."

"No. You made your decision. You must pay the costs of those decisions even if the cost is death," Kwa said. "The only thing you need to apologize for is your apology."

"Kwa is correct," Caraiden said. "You show weakness by apologizing. If you make a decision, you must live with the consequences. When you decided to put ashore, you put our lives in danger. If we'd capsized, you would have had to live or die with those consequences, but you must never apologize."

Elān thought about this for a few moments. Though he couldn't say why, what Kwa and Caraiden had said felt wrong. Apologizing didn't mean one was weak. *Perhaps,* thought Elān, *apologizing is a sign of humility, and humility a sign of strength.*

"There's a hole in the front starboard hold," he said. "We'll set sail for Deshu on Kéet's Island tomorrow. We need to get *Waka* repaired. I was there last summer. They'll welcome us. We can stay at the same pub my father and I stayed at. And their master canoe-builder does excellent work. *Waka* will be good as new."

Nobody spoke. Kwa scowled and Caraiden shook his head.

WHEN THE EVENING turned late and the fire fell low, Hoosa excused himself and set off for the woods. "Should we set a watch tonight?" Elān asked.

"We've taken care of it," Caraiden said. "Kwa, Ch'eet, and I will take turns."

"I can take a shift," Elān said.

"No. We've taken care of it," Kwa said. "We've been trained to take watch. Bookeaters don't stand watch. It's tradition."

Elān felt more embarrassed about the punctured outrigger—and very upset he'd damaged *Waka*—and he felt his youth keenly as he sat next to Kwa and Caraiden. His anger rose. "I don't care about tradition. I expect to do my part on night watch," he told his crew, using as firm a voice as he could. "If not tonight, then on other nights."

"Go eat a book," Kwa said. "I do care about tradition."

"'Eat a book,'" raven laughed from his mast-nest. "That's a good one, you old, traditional sour bag. Give young Crapshack here a piece of what little mind you have. Yéil knows he could use it. When it comes to lack of brains, you two are the opposite twins." Raven cackled at his own joke. "Young Crapshack is stupid where you're smart, and smart where you're stupid."

"Shut up, you annoying and unwelcome bird," Kwa said to raven. "You won't talk such nonsense with an arrow through your throat."

Raven laughed. "Yes! That's it, the traditional sourness. When the bookeater gets you killed, I'll take your traditional bitter skull and fill it with honey from those idiot bears Hoosa hangs out with. For once you'll have a little sweetness in your sour head." He turned in his nest and looked at Elān. "But there's one here," raven drawled in a comic voice, "who likes to ask difficult questions about tradition. There's one here who wants to become what tradition says he shouldn't become. To learn what he shouldn't learn. To go where he shouldn't go. To speak with those with whom he shouldn't speak. Isn't that right, Fathead?"

Elān remained silent, but inside he raged with anger.

"And no matter what any sack of ancient dog turds elder says, there's one here who will ask difficult questions that pick at the threads of tradition until it unravels. Even when his sibling in all but blood, his opposite twin, sour old miss traditional here, threatens to kill him to save tradition, he'll still ask questions. It's in his nature to do so. Isn't that about right, Fathead?"

Elān wrapped himself in his bedroll and lay down with his back to the fire and his companions. His face was flushed and hot with anger. He fell asleep amid a fury and desire to wake up far away from Kwa and that lousy raven.

ELĀN WOKE TO a gray, drizzly morning. He felt as though he hadn't slept at all. The fire was out, the charred logs slick with rain. Though his bedroll was waterproof and had a padded hood on it that kept his head covered during the night, Elān felt a chill. Perhaps it was the coin-mail shirt that held the cold to him. He didn't want to take it off, though, as he felt safe in it, especially when he lay down to sleep at night.

Elān was the last person to wake. His crew was up eating and stowing bedrolls back into *Waka*. Chetdyl was down at the end of the beach with Hoosa. Elān saw them disappear into the forest. The sea was alive, and *Waka*'s stern swayed up and down with the waves at its bow, tied off to a fallen log on the shore, which slid back and forth on the wet seaweed at the ocean's edge. He could hear Kwa talking to Caraiden down the beach beside *Waka*.

"I should be with my crew hunting these large canoes, but instead I'm babysitting a captain who puts all our lives in danger," Kwa said in an urgent yet quiet voice. "Don't tell me you disagree, Caraiden. He's no warrior. I have nothing against him as a person; he will be a good bookeater, I'm sure. But just as I shouldn't teach in his longhouse, so shouldn't he pretend to be a warrior. Especially when true warriors make up our crew. I'm begging you to take over the captaincy of this crew."

"We have our orders, Kwa, from our Hits'aati," Caraiden hissed. "Do you wish to bring dishonor to your longhouse and clan by disobeying? I will become captain in battle, but at all other times we must help him act as befits a warrior and captain. He's smart and can learn."

"Yes, he could learn, Caraiden, if we had long moons to teach and train him, and were we on Samish Island in the same village he and I could become silence-sharing friends," Kwa replied. "But a warrior's voyage is not the place to learn to be a warrior. Please be realistic when it comes to our lives."

Kwa's words stung. Elān rolled his bedroll, stood, and walked to *Waka*. Kwa and Caraiden fell silent and walked away from each other and the canoe. Elān examined the wound to *Waka*'s outrigging. The beautiful, black matte wood on the outside of the starboard outrigger was shredded and raw scrapes ran down its side. The hole was big enough for Elān to put his fist through. The hole would slow them down. Not greatly, but perhaps enough to make them vulnerable at sea.

"When Old Man Bellyache warns you not to put ashore, you should listen to him next time, Craphead, and never trust Zero to guide you anywhere."

Elān looked up to see raven peering down at him from his mast-perch.

Elān was angry. "You are here to help me," he told raven, "and all you do is complain. You argue with the crew, you won't translate, you don't use our proper names, and you fly away at any sign of trouble. You could have helped me guide the canoe ashore last night, but you chose to flee like a coward. You have a mean heart, and I want nothing more to do with you. I will not speak to you anymore until we get to Botson's Bay, and once we fulfill our mission you're no longer welcome aboard *Waka*."

Raven, his beak slightly open, stared down at Elān for a moment and then fell back into his nest, screeching a peal of laughter that echoed over the water and around the beach. "That was wonderful, Crapshack," raven said between caws of laughter. "Say it again."

Elān ignored the bird.

"Come, Crapshack, say it all again with the same anger."

Elān opened the lid of the damaged hold to see about a temporary repair. He was determined not to speak to the bird again.

"Come on, Crappy Shack," raven continued. "Say it all again like you did." Raven changed his voice in imitation of Elān's. "I, Crapshack, nearly killed my crew, therefore I am angry at a bird and I refuse to talk anymore because I'm an idiot in a metal shirt. Say it like that."

Elān ignored the annoying bird. He took a piece of waterproof sail-repair cloth and wrapped it around the damaged outrigger. He tied it tight. It would keep the sea from pushing into the hole and slowing the canoe. Once they arrived at Deshu they'd need to get it repaired proper.

"Oh, Crapshack," raven said. "What was that rotten old man thinking when he sent you on this death trip? Before it's all over, I'm going to poop on your pretty metal shirt."

"I hate that bird," Ch'eet said. "Don't listen to him."

"I'm trying not to, but he doesn't shut up."

Ch'eet looked over Elān's repair. "That should hold for a while," he said, nodding at the waterproof cloth tied around the outrigger. "Don't worry about the damage. Every warrior I know has damaged a canoe at least once. Some warriors many times."

"Gunalchéesh," Elān said. He appreciated Ch'eet's kindness. Elān stowed the sail-repair kit and trudged back up the beach and sat down on the cold, wet sand.

"Are we all ready to put asea?" Caraiden asked.

"I think so," Ch'eet replied. "That repair should get us to Deshu. Any news from the forest?" he asked Hoosa.

"Nothing," Hoosa replied. "The trails haven't been used."

"Strange no Aaní have been here this spring," Caraiden said. "Let's put out to sea. The tide is high enough that we can sail straight out without scraping. We'll stop at Deshu for repairs." All of the crew except for Elān walked down the beach to *Waka*. Caraiden turned to Elān. "Let's go."

Elān felt the tears building behind his eyes. His nose felt plugged.

"Elān," Caraiden said. "We must be going."

"Leave me," Elān replied.

Raven cawed laughter from his perch.

"Elān, get in the canoe," Caraiden barked.

"I said leave me," Elān replied. Tears fell.

"For Yéil's sake, Caraiden, let's leave the bookeater here," Kwa said. "He could've killed us last night."

"Come now, Elān," Caraiden yelled. "Or I'll come up there and knock you out and drag you into this canoe."

Elān cupped his head in his hands. *I can't do this*, he thought to himself. *The whole crew hates me. They will never respect me.*

"The bookeater will get us all killed, Caraiden," Kwa said. "Leave him. Aaní fishing and military canoes patrol these shores all the time. He can get a ride home with one of them."

"I'm oath-bound to bring him home safe," Caraiden said.

Raven cawed a peal of laughter. "Come now, Sleepy Old Man Bellyache, this stupid death canoe will never be safe."

"I designate you captain, Caraiden," Kwa said. "You are a warrior and mentor-uncle and an elder. Forget your oath. Take charge of this canoe and leave the bookeater ashore to pout alone."

"I do not accept your designation, Kwa, so keep your mouth shut," the old warrior snapped. "I am oath-bound, and for the sake of his grandfather I will not accept his captaincy. Elān is our captain and will remain so throughout our journey. If you don't accept that, Kwa, you can stay ashore here. You are not needed."

Raven laughed again. "Nap time, Old Man Bellyache."

"Shut your stupid beak, bird. You're not needed either," Caraiden said. He turned to Ch'eet. "Go get our captain."

Ch'eet walked up the beach to Elān. Elān felt a hand on his shoulder and looked up. Ch'eet squatted down next to him. "I understand now," Ch'eet said to Elān. Elān remained silent. "At the Atx'aan Hídi archery competition you had the physical strength to send three arrows at once as far as I can send one arrow," Ch'eet continued, "yet you pity yourself. I heard you upset all the students and teachers in your longhouse with one story crafted with little forethought, yet you pity yourself. Pity comes from comparing yourself to others. Stop it. You have all the strength you need. Get into the canoe and prove that to yourself."

Elān looked at Ch'eet. Ch'eet had been nice to him, like an older brother, but Elān had been betrayed by Ch'eet's family.

His separation from Ch'aal' still stung. "Why are you being nice to me?" Elān asked.

"I'm being honest with you." Ch'eet laughed. "And I don't care what happened between you and my brother."

"He lost respect for me when I became a bookeater," Elān said. He looked out at the crew waiting beside *Waka*, which was now floating in the tide. "They have no respect for me."

"Then get in the canoe and earn our respect," Ch'eet replied. "Respect yourself and earn ours."

Elān stood up and took long, deep breaths and walked down the beach toward *Waka*.

"Nap time is over, Old Man Bellyache," raven cawed from his mast-nest.

Elān ignored the bird. He walked into the sea and vaulted into the stern of the canoe. "Bow forward. Push us off," he yelled to the crew.

ELĀN'S SOLE PIECE of luck that morning was the wind: it had shifted and came in from the northwest, slanting the rain and pushing the canoe toward Kéet Island, where the village of Deshu lay on the southern end. The crew used paddles only once, to get *Waka* out into the ocean. The rest of the morning into the early afternoon they sailed through the rain and the large, choppy swells that grew as the afternoon wore on. By the time they sighted Kéet Island over the front port side of the canoe, the sea was angry. Large, white-misted swells lifted *Waka* up, raced it forward, and slammed it down in the furrows between crests.

The crew was drenched and the rollers still towering when they came in sight of the village. Deshu, like Naasteidi, had a southern spit which sheltered a short bay and harbor. In the gray, rainy, late afternoon they approached the village, and though Elān had been there only a winter ago, he was shocked to find Deshu unrecognizable—squat and hidden behind a stockade of freshly cut trees with barkless sharpened tops pointing up into the sky. It was Aaní custom not to cut living trees from the forest. For some reason, the Aaní at Deshu had broken custom and ringed their village in a newly-cut stockade.

Two large doors on the stockade opened and a host of armed warriors filed out along its walls. They had bows with arrows at the ready and lanterns to set the arrows alight. "What in Yéil's name?" Elān said.

"They're taking defensive positions," Caraiden said.

Flames spread down the line of warriors as they lit their arrows.

"Laters, fatheads." Raven flew off toward Kéet Island.

"Sails down," Elān yelled. Hoosa and Kwa quickly struck down the main sail, and Ch'eet brought down the jib. Elān tossed Caraiden the screen. "Run it up," he said. Caraiden tied the Aaní flag to the halyard and hoisted it up the mast. A black eagle facing a black raven against a red background flapped with the wind. "Paddles," Elān said, and the crew took to their paddles. "Hold us here."

"We're within range," Kwa said.

"Hold us here," Elān repeated.

The Deshu warriors lit their arrows. The flames whipped in the wind as the warriors laid their arrows across their bows.

"They could easily burn our canoe out from under us," Kwa said.

"Wait until they see the screen," Elān said. He turned the canoe parallel with the shore and floated with the tide along the village edge. One by one, down the line of warriors, they took their arrows from the bows and sunk the tips into the beach sand to extinguish the flames. "Paddle forward slow." The crew paddled as he steered *Waka* toward the village.

"Your ancestors," Elān yelled. He waved a hand at the warriors on the beach.

Ch'eet stood to vault himself overboard as the canoe scraped to shore, but a nearby warrior held up his hand. "Hold right there. Stay aboard. We'll pull you ashore." The warrior, who because of his grayed hair looked older than the rest, nodded to two young warriors who dragged *Waka* onto the beach. Elān was too shocked to speak: never should any Aaní touch another's canoe without permission. With his eyes he pleaded to Caraiden to do something. "This is a violation," Caraiden yelled. "How dare you put hands on our canoe!"

"Stay aboard," the older warrior said, "and don't say a word."

"What welcome is this?" Caraiden asked.

"Don't speak."

Two more warriors wearing uniforms Elān didn't recognize emerged from within the stockade with a massive, leashed dog between them. They led the dog around *Waka*. He sniffed the outrigging, the netting, the air around the canoe, and growled at Chetdyl. The warrior who held the dog's leash looked at the leader and said, "All clear."

"There's no need for the dog," Caraiden said. Elān felt the anger in his voice. "We are not Koosh. If we were, you'd be dead."

The gray-haired warrior glared at Caraiden and spoke to Elān. "Who are you?"

"I'm Elān of Naasteidi. I was here last summer with my father Skaan. This is Kwa of Yelm, Caraiden of Naasteidi, Hoosa of the S'eek Ḵwáan black bear cousins on Samish, Ch'eet of Naasteidi, and Chetdyl of Quintus Ḵwáan on Samish."

"What in the name of Yéil are you doing?"

"We're in need of repair to our canoe." Elān pointed to the damaged outrigger.

"Why are you at sea? We've banned travel to and from Kéet for all but our military."

"How were we to know that?" Caraiden interrupted. "This is Latseen's grandson. But for Latseen, Deshu would be a Yahooni village and all of you slaves."

"Are you captain?" the older warrior asked Caraiden.

"No."

"Then I don't hear you." He turned back to Elān. "Why are you at sea?"

"We're on a mission from Íxt of Samish," Elān said.

"We've heard of no mission, and we've banned all travel around Kéet. It's within my duty to confiscate your canoe and place you and your crew in the forest cells."

"You would punish us for doing nothing wrong?" Elān asked.

"You've ignored a public ban."

"We've had no news of the ban," Elān said. "The only news we've had since we left Samish is this letter from Íxt." Elān took Íxt's letter from his pocket and held it out to the gray-haired warrior.

"That wasn't for his eyes," Caraiden said to Elān.

"Since when do the Aaní keep secrets from each other?" Elān asked Caraiden. "Here. Read the letter," he said to the older warrior.

The older warrior took the letter and read it. He frowned, and then handed the letter back to Elān. He turned to the warriors lining the beach—their bows still in hand, the arrows sticking out from the sand. "The fort at Daadzi is lost." Many warriors groaned. The gray-haired warrior turned and looked at Elān. "Latseen's grandson?"

"Yes."

"I don't know you, but I knew your grandfather," the warrior said. "He commanded me when I was a young warrior. I was part of the Samish–Kéet contingent in the Battle of Heeni. I was one of five hundred that crushed the three thousand warriors of the Mainland Yahooni northern army. Five hundred against three thousand. It was your grandfather's greatest victory."

"I've often heard so," Elān said. "I never got to meet my grandfather. He died in the war against the cannibal giants before I was born." On a strange impulse, Elān took off his sea coat and sea shirt, and exposed his grandfather's coin-mail. "This was my granddad's."

The old warrior's mouth opened. "The flicker tail coin-mail. He wore that during the Battle of Heeni. I never thought I'd see it again." He stared at Elān's coin-mail a moment longer, and then turned to the two warriors who wore strange uniforms and still held the large dog leashed between them. "Tell the Harbor Master we will lift the ban for the grandson of Latseen and his crew. His canoe is in need of repair, so notify Jiyee we're bringing a canoe to him. He's to drop all he's doing and have this canoe fixed by tomorrow, if possible. Two days at the most." They nodded, turned, and headed through the city gate with the large dog. "You may stay in Deshu to repair your canoe, after which you're free to leave. My name is Kooyu and it's my honor to welcome Latseen's grandson to our village."

Deshu's warriors pulled *Waka* ashore and Elān and his crew jumped onto the beach. "Thank Yéil for your old granddad," Caraiden whispered.

CHAPTER 17

ELĀN COULD FEEL it the moment he stepped through the stockade gate of Deshu: the village was tense. After *Waka*'s crew was inside, the warriors shut the gate and ran a locking bar through it. The village looked much the same as it had the previous summer, but darker under the shade of the wall, and the villagers wore worried, haggard expressions. The gate opened onto the main intersection in the village, and *Waka*'s crew, accompanied by a dozen warriors, walked toward the village Harbor Master's house, which sat attached to the new wall down the beach road.

"We're constructing metalworks that will enclose the village," Kooyu told the crew. "Until that's finished, we've put up this wooden barricade." He gestured with his arm to the stockade behind them.

"Metalworks?" Caraiden asked. "Do you mean to build a metal barricade around the entire village?"

"Yes."

"Why?" Elān asked.

"You should know from that note you showed me. The Koosh have come. That Koosh canoe attacked several of our military canoes north of Kéet."

"But you don't cage yourself in a metal pen simply because of a threat," Caraiden broke in.

Kooyu stopped. He looked around and spoke with a lowered voice. "Don't think the Deshu warriors approve of this barricade. You should know warriors don't make such

151

decisions. Our Aankaawu ordered it after the villagers ran crazy with fear about the Koosh. We warriors find it sickening to see these villagers trembling, so fearful they don't care about being penned up. They choose to live in fear behind a wall."

Elān looked up at the wooden stockade. "Who are those warriors with the dog?"

"The Aankaawu's Guard," Kooyu said. "He took our best warriors from the Longhouse of War and turned them into his own personal guard. We have very few warriors now. Let's keep moving. You never know who's listening."

"Dláa! Who in Yéil's name would care what we say? Is it a crime to speak one's mind?" Caraiden said.

"Yes. In Deshu it is," Kooyu replied. "While you're here, you'd best keep quiet."

They walked along in silence for a few moments.

"That letter you showed me when you arrived?"

"Yes?" Elān asked.

Kooyu whispered, "Burn it. Whatever you do, do not show it to anyone, especially the Aankaawu's Guard. If you do, you will be interrogated about your journey's purpose and may never leave." In a normal voice he said to Elān, "You look young to be a warrior captain."

"No, no. Crapshack is no warrior. He may be a useless chalky turd, but he is no warrior." Raven sat atop the Harbor Master's house.

"You're not a warrior?" Kooyu asked Elān.

"No, I'm not. I'm finishing studies at the Longhouse of Service."

"How then is it you are captain?"

"Old Íxt made that determination."

Kooyu nodded as though satisfied by the answer. "You all may enter the Harbor Master's house, even our wolf friend here. I'd prefer the raven stay outside."

"We would too," Ch'eet said.

Elān and his crew entered the house.

"I hope it burns down while you're all in it," raven said. He stayed perched as the crew entered the Harbor Master's house. Several of the Aankaawu's Guard stood in the house. A small, fat man sat at a desk and turned to look at the crew as they entered. "Which is Latseen's grandson?"

"I am," Elān said. "My name is Elān. Your ancestors."

"Yes. I'm Deshu's Harbor Master." The fat man looked at each of the crew. "What is your reason for coming to our village?"

"Our canoe is need of repair."

"Ah, so we've been told. I will order the repairs immediately. But why were you at sea?"

"We are on a mission on behalf of Íxt of Samish."

"A mission? What mission?"

"To gather information around Aaní land," Elān said.

"And to find out why we've had no visitors from Kéet this spring," Caraiden added.

The Harbor Master appeared uninquisitive. "Are you all from Samish Island?"

"We are," Elān replied. The Harbor Master wrote down the names of the crew in the large register book. After he was done writing, he looked to one of the Aankaawu's guards. "May we welcome them or offer them some pine needle tea?"

The Aankaawu's guard shook his head.

The fat man looked back at Elān. "We're all a bit unnerved here, I'm afraid, so you'll find our hospitality diminished. Our public houses have closed for the time being, but I'd be happy to have you stay here in the Harbor Master's house."

The Aankaawu's guard spoke in a whisper to the plump Harbor Master, who then frowned and looked at Elān. "May I ask for all of the details of your mission? What information are you gathering?"

Caraiden spoke before Elān could. "By custom you cannot ask such things, as you well know. But our mission is no secret: we heard of enemy action in Aaní waters. We are simply gathering information."

The Aankaawu's guard whispered again, and the Harbor Master spoke. "If that is the case, we—I mean I—find it strange that your mission is led by someone who isn't a warrior. And why is this odd bear man among your company?" The Harbor Master nodded toward Hoosa.

"Our mission is led by Latseen's grandson. That should satisfy you. And why not the bear man, whose name is Hoosa, and who can speak bear languages?" asked Caraiden.

The Aankaawu's guard leaned toward the Harbor Master. Again Caraiden spoke first. "How is it your Aankaawu created his own guard force?" Caraiden asked. "And need you consult with them to determine if you can sing a welcome song or serve tea in your own house?"

The fat man looked frightened by Caraiden's question. The Aankaawu's guard whispered in his ear. He shook his head slightly. "I'm afraid it's against policy to allow strangers to sleep in the Harbor Master's house. Our Longhouse of War will be glad to provide you accommodation during your stay in the village." The fat man walked to the door. "Kooyu? Will you accompany Latseen's grandson and his crew to the Longhouse of War? They will be accommodated there."

"The Longhouse of War?" Kooyu asked.

"Yes. The Aankaawu's Guard here will also accompany you," the Harbor Master said. He turned and walked back to his desk and sat down. He looked at Elān. "It's a pleasure to meet Latseen's grandson and his crew. The guards here and Kooyu will take you to the Longhouse. I will inform you when your canoe has been repaired."

Kooyu, followed by the suspicious, watchful Aankaawu's guards, took Elān and the crew to *Waka* to fetch their seabags. The crew hoisted their seabags and followed Kooyu to the center of Deshu, where stood the village Longhouse of War and Diplomacy. Kooyu took his leave at the door. "I must go back to the beach, but when my duty is over for the evening I'll come and visit you," he told Elān.

The Aankaawu's Guard led them through the longhouse and out into the back courtyard where the warriors-in-training barracks stood. One of the guards spoke to the crew. "Under the orders of our Aankaawu, you are to remain in these barracks or the courtyard while in the village. You will have meals brought to you." He turned and walked away.

The crew stored their gear on the barrack bunks and went outside again. Dusk was coming on, and the rain had stopped, but the leaden clouds were still swollen. The courtyard was empty: no Deshu warriors-in-training. An unnerving silence enveloped the longhouse. In the doorway stood one of the Aankaawu's guards, watching the crew. Ch'eet and Caraiden wandered around the courtyard looking at the barracks, and Elān, Hoosa, and Kwa sat down on wooden benches surrounding a blackened firepit. Chetdyl stretched out on the lawn in the center of the courtyard.

"Have you been to Deshu before?" Elān asked Kwa. Elān couldn't think of anything to say to her, but he needed to find a way to melt her unfriendliness.

"Yes," Kwa replied. "A number of times."

"Have you ever seen it like this?"

"Of course not," Kwa said.

"I have never heard of an Aaní village not singing welcoming songs, or closing pubs, or kept in fear behind metal fences."

"Nor have I," Kwa said. She looked directly at Elān. "But I am no Harbor Master and I have never been kept prisoner before in an Aaní village. I would appreciate it if you told me the truth. Why am I on this journey captained by a boy who can neither fight well nor sail deftly, heading to a place few Aaní have been?"

"We are sailing to reconnoiter Éil' and gather knowledge," Elān answered in a whisper.

"What knowledge?" Kwa asked. "And why send a bookeater to gather that knowledge?"

Elān paused in thought. He lowered his voice even more. "I'm not supposed to tell you this, but I'm considered an expert in my longhouse on the languages, cultures, and geography of the mainland." Elān looked around as though Deshu was listening. "I'm second only to the great scholar Snaak̲ in such knowledge. Our mission is this: we are to reconnoiter around Latseen's Line and Botson's Bay. I'm to verify topographical features of the mainland, fathom depths, and any new forts or settlements so we can update our military maps at Naasteidi."

Kwa kept her intense eyes peering deep into Elān's until he turned away. "You do know we warriors are taught to interrogate, right?" Kwa said. "There was nothing true in what you just said. It was all story. I don't know if Íxt has lost his wits or if your lying and storytelling has convinced him to allow you to resurrect the lost glory of your Flicker clan, but I don't care who your grandfather was. You are not your grandfather. Don't lie to me."

Elān trembled. "I'm sorry."

"Don't try it again." Kwa stood up and walked away.

Caraiden and Ch'eet returned from searching the barracks. "No sign of any warriors-in-training. Nothing at all," Ch'eet said. "It's as though they've closed this part of the Longhouse."

Elān watched Kwa walk into one of the barracks and close the door.

"Is Kwa not staying with us?" Caraiden asked.

"I don't know," Elān said. "She's angry I won't tell her the all the reasons Íxt sent us on this journey. Can you talk to her, Caraiden? She's not friendly to me."

"I think it's your age more than not knowing the purpose of our journey that bothers Kwa. And you're a bookeater. Besides, I don't think words will help. Earn her respect through your actions."

* * *

KOOYU CAME WITH dinner. It was dark and Elān had a large fire going in the firepit, and his crew sat around staring into the flames, saying little. The guards, Elān was certain, hadn't seen him use Íxt's letter to start the fire. Behind Kooyu several of the Aankaawu's Guard brought small platters of food—old mussels, smoked steelhead, dried seaweed, and venison stew in mugs. Elān asked one guard for leave to check on *Waka*.

"You will stay here at the barracks," the guard replied, "until your canoe is repaired and then you will leave."

Kwa emerged from the empty longhouse and the crew fell to eating. They talked in low tones so the guards wouldn't hear. "Join us," Elān said to Kooyu.

"No, thank you," Kooyu replied. "I've eaten already."

"Could you see that our canoe is safe and accounted for?" Elān asked.

"You needn't worry. The Deshu Yadi have never been thieves," Kooyu replied, "regardless of how the village may appear to you now."

"I didn't mean to offend," Elān said.

"Where are your warriors-in-training?" Caraiden asked. "Your barracks here look as though they've been empty some time."

"Not many young people joined the Longhouse of War in Deshu this past winter. The few who did join stay with mentor-uncles in the main barracks." Kooyu lowered his voice to barely audible. "And the Aankaawu's Guard is quite large and trains their own warriors now."

"Are there other Aaní villages like this?" Ch'eet asked.

"Perhaps," Kooyu said. "All eastern Aaní islands have a travel ban. It'd be best to stay in the wild if you have to stop during your journey. And, when you leave Aaní lands, wherever your southern route takes you, trust no one. By the letter you showed me, I fear you intend to go to the mainland. Yéil only knows what you will find. Personally, I think it mad to go beyond Latseen's Line. Our Aaní cousins closest to the mainland guard that line well, as do our Deikeenaa allies to the south. And I doubt any Aaní have been on the mainland since your grandfather's time, except the Far Out Fort contingent your grandfather left to guard the wall. We don't hear much news from them."

"I don't know what madness drives you westward," Kooyu continued. "But you will find no friends on the mainland. The Yahooni resent the thumping your granddad gave them all those winters ago, and the cannibal giants hold no love for the Aaní. Even our Far Out Fort relatives have grown strange. And, if the Koosh have come in large numbers to our world, you will find nothing but enemies the further south and east you travel."

Elán liked Kooyu. "Why don't you come with us?" he asked. "We have room for one more warrior in our canoe."

Kooyu laughed. "I appreciate the offer but I did just say it would be mad to head to the mainland."

"Yes, come with us," Kwa said. "We have room and could use another sword. We could convince your Hits'aati to loan you to us for a short trip."

Kooyu frowned and lowered his voice. "Our Aankaawu removed our Hits'aati and placed himself in charge of our Longhouse of War."

The crew was taken aback. "By what right?" Caraiden asked.

"Fear," Kooyu replied. "Fear of the Koosh, fear of the Aankaawu's Guard. My village is full of the fearful."

"All the more reason to join us," Elán urged.

"I appreciate the offer, but I must remain and do what I can to prevent the Aankaawu from destroying Deshu."

"I think it's too late for that," Kwa said.

CHAPTER 18

IT TOOK TWO days to fix *Waka*. The crew waited in the barracks yard the entire time, though late on the second evening Elān alone was escorted by the Aankaawu's Guard to the town hall. Several dozen of the Aankaawu's guards stood at post around the building. They shoved Elān into the Aankaawu's office and ordered him to remain standing. Two guards stood behind him. The Aankaawu entered through a back door.

"Your ancestors," Elān said.

The Aankaawu didn't honor the salutation. He simply sat at his desk, glared at Elān, and demanded the letter.

"What letter?" Elān asked.

"The letter you showed Kooyu when he interrogated you on the beach," the Aankaawu said.

"I don't know what letter you're talking about," Elān said.

"Take off his things and search him," the Aankaawu told the guards. Roughly, they grabbed Elān and tried to yank off his sea coat. "Wait, wait. I'll take them off myself," Elān protested. He took off his waterproof sea coat and his sea shirt.

"That pretty metal shirt, too," said the Aankaawu. "And the pants."

Standing in his underwear, Elān watched the guards pawing through his clothes. They found nothing.

"It's not on your canoe," the Aankaawu said, "not in your bags back in the barracks, and not on your person." He stood from his desk and walked over to where Elān's coin-mail shirt lay on the floor. He hoisted the shirt. "My size." The Aankaawu removed his jacket and put on Elān's coin-mail. Unlike on Elān, the shirt fit the Aankaawu well. "Armor can be so heavy. And expensive." The Aankaawu held out his arms, admiring the shirt. "To think I'm wearing the very armor that Latseen wore when he led his five hundred against the Yahooni and thrashed them so thoroughly they've never returned." He shook his upper body. The coins clinked. "Tell me where the letter is or I keep your grandfather's armor."

"I burned the letter in the courtyard of your Longhouse of War."

The Aankaawu sighed. He ran a hand over the shirt, turned, and walked back behind his desk and sat down. "Your canoe is fixed. You can leave in the morning."

"And my armor?"

"My guards noted very little coinage among your effects. How shall we reckon the bill for fixing your canoe?" the Aankaawu asked.

"What do you mean?" Elān asked. "Your Longhouse of War should pay for my canoe's repairs, as is customary, as the longhouse in Naasteidi would pay for yours were you our visitor."

"Yet you are no warrior," the Aankaawu said. "I accept your grandfather's armor as payment for the repairs to your canoe and two nights' lodging and meals in our longhouse." Before Elān could protest, the Aankaawu's guards grabbed his arms and dragged him out of the town hall and back to the barracks.

TWO DOZEN OF the Aankaawu's Guard came into the courtyard early the next morning and called for Elān and his crew to assemble. Elān still raged. He had slept fitfully during the night, alone in an empty barrack, for he wanted none of the crew around. Whenever he drifted off to sleep, the image of the Aankaawu would come and wake him. He would yell and clutch at the Aankaawu's throat, only to wake into darkness.

Elān walked out of his barracks carrying his seabag. His crew stood before the Aankaawu's Guard. "I demand to see your Aankaawu," he yelled at the guards.

The guards said nothing.

"Take me to your Aankaawu," Elān yelled.

"You're to be escorted to your canoe. Your time in Deshu is at an end," one of the guards said.

"I demand my armor be given back," Elān roared. "Your Aankaawu is a thief. You're all fearful cowards."

"Bind them," the guard ordered his comrades. "Drag them to their canoe if you have to."

Their hands bound, Elān and his crew stumbled through town toward the front gate. The Aankaawu's Guard shoved them through the open gates, tossed their bags after them, and closed the gates behind them. Along the beach stood a line of warriors with fire arrows at the ready. *Waka* lay bucking in the surf. Kooyu stood on the beach, holding *Waka*'s bowline.

"Unbind them," Kooyu said to a nearby warrior, "and help them store their bags aboard."

Unbound, Elān looked down the line of warriors. "Your Aankaawu and his guards are cowards." He looked at the gate and turned to Kooyu. "He stole my grandfather's coin-mail shirt."

"I heard," Kooyu said.

Elān heard a cackle from *Waka*. Raven peered down from his mast-nest. "Crapshack lost his granddaddy's metal underwear? And I hadn't a chance to soil it. Missed opportunities. Turds in his Hair can give you one of his stinky bearskins."

Elān picked up a rock and threw it at raven. It caromed off the mast below the nest. Raven laughed.

Kooyu handed *Waka*'s bowline to Elān and leaned close. "It's an outrage he kept your coin-mail," he whispered into Elān's ear. "I don't have enough warriors to challenge the Aankaawu's Guard, or I would see it returned. Tell your clan my clan is sorry that such powerful at.óow has been dishonored." *At.óow,* as you know, is sacred Aaní clan property. At.óow can be clothes, carvings, songs, lands, lakes, rivers, mountains, or even stories, and must be treated with great respect. Stealing at.óow, as you're well aware, brings disharmony to the Aaní world.

The repair to *Waka*'s outrigging had been expertly done. Kooyu held the canoe as the crew settled into *Waka* in the usual order—Elān, Kwa, then Hoosa behind the main mast, Caraiden and Ch'eet in front of the main mast and behind the jib, and Chetdyl in a blanket bed atop the boxes in front—and grabbed their paddles. "If you can, come back with a force of warriors and liberate your at.óow armor," Kooyu said. He pushed *Waka* out toward open ocean. "Liberate Deshu."

They paddled in silence out of Deshu Harbor. Elān still raged inside. He kept the crew paddling far too long out into the sea while he brooded until Caraiden said, "The loss of your grandfather's coin-mail is grievous, but you must now put your mind to the task ahead. Where are we headed? Do we paddle all day, or spread sail?"

Elān shook his head.

Kwa pulled up her paddle and turned to look at Elān. "This sea is too dangerous. I need a captain now and not a bookeater."

"We make for Shanaax Island today," Elān said, "sailing when we can. The wind is against us. We won't make good distance today. We'll sleep in the wild or aboard. I don't want to go to any other villages. After we get close to Shanaax we stay asea and plot a course for Lookaana Island."

"I did my kwalk in Naakw village on Shanaax," Kwa said. "I can assure us safe entry."

"A summer ago I could have assured us safe entry into Deshu," Elān mumbled.

"Naakw is safe," Kwa said.

"Kwa, the captain has spoken," Caraiden said. "We sleep in the wild or aboard *Waka*."

The morning held drizzling until lunch. The rough weather forced Elān from his self-pity. He kept the sails up but had to tack against the wind, zigzagging back and forth southward toward Shanaax Island, with the wide and rising tide behind him. By noon, the sun shot through gaps in the rain clouds. Elān struck down the sails to float with the tide while they ate. Ch'eet opened a bentwood, retrieved several large chunks of smoked salmon, and handed them out. Even raven came down from his perch to take a large piece. He struggled and flapped to get it back to his nest. Hoosa fetched a skin of water, shot a spurt into his mouth, and passed it around *Waka*. Ch'eet sprayed a long stream of water into Chetdyl's mouth.

Elān pulled a quill and inkpot from his pack, turned around to the stern of the canoe, and spread a piece of paper across one of the bentwoods and wrote a letter to Íxt.

The Aankaawu of Deshu has stolen Latseen's armor. He has created his own personal guard, who are holding the village hostage and have banned travel around Aaní islands. They have built a wooden stockade around the entire village. Will soon build a metal wall. Warrior Kooyu asks for help liberating Deshu. Rumor of the Koosh canoe abounds, but we haven't seen it since the day we arrived in Yelm. Tell my parents I am well, but sad about loss of armor. We are a day from Deshu.

Elān didn't specify any direction or destination, should his letter be intercepted. He turned to look at his crew. "I'm writing a letter for Íxt, should we find any eagle messengers."

Elān read the missive aloud. "Is there anything any of you would like me to mention?"

Raven looked over his perch. "Tell that bag of decrepit bones he's going to regret sending a bookeater on this journey."

"Shut up, bird. I recommend removing that bit about Kooyu asking us to liberate Deshu," Kwa said. "It could get him in trouble if this letter is intercepted."

"You're right," Elān said. He crossed out that part of the letter. "Anything else?"

"Tell Íxt that every island and village east of Samish Island should be considered hostile," Caraiden said.

Elān wrote that at the end of his letter and it saddened him to do so. The thought of the Aaní world being hostile felt wrong. Did the bonds of the Aaní fray so easily, like an old sea-bitten rope unraveling at the ends? Elān signed the letter with a small, timid *E* and rolled it up. He put his letter in the same small, leather scroll-holder Íxt had used for his letter. "Chetdyl," he yelled up to the wolf standing on the bow of the boat. "Keep an eye out for an eagle." Chetdyl lowered his eyes in acknowledgment. "All right, sails up. Let's make for Shanaax."

The crew of the *Waka* continued their zigzag course southward toward Shanaax. You know if you've ever tried to tack against a shifting wind how frustrating it can be. Now imagine having one of your most valuable possessions, perhaps a gift from your ancestors, stolen before you had to tack against that shifting wind. You know then how angry Elān was that entire afternoon. The wind would creep around the portside of the sail, Elān would shift the tiller to fill the sail, *Waka* would surge forward for a few lengths and then the sail would fluff empty and billow backward and Elān would have to quickly adjust his tiller before the progress of the canoe was halted altogether. The wind would shift, Elān would rage inside, he'd think of his beautiful stolen armor and seethe, and the wind would shift again. His anger echoed back and forth between the unpredictable wind and stolen armor.

The northern end of Shanaax appeared with dusk on the horizon. Chetdyl turned to the crew and yapped.

"Crap Eater says some stupid eagle nears," raven said from his perch atop the mast.

Elān and the crew searched the skies. It took a while, but they saw a small dark spot in the dusk sky growing larger as it flew toward them.

"Bird," Elān yelled up to raven. "Tell him I have a letter for Íxt. Tell him the truth. I'm in no mood for your tricks."

"Still mad about losing your metal diapers?" raven mocked. "Sour miss traditional would say a bookeater shouldn't be wearing a warrior's armor. She fears her life will unravel without her traditions. But you're doomed to bookeating unless tradition unravels. I for one can't withstand the tension." Raven flopped down in his nest. "Stupid Aaní."

"Bird, you are here to translate for me," Elān said angrily. "Keep that in mind if you wish to taste salmon again on this voyage."

The eagle circled above *Waka*. Elān held up the leather scroll-holder. The eagle glided downward, flapping his powerful wings to steady himself at a slow pace, and landed on the stern of *Waka* next to the tiller arm. Elān was amazed at his size. He'd seen eagles his whole life, but never this close. He handed the leather scroll-holder to the eagle, who grasped it in his massive talons. "Could you bring this to Íxt?" Elān asked. The eagle stuck his head forward.

"Bird," Elān yelled up to the mast-nest.

Raven leaned over his nest edge and said something to the eagle in eagle language. The eagle raised its massive wings and lurched off *Waka*. Elān felt the rush of air pushed by its wingbeats. The anger he'd felt all day was gone, leaving a sadness he felt in his stomach. He wished only to join the eagle in flight.

CHAPTER 19

THEY APPROACHED THE northwestern end of Shanaax Island as night settled in. No lights shone on the island. Elān had the crew take down the sails and light lanterns. It was quiet. There was no human settlement or village around. The only sound was the soft slosh of paddles as the crew brought the canoe to shore. Unlike Kals'aak, Shanaax had many smooth, sandy beaches. One large Aaní village called Naakw sat in a sheltered bay at the southern end of the island, far away—a half day's paddle—from the northern beach where *Waka* came ashore. "I think it's safe enough to have a fire to cook dinner," Elān said, "but we should set watch. I'll take the first watch."

"Have you ever stood watch before?" Kwa asked.

"No," Elān said.

"We shouldn't risk our lives on a would-be-warrior bookeater who might fall asleep during watch," Kwa said.

"Would-be-warrior bookeater," raven cawed from his perch. "That's a good one. You do have your moments, even though you are a large crap sack of sourness."

"Speak again, foul bird, and I'll have your head," Kwa said.

"Sour sack of crap," raven replied.

"I'll stand watch with Elān," Caraiden said, "and show him what he needs to know."

Kwa shook her head, turned abruptly, and scuffed through the wet beach rocks toward *Waka*. She grabbed her bedroll and pack from the canoe and stomped back to shore. Elān could tell she was angry, but he didn't care. He'd been angry all day. And Kwa was a sour person, Elān thought to himself, raven was right about that.

Ch'eet had already made a rock ring for the fire and was gathering wood. He dumped an armload of wood into the ring and smiled at Elān. "You did well handling *Waka* in rough seas today."

"Gunalchéesh," Elān said. He liked Ch'eet. Ch'eet was close to Elān's age and not sour at all. He was easy-natured, affable, and was happy to be on this journey. He looked around for Hoosa but didn't see him; Hoosa was already up into the woods for the night. Elān neither liked nor disliked Hoosa. He was odd and quiet. He never said a word. Elān wondered, deep down in a locked chamber of his mind, if Hoosa was even needed for this journey. Elān felt a hand on his shoulder. It was Caraiden.

"Let us stand watch," he said. "Grab your weapons and come with me."

Elān retrieved his sword, bow, bowstring, and a quiver of arrows from *Waka*, and jogged to catch up with him. The sand squished beneath his boots. He walked with Caraiden a long distance from the beach where *Waka* sat. Elān could still see that Ch'eet had the fire going. It flickered shadows in the forest behind the crew.

"First lesson for standing night watch: don't look at the fire," Caraiden said. "It will take away your night eyes. Never look directly at any fire or lantern when on night watch."

They sat down inside the forest line in the darkness under the long, wet branches of a spruce tree. "Are you cold?" the old warrior asked.

"Not yet," Elān replied.

"You will be," Caraiden replied. "That's the main difference between youths who have been through the Longhouse of War and those who have been through the Longhouse of Service."

"What's that?" Elān asked.

"The Longhouse of War trains you to ignore the cold. You can train anybody to handle a sword, to use a bow and arrow, to remain calm in battle, or to sit night watch over a village or crew. But it takes winters to handle the wet, thick cold of these islands. When our youths first come to the longhouse, we force them to submerge in Naasteidi Bay every morning for the first few winters of their training. Every morning. Five, ten minutes. When they get out, we whap them with tree branches. After a few winters, they no longer feel the pain of cold." Elān knew that was how they trained future warriors. Many mornings, as he lay in his warm bed, he could hear the shouts of the mentor-uncles telling the warriors-in-training to get into the freezing water. Elān was happy, those times lying in bed, to be in the Longhouse of Service and Trade. However, as the cold set in on Shanaax, he wished slightly he had done the cold water training.

It was so dark now that Elān could barely make out the outline of Caraiden's body and face, even though he was sitting a few feet from him under the tree. "I saw your sword and bow," Caraiden said. "But I didn't see any armor. Do you not have armor? Head armor at least?"

"No," Elān said. "All I had was my grandfather's flicker tail coin-mail shirt."

"I'm sorry about the loss of that shirt," Caraiden said. "I know that armor well. I'd like to say you'll get it back, but I don't want to lie to you. You do need armor, though. We teach our warriors-in-training to make wooden slat armor in case they have no metal armor. I can teach you how to make wooden armor if we stop in one place long enough. It'll provide you a little protection. But, if we get into a fight, I don't want you joining in. We all have armor. You don't. We'll protect you. Now, you should string your bow and get an arrow or two at the ready. Always have your quiver and sword at hand while on watch. I don't expect any trouble, but you always must be ready."

Elān took out his bowstring, ran it through his pinched fingers to get some warmth in it, bent his bow with his foot, and strung it. He took an arrow and laid it across his bow, holding it with his left hand. "Are you confident with your bow?" Caraiden asked.

"No," Elān said. "You saw how I did at the archery competition."

"I'd never seen any student throw arrows before," Caraiden laughed. "You need to become confident with your bow. You need to train to the point where you know you can hit a moving target at one hundred paces. Don't you hunt?"

"Not anymore," Elān replied.

"And your sword?" Caraiden asked. "Are you confident with your sword?"

"No." Elān felt a tinge of shame. He had never learned to handle a sword.

"I can train you, but first you should train on your bow so you can rely on your bow for protection," Caraiden said. "As for night watch, we do four-hour shifts. Part of warrior training is knowing the passage of time. We know, to the precise minute, when an hour has passed. And we know even better when four hours have passed. You do night watch with me or Ch'eet and we'll tell you when four hours are over. Falling asleep on watch is one of the greatest violations of the warrior code. Betraying your fellow warriors, disobeying orders, and falling asleep on watch. In the days of *looong* ago, those were punishable by death."

"I'll never fall asleep on watch," Elān said.

"You say that, but you'll learn it's not so easy after a twelve-hour paddle and little food. When I was a youth at the Longhouse of War, we were forced to sleep sitting up in a canoe. Now, as for what to watch for when in hostile territory, you want to watch for movement. Any movement at all. Unlike daytime, at night the sides of your vision are the keenest. You may have noticed if you've tried to watch a canoe come ashore at night that it can disappear if you look straight at it. Look to the left of it, or to the right, and you'll see it. Even if you see a light from a distant lantern on a canoe, don't look straight at it. Look to the right or left of it. When you're scanning the sea at night, focus wide not narrow by paying attention to the sides of your vision. Start by looking as far as you can to the left, cover your left flank, but keep your head mostly still because someone may be looking for you and even the slightest movement of your head can expose you. When at watch, move your head very little. If you have to move your head, move it slowly. Move your eyes, not your head. Focusing on the edges, move your eyes slowly from left to right. It should take you five, six heartbeats to move your eyes from far left to straight ahead, and another five, six heartbeats to move from straight ahead to far right. Turn your head slowly a little when you get to the right to see what's on your right flank. Then start over, going from right to left. Movement. Watch for movement."

Elān did as he was instructed. He moved his eyes slowly, paying intense attention to the edges of his vision. After a few minutes, Caraiden spoke again. "After you strengthen your wide vision to the very edges of your sight, and that takes moons of practice, you will see all sorts of movements you've never noticed before. You'll never walk the same through the world. You'll be aware of what's going on in a greater circumference around than you've ever been aware of before. The world will be expansive and more active in your vision. You of the Longhouse of Service and Trade have the expanded world of books, but we warriors have the expanded world of vision."

"I'll practice expanding my vision every night," Elān said.

"Good," Caraiden replied. "As important as your vision is your hearing. As I'm watching the waves in front of us, so I am also watching the world behind us. My ears are searching for any sound in the forest behind. I'm listening for sharp branch cracks that usually mean an animal or person is near, or breathing or growling. You know this from when you used to hunt, so I need not explain in detail. Most importantly, I'm listening for that false stillness of an enemy before attack. Any time you feel a shudder or your hair standing up along your neck or arms, you must pay heed. You are about to be attacked. Grab your knife, sword, any weapon, and be ready. Even if it's nothing, best be prepared on such occasions for attack. Nine out of ten times it is nothing. A true warrior stands ready on the one time in ten when it is something."

"I understand," Elān said.

"Last but as important," Caraiden said, "is smell. As with hunting, a warrior's nose is of utmost importance. I assume you've located moose and deer by smelling them?"

"Yes," Elān said. When he and Ch'aal' used to hunt together, he'd located many deer and moose with his nose. Getting close enough to them to loose an arrow, especially in the woods, wasn't as easy as smelling them.

"Your enemy can be located the same way," Caraiden said. "Especially if they're human. They'll smell of sweat, smoke, and human stink. As with hunting, as with sailing, always be aware of the direction of the wind. You notice I walked downwind from our crew? The wind is blowing up the beach from them to us. I assumed if any animal or enemy scented them it would be from downwind, and chances are that enemy would have to pass by us to attack our crew. Always, always, be aware of the wind."

Elān had to admit to himself that there was indeed more than he expected to a night watch. He was grateful Caraiden had been willing to stand watch with him. He felt close to the old warrior. "What was it like to serve with my grandfather?" Elān asked.

Caraiden sighed. "He was the greatest warrior I've ever known. There's no other warrior who could compare. He could look at a landscape and guess where the enemy were, and where and how the enemy would attack. He said he had the ability to see the land from the ground as a bird does from the air. The land bloomed and unfurled in his mind as though he were gliding above." Caraiden chuckled.

"What was he like as a person?" Elān asked.

"He was a marvelous storyteller," Caraiden replied. "Nobody ever mentions that, but he could craft a story that would weave a spell on listeners. Dozens of his stories played in my head as though they were alive and happening in the hours I was with him listening. I wish those stories still played in my head. I wish him here with us now. I would want to see and speak with him of the things I left unsaid."

Elān smiled at Caraiden's words. "Was my grandfather your mentor-uncle?"

"No, but he was like a mentor-uncle to me." The old warrior laughed. "I've seen so many winters I can't even remember who my mentor-uncle was."

"You're a mentor-uncle to me," Elān said.

"I'm not sure if Aaní tradition allows that," Caraiden replied. "But I appreciate the sentiment."

"Aaní tradition is full of things we're not supposed to do and lacking reasons *why* we are not supposed to do them."

Caraiden chuckled. "Don't let Kwa hear you say that."

"Aaní tradition is a bunch of stories about how to behave and how not to behave."

"Is that a problem?"

"Have you ever wondered where all those stories came from?" Elān asked. "They had to start somewhere in the *looong* ago."

"Tradition has helped us survive for generations and generations," the old warrior replied. He softened his voice. "Just because one young bookeater can't find much sense in tradition doesn't mean we should put it all to the torch. Yéil only knows what would become of us then."

That's what every elder says, Elān thought to himself, *when they don't have answers and want inquisitive youth to be quiet.*

They sat a long time in silence, watching the world in darkness around them. Elān stretched and yawned. "Have you ever fallen asleep on watch?" Elān heard a branch crack as Caraiden turned toward him.

"Why do you ask?" Caraiden hissed. "What have you heard?"

Elān froze. Caraiden's voice was thick with anger. "I didn't mean anything," he pleaded. "I yawned and realized I was tired."

"No more talking tonight," Caraiden said. "Warriors don't talk or fall asleep on watch."

Silence fell between them and Elān couldn't hear Caraiden's breath over the sound of the waves crashing and receding. He was worried he'd angered Caraiden, but was too afraid to speak.

The hours passed in silence. Elān didn't fall asleep during the entire watch, not because he saw any movement or smelled an enemy, but because he couldn't stop shivering from the cold. After four hours' watch, Caraiden said, "Our duty is over. Let's wake Ch'eet and Kwa for their watch and get that fire piled high before you freeze to death."

Elān was so cold he could barely stutter in agreement. He grabbed his weapons and stepped out from under the tree. His sore legs tingled with needles of pain as the blood coursed through them. His eyes hurt even more. He'd spent four hours looking back and forth slowly, left to right, right to left. The muscles behind his eyes and in his temples ached. He walked with Caraiden to the fire, around which the crew lay sleeping. Caraiden made a noise, a strange owl-sounding noise, which woke Kwa and Ch'eet instantly. They opened their eyes and stood up by the fire. Elān went to *Waka* to retrieve his bedroll and clothes pack. He overheard Kwa ask Caraiden, "How did the bookeater do on night watch?"

"Grab your weapons and take watch," Caraiden growled.

"Don't think he's a warrior," Kwa replied, "after one night of watch."

"He's not a bookeater either," Caraiden replied gruffly. "Grab your weapons and take watch."

CHAPTER 20

ELAN WOKE WITH the sun. The dawn sky in the east glowed crimson. Spidery red clouds streaked the horizon. He raised himself on his elbows and looked around. Caraiden and Ch'eet were already awake and packing *Waka*. Hoosa and Chetdyl walked together far down the beach, returning from watch. Elān felt strong even though he hadn't slept as long as he usually did back home in the Flicker House. The pain around his eyes had gone. The wind tumbled down the beach east by southeast—the very direction they had to travel. It was a good sign, Elān thought. The sun would rise in front of them and the wind would be behind them.

Kwa sat close by Elān, running an oiled cloth up and down her bared sword. "I gave you much thought during my watch," she said to Elān. "I don't like being mean to you, but you hold our lives in your hands. Our warriors train for years to be warriors, and train for many more years to be captain, and then train again for as many years to be leaders and elders. Caraiden is a captain and leader, so it baffles me why a boy has been made captain of our crew. But I had no control over that decision and so I must face my reality as it is, rather than how I would have it be. That means I must help you become a captain in a breath of time, even though I know it's an impossible task. Do you understand my dilemma?"

"Yes," Elān replied.

"It's not that I don't like you as a person," Kwa continued. "I don't like the impossible position you've been put in because it puts me, and all of your crew, in an impossible position. Along with this impossible position, I'm oath-bound to protect you and even sacrifice my life for yours. All of this, then, is made much more difficult when the true purpose of our journey is hidden from me. Can you understand this as well?" Kwa asked.

"Yes," Elān replied. "What do you want me to do?"

"Get me out of this impossible position," she replied.

"How?"

"Tell me the truth," Kwa replied, "and make Caraiden captain."

"I can't," Elān said. "I'm sorry."

Kwa closed her eyes. Elān could see the muscles in her cheeks clench taut. She stood, sheathed her oiled sword, stuffed the oil cloth in her pocket, and walked away.

While the crew packed and made *Waka* ready, Elān dug through the firepit and grabbed a few still-smoking coals in a piece of leather and stored them in the sand-lined cooking box. "I thought we could set fishing lines out and maybe catch some salmon as we go along the coastline of Shanaax," Elān said. "I've heard there's a large salmon run between here and Lookaana Island."

"Metal Diapers thinks he can do some fishing, does he?" raven laughed and cawed. He'd stuck his head over the side of his mast-nest to watch the proceedings below.

"You should appreciate the chance to get more salmon, you stupid bird," Ch'eet said to raven. "Are we going to Sheet'ka?" he asked Elān. Sheet'ka was the largest Aaní village on Lookaana.

"Has anyone ever been to Sheet'ka?" Elān asked the crew.

"I've been," Caraiden said. "Many winters ago. Ten or fifteen. If Deshu is now the example of how our eastern Aaní relatives behave, Sheet'ka may be closed to visitors, too."

"I agree," said Ch'eet. "We were lucky to have been allowed to leave Deshu. We might not be lucky with other villages."

"Agreed," Elān said. "We'll hug the coastline south along Shanaax this morning until we near Naakw, and then set course due east for Lookaana. We'll sleep in the wild on the west side of Lookaana or aboard *Waka* tonight."

Elān tied metal spoons with hooks to the end of the fishing lines and set them out in the sea while the crew paddled *Waka* southward just outside the kelp beds offshore. The wind rose. Ch'eet set the jib and Elān held the mainsail full, and *Waka* ripped southerly along the coast of Shanaax.

Have you ever trolled for salmon? You know then that you shouldn't travel very fast. Definitely not the speed that *Waka* was traveling that morning. For bait you can use metal spoons, real or fake herrings or squids, or even spinners, but you need slowness. Slowness and depth. Other fish like tuna don't mind a faster speed, but there's no tuna in Aaní waters, as you're well aware. For salmon, you'll want to troll about the speed of a quick stroll along the beach. Have you ever walked the beach, startling seagulls, enjoying clam squirts and shore crabs scuttling under rocks? That's the speed for salmon. And you don't want the hook bouncing along the surface of the sea. You want it down deepish. You can see, then, Elān's embarrassment when he looked back that morning to see his spoons and hooks dancing upon the ocean. Elān shook his head as he looked back behind the canoe. He hoped Kwa wouldn't notice.

"What fish are you planning on catching, Crapshack?" raven cawed to Elān as he peered over his nest at the hooks bouncing along the waves behind *Waka*. "Fish as stupid as you? The legendary Dumbass fish?"

The entire crew turned as raven spoke. Kwa shook her head when she saw the dancing hooks. Hoosa knocked his paddle against the mast. Raven tumbled backward into his nest. A moment later, Elān saw raven's tail feathers poking out over the edge of his nest as he tried to position his bottom above Hoosa. The foul string of poop landed on the canoe floor between Kwa and Hoosa. Hoosa reached down and grabbed a large *sú*—also known as bullwhip kelp—from the sea, and with great precision whipped the bottom of raven's nest. Branches exploded and raven screeched as he flew up into the air.

"No more, bird," Hoosa said. He tossed the bullwhip kelp back into the sea.

Raven flew a circle around *Waka* and landed back in his nest. The nest wasn't destroyed, but the whip had ripped a small opening. "Ha, dumbass. I needed a front door. And it'll be easier to crap on you."

THEY MADE THEIR way south for most of the morning. Kwa asked, "When do you want to turn east?"

The wind had held steady southeasterly. The sun was making its way mid-sky. If they continued along the coastline, Elān figured, once they got clear of Shanaax and out on the open ocean south of the island, the wind would come from the west. They could ride that wind due east to Lookaana. The only potential problem would be the village at Naakw. True, it was an Aaní village and Kwa had lived there. But what if the Naakw Aaní wanted to interrogate the crew? Elān could run up the Aaní flag and perhaps the folks at Naakw would leave them alone. If that didn't work, Elān felt sure *Waka* could outrun any Naakw canoe.

"Well?" Kwa said.

"We're making good time with the wind directly behind us," Elān said. "We'll ride this wind while it lasts. I expect once we get on open ocean south of this island we'll get a wind straight out of the west. We'll ride that to Lookaana." Elān retrieved the Aaní flag from underneath the stern. He tossed it up to Caraiden. "Run up the flag in case we meet any canoes from Naakw."

Waka cut the water, traveling swiftly along the coast of

Shanaax. The village of Naakw was at the very south end of the island up a large bay surrounded by sandstone seacliffs that extended pincer-like out into the ocean. Elān could soon see the greenness of the forest coming to an end and the cliffs coming into view. "I imagine the warriors at Naakw have watchtowers atop the cliffs surrounding the village?" Elān said to Kwa.

"Yes," Kwa replied, "and you can be sure they've seen us and are lighting a signal fire. I expect we'll meet a Naakw canoe as soon as we sail past the cliffs."

"You think they'll see our flag and let us pass through their territory?" Elān asked.

"We'll find out soon enough," Kwa said in a sharp tone.

Elān smiled at her sharpness. *Get me out of this impossible position*, she had said to him. Elān laughed aloud. The crew turned and stared at him, and Elān laughed aloud again.

"I don't see anybody on the ocean or cliffs," Ch'eet said. Elān had steered *Waka* close to the cliffs as they neared the end of the island. The cliffs stood several hundred feet high, and they could see the lookout tower at the end of the military houses atop them, but there appeared to be no people walking along the cliff top. There was no alarm, no call, only the sound of *Waka* ripping the sea. No Naakw canoes appeared. As they approached the open ocean, Elān yelled up to Ch'eet, "Loosen the jib and prepare to tack westward into Naakw Bay."

"What?" Ch'eet asked in disbelief. "Aren't we going the other direction to Lookaana?"

"Yes," Elān said. "After we leave Kwa at Naakw. I'm removing her from an impossible position."

Caraiden protested, but *Waka* had cleared the cliffs out into open ocean and a strong westerly wind rattled the sails. Elān adjusted the mainsail to tack southwest against the wind. Chetdyl stood up on the bow and held his nose high. Lost in the thought of being rid of Kwa, Elān didn't pay attention to Chetdyl's growls. *Waka* ran southwest at a rapid clip, and then Elān tacked northwest toward the opening between the cliff pincers into Naakw Bay. The boom swung starboard-side and *Waka* lurched as Elān pulled the tiller. Chetdyl howled, startling the whole crew.

"Humans coming," raven croaked. "And something else."

Elān tried to look around the mainsail toward Naakw Bay. He couldn't see anything.

"Trouble comes from Naakw," raven said. "Go the other way!"

"Canoe spotted," Ch'eet yelled.

Elān looked under the boom to see the canoe emerge from behind the cliff's western pincer. One sail showed, a small one on the bow, then two, three, four large sails, then five six seven sails on two masts. Humans scrabbled around the deck and up in the sail-rigging. The large canoe turned head on toward *Waka*.

"Laters, fatheads," raven cried. He flew from his mast-nest south toward the open sea.

Elān felt fear spread from his stomach up to his throat. "We need to escape." He shoved the tiller starboard. "Mind the boom," he yelled. The mainsail boom swung back to port, the sail filled, and *Waka* turned in the opposite direction and headed southwest. "Lock the jib," Elān yelled. He held the tiller out and the mainsail sheet taut against the cleat. The large canoe was out of the pincer mouth and gaining portside on *Waka*. If Elān headed east, the large canoe could intercept them. Southwest was the only option. Wind rippled the sails, and *Waka* flew and soon outpaced the big canoe.

"That's like the canoe we saw near Daadzi," Ch'eet said.

After tacking southwest a yaakw, Elān calculated the progress of the big canoe in his mind. *I think we put enough distance between us and them*, he thought to himself. *It's worth a try.* "Mind the boom again," Elān yelled.

"What are you doing?" Kwa said.

Elān didn't answer. He changed direction and now headed southeast. His course would be dangerous, but if he could get east of the large canoe without it destroying *Waka* with fire arrows—or worse—he was certain he could outrun it to Lookaana Island and maybe take shelter at Sheet'ka. *Waka* slowed in the turn as the wind spilled from the sails.

"Caraiden, relieve Elān of his duty and take over as captain," Kwa said.

"He's doing fine," Caraiden said. "You're a warrior. Act like it."

"You are captain in case of battle," Kwa replied. "This is going to be a battle. I demand you relieve the bookeater of his command."

Waka's course adjusted east by southeast and its sails filled with the wind once again. *Waka* lurched and then sped off southeasterly. The large canoe made a small shift southeast as well, trying to intercept *Waka*. "Armor and bows," Elān yelled.

"Yes, Captain," Caraiden said. He, Ch'eet, and Kwa scrambled to put on their armor and string their bows. *Waka* lashed through the sea. Over his left shoulder Elān could see the large canoe bearing down on them. "Hoosa, adjust the jib sheet. We need more speed." Hoosa stood and loosened the portside jib sheet. Elān pulled the tiller slightly, hoping to get more speed, and the jib snapped tight. *Waka* was flying southeasterly, but the large canoe was cutting down *Waka*'s angle by heading due south. It had a shorter distance to travel to the impact point and didn't need to match the speed of *Waka*. Elān looked at the large canoe. He could see armored but unhelmed men lining the starboard side, with bows ready. Their hair was cut Yahooni-style: long to the shoulder on one side, close shaved on the other side so as not to get tangled in their bow strings when they loosed arrows.

Elān held his southwest course. He could see in the far left of his wide vision the Yahooni canoe closing in. "Look there, toward the stern." Ch'eet pointed to the Yahooni canoe. "The thing without hair." The crew looked where Ch'eet indicated. A tall figure stood on a raised deck. The figure wore strange garb that glittered and changed colors. Chetdyl growled.

"Is that...?" Ch'eet's tongue faltered.

"I think it is," Caraiden said.

"Will it have a dzanti?" Ch'eet asked.

"I don't know," Caraiden replied. "I've never seen one before."

"We can't get by them to the east," Elān said. "We're going to have to outrun them south." He pulled the tiller toward himself and let out the mainsail sheet. *Waka* veered starboard and headed due south. The sails caught more wind in their pockets. The Yahooni canoe adjusted its course, traveling from *Waka*'s rear portside directly into *Waka*'s wake. Elān looked over his shoulder and saw, blurred at this distance, Yahooni warriors side by side up on the bow. They raised their bows to the sky. Elān could see blurry fire flickering from the arrow tips.

"Incoming," Caraiden yelled. "Helmets on."

"Are they in range?" Kwa asked.

"We'll find out," Caraiden said. The crew donned their metal helmets and tied them tight under their heads. Only Elān remained bareheaded.

Most of the arrows fell short. It sounded, behind Elān, as though handfuls of small beach rocks had been thrown into a calm bay. A few arrows thwacked into *Waka*'s outrigging and body. Hoosa scrambled out of *Waka* onto the netting and splashed water on the arrows before the fire could catch. A host of arrows slitted through the mainsail into the sea below, and a few hit the mast. Caraiden and Kwa used their paddles to knock out the fire. Elān looked back: the Yahooni canoe was directly behind *Waka*, close but not as close as before. It may have lost speed as it turned into *Waka*'s wake, or *Waka* was outrunning it, or both.

"Incoming," Caraiden yelled. Again, Elān heard the soft *plooshing* of dozens of arrows slicing into the water behind him. One arrow thwacked into the stern next to the tiller arm, startling him. He jumped, but he hung on to the tiller and mainsail sheet. "Recurved longbows," Caraiden said to Elān. "Only a recurved longbow could send an arrow that far." He pointed the end of his bow at the arrow stuck into *Waka*'s stern. "The fire went out before it hit. You did well, Elān. You didn't panic and lose control of the canoe. Had you let go the tiller or sheet, they would have closed enough sea to send hundreds of fire arrows into us."

Elān used both hands to yank the Yahooni arrow out of the stern. Its tip was honed to a keen sharpness. "A few inches more, a stronger pull of that longbow, and that arrow would've gone straight through you," Caraiden said.

Elān's throat constricted at Caraiden's words—his life had been out of his control and in the arms, literally, of his enemy. He pushed the thought away.

"Incoming," Ch'eet yelled. The entire third volley of fire arrows fell far short of *Waka*. The large canoe was far behind. Elān looked at the mainsail. The wind buzzed through a dozen holes. A small section near the mast had been burned. *Waka* would be slowed, and if the sail wasn't repaired soon, the holes would rip and expand and slow *Waka* even more. Violent winds could shred the sail.

But *Waka* was still gliding over the ocean at an incredible speed, opening up a great distance between it and the Koosh canoe. They were out of trouble, for now. Elān stored the Yahooni arrow that nearly killed him in the storage space underneath *Waka*'s stern. He would keep it as a reminder of his first meeting with the Koosh.

CHAPTER 21

ALL LAND HAD disappeared from sight except for the snow-peaked mountaintop of one island far to the northwest. The wind blew hard south. *Waka*'s sails billowed as it outpaced the large Yahooni canoe, but the wind whined through the mainsail's holes. *Waka* was wounded.

Elān pulled the navigation map and jishagoon from his sea coat. They were about a yaakw away from Xoots Jin Island. If they could lose the Yahooni canoe, maybe they could hide on Xoots Jin and repair the mainsail. The beings on that island, though, might not appreciate a visit.

"Hoosa, have you ever been on Xoots Jin Island?" Elān asked. His pulse still raced with the exhilaration and danger of being chased by the Koosh.

"No. They are not my relatives," Hoosa replied.

"Can you speak their language?" Elān asked.

"I don't know. We used to speak the same language but that was *looong* ago. Languages grow apart."

"Has anyone been to Xoots Jin?" Elān asked the crew. "Are the Xoots allies with the Yahooni?"

None of the crew had been to Xoots Jin.

"The Xoots keep to themselves," Hoosa said. "I doubt they have any allies."

"Because nobody is foolish enough to visit their island," Kwa said.

"Nobody but our dear Crapshack, of course," raven said. He circled above *Waka*, round and round, descending to his mast-nest. He landed and knocked an arrow from the mast onto the canoe below. He peck-fluffed his nest a bit and then smugly perched himself. "I'm surprised to find you still among the living."

"Your cowardice is disappointing," Elān said.

Raven cackled. "Where we headed?" he asked. "A party on Xoots Jin? Are you snagging some of Hoosa's unwashed cousins?"

"Shut up, you coward's excuse for a bird. Do you speak the Xoots language?" Elān asked.

"Oh, probably."

"If we put ashore at Xoots Jin, can you translate with the Xoots for us?"

"Let me think," raven replied. He sat silent in his nest for a moment and then said, "Nope. You'll have to make your own introductions."

"Elān, the Claws of Xoots Jin are in the distance," Ch'eet said. "What's your plan?"

"We need to repair the mainsail or it'll soon be shredded," Elān said. The fate of the crew depended on his actions—and his decisions. His hands on the tiller and sheet shook with nervous excitement. "We'll sail through the Claws and land in one of the shallow bays on the north of Xoots Jin."

Five large, barren, stony, claw-like islands known as the Claws lay due north off the main body of Xoots Jin. The south end of the Claws opened to a series of large bays on the north side of the main island. Elān thought they could hide in one of those bays, take shelter, and fix the mainsail. With any luck, the Yahooni canoe would sail on by Xoots Jin, thinking *Waka* had stayed at sea. They wouldn't expect Elān to put ashore—he had a faster canoe and was greatly outnumbered. They would expect him to stay asea. Elān looked behind him. Only the very peak of the main mast of the Yahooni canoe could be seen, far in the distance. The Claws lay starboard, to the south of *Waka*. He would hold his course until he could no longer see the Yahooni canoe, and then he'd make a run for the Claws.

When they neared, Elān checked behind him again. He couldn't see the Yahooni canoe. He pulled the tiller a few degrees port and pointed *Waka* toward the Claws. "We make for the Claws," he told the crew. "We'll go between the middle claw and second claw to the right. The chart says it's a fathom to a fathom and a half deep. *Waka* draws less than a fathom. Let that canoe try to follow *Waka* through there."

Waka sailed into the Claws without slowing down. Elān had never been in these waters, so he had to trust his charts. There was still no sign of the Yahooni canoe behind them. The Claws stood fifty, sixty feet high, made of slate rock. The distance between each claw differed, but *Waka* sailed around both the shallowest and narrowest of the islands. Thirty feet to either side of *Waka*, big knife-like chunks of slate leaned out into the sea. The Claws pinched and intensified the southerly wind. *Waka* flew at a rapid clip between the ominous slate crags.

Once out of the Claws, the thick-forested, mountainous island of Xoots Jin lay a short distance south. From the chart, Elān had selected a nameless, long bay off to the northwest side of the island. If the chart was correct, the bay had a narrow entrance: a steep forest cliff to the west and a long spit of land coming from the east, nearly touching the cliffs. *Waka* should be able to enter that narrow opening—it was a fathom and a half deep—but Elān was sure that the Yahooni canoe couldn't. He double-checked his jishagoon with the chart, and then pulled the tiller further port and aimed the prow toward the northwest side of the island. *Waka* slowed a bit without the full force of the wind. "Paddles," Elān said to the crew.

"What's the plan?" Ch'eet asked as he dug his paddle deep into the sea.

"There's a sheltered bay close," Elān said. "We'll hide there and repair the mainsail."

"Good," Caraiden said. "That large canoe won't expect us to pull up. They'll pass by this island thinking we're still asea."

"Exactly," Elān said. "We may have more trouble from the Xoots than from that canoe. Hoosa, when we land ashore would you head inland and try to make contact with the Xoots? Tell them if you can that we don't intend to stay long."

"You should send that stupid bird with him to translate," Kwa said.

"I need that stupid bird to be our cloud-eyes," Elān said. Raven peered over the edge of his nest. "You hear that, bird? I need you up in the air between here and the Claws to keep an eye out for that large canoe."

"Not for nothing," raven said.

"I'll give you a big piece of salmon when we get to shore," Elān said. Raven disappeared back into his mast-nest. Elān checked his jishagoon again. "Chetdyl, we're looking for a little opening into a large bay. Should be straight ahead but it might be hard to see from the sea. From the chart it looks like a cliff or steep forestland on the west. A long spit of land— either rocky or forested, the chart doesn't specify—curls out from the mainland and almost touches the cliff. I'd take us closer to the island, but I'm worried my chart might not specify underwater rocks." The wolf stood up on the bow. He scanned the shoreline with his keen eyes. He looked back at Elān and made a low grumble.

"You see it?" Elān asked. Chetdyl pointed to a spot on the island with his long snout. Elān turned *Waka* in that direction.

Soon, the crew could discern a rocky cliff running steeply from the ocean a long ways up to a snowcapped mountain. As *Waka* glided toward it, a small opening appeared as the cliff separated from the trees on the opposite side. "The spit is forested," Ch'eet said. "That's good. If the large canoe decides to sail by here, we'll be hidden in the bay behind the trees."

Elān pulled *Waka* into the narrow entrance of the bay. "Take down the sails," he told the crew. "To your paddles." *Waka* ran quietly between the cliff and tree-lined spit into a large, calm, shallow bay. The water was so clear Elān could see the bottom. It looked sandy and seaweedy. "Chetdyl, keep watch for underwater rocks or water-sogged logs." The wolf edged atop the eagle head on *Waka*'s prow and looked down into the sea. It took about fifteen minutes' paddle to reach the shore from the mouth of the bay.

The sun was on its descent, but still high above the western horizon of the island. Elān held out his right hand toward the sun, fingers tight together, arm fully extended. He closed his left eye, lay his little finger along the horizon tree line, and looked at his hand with his right eye. The sun was still high above his four fingers. He placed the four fingers, again tightly together, of his fully outstretched left hand atop the four fingers of his right—left little finger laying along right index finger—closed his left eye and looked at both his hands with his right eye. The sun now touched the index finger of his left hand. That meant there was still two hours of sunlight before the island fell into shadow. Each finger held arm's length away from the eye equaled fifteen minutes of the sun's descent.

Ch'eet pulled *Waka* ashore. "Okay," Elān said. "Quiet now. Weapons and armor. Hoosa, make your way inland and locate the Xoots. Tell them we'll leave tonight. Ch'eet, gather branches and then camouflage *Waka* as best you can. If you need to use your axe, use it as quietly as possible. Chetdyl and Kwa, set a lookout around the mouth of the bay. Caraiden and I will remove the mainsail and repair the holes. Bird, grab yourself some salmon and then I want you up in the air looking for that large canoe."

The crew did as Elān asked. Even the rotten bird didn't protest. Caraiden fetched him a large piece of salmon from the box, raven ate it, and he then flew off high northward to keep watch for the Yahooni canoe. Hoosa made his way inland as Chetdyl and Kwa walked out to the forested spit to stand watch. Ch'eet worked nearby trying to gather branches large enough to hide *Waka*. Elān grabbed the sail-repair cloth, needles, thick thread, and patching glue from the waterproof bag in the outrigger as Caraiden unhooked and took down the mainsail. He dragged the sail a short distance into the woods. Elān followed with the repair tools.

"Ten arrow holes and a small, burned section," Caraiden whispered to Elān. "When do we lose the light?"

"About two hours before this bay is in the shadow of the island's mountain," Elān said. "Probably four hours before sunset on the open ocean."

"Five holes each to fix. Two hours before it gets dark here. We can get it repaired well before dark. I don't want to light lanterns. Yéil knows the trouble that might bring to us. I'll take care of the small, burned section. Let's get to work." Elān set down the repair tools and sat next to the sail.

It was quiet in the sheltered bay. He could hear Ch'eet off in the distance collecting branches. He listened for movement or sound in the forest behind him, but could hear none. Elān ran the coarse, nearly unbreakable thread through the sharp metal needle and began sewing holes shut. It was quick work sewing shut the rent mainsail, for the arrow holes were small and clean. Gluing cloth patches on both sides of the hole and feathering the edges of those patches smooth against the sail took a bit more time and skill. Yet Elān and Caraiden, indeed every Aaní, were skilled at sail repair.

They repaired the arrow holes in under an hour, and Caraiden had finished gluing a patch over the burned section when raven came screeching into the sky above the sheltered bay.

Elān ran to the beach. "Shoot him," raven cawed. "Shoot him, he's a spy, shoot him!"

Elān looked beyond raven and saw a massive sea eagle with a yellow beak and large, blood-red eyes bearing down on raven. "Shoot shoot shoot," raven cried. "Don't let him go!" Elān looked around the beach for his bow, but Kwa and Ch'eet across the bay stood armed and ready. Raven dove madly through the air toward *Waka*, which was only partially covered with branches. Ch'eet hadn't had enough time to cover the canoe entirely.

Kwa and Ch'eet loosed their arrows. If you have ever tried to shoot a fast-diving bird with an arrow, and hopefully you haven't, but if you ever have you know it is near impossible to hit the target. The arrows sang past the giant sea eagle. The sea eagle fluttered his massive wings, pulled out of his dive, and then spread his wings into the wind to gain altitude. Kwa and Ch'eet's next arrows fell short.

Raven landed on the shore next to Elān. "He tried to kill me," raven screeched. "He's crazy. He's from the large canoe. The Koosh controls his mind." Elān watched the sea eagle circle the sheltered bay a few times, well out of arrow range, his keen eyes watching all that was going on below. The sea eagle noticed *Waka*, it seemed to Elān, and then shot off toward the Claws. "He's gone," said Elān. Ch'eet and Caraiden came over to where they stood. "What happened?" Elān asked raven.

"As I flew over the Claws, I spotted that foul canoe heading south. It looked like it was going to stay east of Xoots Jin and keep going. Then that crazy bird came at me. I need some salmon before I can say more."

"We have no time," Elān said. "Finish your story and then you'll get salmon."

"He was circling above the Claws. At first, I thought he was a normal sea eagle. You know, big and stupid and full of crap. Like any other eagle. Or Hoosa. I went to talk to him and he taloned me. Lousy crapbag. I lost a feather or two. Then he darts off to the Koosh canoe and raises the alarm, screeching his stupid eagle screech. You know, for a big bird they sure can't caw proper. I bet they fart louder than they screech—"

"Bird," Caraiden yelled. "Where is the Koosh canoe?"

"Oh, it'll be here soon, no doubt, thanks to that rotten bird. When that stupid bird raised the alarm, the canoe turned westward between here and Xoots Jin. It was coming toward this bay when that lousy bird decided to attack me again. I thought if I brought him here, you'd kill him with your arrows. I didn't know Old Sourbag over there and young moron Zero"—he pointed with his wing at Ch'eet—"were bookeaters like Crapshack. I thought we had some warriors in our crew."

Elān ignored the insult. "Caraiden, do we have time to get *Waka* ready and outrun them?"

"No," Caraiden said. "And we can't leave Hoosa behind on this island."

"Why not?" raven asked. "Leave Turds-for-Hair here. He can live with the Xoots. They share the same distaste for bathing." Elān was also thinking they could leave without Hoosa, and he felt ashamed for thinking it, but unlike raven he would have never said it out loud.

"We don't leave a crew member behind," said Caraiden.

"Crapshack was going to leave Old Sourbag behind at Naakw," raven said.

"Would you shut up?" Caraiden barked. "Go eat your salmon now that your story is over." Raven hopped off toward the salmon box.

"A few of us could get *Waka* out into the ocean and escape the Koosh canoe and come back for the others later," Elān said.

"No, Elān," Caraiden said. "We shouldn't split up the crew. We have a fight on our hands now."

"This is a battle situation, then," Elān said. "Caraiden, you should captain us now."

"Very well," Caraiden said. "Fighting from sea is the worst option. The wind doesn't favor us so we can't outpace them, and the Koosh canoe can inflict far more damage on us than we can on them. In my opinion, we can either fight from the shore or retreat inland. If we fight from the shore, we're heavily outnumbered. We wouldn't stand much of a chance. If we retreat inland, they'd come after us and most likely set fire to Waka. We could be beset by the Koosh and his slaves from one side, and the Xoots from the other. And should we survive, we'd have no canoe to get home."

"Let's fight from shore," Ch'eet said.

"I agree," said Caraiden. "That Koosh canoe cannot enter this bay and I don't think it can beach on the shore outside of the bay. It will have to anchor close to shore out there and attack from open sea. That's difficult. The Yahooni slaves will have to climb down into the ocean and swim to shore, which isn't easy in armor. I'd guess they'll be wearing floats that will slow them down. That's when they'll be most vulnerable. If we can kill most of them in the ocean, we may be able to fight off the few that make it to shore."

"Have fun," raven said. Bits of salmon hung from his beak. "If you need me, I'll be far away in a tree, sleeping." He ruffled his feathers, crapped on the beach, and then flew off inland.

"I hate that bird," Ch'eet said.

"We'll fight them from the beach along the spit out there. Weapons and armor," Caraiden ordered. "Bring all the arrows and fasten on your swords. Elān, without armor you'll be exposed. Use the trees for shelter to loose your arrows from. Let's move."

Elān's stomach hurt and his throat felt tight. He had never been in a battle before. He'd never seen somebody die in battle. He strapped his sword belt around his waist and then grabbed his bow. It felt heavier than usual. He gathered arrows and shoved them into a quiver which he slung over his back. Íxt had said they shouldn't have any trouble getting to Botson's Bay. They'd had nothing but trouble the whole trip, and he'd lost his grandfather's coin-mail shirt, and now there was a good chance their journey would end here on a nameless bay on a stupid island thanks to a stupid bird. Elān could feel tears crowding the corners of his eyes. He couldn't help but think of his parents. They'd never find his body here.

"Come on," Caraiden hissed at him. "Let's go."

CHAPTER 22

THE LARGE KOOSH canoe lay anchored about five, six hundred feet offshore from the beach where Elān and the crew hid. "They're beyond our range," Caraiden said. "We'd need recurved longbows to reach them. Hold your arrows until they're closer." They crouched, hidden behind the tree line along the spit, watching the large Koosh canoe. As it had come near the sheltered bay, it had lowered all its sails and glided to a stop straight out from where Elān and the crew waited. The big canoe had lowered stern and bow anchors. Elān could see the Koosh standing in the bow. There was a loud whistle—low, high, low—and the canoe came to life with Yahooni slaves.

"Here they come," Caraiden whispered. "Weapons ready. Hold fire until I tell you to release." The crew readied their arrows against their bows and waited. And waited. The Yahooni slaves busied themselves on the far side of the canoe. "They must be disembarking starboard."

Elān thought he could see small, light canoes being lifted over the starboard side.

"Those look like canoes they're putting in on the far side," Elān said. Chetdyl growled something which Elān took to be agreement. "The Koosh canoe carries its own small canoes that look like ours."

"If that's the case," Caraiden said, "they'll make it ashore much quicker than we expected. We send as many arrows as we can while they're asea, but we must be ready for swordplay

197

sooner than we expected." Elān grabbed the hilt of his sword and made sure it slid easily from in its scabbard.

"Look," Ch'eet whispered. Small canoes appeared from behind the Koosh canoe. In a minute, three paddled out from behind each side. "Six canoes," Ch'eet said. "Chetdyl, can you see how many warriors each of them holds?" The great wolf narrowed his eyes at the canoes. He stamped his paw six times into the ground. "Thirty-six," Ch'eet said.

"Seven for each of you," said Caraiden. "Eight for me."

"That's insulting," Kwa said. The crew looked at her. She smiled the first real smile Elān had ever seen from her. "I'm worth ten warriors at least."

Kwa found some humor, Elān thought. He couldn't help but smile back. His tension lessened and his stomach eased a bit. He had to admit to himself he was glad to have Kwa here with him and not ashore at Naakw.

Five of the enemy canoes spread out wide across the sea and made their way toward shore. One canoe held back. Chetdyl sniffed the wind and growled. Elān looked at the canoe lingering behind. A figure stood in the very front of the canoe. It wore no helmet. Even with his bad vision, Elān could see the thing's hairless skull in the distance. The thing appeared to be covered in multicolored scales or clothing.

"The Koosh stands in the bow of the far canoe," Ch'eet said.

"They are said to be able to shape-shift," Caraiden said. "Chetdyl, only your nose may be able smell through Koosh trickery. Your job is to know where that Koosh is at all times. Attack and kill him if you can. When we're done with the Yahooni, we'll come to your aid." Chetdyl growled in agreement. Caraiden nodded and looked over at the others. "We kill as many as we can while they're in their canoes. Elān, take the canoe to the far right. Kwa, second from right. Ch'eet, middle. I'll take the two canoes on the left. Arms to the ready." The crew stood and notched arrows in their bows. "Step out and find your range."

Elān looked at the canoe on the far right. Paddles flashed along the side of the canoe in unison as the warriors dug hard into the sea. He could hear a low chanting coming from the canoes as the warriors timed their strokes to their chants. He estimated their distance to be about four hundred feet. He stepped out from the tree he'd been sheltering behind and pulled the arrow taut in the bowstring, pointed the arrowhead at the canoe and then slowly lifted above the prow.

"Three hundred and fifty feet," Caraiden said. "Hold."

Elān's forearm trembled. He tried to recalculate his trajectory. The chanting grew louder, faster.

"Three hundred feet. Hold."

Elān pointed the arrow tip at the canoe again and slowly leveled the tip up above the prow. One of the canoes raised an alarm.

"Release."

Elān loosed the arrow. He stood and watched it sail through the air. Up, up it went. He lost track of it when he was nudged on the shoulder by Kwa at his side. "Ready another arrow while you watch." She'd already notched and loosed her second arrow as Elān stood and watched his first, and now she was pulling a third from her quiver. Elān did the same.

"Two hundred feet," Caraiden said.

Elān notched another arrow, targeted his canoe, and let loose. He notched a third, then a fourth, and a fifth. He didn't notice any effect on the canoe. The flashing paddles kept plying the water. Elān could hear shouts and groans coming from the other canoes. He reached behind his shoulder and grabbed another arrow. "You're holding your breath," Kwa said, calm and quiet. "Breathe deep. Relax. Exhale when you release."

"One hundred fifty."

Elān took a deep breath and tried to calm his racing heart. He notched the arrow, brought the bowstring back till his right thumb felt the small indentation on the back of his jawbone, lowered the tip of the arrow directly at the metal helm of the warrior in the front of the canoe, led him slightly, and released. He reached for another arrow as he watched. The warrior he aimed at splayed his arms and tumbled backward. His paddle dropped into the sea and the canoe turned. The warrior popped back up and looked over the canoe edge for his lost paddle. Elān notched another arrow, breathed deep, exhaled halfway out, swung the arrow point to the warrior in the stern who was steering the canoe, again leading slightly, and loosed. His arrow sliced high into the warrior's armored chest. The force knocked the warrior down in the canoe. Elān notched another arrow. The canoe veered sideways. The steering warrior didn't get up. It felt as though needles pierced every hair follicle on Elān's head and arms. Had he killed the warrior?

"One hundred."

He'd never killed anyone before. His face bloomed hot and flushed. He loosed another arrow, and another, and another, and another. One more warrior fell into the canoe and this time Elān could see a bright rope of blood spurt up as the warrior fell back. He loosed one more arrow. It shuddered into the hull of the canoe with a loud knock. Elān noticed the canoe with the Koosh advancing slowly behind the leading canoes.

"Fifty feet. Prepare to fall back into the trees."

Elān could hear the angry determination of the Yahooni warriors as their chanting grew louder and more frantic. He could hear their paddles digging deep into the waves. He shot his last arrow and it tore into the bicep of a warrior near the stern as he was pulling on his paddle. He too dropped his paddle in the ocean. Elān slung his bow over his back and pulled out his sword. The palm of his hand was sweaty. He could hear canoes scraping ashore to his left. "Fall back," Caraiden yelled. "Battle positions." Caraiden, Ch'eet, Kwa, and Elān turned and ran back through the tree line along the edge of the spit to a small clearing. They formed a half-moon shape an arm's distance apart, facing the oncoming Yahooni. "Swords on guard," Caraiden said.

Through the trees Elān saw four warriors leap from the canoe he'd been sending arrows into, splash knee deep into the surf, and race up the beach toward the trees. "Four Yahooni to the right," he yelled, his voice was pinched and tense.

"Two," yelled Kwa.

"Three," yelled Ch'eet.

"Seven to our left," yelled Caraiden. "Spread out and engage."

Elān raised his sword. His throat was dry and his heartbeat thudded in his ears.

In thinking back, Elān was certain he noticed the smell first. An acrid, wet-fur stench. He realized he'd smelled it as he was firing arrows. The second thing he could recall, thinking back over that day on the beach, was the lack of noise when they struck. One second Elān's sword was up at eye level, ready to meet his first attacker, and the next second his sword tip was lowered to the ground as he watched the largest bear he'd ever seen crash into the wall of four warriors at amazing speed. The warriors were nearly at the tree line—trees they'd never reach, the last trees they'd ever see. *The impossible-to-reach trees they should be called*, Elān thought. The enormous bear knocked all the heavily armored Yahooni senseless onto the beach. They rolled about, dazed, over the rocks. The bear lashed out with both paws at the prone warriors and Elān would never forget the horrid sight. The bear's claws sliced right through the metal armor and mangled the flesh underneath.

Elān ran to the tree line, where he'd stood only moments before. Bears charged all over the beach. Two dozen or more. More bears than Elān had ever seen together. The Yahooni, whose angry faces he'd seen only a minute earlier, were corpses ripped apart and strewn across the beach. The bears didn't stop. They crashed into the sea and began to swim out toward the remaining small canoe that held the Koosh. It was about one hundred feet from the shore, coming in quick. Heavily armored Yahooni warriors paddled furiously, and the Koosh still stood in the bow. The Koosh wore clothes that resembled human clothes, except for the constant shimmering of colors. It wore no helmet. Its bulbous head, or the head-like thing atop its body, lacked hair, but had what appeared to be eyes, ears, and a nose.

Elān heard three whistles—low, high, low—and then something happened that Elān could never quite capture in words when he storycrafted about it later on: the Koosh's clothes changed colors and appeared to whirl around him and the air... *melted* (that was the best word to describe it). All the swimming bears stopped momentarily, and then swam away from the canoe. The canoe came on. Its Yahooni warriors bore down hard on their paddles. Hoosa burst from the woods to Elān's right. He growled at the mob of bears floundering out in the ocean and then growled at the oncoming canoe. Elān realized he was speaking the bear language. The Koosh came on and its strange clothes changed colors, and Hoosa collapsed to his knees on the beach.

The Koosh approached the shore in the melting air. Elān watched as the Koosh's clothes continued to change colors. An odd sensation washed over Elān's body and a strange vibration buzzed in his head. The Koosh was no longer the Koosh: Before Elān stood his grandmother, his mother's mother, the old woman who had made Elān clothes and moccasins when he was a child, the old woman who had taught Elān how to smoke salmon and tell stories, the old woman whose death ten winters earlier had made Elān so upset, he couldn't attend her funeral.

"Grandmother," Elān said. "I'm sorry I missed your burial." The old woman smiled at him, now very much alive in the prow of a canoe. "Grandmother. It is I, Elān."

Caraiden, Ch'eet, and Kwa also fell transfixed onto the beach as the Koosh drew close. Only Chetdyl was aware. When the canoe was only ten twenty paces from the beach, the armored wolf flew past the stunned crew out toward the sea and hurled himself in a giant leap over the bow. He caught the Koosh's neck in his massive jaws with a sickening crack, and both wolf and Koosh crashed into the sea behind the canoe.

The collision broke the crew's trance. "Attack," Caraiden cried. He upped his sword and ran down into the surf. Elān looked around for his sword. It was in his hand. His grandmother was gone. Elān heard the hiss of arrows. Kwa and Ch'eet loosed at the confused Yahooni warriors in the Koosh's canoe as they leaned over the port gunwale, looking for the Koosh. The canoe blocked Elān's view, but a great commotion was taking place where the Koosh had fallen. The ocean was being torn up.

Kwa and Ch'eet quickly loosed a few more arrows into the Yahooni and then ran down toward the canoe. Elān followed. Chetdyl and the Koosh churned the surf in a deathly embrace. Chetdyl's jaws were locked on the Koosh's throat, trying to hold it underwater. The throat-held Koosh flailed, leapt, and clawed, trying to get free. Caraiden waded into the sea with his sword out, trying to find an opening, but the thrashing was too erratic to land a blow.

"Chetdyl," Caraiden yelled. "Chetdyl!" Chetdyl sensed what Caraiden wanted and, with incredible power, his jaws still clenched around the Koosh's throat, he raised and held it up almost entirely out of the water. Caraiden skewered the Koosh through the armpit and down into its lungs and heart. Chetdyl unlocked his bite and dropped the Koosh. Caraiden withdrew his sword and in one smooth, arcing movement brought it down on the back of the Koosh's neck. The Koosh's body and severed bald head splashed down into the sea.

CHAPTER 23

NOBODY NOTICED THE large Yahooni canoe hauling sheets and raising sails. Elān and the crew, and the bears who had now swum back to shore, stood in the surf looking down on the decapitated Koosh. It was both human-like and yet very unhuman. Its craggy skin was the color of the smoke off damp evergreen boughs. Except for its unhelmed head, the Koosh wore body armor made of small squares that looked as though they were made from abalone shell. The squares in the armor gave off a faint, multicolored glow.

"The legend isn't true. Its body isn't made of scales," Elān said, surprised. "That's armor." He touched his sword tip to the Koosh armor. It clinked as though it were metal, but Elān had never seen a metal that resembled the inside of an abalone shell. He turned to Chetdyl. "Thank you. Are you hurt?"

Chetdyl growled low. Dark blood, almost black in color, streaked his armor and dripped from the fur around his muzzle. The war-wolf dipped his entire body into the sea and shook to clean himself. He resurfaced and Caraiden examined him. "He looks fine. The blood was not from Chetdyl."

"The Koosh have blood, then?" Kwa asked.

"Blood or something like blood," Caraiden said.

"Do we burn it or sink it?" Ch'eet asked.

"Don't bring it ashore," said Hoosa.

"Can it come back to life?" Elān asked.

"I don't know," Hoosa said. "But we don't want to offend

205

the Xoots any more than we have already. They're not happy with us being here."

"I don't like having this thing on land," Caraiden said. "Let's weigh it down with rocks as a feast for crabs. We can tie a rope around it and use one of these small canoes to drag it out there to the depths. Look." He pointed to the large Yahooni canoe. The mainsail was raising. The Xoots bears growled among themselves.

"Hoosa," Elān whispered, "what are they discussing?"

"They want to go destroy the large canoe," Hoosa said. "They don't want it leading any more like it to their island."

"Can they swim that far?" Elān asked.

"Of course," Hoosa said. "That's no distance for the Xoots."

"Tell them not to sink it," Elān said. "I want to go aboard and search it first."

"They don't care about that," Hoosa said. "They want it at the bottom of the sea."

"Tell them we need to retrieve something important," Elān said. "Or, that we want one of the Yahooni for a captive. Tell them anything, just don't let them sink it. Tell them we'll burn it when we're done."

"That's a good idea," said Kwa. "We need to search that canoe, Hoosa."

Hoosa growl-spoke with the Xoots. "I asked them not to sink it and to leave one Yahooni alive for us to talk to. I said we'll burn the canoe when we're done."

Twenty Xoots bears stormed to sea, swimming out to the large canoe, their massive paws raking the ocean in large strokes. Elān looked at the crew. "Let's take one of these canoes out to it. I want to go aboard and see it from the inside. On the way, we can drag this Koosh out and sink it in the depths."

A few of the Yahooni landing canoes had floated off with the tide, but several still lay tilted, beached on the sand. Elān

went to the closest—the canoe that had held the Koosh—
and looked inside. Five corpses sprawled in terrible visages of
death with arrows through their necks. Blood had pooled on
the floor and spattered red the walls and seats.

"Dump them in the sea," Caraiden said. He turned to Elān.
"You should take the armor of that one there." He pointed to
a Yahooni corpse in the stern. "He's about your size." Elān
untied the metal chest plate, gorget, and helmet and tossed
them on the beach. He despised the notion of wearing armor
stolen from a corpse, but the terror of battle showed him
how vulnerable he was without it. They tossed the Yahooni
corpses into the sea, and splashed handfuls of sea water
against the walls of the canoe until it held a bloody red pool.
They dumped out the water from the canoe, roped up the
body of the Koosh and tied a large rock to the other end of
the rope, and put the rock in the canoe. Nobody wanted to
touch the dead Koosh's head, so Caraiden staked it to the sea
floor off the beach with one of the dead Yahooni's swords.
They paddled out toward the large canoe, dragging the
headless Koosh corpse in its abalone-like armor behind them.
The Xoots crawled aboard the large canoe; Elān was amazed
at how fast they swam out to it and even more amazed at how
easily they scaled the outside of canoe with their razor claws.

As the crew neared the large canoe, Caraiden lifted the large
rock from their own and tossed it overboard. The rope went
tight, and they watched the headless Koosh disappear behind
the rope down into the depths of the sea. The shimmering
armor dimmed into darkness as it sank out of sight. "I'm
glad it's gone," Hoosa said. "The Xoots may have killed us
after they finished ripping apart the Yahooni on the beach, but
because of what Chetdyl did to the Koosh, I think the Xoots
will let us go. The Koosh terrified the Xoots, and I don't have
the words to even explain to them what the Koosh is."

"All the horror stories I've heard about the Koosh are
children's tales compared to seeing a real one," Ch'eet said.

"My father died five winters past," Hoosa said in a quiet, flat voice. "But I saw him alive on the prow of this very canoe. He spoke to me—the very voice of my father. He said he missed me. Tears were in his eyes."

"Koosh trickery," Caraiden said. "The old legend of the Koosh appearing as our loved ones is true."

"Yes," said Hoosa. "I couldn't move. I saw a dead relative living."

"So did we all," Caraiden said. "Thank Yéil for Chetdyl. He was the only one…" Caraiden shook his head. "We'd all be dead without Chetdyl." He patted Chetdyl's paw. Chetdyl growled a low, pleased growl.

They reached the large canoe and paddled around to the far side. Rope ladders ran down the side of the canoe. Elān grabbed the end of one of the ladders and handed it to Kwa. She held it tight as Elān climbed. Once over the side of the large canoe, Elān saw a group of Xoots prowling the main deck. The deck was awash in blood and slick with entrails. Elān felt sick to his stomach. Hoosa was next aboard the large canoe followed by Ch'eet, Caraiden, and Kwa. Chetdyl came last, climbing the rope ladder using both his mouth and paws.

Hoosa spoke with the Xoots in a low, growling language. He pointed to Elān. The Xoots turned and looked at him. Hoosa did the same with the rest of the crew and Elān realized he was introducing the crew to the Xoots. Afterward, Hoosa turned to Elān. "There was a crew of twenty, thirty Yahooni aboard. All are dead and tossed overboard except one who is in that small cabin near the stern, badly injured but still living, or so he was a little while ago. There's a deck below this one, but they didn't find anyone down there."

"Chetdyl," Elān said. "Check the below deck for human or Koosh." Chetdyl growled and trotted off toward a set of stairs leading to the below deck. Elān walked to the mainsail and felt its fabric. "What is this?" he asked the crew. They ran their hands along the strange sail. "I've never felt anything like it."

"Ch'eet, you have your knife with you," Elān said. "Could you gather enough of this sailing to outfit *Waka*?"

"Yes," Kwa said. "Good idea."

"Good as done," replied Ch'eet.

Elān looked to the others. "Let's go talk with the Yahooni."

They walked to the cabin in the stern and through the broken doorway. The door had been knocked down and shredded by the Xoots' massive claws. The cabin held a large table with a map tacked across it, several lanterns, two small chests, several chairs, something that looked like a sword storage box, and a low bed on which lay a heavily bleeding, moaning Yahooni slave. His legs had been slashed by the Xoots' claws. "Kwa, could you see to him? Maybe get him some water?" Elān asked. "Maybe we can wrap his legs."

Kwa nodded and went to the Yahooni on the bed. Elān walked to the table and examined the navigation chart. It was made of a strange material similar to the sail. The map showed all the islands of the Aaní, Deikeenaa, Yahooni, and the mainland including the Far Wilds in the east. It also had a detailed inset of the Koosh island of Saaw and something Elān had never seen before: chartings of the Fire Islands, far, far to the west. Many strange symbols covered the map. Elān assumed it to be Koosh writing. He untacked the map and folded it. He would keep it in his lockbox. Perhaps, back in Naasteidi, Íxt or one of the scholars at the Longhouse of Service and Trade could read it.

Caraiden brought the two chests to the table and opened them. One chest contained metal coins. "What use would coins be to the Koosh?" he asked.

"I don't know but it's ours now," Elān said. "What's in the other box?"

Caraiden opened it and pulled out a strange object none of the crew had seen before. It was hand-sized, square and flat and thin as a sword, except for a small orb stuck into its middle. The whole object was made from strange, slate-colored metal. Caraiden put a hesitant finger to it and the metal orb glowed. He dropped it in alarm. It banged back into the chest.

"Is it a dzanti?" Kwa asked. She was helping the wounded Yahooni drink from a metal goblet.

"I don't know," Caraiden said. "I've never seen a dzanti before."

"Let's try to use it," Kwa said.

"It's not a dzanti," the injured Yahooni slave said in a weak voice. "The Koosh use it like a jishagoon, but it connects with other Koosh things."

Elān turned to the man. "How do you know?"

"Very few Koosh have a dzanti," he said.

"How many dzanti are there?" Caraiden asked.

"I don't know," the Yahooni said. "They call it a xahaat in their language, not dzanti."

"What's your name?"

"Goox," the man said.

Elān pulled a chair next to the bed. "You are Island Yahooni?" he asked the man.

"Yes." His voice was thin, barely audible. He'd lost a lot of blood. Kwa had tried to bandage his legs with a bedsheet, but the legs looked too torn up to be able walk again.

"How long have you been a slave to the Koosh?"

"I don't know," Goox said. "Time makes no sense anymore."

"How many Koosh have returned to this world?"

"I don't know. Dozens, maybe," Goox said.

"How many canoes like this do they have?" Caraiden asked.

"I don't know. I've seen fifty or sixty. The Koosh call them ships. They enslaved my people. All my people. We have to work their ships."

"What do they want?"

Goox laughed. "Your soul. Everyone's soul. They want to enslave this world entire."

"Why?"

"Greed. Hatred. They don't think like the Yahooni or Deikeenaa or Aaní. We all think alike to them, and they don't like how we think." This puzzled Elān. What did he mean the Koosh didn't like how the Yahooni, Deikeenaa, or Aani thought? Those three nations could hardly agree on anything.

"I don't understand," Elān said.

Goox laughed weakly again. "I don't either."

"You don't have any idea how many dzanti the Koosh have?"

"I don't know," Goox said. "Not many. We heard they come from the otherworld but may not be Koosh-made. I've only seen one. The Koosh who attacked my homeland had one. He wore it on his hand like an evil mitten. Our entire village was destroyed in minutes. We stood no chance. Those of us left alive surrendered."

Caraiden picked up the Koosh jishagoon. "You said this Koosh jishagoon is connected to other Koosh things. What things? And how is it connected? I see no connection."

"I don't know," Goox said. "I overheard the Koosh that captains this ship say something about it. The Koosh keep those jishagoon with them all the time unless they go ashore. They don't want them falling overboard. The Koosh that captains this ship always kept four guards at its cabin door to protect that jishagoon." Goox tried to sit up and groaned in pain. "Ach. I need help. I'm tired."

Elān felt sorry for Goox. He wasn't young, but he wasn't old, and now his life was draining away aboard a Koosh slave ship. "We can take you to shore and give you a paddle and one of your small canoes."

"I need to rest," Goox said. "Ach, please let me rest."

Elān stood and turned to the others. "Let's let him rest." He walked over the odd-looking sword storage box and picked it up. It was much lighter than it looked. He unlatched the box. Inside was a thin-necked, wooden-bodied instrument with strings woven from thin metal running the length of its neck and body. Elān plucked one of the strings with his finger and it rang with a high yet pleasing sound. "I think it's a musical instrument," Elān said. "Like our Tas back home, but stranger and with more strings." He lifted the instrument and examined it in the sunlight streaming through a window. There were strange carvings in the wood, but the wood itself was familiar. "Shéiyi wood from our world." Shéiyi is the Aaní word for a special kind of spruce tree that grows in Aaní territory. Elān ran his hand over the wooden body of the instrument. "Rough. Our carvers in Naasteidi can make better."

"Music," Kwa said in astonishment. "The Koosh make music?"

"If so, it's the only thing about the Koosh I understand," Caraiden said.

"I don't understand anything about the Koosh," Kwa said.

"Let's keep it all," Elān said. The strange Koosh things excited him. "Kwa, bring the coins. Caraiden, bring the Koosh jishagoon. I'll bring this Koosh Tas. Let's search the rest of the ship. We'll be back for you, Goox."

The below deck was for the slaves. Hammocks swung back and forth with the waves, dining tables still held plates and utensils. There was a small forge for repairing weapons, a cache of extra armor, dozens of well-made recurve bows both short and long, and thousands of arrows in small wooden barrels. Elān took one of the short recurve bows and the crew carried a few barrels of arrows up to the top deck and lowered them into the small canoe. Ch'eet had already placed one of the ship's sails into the bow of the canoe. The fabric was so strong, he'd told Elān, it couldn't be cut with a knife, so he found a small staysail that looked like it would fit *Waka*. It was easy to fold, though, and not bulky. They tossed everything down into the canoe. It would be a cramped ride back to shore. The crew would have to sit on barrels and chests and folded sail as they paddled.

"Hoosa," Elān said. "Tell the Xoots we're ready to go. We'll burn this canoe as we leave." Hoosa nodded and walked to the bow where the Xoots had gathered. Elān turned to the crew. "I'll fetch a lantern from the Koosh's cabin and start the fire below deck. Caraiden, Kwa, and Ch'eet, can you retrieve and try to lower our prisoner into the canoe?" They walked to the Koosh cabin. Goox was dead.

CHAPTER 24

AN UGLY, CHARCOAL-COLORED smoke filled the sunsetting sky. Elān and the crew watched the Koosh ship burn as they paddled back toward the sheltered bay. The Xoots had already made it to shore. Elān could see them cleaning up the beach where they'd battled the Yahooni force. They dragged armored corpses, canoes, and weapons off the beach and out into the sea. Elān felt exhausted and depressed. The day had been impossibly long and now, as night fell, wearing away the shock of the day, he was physically exhausted, but he also carried a heavy weight of sadness low in his chest. As he paddled toward the sheltered bay, he tried to understand that heavy sadness. When had he felt that before? It was the same feeling he'd had when he used to hunt and he'd sent an arrow into a deer or moose or mountain goat. Or any animal. Even though he appreciated the meat that kept him and his family fed, for at least a moon after he'd taken any animal's life he grew depressed and sad, with a heavy hollowness in his chest.

He could never evade the memory of his arrow slashing into a mountain goat or deer. Those memories always came unbidden to him as he lay down to sleep. Elān worried that tonight when he lay down to sleep, the memory of the Yahooni warrior he'd hit falling backward into the canoe with bright blood spurting above him would come to him in the dark, along with the memory of Goox's shredded legs, and mingle with the memory of what the Xoots did to the force on the beach.

He understood: the heavy weight he carried low in his chest came from taking life. *No*, Elān thought, *I should be honest. It comes from killing. Every time I kill, the weight gets heavier and hollower.*

He thought of what Goox had said: *Time makes no sense.* Killing also made no sense. *It's all related*, Elān thought, *the loss of sense and meaning to this heavy, hollow feeling. My father was right. I'm no warrior. I can't kill. I'm a bookeater. I'm just a bookeater.* He tried hard to keep the tears within, and as they paddled through the small opening into the shallow bay, Elān knew what he had to do to bring meaning back to his world. First, he'd have to find the right rock.

DARKNESS ENFOLDED THE sheltered bay under the shadow of the Xoots Jin mountain. Elān passed a lit lantern up to Kwa in the bow and she guided the small canoe to the beach next to *Waka*. *Waka* was still half covered in branches. The crew jumped out into the bay and pulled the canoe ashore.

"I would say it was good to see you, Crapshack, but we both know I'd be lying."

Kwa held the lantern up. Raven lay on his back on the beach with his wings out wide—an unusual position for a bird. Bits of salmon had fallen on his feathers. His stomach bulged out.

"He looks pregnant," Kwa said.

Raven cawed with laughter. "Old Sourbag, I missed your stupidity. When I feel better, remind me to show you where babies come from."

Caraiden lifted a bentwood box that, until that evening, had held a large amount of smoked salmon. "The stupid bird has eaten a three-day supply."

Raven patted his bloated stomach with his wing. "I'm going to name this baby Caraiden."

"You call me Crapshack," Elān said. "Look what you've done."

216

Runny, grayish poop lay in globs around raven's ass. "Turds-For-Hair wasn't here for me to crap on," raven said.

"My name is Hoosa, bird. It's the traditional name of my clan and was gifted to me by my grandmothers. I know you have no respect for my traditions, but you will call me by my name."

Raven laughed. He tried to sit up but couldn't. "'You *will* call *me* by *my* name,'" raven laughed, imitating Hoosa. "Hey, Miss Sourbag," he said to Kwa, "it just occurred to me: tradition is like our friend here."

"What nonsense do you mean by that?" Kwa asked.

"Bears are bears by nature," raven replied, "and while they're dumb as driftwood, they are who they are. But him and his stinking human cousins pretend to be bears because of some silly stories and songs from the *looong* ago. That's tradition."

"If that's tradition," Kwa said, "then I see nothing wrong with being traditional."

"Of course you don't," raven replied. "Like him, you love to play pretend. So, tell me, sour Miss Traditional, who is dumber: Beings who are who they are by nature, or beings who pretend to be something else?"

"Ignore the stupid bird, Kwa," Caraiden said.

Elān saw anger in Hoosa's eyes. Hoosa's hand went to the sword on his belt but paused. Again, the smell hit Elān before the bears appeared. The Xoots had come. About thirty of them emerged from the woods around the sheltered bay. They looked even larger in the shadows cast by the lantern. Raven was startled. He stood up, hopped into the air, flapped his wings, and tried to fly, but he'd eaten far too much salmon. After trying several times to take flight, he gave up and collapsed, wings out, beak down.

Hoosa spoke to the Xoots. Elān listened and again was amazed at the growling language. The crew waited. Hoosa pressed his forehead to one of the Xoot's foreheads, turned to the crew and called for Chetdyl. "They want to show their appreciation for what you did today," Hoosa explained. "Press your head to theirs and breathe in. All of them." It took several minutes to perform the ceremony. When it was done, the Xoots disappeared back into the dark forests of Xoots Jin.

"We can stay here for the night," Hoosa told the crew after the Xoots had left. "But we must leave in the morning. We can use our lanterns but we cannot make a fire. They'll kill us if we make a fire. Hereafter, Chetdyl is welcome to stay on the island wherever and whenever he'd like. He has forever permission. I have permission to visit this island again but only in this bay, which they call 'Out of the Claws Bay' in their language. If any of you visit this island again without me or Chetdyl, the Xoots will kill you and feed your corpse to the waves as they did the dead Yahooni."

THE CREW ATE a meal of smoked salmon and dried berries and unrolled their bedrolls on the soft sandy beach of Out of the Claws Bay. "Ch'eet, could you help me retrieve the armor I left on the beach?" Elān asked.

"Yes," Ch'eet replied. The two left the crew and walked along Out of the Claws beach toward the spit and the open ocean beyond. Once out of earshot of the crew, Ch'eet said, "I've never been to battle with a bookeater, but you did well. You followed orders and were willing to die to defend your crew. You've honored your grandfather today. Old Latseen would have been proud to see how you handled yourself in battle."

"Thanks," Elān replied. "But he might not feel honored by what I'm about to do. That's why I wanted you to come with me. I need a witness. I'm going to make a sea bond."

Ch'eet halted. "What?"

"I'm going to make a sea bond," Elān repeated. "I killed a human today with an arrow, or I think I did. I didn't see him get out of the canoe. I can't explain, but meaning is unraveling inside me. I felt this way when I killed a deer or mountain goat. I don't like this feeling. I'm no warrior. I'm going to take a sea bond not to kill."

Ch'eet put his hand on Elān's shoulder. "Your enemy didn't take a sea bond not to kill. The Yahooni tried to and would have killed you this afternoon."

"They're not my enemy," Elān said.

"You should inform them of that," Ch'eet said emphatically. "What about taking a life in your own self-defense? Or protecting your crew? I don't want a crewmate who won't protect my life. What about mountain goats or birds? Or fish, crabs, even clams? They have life. Will you not take life to eat?"

Elān thought for a moment. How could he live without food from the sea? Without salmon? "You have a point," Elān said. "I'll make a sea bond not to purposefully seek to kill another human, nor hunt and kill any animal of the land. I'll protect myself and my crew, and I'll actively seek to kill Koosh, but I will not kill without meaning."

"I'm not sure what meaning has to do with it," Ch'eet replied. "Seems to me you're making up a story about when you can kill and when you can't."

"Maybe that's the meaning," Elān said. "Stories give us meaning."

"You're still thinking like a bookeater," Ch'eet scoffed. "A warrior doesn't need to make up stories for his behavior. A warrior acts and serves his people."

"Perhaps the stories were made up *looong* ago and warriors don't realize they're following them," Elān said. "But you're following them just the same, and they give you meaning."

Ch'eet laughed. "Warriors have little time to make up stories when facing an enemy in battle."

"Warriors who survive make them up after the battle," Elān said. "That's what I'm doing. I'm making up my own stories now."

"A sea bond is a serious thing, Elān. Where are you going to sink your rock?"

"Out in the ocean somewhere."

"I suggest you sink it in Out of the Claws Bay," Ch'eet replied. "It's shallow and it'd be easy to retrieve if you change your mind or your stories." He smiled at Elān.

"Yes, I suppose you're right."

They walked to the shore. The moon was out and Elān could see the yellow glow of the remnants of the Koosh ship smoldering in the distance. A dark funnel of smoke wound up into the night sky. He and Ch'eet retrieved the Yahooni armor. Elān washed it in the surf, scrubbing it thoroughly with handfuls of sand. He put on the breast plate. It fit fairly well. The gorget and helmet were large. Elān tied tight the thongs of the Yahooni helmet under his chin. "Even a Yahooni thong can break," Ch'eet said. "You can pad the inside of that helmet with rags or spare sail patch. That should help keep it tight to your head."

Elān then selected a large, flattish rock, about the size of a gluuch ball, and carried it back to his bedroll at *Waka*. In the flickering light of a lantern, he used a short knife to carve the figure of a man and deer across the rock.

When done, he took the rock and, instead of throwing it out into the ocean, he walked it out thigh deep and set it on the floor of Out of the Claws Bay. Ch'eet was right—he might have to retrieve the rock one day. The rock now held his sea bond. He couldn't break his bond without first retrieving the rock. The sea would bring shame, dishonor, bad luck, drownings, storms, everything awful to him and his family if he broke his bond without that sea bond rock in his possession.

ELĀN SLEPT DREAMLESSLY that night, whether because of his sea bond or sheer exhaustion he didn't know. He was grateful not to be haunted by visions of death. Caraiden had the crew up early preparing *Waka* to depart. They removed the branches, outfitted the mast with the Koosh staysail of strange fabric, loaded the repaired mainsail with the rest of gear in the outriggers (keeping weapons in the canoe, of course), donned their armor, and readied to take to sea once again.

Elān felt secure in his armor. His depression had lifted, maybe because of his sea bond, and he stood on the shoreline and admired his helmeted visage and metaled body in the reflection off the bay. He looked more warrior than bookeater.

"Crapshack found some metal diapers." Raven looked down from his mast-nest. He had recovered from his excess the night before.

The crew pushed *Waka* out into Out of the Claws Bay and paddled toward the bay's mouth. Once on the open ocean, Elān had the crew run up the sails and store paddles. The sun was up in the east, the wind blowing southeast, and it looked to be another warm day at sea.

The Koosh ship's sail was an arm's length longer than *Waka*'s boom, but it was lighter and stronger than *Waka*'s original skin sail and held the wind better. *Waka* flew eastward and the outriggers sizzled through the calm sea. Xoots Jin Island straddled the boundary between Aaní and Deikeenaa territories. The Aaní and Deikeenaa had been allies since time immemorial and, in normal days, Elān and the crew could stop in at any Deikeenaa village and be welcomed as though they themselves were Deikeenaa. But these were not normal days. The dozens of Deikeenaa villages on dozens of Deikeenaa islands between Xoots Jin and Botson's Bay could be as hostile as Deshu.

Elān cleated the mainsail sheet and locked the tiller. He pulled out his navigation map and, out of curiosity, took the Koosh navigation map out from the lockbox under the stern. He folded both maps to show Deikeenaa territory and held them together. The Koosh map, so it appeared, was more detailed. Strange symbols recurred along the seaways, inlets, and bays, but not on land. Elān assumed they'd be depth markers. Perhaps Íxt could compare them to the fathom numbers on his map and then translate the symbols. He noticed the Koosh map contained all the island villages of the Aaní, Deikeenaa, and Yahooni. He assumed the strange writings next to the villages were the Koosh names for them. Even Naasteidi was noted on the map. On the mainland, the Koosh's map showed Latseen's Wall that separated the Mainland Yahooni from the Aaní in the north and cannibal giants in the south. The Koosh's map also appeared to mark the cave dwellings of the cannibal giants. Íxt had doubted many, if any, cannibal giants were left. Elān hoped Íxt was right.

Elān guided *Waka* out into the open ocean east of Xoots Jin and turned southward. The wind was heavier in the open seas, but not unpleasant, and *Waka* made good speed. "Caraiden," Elān called up to the old warrior. "Were you with my grandfather on Kasaan Island for the treaty signing?"

"Yes, that was many winters past," Caraiden said. "I don't know the island well, though. I was part of your grandfather's guard. We stayed in a Deikeenaa village called Choosh at the south end of Kasaan. It's one of largest and most beautiful Deikeenaa villages."

"I saw Choosh on the map and recalled that was where the official Yahooni surrender and treaty signing took place," Elān said.

"That's true," Caraiden said. "That's where your grandfather established Latseen's Line. Are you thinking of putting in there?"

"Yes," Elān replied. "I was thinking we could rest there for a day or two. We have the coin for lodgings and replenishing food stores. From Choosh it's only two days to Botson's Bay. You think we dare put in at Choosh?"

"While I have fond memories of Choosh," Caraiden said, "I was there in much happier and safer times, at least for Aaní people. Choosh is unimaginable until you see it, carved into the rock of giant seacliffs. The houses and buildings are made of stone. All people should see Choosh once in their life. But we don't know if it has been destroyed by the Koosh or, if it's still there, if the villagers would allow us in. I do like the idea of a short rest on land. And we need food, especially if that stupid bird is determined to eat like he did last night. If up to me, I'd risk putting in at Choosh."

"I agree," said Elān. "We'll make a course for Kasaan Island, then. We should be there by afternoon tomorrow if winds hold. We can sleep aboard *Waka* tonight and travel under moonlight."

"Look," Ch'eet said. "An eagle approaches." A great bald eagle traveling at an incredible rate was diving from the heights straight toward *Waka*.

"Bird," yelled Elān to raven. "Speak to him. Find out what he wants."

"No," said raven.

"I think it's the messenger bird," Ch'eet said, "from Samish."

The eagle pulled up above *Waka* and dropped a leather scroll-holder down into the canoe. Caraiden picked it up.

"Wait, wait, wait," Elān called up to the bird. He pretended to write on his hand. "I'll give you a message to take back to Íxt." The eagle seemed to understand. He flew in circles about the canoe. "I should have written before we left Out of the Claws Bay." Elān took a quill, ink pot, and a small scrap of paper from his sea coat. "Read the scroll, Caraiden."

Caraiden unfurled the scroll and read aloud. "It's from Íxt, I think. It's signed with an I. It says, 'Letter received. Sorry for Latseen's armor. Rumor of Koosh attacking Aaní villages far east and Deikeenaa villages far south. Yelm warriors burned and destroyed large Koosh canoe off Daadzi. Rumors of

Koosh canoes across Éil'. Naasteidi safe for now. Mountain strongholds prepared for retreat. Hurry home. I.' This letter reads as though it was written in haste."

Elān wrote a short note:

We destroyed & burned Koosh canoe in southern Aaní territory. Killed Koosh by decapitating. Have much to tell about them. Journey continues now in Deikeenaa territory. Crew is well. Four, five days from destination. Keep messengers coming. Will send message on return journey. E.

Elān read the letter aloud to the crew. They thought it vague enough not to cause any trouble if an enemy captured the eagle. And the eagle would inform Íxt of where he had found them, Elān was certain, so the old man would have a good idea of where they were. He curled up the letter and put it in the leather scroll-holder and lifted it up to the circling eagle. The eagle veered down to the canoe. Elān put the scroll-holder on the stern, and in a deft movement the eagle grasped it in his claws without landing and flew off toward the northwest.

CHAPTER 25

ELĀN GUIDED WAKA through the open ocean and, toward
sunset, along the eastern coast of Kaltask Island. Noticing
thick beds of bullwhip kelp floating offshore in a cove, they
anchored briefly to bottom fish and within a half hour had
pulled up three long *xaax'w* fish (which you, of course, know
as lingcod) and one large *ish̲keen* (which you know as black
cod). Caraiden got a fire going in the bentwood cooking
box as Elān hauled anchor and set sail southeasterly. Ch'eet
filleted the xaax'w fish first and handed the raw, bluish fillets
to Caraiden, who placed them on the grill of the cooking
box. The fillets turned milk white as they cooked.

Night sailing can be enjoyable if the moon is out and the sea
is calm, and it was calm that night. The crew passed around
slabs of grilled fish and leaned back against the gunwales as
they ate. The sun was down, the moon was up, and the sea
was dark. They chatted about the brutal events of the day
before, about what might await them in the journey ahead,
and about home. Even raven was as agreeable as Elān had
known him to be. He rested in his mast-nest and pecked at
the large piece of xaax'w fish Elān had given him. But a calm
sea also means little wind. *Waka* slowed down, the Koosh
sail pocketing what little wind there was, and glided leisurely
along the coast of Kaltask.

After their supper, of a sudden, the crew fell silent. Elān
said, "Why don't you get some sleep Kwa, Caraiden, and
Chetdyl? Ch'eet and I will sail and stand watch first. Hoosa,

you take the first watch with us. We'll wake the rest of you up for second watch. Kwa can take the tiller then." The crew murmured their agreement. Kwa and Caraiden wrapped themselves in their sea coats and tried to rest against the sides of the canoe. Chetdyl curled up on the bow. If you've tried it, then you know sleeping aboard a canoe is not pleasant, but it's not entirely unpleasant on a calm, not-too-cold, moonlit night. You would also know that one doesn't sleep so much as doze.

Elān left the mainsail sheet cleated but held the tiller and guided *Waka* over the dark sea. The moon provided enough light to navigate by, but Elān kept the canoe well away from Kaltask to avoid any rock outcroppings. It was peaceful as long as he didn't think of the dead Yahooni warriors, or Goox, or the corpses on the beach. If his mind brought those images up, he thought of the rock that held his sea bond sitting in quiet water under Out of the Claws Bay.

Or he tried to imagine what his parents were doing. The village of Naasteidi would be peaceful on a night like this. There'd still be some people in Gooch's Dad or Raven's Tail or the Longhorn, drinking ale and gambling and laughing and singing songs. Or young people taking an evening paddle around Naasteidi Bay. The thought made Elān smile with homesickness. Íxt's letter said the Koosh had attacked villages all over Éil'. He didn't want to even think about what might happen to Naasteidi. If the dzanti were as rare as Goox said, if he could bring one back to Naasteidi, maybe they'd have a chance against the Koosh and their Yahooni slaves. *The Koosh are our enemy, not the Yahooni*, Elān thought to himself. Now that he'd seen what a Koosh could do, he knew the Yahooni were not to blame, even though they fought a many-winters war against the Aaní in his grandfather's time. Ch'eet's voice startled Elān from his thoughts.

"It's time to switch the watch," Ch'eet announced. Kwa

and Caraiden stirred from their sea coats. Elān took off his breastplate armor.

"Were you able to sleep?" he asked Kwa.

"In fits and starts," she replied.

"I've locked the mainsail sheet and tiller. We're heading south by southeast. I've been keeping the prow toward where the Southern Spar star will disappear at the horizon. You'll need to head east toward Kasaan around sunrise, or before if the wind picks up. Kasaan looks to be a large island. I've circled it on the navigation chart, which is on top of the lockbox in the stern. I put the jishagoon with it. There's a lantern there too if you need light. *Waka* is all yours to command. Wake me if you have questions." He stood and stretched his legs. He was going to sit on the gunwale to make way for Kwa to take the captain's seat, but as he looked at the netting between the port outrigger and canoe, he remembered what his father had said when Elān first brought *Waka* home. "I'm going to sleep on the netting," he said to Kwa as she shuffled by him to take control.

"What?" she asked, as though she hadn't heard correctly.

"I'm going to sleep on the netting. The sea is calm enough I shouldn't get wet." He kicked off his boots into the bottom of *Waka* and crawled out onto the netting. It was like a hammock. It felt so good, after a long day sitting in the canoe, to stretch out fully. He looked through the netting. The dark sea, silver-tipped with moonlight, slipped by. The only sound was the soft murmur of the outriggers hissing through the ocean. Elān pulled his sea coat around him and fell asleep.

"YOU SHOULDN'T PEE in your metal diapers. They'll rust."

Elān sat up, unsure where he was. Why was he sleeping outside in the rain in a strange hammock? He saw the sun over the edge of the eastern horizon slightly portside of *Waka*'s bow. His pants and socks were soaked.

Raven was looking down at him from his mast-nest. "You'll rust your diapers, Crapshack. What happened, did Sleepy Old Man Bellyache get tired and kick you out of the canoe? Or did Old Sourbag take revenge for you almost leaving her at Naakw and banish you to the netting?"

The annoying bird brought sense back to Elān's mind: he was aboard *Waka*. The wind had kicked up and the waves splashed through the netting. Elān climbed back into the canoe. "How did you sleep?" Kwa asked.

"Fine," Elān said. "I feel great."

"Then you can take over the tiller," Kwa replied. "I'm exhausted. I need to sleep."

"Where are we?" he asked.

"That's the north end of Kasaan ahead in the distance," Kwa said. "Once we cleared the lee of Kaltask and Kanata islands, the wind shifted easterly. I've been riding that wind. This canoe can fly." She stood up, stretched, then sat down on the floor of the canoe in front of her seat and rested her head against the side of the canoe. Elān pulled on his boots and then took his captain's seat and pulled out his map and jishagoon. Ch'eet had already relieved Caraiden. Caraiden was resting with his back against the mast. Chetdyl was still curled up in the bow. He looked to be asleep. Hoosa was sleeping with his head on his folded arms, leaning against the mast. Elān woke him to take watch.

"How was the netting for a bed?" Ch'eet asked.

"A little cold," Elān said, "but I haven't slept that well in a long time."

"I might try sleeping on the netting next time we overnight aboard," Ch'eet said.

"You should," Elān said. "You should try it too, Hoosa."

"I'll sleep where I will," Hoosa said.

Behind Hoosa, Ch'eet gave Elān a glance that betrayed the awkwardness Elān felt in Hoosa's response. Elān changed the subject. "You've never told us about S'eek Ḵwáan."

"Why would I?" Hoosa asked. Elān was taken aback again by the awkwardness and sat for a moment in silence. He realized that Hoosa didn't mean to offend. Rather, it was an honest response to Elān's question.

"Because we are your crewmates, Hoosa," Elān said. "We are your friends."

"Friendship has a different meaning to my black bear relatives and cousins," Hoosa said.

"I don't understand," Ch'eet said. "Friendship is friendship."

Hoosa remained silent for a long time. "It's hard for me to explain in human language. My black bear relatives have a better language. We can express what we mean in more ways than just sounds."

"Now I really don't understand," Ch'eet said.

"Think of it this way," Hoosa replied. Elān could see him struggling to get the sense of his words across. "Imagine you are dying of thirst and have only a fishing net to catch the rain when it falls. Human language is a net trying to catch the rain. Most of the meaning falls through it. Human languages use sounds that struggle to impart meaning. But my black bear relatives' language is a bucket in the rain. Full of sounds, smells, and emotions. Full of meanings."

Hoosa's words struck Elān. Most humans talked so much because of the inadequate net of their languages. They had to scoop and scoop again to get but a small dampness of meaning. Hoosa wasn't silent because he was arrogant, disliked people, or didn't want to be part of the crew; Hoosa was silent because he had knowledge of a better, more meaningful language that could describe reality far better than any human language. "I think I understand, Hoosa," Elān said. "It's like having only two colors to paint with, or a one-string Tas to play, when you're used to hundreds of colors or a many-stringed Tas. I would find that frustrating."

For the first time on the voyage, Hoosa smiled. "Yes. You now understand what many do not."

"I would like to learn the black bear language," Elān said. The thought of the black bear language, filled with smells and emotions, intrigued Elān.

"I will teach you a little on this voyage," Hoosa replied. "And you would be welcome to come to S'eek K̲wáan to learn when we return from our journey."

"Your ancestors," Elān replied.

"And yours."

ELĀN RODE THE eastern wind and Kasaan Island grew closer and clearer. It was a large island. Even from a distance he couldn't see the southern end of it. He pulled the tiller portside and *Waka* veered off to the south. With the wind pushing southeast, he'd aim for the southern end of Kasaan. He checked the map and made a bearing and estimate with the jishagoon. If the wind held, they'd be at Choosh in the early afternoon. Elān was excited, after hearing Caraiden's description, to see Choosh—if the village was still there.

The wind died when the sun was straight up in the sky. The Koosh sail, adept at capturing the wind, drooped emptily along the mast. The crew had to take up paddles. Elān set time with a quiet two-beat sea chant of the sort every Aaní child is taught when young. Kasaan Island rose steadily in height until, around midafternoon, the crew could see the Cliffs of Choosh at the south end. Hoosa ran the Aaní flag up *Waka*'s mast. Elān upped the pace of his chant and urged the crew on. As they neared the cliffs, Elān could see staircases spiderwebbing up the sides of the rock. Pillars, terraces, balconies, and windows were carved directly into the cliffs all the way to the top, some four, five hundred feet.

A massive sea wall, forty, fifty feet high and made of stone fitted atop a thick base of riprap, extended far out into the ocean and curved around to meet the other side of Choosh. In the middle of the sea wall, directly out from the center of the village, was a metal sea gate. "This sea wall and gate weren't here the last time I visited," Caraiden said. "Protection against the Koosh, I would guess."

"Canoe off the portside bow," Ch'eet said.

A small, military canoe approached, bearing the standard of the Deikeenaa: a black eagle and black raven standing back-to-back together on a red background. "Paddles up," Elān said. The crew held their paddles tip up in their right hands. It was the universal gesture for peace in Éil'. And it also showed you didn't have a sword or bow at the ready.

The Deikeenaa canoe drew close. It held a crew of six warriors and a large wolfdog. As it neared *Waka*, a warrior in captain's armor stood up in the bow. "Hold," she said to Elān. "Stay where you are." The wolfdog jumped up onto the prow. The Deikeenaa warriors paddled their canoe around *Waka* entirely, allowing the wolfdog to use his nose at all wind angles. When the canoe had made a full circle around *Waka*, the wolfdog lowered its massive head to the standing warrior and sat back down.

"State your names and business," the warrior said to Elān.

"I am Elān from Naasteidi on Samish Island. This is Kwa, Hoosa, Caraiden, Ch'eet, and Chetdyl, all from Samish Island. Our canoe is called *Waka*. We seek entry into Choosh to stay a few nights, rest, and replenish our stores."

"What in Yaahl's name is a canoe from the northwest doing here?" the warrior asked. Elān heard more curiosity than annoyance in her voice. "Have you run out of sea? State your business."

"We seek entry into Choosh to rest and replenish—"

"Why are you in our waters, young Elān of Samish?"

"We have been charged by the Hits'aati of Naasteidi to reconnoiter Éil' from Samish Island to Latseen's Line, to assess the strength and numbers of the Koosh and their movement, and to determine which villages still remain extant and which, unfortunately, have been destroyed and displaced, upon which we are to return said news to Naasteidi with the greatest dispatch."

The warrior chuckled and took off her helmet. She had long, dark brown hair streaked with gray pulled loosely back behind her head. "You sound more bookeater than warrior. Is that the nonsense they teach in your Longhouse of War, or has your sea-road addled your brains?"

Raven cawed in laughter atop his mast-nest.

"We're surveying the damage the Koosh have done," Elān said. "Koosh canoes have been spotted across Aaní waters. The elders of Naasteidi charged us to do reconnaissance around Éil' and return with the greatest dispatch."

"Just learn the word *dispatch*, did you?" the warrior asked. Her Deikeenaa crew and raven laughed. "Why not send a messenger bird? Why send a crew in small canoe?"

"Naasteidi has sent birds, but some haven't returned and the information they did return with couldn't be verified," Elān said. "So, they outfitted us with this canoe. It can outrun any Koosh canoe."

"With the help of a Koosh sail, I see," the warrior said.

Elān was taken aback. The warrior was observant. Sea negotiations for entry into a strange village were always delicate. Elān didn't want to give too much information, but he really wanted to visit Choosh. From the sea it looked to be larger than any village he'd ever seen. "We were attacked by a Koosh canoe near Xoots Jin. We burned it and took its sail."

"If it were that easy," the warrior replied, "for a meager crew to defeat and burn a Koosh canoe, we wouldn't have a Koosh problem." The warrior put her helmet back on. Her crew readied their paddles. "You have no cause to be untruthful. The Deikeenaa and Aaní have been allies from time immemorial. Yet I have received nothing but dishonesty from you. You're not welcome in Choosh. Depart and you won't be harmed. Come close to our gates and we'll torch you and your canoe to ashes." She sat down and the warriors started paddling.

Elān's stomach sunk. He wasn't being untruthful, he just wasn't offering *all* the truth. He quickly decided to offer a bit more. As the Deikeenaa canoe turned toward the sea wall, he yelled out, "The Xoots of Xoots Jin helped us destroy the Koosh and his slaves."

Nothing. The Deikeenaa canoe kept going. Elān decided to offer another parcel of truth—but he wouldn't offer any more. If it didn't work, they'd have to continue their journey without seeing Choosh.

"With the Xoots' help we killed the Koosh and raided his canoe," Elān yelled to the departing canoe. "I took his navigation map but I can't read it. I thought someone in Choosh might be able to read it."

The warrior in the front of the Deikeenaa canoe held up her hand. Her companions turned the canoe around and came back to *Waka*. She stood up and took her helmet off. "Show me the map."

Elān grabbed the Koosh map from the storage box and held it up. The warriors in the Deikeenaa canoe murmured, but Elān couldn't hear what they said. "There's symbols and writing I can't decipher," Elān said. "And I wasn't being untruthful. All I said has been truth, but guarded truth. We ran into trouble in Deshu because I didn't guard the truth. They stole my grandfather's flicker tail coin-mail armor, so I now guard the truth. I story the truth."

The murmuring stopped. The warriors lifted their helmeted heads and looked directly at Elān. He could see their eyes narrowed behind their visors. "Flicker tail coin-mail. That means you are of the Flicker clan of Naasteidi?" the standing warrior said, more to herself than to Elān. "Who was your grandfather?"

"Latseen of Samish Island."

There was a pause. "Is this true?" the warrior asked Elān's crew.

"No, it's not true. His name is Crapshack of the Metal

Diaper clan." The sound of raven's cawing laughter broke the tension a little.

"I see Aaní ravens are no more helpful than Deikeenaa ravens," the warrior replied.

"Look," one of the Deikeenaa crew said, pointing to Elān's paddle. "A Flicker paddle."

"May I speak?" Caraiden asked Elān.

"Of course," Elān said.

"Everything Elān has told you is true," Caraiden told the Deikeenaa warrior. "We destroyed a Koosh and burned his canoe, and Elān's grandfather is indeed the famous Latseen who led the combined Aaní and Deikeenaa forces that crushed the Yahooni, the same Latseen who signed the treaty here many winters ago that established the line that bears his name to this day. I was with him in that war and at the treaty signing. Choosh didn't have a sea wall or sea gate then. And the Deikeenaa were more welcoming."

"I too was in that war and at that treaty signing," the Deikeenaa warrior said. She looked long at Elān, and then put her helmet back on. "Stay right behind us in our wake and we'll lead you through the sea gates. You're all welcome to come ashore at Choosh."

CHAPTER 26

CHOOSH WAS AS overwhelming as Caraiden had described. The sea gate opened as the Deikeenaa canoe approached with *Waka* in its wake. Once through the sea gate, Elān beheld a massive village of stone carved into the cliffs. It was alive with Deikeenaa villagers. On the beach in front of the cliffs sat a series of low, wooden longhouses and a large open-air market. The Deikeenaa canoe led *Waka* through the bay and up to the beach in front of a carved longhouse painted black and red on the far edge of the village. When the Deikeenaa canoe beached, the warrior who'd interrogated Elān jumped out and pulled *Waka* ashore. "I'm Xuut, captain of the Choosh Sea Guard."

"Your ancestors," Elān said.

"And yours," Xuut replied. "This is the Harbor Master's longhouse," she said, indicating the carved building. "You can make your welcome, register your crew and canoe, and they can suggest some lodgings and pubs, if you have coin. If not, you're welcome to sleep on your canoe here. There's a longhouse a short ways down the beach for those in need of food but light of coin. But I'd wager if you mention your grandfather's name to any of the old timers in the village, they'll buy you all the food and ale you can hold. He's remembered fondly. There's a statue of him on level five in front of the longhouse where the treaty was signed. You need to go see it. He brought us many winters of peace from the Yahooni."

"Thank you, I will," Elān said. "And we've a bit of coin and can find lodgings in the village."

"My shift isn't over until after sundown but with your permission I'd like call a meeting of the Choosh Sea Guard and Upland Guard, and our Aankaawu and Hits'aati, and have a look at that Koosh map. We'd also like to hear your tale. We can inform you of what we know about Koosh movements, and you can inform your leaders on Samish Island. Maybe we can meet tomorrow after you and your crew have rested and supped. You plan on staying more than one night?"

"We'll stay two nights," Elān said. "And it'd be my honor to meet with you and the leaders of Choosh tomorrow night."

"Send word to the Harbor Master, then, about where you'll be staying, and I'll send word about the meeting."

AFTER SEVERAL WELCOMING songs back and forth between the Harbor Master and his deputies and Elān and his crew, Elān registered *Waka* and the crew members' names in the Harbor Master's log and paid a small canoe beaching fee. The Harbor Master recommended several pubs with lodgings in the village. Pubs grew more expensive the higher up the cliff they were. Elān wanted to lodge in a high-level pub, where he could get a bird's cloud-eyes view of the ocean, but Caraiden pointed out it might be best to lodge in a lower pub with quicker access to *Waka* in case of trouble. Hoosa would stay aboard *Waka*—he didn't like sleeping indoors. Chetdyl and raven, too, would stay aboard *Waka*. Hoosa would make sure they got fed.

They checked their weapons in with the Harbor Master for, like Aaní territory, no weapons were allowed in Deikeenaa villages. Then Kwa, Caraiden, and Ch'eet fetched their seabags and coinage from *Waka*—Elān grabbed his seabag, lockbox, and the Koosh Tas, said their goodbyes to Hoosa and Chetdyl, then walked the cobbled road behind the rows of longhouses toward the cliffs. The received a few "Your ancestors" from various Deikeenaa walking along the road, but mostly they received strange looks. Elān wondered how often Aaní visitors came to Choosh. And, of course, their clothes were dirty and crusted with sea salt and smelled ripe and foul.

A set of stairs carved into the cliff led from the road up to the village proper. They walked up the stairs into a rock tunnel, lit by lanterns hanging from the ceiling, that took them deep into the cliff. Around a long corner, another set of stairs took them up and back out toward the sea; once again back into and out of the cliff and they were at the first level of the village. The ceiling of the first level, which was the floor of the second level, was about forty, fifty feet high, but it fell in a gentle downward slope as it ran into the cliff. It was difficult to tell how far back the first level went, but it appeared to be as large as the entire village of Naasteidi. Cobbled roads led to stone houses that looked like residences, wooden longhouses that looked like business or government buildings, and restaurants, pubs, shops, and open areas with greenery and benches. There was natural light coming in from the oceanside, and lanterns hung on street poles lit the village as it went deeper and darker into the cliff.

Elān walked to the outer edge of the first level—a parapet kept people from falling onto the beach below—and looked up. He counted eight more levels. Each level, it appeared, had stairway access on either side. They ascended another level, and another. Each time they walked to the parapet and looked out over the ocean. At the third level, Elān leaned against the parapet and looked down and up. The height made his stomach flutter. "We should stay on level five," he told the crew. "Do you recall what pub you stayed at with my grandfather?" Elān asked Caraiden.

"We stayed in the Hits'aati's residence somewhere near the top level," Caraiden said. "But a statue to your grandfather is a good sign. We should stay on level five."

Up two more levels, high above the ocean, Elān reached the top of the stairs and looked out over the world below. He thought he could see *Waka* far off on the beach to the left. He turned and looked at the village on level five. It was much like the villages on the lower levels, but it had fewer small, stone homes. The stone buildings were large with pillars beside their entryways and statues out front. "This must be the administrative level," Elān said. Many of the Deikeenaa villagers on this level, hurrying to and fro, wore the formal, non-battle armor of administrators and longhouse worker ranks.

Down the cobbled road which ran alongside the parapet, Elān could see what looked to be a pub—it had an awning sign of two eagles' talons in the shape of fishhooks. It was called the Talons, and was one of the slightly more expensive of the mid-level pubs due to its location near the parapet. Large, colored glass windows ran along the front of the pub, allowing for natural light from the sea. Elān opened the door and walked in. "Your ancestors," said the man behind the bar without looking up. He was washing pint glasses in a tub of steaming water.

"And yours," Elān said. "Have you any rooms?"

The man looked up. "We don't get many boarders these days," he said. "Especially Aaní from the northwest, if I got your accent right. Yes, we've plenty of rooms."

"Can we have four rooms?"

"Sure," the pub man said. "How many nights you plan on staying?"

"At least two," Elān said. As the pub man studied Elān and his crew, his forehead wrinkled and his eyes narrowed. "We'll pay ahead of time for two nights."

Of course, the pub man grew very friendly when Kwa laid out enough coin for two nights. He grabbed four room keys from behind the bar and assigned each of them rooms. "Welcome to the Talons of Choosh. You can lock your things in your rooms and explore Choosh, though we have very little theft and your things are as safe unlocked as they are locked. Supper starts an hour before sundown, but you can get an ale whenever you'd like. Xaal's my name. Let me know if you need anything."

The crew took their keys, agreeing to meet around sundown for supper. Elān opened the door to his room. It was on the parapet side of the pub. Light poured through the colored glass of the window, making his room glow in reds, blues, and yellows. The room had a large bed, a seat and desk with a mirror above it, and—in a small, attached room with a screen for privacy—a large stone washtub with two pipes pointing into it from above and one pipe leading into the floor below. He'd never seen such a thing. The pipes pointing into the tub had handles on them. He turned one of the handles and water gushed out into the tub. Cold, cold, water. He turned the handle on the other pipe and hot water whooshed steaming into the tub.

Elān bathed for the first time in days. Glorious. He washed his sea clothes the best he could and hung them around the room to dry. A thick layer of dirt lined the bottom of the tub when he was done. He sat at the desk and looked at himself in the mirror. The sun had darkened his face. He looked older. Or, perhaps, more weathered. A not-so-thick beard had grown. He decided not to shave it off. It made him look more mature, more like a warrior. He took his quill and inkpot and paper out and wrote his parents a short letter. He left out all the details and dangers of his journey. Those could wait until he met them again in person. He wasn't sure where he could send it from. He'd keep it with him until he found a canoe headed to Samish.

Clean, washed, and wearing his shore clothes, Elān locked his door and walked out into the pub. He pulled a stool up to the long wooden bar. "Could I get a mug of ale?"

"Sure thing," Xaal said. He fetched a pint glass from the shelf and pumped frothy ale into it. "If you don't mind my asking, what's your name and where you from?"

"My name is Elān and I'm from Naasteidi on Samish Island," he said.

"Ah, Naasteidi. That's where the great Latseen was born." Xaal set the ale in front of Elān.

"Yes," Elān said. "I heard he has a statue on this level." He took a long drink of ale. It was cool and heavy and tasted wonderful.

"Yes, not far. Two roads over and then straight back into the cliff about three roads. It's in front of the longhouse where he signed the treaty. I was there that day, just a young kid. I got to see the great Latseen from a distance as he entered the longhouse with the defeated Yahooni contingent. That was the last time any Yahooni dared set foot on Kasaan."

"The older warrior who is with me was here that day, too," Elān said. "He was a member of Latseen's personal guard at the time."

"Those were better days," Xaal said. "May they come again."

Elān held up his pint of ale. "May they come again."

"Your ancestors," Xaal said.

"And yours."

Elān finished his pint and walked outside. The shadows inside the cliff village grew long. He wanted to go all the way to the top level to see the upland, where there was a lake and gluuch field atop the cliffs, but he decided to return to the Harbor Master and check in on Hoosa and Chetdyl. They lounged on *Waka*'s netting, enjoying the last shadows of the setting sun. The evening was even more pleasant, Hoosa said, because raven was not around. He'd gone to the open-air market to steal his supper.

When Elān returned to level five, he was astonished to see a rather average occurrence for the Choosh Deikeenaa: the villagers had pulled chairs and tables up to the parapet and sat looking out over the sea, laughing, singing, playing music, and drinking. He walked toward the Talons and saw his crewmates around a table at the parapet in front of the pub. They had pints and large bowls of steaming food. They wore their shore clothes; Caraiden and Ch'eet had shaved, their faces shone red, and by the volume of their voices Elān could tell that they were on their second pints.

"There he is," Ch'eet yelled out as Elān approached. "Our peerless captain, our whale-road companion, our sail spinner." He hefted his ale and clinked glasses with Caraiden and Kwa.

"Have a seat," Caraiden said. He kicked a chair out from the table and Elān sat down.

Even Kwa was jovial. "I saved you a pint and a bowl of seafood chowder." She passed him a full ale glass and pushed a bowl in front of him. It smelled delicious. Elān downed the ale and devoured the chowder.

"By Yéil," Elān said, "this is the greatest village I've ever seen."

Kwa laughed and kicked his leg with her moccasined foot. It was the first time Elān had really heard Kwa laugh. Her laugh was bright, uncontrolled, and different from what Elān expected. "And how many villages have your visited in your short life, young Elān of Naasteidi?"

Elān smiled. "Not many."

Kwa laughed again. "I've seen many villages. They all look the same. I thought Naakw the greatest village in all of Éil', but even Naakw cannot compare to this village."

Shame surged through Elān. "I'm sorry I wanted to leave you behind at Naakw."

Kwa smiled. "I understand. We've both wanted to leave each other behind a time or two on this voyage. It is hard for me to be patient and generous around bookeaters, and I was wrong to question your captaincy."

"I was wrong to try to leave you behind at Naakw," Elān said. "We need you and your sword and bow. I need you."

"Gunalchéesh," Kwa replied. "And I can admit you have done well, Elān, ever since leaving Deshu. Perhaps I can find some admiration for a young bookeater who wants to be a warrior. We may understand each other's stories yet, young Elān."

"Your ancestors."

"And yours," Kwa said. She looked into Elān's eyes. "So, I ask you one more time to tell me the truth of why we are on this journey."

Elān looked around the table. Caraiden and Ch'eet were deep in ale-fueled conversation about the wonders of Choosh. The sun had disappeared beyond the cliff and lamplighters were lighting lanterns along the parapet. "Look at me," Kwa said to Elān. He peered into Kwa's eyes. "Why are we on this journey?"

Elān knew he could not make up another story again, for Kwa was far too perceptive. He fought the temptation to tell her everything and sighed. "Íxt made me promise not to tell anyone." He held Kwa's eyes with his for a long moment but could not outstare her. He turned away.

"I can see that's the truth," Kwa replied. "I respect Íxt's wish, since he's our island's elder and an over-the-edger, but I worry your storytelling has convinced him to send you to someplace you are not prepared for. You're a skilled storyteller, and I don't entirely mean that as a compliment."

"I won't entirely say gunalchéesh, then," Elān replied.

Kwa laughed. "I bet your storytelling has got you in and out of trouble at Naasteidi, hasn't it? Your story about updating maps is a good one. Use it if anybody asks about our journey. But don't say you're updating military maps. Say that you're updating maps for your bookeater longhouse. That's more believable."

"That's a good suggestion."

"I bet the stupid raven has something to do with this journey, doesn't he?"

"Yes," Elān replied.

"That worries me even more," Kwa said. She released his stare and looked out over the parapet. "But I won't ask again.

I will protect you and if possible see you home safe." She hefted her mug of ale and took a long drink.

Elān looked around the table at his crew. He felt an indescribable bond with them, and wondered if they felt it for him in return. *This is what I am missing in Naasteidi,* he thought to himself. *The feeling that I belong.* He smiled at Caraiden, Kwa, and Ch'eet. Ch'eet caught Elān's smile and smiled back.

"I didn't know people could build a village like this," he said. "I say we end our journey and stay here."

"Yes," Elān agreed. He'd like nothing more than to stay a long while in Choosh. "Maybe I can do my kwalk here," he said to his crew. "Would they let me do my kwalk in Deikeenaa territory?"

"I don't see why they wouldn't," Caraiden said. His graying hair appeared almost youthful in the lantern light. "I'll do a second kwalk with you here."

Ch'eet laughed. "Me too. Let's all do a kwalk here. We can work at the Talons. Hello! Xaal, my dear friend, do you need any workers? We'd like jobs here. We could wash dishes, rough up unpaid boarders, sample ales for quality." Xaal had come out to collect bowls and refill pints.

"Sadly, no," Xaal said. "We don't get many boarders with all this Koosh nonsense going on. I can barely afford the cook on payroll. And I take care of serving drinks. It's mostly cliff folk and uplanders here nowadays. Enough to keep me and the cook, but not other workers."

The mention of the Koosh brought the crew back to reality. As Xaal returned to the pub with an armful of empty bowls, Elān followed him in and went to his room to grab the Koosh Tas. He brought it back outside and pulled it from its case. The flickering yellow lantern light brought out the carvings on the Tas's body. Elān plucked a few notes and the crew fell quiet. He could play a few songs on the four-string Tas back home, but the six-string

Koosh instrument would take some time to learn. He wasn't even sure how to tune it. He tuned the bottom four strings the same as he did an Aaní Tas and strummed a haunting three-beat Aaní sea-road chant. Some of the tables nearby stopped their conversations and listened as Elán played and sang. Nobody here, Elán realized as he was strumming, had ever heard this strange Koosh instrument. Even Xaal, who returned with full pints, placed the ales on the table and stood enrapt, caught in the net of the mournful melody and bright sound of the Koosh instrument.

Elán let the last note of the song sustain before bringing his palm down on the strings to end the song. He enjoyed the smiles of his crew and how he was able to capture them with music. The tables around returned to quiet conversation.

Kwa stood. "I need some sleep."

"We should all get some sleep," Caraiden said. "We'll be busy tomorrow." He leaned over to Elán and whispered, "You play well. But I wouldn't get too comfortable with the Koosh's things."

CHAPTER 27

Two hours before sunset the next day, the crew made their way to Choosh's Longhouse of War and Diplomacy. It was a beautifully carved, massive wooden longhouse on level nine. They were welcomed into the longhouse with song, and Elān and his crew sang an Aaní song in return. They sat on the visitor's side of the longhouse's council fire, and so began the long introductions that included recounting the ancestors of every person present. Xuut spoke for the Deikeenaa and Elān spoke for the Aaní. Elān recounted the ancestors of his crew the best he could, but he didn't know Hoosa or Chetdyl's ancestors, so unfortunately had to omit them. He then recounted his personal ancestry and reluctantly mentioned Latseen.

Elān couldn't recount his ancestors without mentioning Latseen. A murmur went through the gathered crowd when he said he was Latseen's grandson of the Flicker clan from Naasteidi. Elān also added that he was studying to become a teacher like his father, Skaan. He hoped that would dampen the Choosh villagers' expectations that he was the reincarnation of some great warrior, come to destroy the Koosh single-handed. After introductions, each side shared a story from *looong* ago. With the formal welcome ceremony over, the business commenced.

"Thank you for being willing to meet with us," Xuut said. "If you could produce your Koosh map, and if we have your permission, we have a team of language scholars including etymologists here"—a group of Deikeenaa sitting on the Choosh side of the longhouse stood up—"and we've asked them to make a copy of the map."

"That's fine," Elān said. He gave the map to Xuut.

"Thank you. As they're working with the map, perhaps you could tell those of us gathered about your journey."

Elān stood up and faced the audience in the Choosh section. Members of the Sea Guard and Upland Guard sat near the council fire, as did the Hits'aati, Aankaawu, and a host of other village officials and military leaders. Elān told the story of their journey in its entirety since leaving Samish Island. It took over an hour in the telling. Afterward, the Deikeenaa leaders had many questions for Elān and the crew.

"What did it feel like when you ran your sword through the Koosh?" one of the Sea Guard asked Caraiden.

"It went through as it would a human," Caraiden said. "Its armor is strange and strong, unlike any armor in this world that I am aware of. But its flesh, if that is what we can call its body, is as easily punctured as a human's."

"Was it dead then, or did it not die until you cut its head off?"

"It happened so fast I couldn't say for certain. It was certainly dead without its head."

The Hits'aati, who'd been busy taking notes, said to Elān, "We built the sea wall and gate to keep the Koosh at bay and off land. We built it with a network of underwater pipes. We can flood the area in front of the entire sea wall with oil and set it alight. We've burned five Koosh canoes this way. You've destroyed one, and Yelm has destroyed one. That's seven Koosh canoes that we know of. You say the Yahooni slave, this man called Goox, told you there are how many Koosh canoes?"

"He didn't know for certain," Elān said. "He said he'd seen fifty."

"We've heard the Koosh can't die on land and that they can only be drowned, but you say you killed one on the shore— though he was standing in water," the Hits'aati continued. "We also heard their dzanti can't work at sea, but Goox told you they used the dzanti to destroy Yahooni villages."

"I didn't think to ask him if they destroyed his village from sea or from aboard a Koosh ship or if they came on land. I wish I had asked Goox before he died. Now it's a question we need to have answered before we can defeat the Koosh," Elān said.

"So much is uncertain. If the Koosh can use the dzanti at sea, why don't they destroy our villages from the sea? Why haven't the Koosh used them against Choosh outside our sea wall?"

"I don't know," Elān said. "Goox told me they don't have many dzanti. The Koosh don't or can't make them. They come from the otherworld. Goox said he'd only seen one. Maybe there's only one and they've been busy using it elsewhere. Maybe you burned their ships before they could use that dzanti. We were sent from Naasteidi to gather knowledge, but I think we've gathered more questions than answers."

"We thank you for all this gathered knowledge you've provided us with," the Aankaawu said. "One large unanswered question still looms for me, though. What in Yaahl's name is the purpose of your journey? Why send a bookeater as captain to gather information about such dangerous enemies?"

Elān remained standing and looked at Kwa. He drew a deep, dramatic breath and asked Kwa, "Shall I tell them?" *Play along*, Elān begged Kwa in his mind. *Please play along.*

Kwa played her part. "The Deikeenaa have been our allies since time immemorial," she said to Elān. "They fought for your grandfather. Trust them, Elān, for they have as much to lose as we do."

Elān nodded and paused a long moment. "My friends," he addressed the audience, "we travel to the mainland from Botson's Bay up to our cousins at the Far Out Fort." Gasps erupted from the audience. "Yes, I tell you the truth. You may have heard of the great Snaa<u>k</u> at Naasteidi, scholar of languages and cultures of Éil'. I'm his apprentice and cartographer, which is why the Koosh map is of great interest to me. Snaa<u>k</u> and our Aaní Islands Elders' Council have tasked me with fulfilling the purpose of this journey. If asked, I'm to say I'm updating maps for my Longhouse of Service and Trade. Fathom markings, new settlements, geographical features, and such things."

Elān lowered his voice. The audience strained to listen. "The truth is, my friends, I'm charting all the Koosh incursions and settlements on the mainland so we can update our maps and plan an invasion. We heard there was a vicious battle at Botson's Bay and the Koosh have settled there, which is why I travel in a swift military canoe with warriors to guard me. I may be a good cartographer and bookeater, but I'm no warrior." Elān laughed, and the audience responded with laughter. "Trust me, my friends, I will present our gathered knowledge of all the Koosh settlements, both temporary and permanent, to the Aaní Islands Elders' Council and they will devise a plan to invade and defeat the Koosh. Our leaders will send messengers to Choosh and other Deikeenaa villages so we can coordinate battle plans. The Aaní are forever allied with the Deikeenaa, and I am here to honor the memory of my grandfather, Latseen. This, my friends, is the true purpose of our journey."

Elān looked at the audience and then at the Aankaawu. *They all believe me,* Elān thought to himself as he stared into their trusting eyes. With Kwa's help, he had entangled his Deikeenaa audience in his word-netting. He felt a strong urge to spin more stories, outlandish stories, and further enmesh the audience, taking them on a story journey into the depths of the mainland where no Aaní had ever traveled. *Why wouldn't they believe that the Aaní Islands Elders' Council charged me with exploring the mainland?* Elān thought to himself. He looked at Kwa. Her eyes told him to remain silent. He fought the urge to continue storycrafting and sat down beside his crew at the council fire. The Deikeenaa audience stood in response and thanked him, thanked Latseen, and thanked the Aaní for taking the lead in the coming war against the Koosh.

If storytelling is to be my strength, Elān thought to himself, acknowledging the audience appreciation with a wave of his hand, *I will train in it like a warrior, and tonight I just learned my first lesson: knowing when to shut up.* He smiled at Kwa. She smiled back.

"Thank you, young Elān, for this information and for honoring your ancestors," the Aankaawu said. He addressed those gathered in the hall. "Let it be known that young Elān and his entire crew have a forever-welcome at Choosh." He looked at Elān. "You may return and be welcomed in Choosh whenever you desire."

"Gunalchéesh," Elān said.

The Aankaawu turned to Xuut. "And, Xuut, you will see that young Elān receives our Choosh tináa, yes?"

"Of course," Xuut said.

A *tináa* is a miniature shield, usually made of copper or sometimes silver, given as a gift among the Aaní and Deikeenaa. When carved with the image or name of a village, a tináa can also be used across Éil' as you would use a passport in your world, for entrance into villages, Kwáans, and longhouses.

"Don't stray too far into Botson's Bay," the Hits'aati warned Elān. "Our chaatl fishermen who've approached Botson's Bay report that the cannibal giants are enslaved to the Koosh. They now refuse to fish there. Chaatl fish is scarce now and expensive in Choosh. Stay well away from shore and turn northward early."

Xuut handed the Koosh map back to Elān. "Thank you for this," Xuut said. "We have copied all the writing on it."

Elān looked at the table of orthographers. "Can you decipher it?" he asked.

"Not yet," one said. "But we can compare the writing on the Koosh map to the known names on our maps and begin to learn the Koosh writing system. Even though you say you've gathered more questions than answers, this map and the information on it may lead to more answers than you can imagine. If we learn the secrets of this map, we'll be sure to send message to our Aaní allies in the north. Please return the favor if you decipher the map. Victory will come again from the Flicker clan of Samish. Together with your grandfather, we defeated the Yahooni. Together with the help of Latseen's grandson, we'll defeat the Koosh."

THE NEXT MORNING Elān was up with the sun. He put on his sea clothes and packed his bag, and went into the pub. It was dark in the pub's dining room. Xaal wasn't yet up. Elān unlocked the front door and walked outside. It took him about ten minutes to find what he was looking for. He took his quill, inkpot, and a piece of paper from his sea coat and sat down in front of the statue and began to sketch the stone representation of his grandfather. He would tell his parents about the statue and give them the sketch. He didn't know if it was a good likeness of his grandfather or not—he'd only seen him in drawings.

His grandfather became a warrior at the age of twelve and had distinguished himself in battle before he was twenty. He traveled the world protecting the Aaní people. When the Island and Mainland Yahooni decided to invade all Éil' and make slaves of every human, his grandfather organized the Deikeenaa and Aaní forces, crushed the Yahooni invasions, attacked and destroyed the Yahooni fortresses on the mainland, and forced their surrender here at the very longhouse Elān now sat in front of, sketching his likeness. It was now a different world. The Koosh were not the Yahooni.

Footsteps echoed along the cobbled road from the oceanside of the village. Caraiden was dressed in his sea clothes making his way toward Elān. "Thought you might be here," he said. He looked at the statue. "Doesn't quite capture him, does it?"

"I don't know," Elān said. "I never met him."

"There was more life in his face," Caraiden said.

"It *is* made of stone."

The old warrior chuckled. "I mean it doesn't capture the love of life, his mischief or sense of play. He wasn't a reserved, quiet, or proper man. He was full of fire and loved being alive. He didn't do what people expected of him. You got that from him."

"Me?" Elān said in disbelief. "He was a warrior. Warriors always love life because they can lose it so quick. I'm a bookeater, as Kwa would say."

"No, your grandfather was a warrior on the outside," Caraiden said. "It was a skin he wore, an armor he put on to command his warriors. But on the inside, he too was a bookeater, though he was smarter than any teacher. He outthought his enemies. His mind was unpredictable. He storied out possibilities and potential endings and even claimed he heard a voice in his head that gave him direction during his more dire times. I don't know how to put it, other than he thought differently from any other man I've met. You're a bit like him in that way. Maybe you're a bookeater on the outside and a warrior on the inside. The opposite of your granddad."

"Or maybe I'm a warrior at storytelling," Elān said.

Caraiden laughed. "Yes, and that also describes your grandfather."

"The Deikeenaa here in Choosh sure think I'm a warrior like my grandfather," Elān mused.

"No need to tell them otherwise, then," Caraiden said. "If it gives them hope to think Latseen's grandson will save them, let them have their hope."

Elān didn't agree with the old warrior, but out of respect he didn't voice his disagreement. He held his sketch up to the statue. It was close enough. He folded the sketch and put it in his sea coat. He stood up and looked at Caraiden. "I'm ready now. Let's wake the others. It's time to finish our journey."

CHAPTER 28

AT FIRST, IT felt good to be at *Waka*'s tiller, cutting south toward Botson's Bay. But the sunrise soon gave way to clouds that looked as though they were swollen with rain. Cloudy weather on the sea, as you may know, often means windy weather. Xuut had given Elān a fine copper tináa about the size of his palm, etched with the cliffs of Choosh, and then led them out of the sea gate earlier that morning with promises that they'd always be welcome back in Choosh. Elān promised they'd send word to Xuut about what they found on their journey back to Samish. He put the tináa in his lockbox. As they pulled away from the sea gate, Xuut sang them a sea charm song, a song to calm the sea, but soon the wind rose and the sky grew cloudy, and large, white-frothed waves rolled in starboard and rocked the crew in a constant unbalance. Chetdyl had to get down onto the floor of the canoe to keep from falling overboard off his bow perch.

"That hideous Xuut must have sung an anti-charm song," raven yelled.

As Choosh disappeared from view, the ocean grew more violent, lifting *Waka* high on crests and slamming it down into wave-valleys. Elān feared the outriggers would be ripped from *Waka*'s body. He had to be steady with the tiller and quick with the mainsail sheet to collect and spill wind. Shoved by a strong wind from the stern, every time *Waka* climbed to the top of a mountainous wave, gales pulsing into the bow ripped at the sails and threatened to turn the canoe sideways in the deep troughs between waves—which, as you know, is dangerous and an easy way to capsize a sailing canoe. You may also know, if you're of the sea, that outriggers become a hindrance instead of a help if caught sideways in between huge waves. Elān struggled to keep the outriggers and prow of *Waka* forward as it climbed up the steep backs of waves, and then struggled to slack the sails just enough as the canoe crested and fell down wave faces. The rest of the crew labored in repetitious motion, bailing seawater from the canoe floor and tossing it overboard.

Ch'eet sang an Aaní sea charm. He had to yell to be heard over the noise of the ocean and wind. Kwa and Caraiden joined in, chanting the song together in time with their bailing. It was an ancient sea charm begging the waves to fall asleep. Whatever turmoil angered the ocean, the Aaní sea charm said, could be pacified by the lulling motions of a calm sea. Elān, soothed by the repetition of the sound, joined in the song full-throated and unrestrained. The sea charm coaxed his conscious mind away from the tension of captaining in heavy seas and fixed his thoughts on being one with his crewmates. As natural as the wind, the sea charm turned into a round: one of the crew waited for a verse to pass by before starting the song over, then another waited a verse, and another. Soon, four voices sang different rounds in a harmony that echoed inside *Waka*. As naturally as they had separated into rounds, the singers wove the song back together, as if braiding a rope.

Soaked through but lifted by song, the crew toiled through the morning and *Waka* withstood the battering. By the time the sun sat above, the sea had fallen calm and leveled out, and the crew braided the sea charm song into an ending. The sun broke through barred clouds and a steady wind pushed *Waka* toward the mainland. Elān fastened the mainsail sheet, locked the tiller, and rested with his back against the stern. He was drenched to the skin.

"I have been in heavy seas many times, Elān," Kwa said, "but I have never seen anyone as young as you, bookeater or warrior, captain a canoe that well. Our lives were in your tiller and sheet hands. You should be proud." Sea water dripped from her hair and armor.

"We should be proud, Kwa," Caraiden said, "to have him as captain. Well done, Elān. I could have sworn it was your grandfather I saw, not you, guiding *Waka* through the storm."

Raven cackled.

"Gunalchéesh," Elān said. "It was the sea charm. I can't explain it, but somehow that song gave me courage when I needed it."

"That's an old, traditional sea charm," Caraiden said. "It comes from our ancestors of *looong* ago."

"Those traditional songs always work," Ch'eet said.

Raven laughed.

Kwa smacked the mast and looked up at raven's nest. "Why do you mock us, stupid bird?"

"The sea is calm at times and violent at times," raven replied. "And both at the same time, regardless of what silly traditional song you stupid Aaní sing. Tradition is like pictures drawn in the sand at low tide. And Crapshack here is the incoming tide. Isn't that true, Fathead?"

"Shut up, bird," Elān said. The crew stared at Elān as though wanting an explanation. Raven laughed and disappeared into his nest.

"I respect tradition," Elān murmured. "I just wonder sometimes where it came from."

"Stories from our ancestors of *looong* ago," Kwa said.

"So, our ancestors of *looong* ago created tradition. Why can't we do the same now?"

Kwa laughed. "And what new tradition would you create, young Elān?"

Elān hesitated, unsure if he should speak the truth of his thoughts. "Only this," he said. "I would let any Aaní become who they want to become at any time, no matter their age or what others want them to become."

Kwa laughed. Caraiden and Ch'eet laughed too. "That's all?" Kwa said. "You'd throw into the fire almost all of our old stories and traditions?"

"No," Elān said. "I just want to create a new story or two."

"Storycrafting is part of tradition too," Caraiden said. "There's nothing in tradition that prohibits new stories." The old warrior gave Elān a slight smile. *Don't push this conversation too far,* his smile seemed to say, *or you might not like where it ends.*

Raven laughed.

Elān unlocked the tiller. "Very true, Caraiden," Elān replied. "Ignore the stupid bird. Let's set to sailing. Control that jib, Ch'eet. Kwa, Caraiden, and Hoosa, get back to bailing. *Waka* is still flooded up to our ankles."

Caraiden's smile grew. He nodded at Elān's orders and hefted his wooden bailer.

THEY SAILED ALL day into dusk along the western side of Jinahaa Island—the last island they'd encounter before Botson's Bay on the mainland. Rain drizzled the entire journey. The crew stayed wrapped in their sea coats and waterproofed sea hats. Shortly before the sun set behind the dark clouds to the west, Elān pulled *Waka* into a cove near the southern end of Jinahaa. They'd spend the night in the wild and plan for the next day's journey into Botson's Bay. They tied the spare sail in the trees above them and sat under its shelter out of the rain. Shortly after sundown, the rain stopped and the clouds broke. The moon and stars came through. The crew spread their bedrolls under the sail in case the rains returned.

Though they had not asked directly, as Botson's Bay drew close, Elān sensed the crew wondering about the purpose behind going there. He thought about telling them the truth, but had held back for some reason he couldn't express. He had to admit there was part of him that enjoyed having secret knowledge. Raven knew about the dzanti, of course, but hadn't revealed the secret. In fact, raven fell quiet as they grew closer to Botson's Bay, staying within the recess of his mast-nest.

"Raven and I will take first watch," Elān said. The crew agreed without hesitating. Elān took a lantern with him—the beach was rocky and treacherous—and walked downwind a ways from the crew. He stepped back into the trees and sat on the damp ground underneath a massive cedar tree. Raven sat in the beach grass nearby. "When we get to Botson's Bay, I need you to show me where it is."

"Where what is?" raven asked.

"It."

"What?"

"You know what I mean," Elān said.

"I have no clue what goes through your feeble, crap mind," raven replied.

"Quit fooling. This is serious. Show me where to find the dzanti."

"Do you have your map?" raven asked. Elān brought out his map and spread it across the beach. He opened the shutter of the lantern a sliver to spill light onto it. Raven looked over the map. "It's here." He pushed his beak straight through the map.

"Why did you have to do that?" Elān said. "You could have pointed with your beak." He peered at the point raven had punctured.

You can see Botson's Bay by making a U shape with your index finger and thumb on your right hand. Now turn the opening northwestward. Inside that U is the sea. Your fingernails are peninsulas out into the ocean—your thumb fingernail the southern, your index fingernail the northern.

To sail across from fingernail to fingernail takes about fifteen, twenty minutes with a strong wind. From your fingernails down to your hand are heavily forested seafronts leading to the mainland behind. The fleshy web between your index finger and thumb are rocky ledges, and off the middle of that web is where the dzanti lies, according to raven.

"That's where it is? Offshore in the middle of Botson's Bay and not on the northern or southern peninsulas?"

"Right in the middle. And it's not on the beach," raven said. "There are rock ledges all around that area. When I last saw it, it was deep underwater. It glows. A bluish-white light. The color of xaax'w fish flesh. We should try to retrieve it at night. I'll fly across the bay and see if I can locate it again. If it's still there, I'll let you know. If the giants are around, we shouldn't go ashore. We should keep the canoe in the bay and you can swim in and get it. I doubt a craphead like you could even touch it, though. I flew down next to it, tried to pick it up and it knocked me senseless."

"We'll approach it at night then," Elān said. "How long would it take you to fly there tonight? You could surveil the area for us and meet us at sea on our way there."

"Have you lost the last bit of wits in your craphead?" raven replied. "It's nearly a seet's distance from here to Botson's Bay. Look at your map. It's eight yaakw. Eight hours sailing with a good wind. And unlike a canoe, I need to take bath breaks, crap breaks, meal breaks, rest breaks, and what happens if I meet another raven of amorous intent? Fly there yourself if you want it surveilled."

"Okay, but I want you to be our cloud-eyes when we get close," Elān said. "Our approach all depends on the wind. Since it's late spring, I expect it'll still be running southerly as it has most of our journey. We'll approach Botson's Bay from the north. But if early summer northern winds come tomorrow, we'll approach from the south. I want you in the air the second we see either peninsula leading into the bay. We'll wait outside the bay for night and your return. Once you let us know if it's clear and safe, we'll sail into the bay and retrieve the dzanti."

MORNING CAME GRAY, foggy, and drizzling. The fog had come overnight and draped itself upon the sea. The crew stowed their gear aboard *Waka* and pushed off into the steady southward wind. It was open sea between Jinahaa and Botson's Bay, so they weren't in danger of running aground in the fog.

"With this wind," Elān told his crew, "we'll pull in north of Botson's Bay behind the northern peninsula. The bird will scout the area for us. Our goal is the shore at the middle of the bay. I want to be there at night. If all goes well, we won't have to stop very long."

Up in the mast-nest, raven let out a caw of laughter. "If all goes well…"

The morning remained foggy and rainy, but the fog lifted by midday. Elān took a bearing and estimate from his jishagoon and then angled *Waka* north of Botson's Bay. By late afternoon, they could see the edges of the mainland. Elān had never been to the mainland. It was said to go on eastward for many moons, winters even, of foot travel. He wondered where, if at all, it ended. A few hours before dark, *Waka* neared the northern peninsula of Botson's Bay. The shoreline above the beach along the mainland was heavily forested. They saw no lights, smoke trails, or signs of movement.

Elān found a rocky beach near the northern peninsula and glided *Waka* toward it. Ch'eet pulled *Waka* ashore. "Armor and arms," Elān whispered to the crew. "Now is the time, Bird. Go," he said to raven. Reluctantly, raven stood in his nest, preened his feathers, and flew off south toward the bay.

"Let's stay aboard *Waka* in case we need to flee," Elān said. He put on his Yahooni armor, fastened his sword belt around his waist, pulled his waterproof sea coat over his armor, and hung the Yahooni recurved bow on the tiller arm. A quiver of arrows lay under the cover of the stern. The key to the lockbox hung around his neck. He took off the key and unlocked the lockbox and put the Koosh map, quill and inkpot, and the letter to his parents inside. He put the key inside and left the box unlocked, for Elān was certain it would soon hold a dzanti.

It was dark but they dared not light a lantern. The rain fell steady as it had all day. Nobody spoke. The crew sat aboard beached *Waka* and waited. After a few hours, raven returned. He landed on the gunwale next Elān and shook the water from his feathers. "Miserable weather," he said. The crew waited for him to say more, but he kept quiet.

"Well?" Elān said.

"Well, what?" raven asked.

"Give us your report," Elān said.

"My report? Oh. It's going to rain through the evening and then there will be some weather tomorrow, no doubt. And more weather most likely the day after."

"You know what I mean," Elān hissed.

"Oh, Botson's Bay, you mean?" raven said innocently. The crew waited. Raven scratched his chest with his beak.

"Yes, Botson's Bay," Elān said.

"Oh. You're not going to want to go there," raven said. "It's full of Koosh ships. Can I have some salmon?"

"Koosh ships?"

"You bet. Koosh ships. Oh, and they've got dozens of Yahooni slaves down in the bay there too. And then there's the cannibal giants, of course. Can't forget about them. And where there's cannibal giants, their foul mosquitoes are sure to be biting asses. And, of course, all of you are asses. Can I have some salmon?"

"I'll give you all the salmon you can stuff in your stupid beak if you tell me what you saw," Elān said.

"Too crapheaded to make meaning out of it? I'll speak slow, in small words. The bay is occupied, that means full, with Koosh ships. I counted five ships, that's the number that appears when you lift up your hand, but I didn't see how many Koosh. Their Yahooni slaves, that means morons forced into servitude, are standing armed guard, that means with bows and arrows at the ready, as cannibal giants, that means real tall human-flesh-eaters, are bringing trees they've felled, that means cut down, to shore, that means the beach, and floating them raft-like out to the Koosh ship, where other cannibal giants on those very Koosh ships are loading them aboard, that means the cannibal giants are providing lumber to the Koosh, probably so they can build more canoes. Anything else about this simple scenario you can't get through your fat, crap head?"

Elān couldn't believe it. His throat felt tight. He lowered his voice to a whisper. "What about the purpose of our journey? Is it still there?"

"What's that?" raven said loudly, feigning ignorance.

"It. Our journey's purpose," Elān hissed. "Is *it* still there?"

"I don't quite catch on, my dear boy. What do you mean?"

Elān couldn't believe that raven would choose this time for trickery. The crew was listening. They had strange looks on their faces. "You know very well what I mean."

"I'm afraid I haven't a clue. I swear I must have crap for brains. Could you spell it out for me? What is this *it* to which you're referring?" Elān grabbed the Yahooni arrow from under the stern of the canoe and pointed the razor tip at raven. "All right," raven cawed. "Dumbass. Yes. It is still there, unnoticed by the moronic mass of giants and Yahooni. It lies fathoms deep, a ways down shore from the beach where they're loading trees, as far as salmon sits from my stomach about now."

"Get him some salmon," Elān said to the Caraiden, ignoring the inquisitive looks of the crew. "Ch'eet, push us off. To paddles." Elān turned *Waka* and headed north along the mainland coast. "We have to find a place to hide for the evening. Tomorrow, I want to scout Botson's Bay by land."

"We're not going home?" Kwa asked.

"No," Elān said. "I need to go to Botson's Bay."

"You heard what that foul bird said," Kwa replied. "You'll get killed if you go to Botson's Bay. I'm shocked to be the one recommending we avoid confrontations, but I see no reason for us to go there. We have the Koosh map and strange jishagoon. Let's head home. Our orders are to not engage the Koosh."

"I have to agree with Kwa," Caraiden said. "Surely Íxt can't expect us to engage five Koosh ships in battle at Botson's Bay? We should return to Samish Island." Hoosa and Ch'eet agreed with Caraiden and Kwa's assessment. Surely a small force such as *Waka*'s crew couldn't be expected to battle a massive Koosh force. "We must head home now," they said.

"Ha, Craphead," raven cawed. Bits of salmon flew from his mouth as he talked. "Looks like you'll have to tell them about *it* after all or you'll have a mutiny."

"Shut up, stupid bird," Hoosa said.

"No, the bird is right," Elān said. He took a deep breath. Íxt had warned him not to tell anybody, but he felt obligated to tell Caraiden and Ch'eet—his fellow Naasteidi companions-turned-silence-sharing-friends—the truth, since they were all willing to sacrifice their lives for his safety. Kwa deserved the truth.

"Underneath the sea at Botson's Bay lies a Koosh dzanti. I've been charged by Íxt to bring it back to Naasteidi to aid in our upcoming war with the Koosh."

The entire crew stopped paddling—very un-warrior -ike, as warriors are trained not to stop paddling until given the order. Even Chetdyl turned and looked at Elān. Silence. Elān explained, "For five moons, Íxt and the Aaní Islands Elders' Council and their allies have been traveling Éil' gathering knowledge, meeting together, and planning how to overthrow the Koosh. This isn't our stupid bird's first trip to Botson's Bay. He was here two moons ago. He witnessed a battle between the Koosh and cannibal giants. A cannibal giant crushed a Koosh's skull with a boulder and the dead Koosh dropped his dzanti. Our stupid bird knocked it off a rock ledge and into the sea. The stupid bird told me about it and Íxt took that as a sign I was chosen to retrieve it. The dzanti sits there still, giving off a faint glow deep underwater." He looked at Kwa. "This is why, Kwa, I was made captain and why you are in the position you're in. If I weren't captain, and if I hadn't divulged this secret I promised Íxt I would keep, we'd be headed home right now. I wouldn't be able to convince you otherwise. I am just a bookeater, after all."

More silence. The crew exchanged amazed looks. The rattling of rain falling upon ocean echoed around *Waka*. Caraiden spoke first. "This knowledge changes everything. We cannot turn away from this opportunity."

The crew all agreed. "A dzanti," Kwa said. Her eyes glowed in the showery dark. Her voice was bright. "A dzanti in the hands of an Aaní warrior. We could destroy the Koosh forever."

"Yes." Elān felt better now that he'd let such a heavy secret out. "Let's find a place to put ashore for the night and hide *Waka*. Tomorrow, I'll go on foot to scout Botson's Bay."

CHAPTER 29

FOR THE SECOND morning in a row, the fog had come in the night. The crew spent a cold, rainy night wrapped up in their sea coats aboard *Waka*, which they'd anchored offshore of the mainland. They dared not make a fire or light a lantern, so they ate cold salmon and slept fitfully. At first thinning of the darkness, they paddled *Waka* ashore and set to camouflaging it with branches and seaweed. Chetdyl and Hoosa patrolled the mainland forest nearby.

Raven slept through the entire morning in his mast-nest, but when Chetdyl and Hoosa returned, he joined the crew, sheltering under the trees above the beach. "We saw and heard nothing," Hoosa said. "There are animal trails in the woods back there, but they haven't been used recently. And there's a wide, hard-packed dirt road that runs north–south, made for either giants or humans, but Chetdyl didn't smell human, giant, or Koosh presence on it over the past few days. Now would be the time to scout the bay. The fog will hide you well in the woods."

Elān thought for a moment. "Ch'eet, Chetdyl, and Hoosa, why don't you stay with *Waka*? If there's trouble from sea or land, get in and fly. Kwa, Caraiden, and the stupid bird will come with me to scout the bay. If we get in trouble, we'll make for the northern peninsula. I'll send the bird to fetch you."

The thick forest on the mainland made for slow going, especially in the fog, but Elān, Kwa, and Caraiden quietly,

265

as though hunting, wound their way through ancient cedars toward the north end of Botson's Bay. They made it to the edge of the forest and waited for the fog to lift. Like the day before, the fog hung overhead until midday then cleared. Elān crawled out from the trees into the sea grass on the beach. He removed his helmet in case there was any reflection—he needn't have worried as the sun was behind the rain-swollen clouds—and peeked up above the grass.

The stupid bird was right. Far in the distance, he could see the Koosh ships across the bay. He ducked back down in the grass and motioned the others forward. They too removed their helmets and observed. Five Koosh ships. From the distance, they couldn't see the Yahooni or the Koosh, but they could see the cannibal giants, tiny-looking from across the bay, hauling limbed trees down to the beach. Their body language said they pulled the trees with ropes—both hands up to their shoulders, heads down, bodies leaning forward. The land around that middle section of Botson's Bay was an ugly brown scar. All the ancient evergreens had been torn down and the destruction was expanding outward and upward.

Raven landed atop Elān's right shoulder in the tall grass and whispered into his ear. "On the far left are the camp tents for the Yahooni slaves guarding the giants. Do you see the Koosh canoe anchored on the far right waiting its turn to load?" Elān noted the ship. Its sails sat wrapped up and tied along the booms.

"I see it," Elān whispered.

"From that canoe, keep looking off to the right. Go past the end of the beach, past that long, yellow patch of beach grass, keep looking right, you'll see the grayish rocks. Those are the ledges that stick out over the sea. Look to the far right side of those ledges and straight down from the mountain peak on the horizon. That's where it is."

"How deep?" Elān asked.

"Far too deep for a craphead like you to dive," raven replied.

"How deep?"

"Three, four fathoms, I'd guess."

The crew watched the Koosh ships for a long while before Elān signaled them to back slowly out of the grass and into the forest behind. They made haste back to *Waka* to find Hoosa, Ch'eet, and Chetdyl sheltered in the forest off the beach. "The stupid bird was right," Elān told them. "Five Koosh ships are being loaded with trees. Yéil knows how many beautiful living trees they've killed. They're destroying the mainland."

"What's your plan?" Ch'eet asked.

"I think we wait until the ships leave," Elān said. "It shouldn't take them long to load the trees. After they're gone, we'll sail in at night and retrieve the dzanti."

"What if more ships come?" Ch'eet asked. "Or what if the Koosh keep a small force here permanently? And what about the cannibal giants?"

"Those last two we can overcome by sailing stealthily into the bay at night," Elān replied. "As to your first question, the only answer if that happens is that we'll have to rethink our plan."

OF COURSE THEY had to rethink their plan. Nothing, as you've seen, in the journey of *Waka*'s crew was easy. Two days they waited, taking turns watching the bay through the sea grass. In their time away from watch, sitting aboard or near *Waka*, Elān and Hoosa practiced the black bear language. It took Elān hours to learn the simplest greeting phrase. He didn't have the honed ear to hear the slight differences between the guttural growl tones of the language. Rather than discouraging him, his struggles made him determined to learn.

On the morning of the third day, four Koosh ships sailed out of Botson's Bay as three more arrived. Later that afternoon, one more ship sailed from the bay. "There's some portside positivity in this," Ch'eet told Elān when back in the forest behind *Waka*. "That's two fewer ships than yesterday."

Elān laughed and took off his helmet and stared into its bowl. "Time to rethink the plan. Any suggestions?"

"We could wait for these new ships to leave," Ch'eet said.

"More ships might come take their place," Caraiden said. "The longer we wait, the more likely we'll be found out."

"We could sail *Waka* into the bay late at night when they're asleep," Kwa offered. "Or sail across the peninsulas and try to come in from the south."

"Too risky," Caraiden said. "We can't afford to lose our canoe. We need it to get us and that dzanti home. They're sure to have lookouts, and I don't think they allow the giants to sleep. It looks like they're being worked to death, day and night."

"We could try to fire the Koosh ships," Hoosa said. "There's five of us with bows; we could send fire arrows into them."

"It's hard to fire on a ship that size from the sea," Caraiden said. "They'd raise an alarm and we'd have a battle on our hands. We need to avoid a sea battle."

Elān spun his Yahooni helmet around and brought it down onto his head with a laugh. The solution was in his helmet all along.

"I'll go," he said.

"What?"

"I've got Yahooni armor and a helmet and bow. I'll cut my hair Yahooni fashion and tonight, late, I'll walk in my helmet and armor around the bay, through their camp, and out to the ledges. The stupid bird can wait in the trees across the bay. I'll bring a lantern and signal him when I get to the ledges. He can fly across and help me locate the dzanti. When I locate it, raven can fly back and have you bring *Waka* across the bay to pick me up. I'll swim to you if I have to."

"Too dangerous," Caraiden said. "If you have to talk to the Yahooni, your accent will give you away. The Koosh might not be so easily fooled. There are too many risks."

"No," Elān said. "It might work. I'll walk through the camp and not say anything. I'll keep going. I can do it."

"What if there's trouble?" Ch'eet asked. "What about your sea bond?"

"Sea bond?" Kwa asked. "What sea bond?"

"That's between Elān and the sea," Ch'eet said, "but it could get him killed."

"I'll go," Elān said. "Prepare *Waka*. I leave when it's dark."

ELĀN AND THE crew ate the last of their dried berries, large portions of salmon—they didn't know when they'd get the chance to eat again—and drank enough water to bulge their stomachs. Elān shaved the right side of his head in Yahooni fashion—his head was cold without his long hair—donned his gorget and helmet, and slung his Yahooni short bow over his shoulder but left his sword in its sheath in *Waka*. It was of obvious Aaní make and could raise questions in the Yahooni camp. He hung a lantern from his sword belt. "Go now and wait in the trees across the bay. I'll light the lantern when I'm on the ledges," he told raven. "When you see it, be quick and come help." He bid his crew a goodbye and headed south in the forest beyond the beach.

Before he was out of earshot, he heard Caraiden say, "Your ancestors."

The forest was quiet and dark. The only sound was the incessant crash and retreat of the waves just beyond the forest's edge. He veered left when he came to Botson's Bay and walked even more warily toward the Yahooni tents far in the distance. He walked slow, often stopping to hide and observe.

It took a few hours for Elān to reach the camp. As he neared the row of tents, he could hear voices and smell the stench of humans. Now that he was closer, he could see the cannibal giants better. They stood about twice the height of the average Aaní and were proportionally broader, but they looked human. They were different from the hideous monsters he expected or had been taught to expect in the stories he'd heard growing up. The cannibal giants could be human.

He kept in the trees until he came to the torn up, treeless ground. He then moved into the tall beach grass and walked quietly to the edge of the closest tent. He could hear the Yahooni inside, drinking ale and gambling. He crouched down in the grass and listened hard to their accent, to how they pronounced certain words different to the Aaní.

Elān hid a while in the grasses near the tents. There was a lot of commotion in the forest beyond the camp. The night was full of shadowy light, wet with rain. Lanterns hung from high poles lit the skid road along which the cannibal giants hauled their trees down from the forest above. Lanterns also lit up the Koosh ships, and dozens of small canoes holding Yahooni guards outfitted with bows and arrows flitted around the bay with lanterns fore and aft. Elān could see two giants on the Koosh ship hauling trees aboard with ropes.

He counted sixty Yahooni guards on the beach watching over the work of a dozen or so giants, and half as many more guards in the small canoes and aboard the large Koosh ships. He wasn't sure how many more Yahooni remained in the camp tents. He couldn't see any Koosh but assumed they could be found in their cabins aboard ship. A loud voice came from outside the tent closest to where Elān hid. "Midnight watch, take guard." There was shuffling in the tent, and a large group of armed and armored Yahooni walked outside. Elān stood, hesitated and crouched, stood again and slowly followed the Yahooni warriors. A voice from inside the tent growled, "What you doing back there?"

Elān froze. He turned and saw a large Yahooni in captain's armor standing in the doorway of the tent. Behind him stood a group of Yahooni with ale mugs in hand peering over the captain's shoulder. Elān wobbled as though he had drunk too much ale. He took a few steps, wobbled out toward the sea, bent over hands to knees, and pretended to puke in his helmet with an awful retching sound. He heard laughter from the men inside the tent. "Midnight guards," the captain scoffed. "Never can handle their ale." More laughter from the tent. "Clean out your helmet and get going."

Elān stood up and hobbled on toward the midnight guard. His heart was beating so hard he could feel it against his breastplate. He tried to imitate the tired-looking stooped posture of the midnight guards in front of him. He trudged, tripped over rocks, and dragged his feet through the wet sand. The midnight guard got to their guard stations—small, raised watchtowers and platforms either side of the skid road—and lined up to load arrows from a large barrel into their quivers. Elān got in line and waited. The guard in front of Elān took the last arrows. "Ach, we're out of arrows. Goosa!" he yelled to a captain standing atop a watchtower, observing the giants. "We need more arrows."

The captain looked down from his watchtower. "You." He pointed to Elān. "Fetch another barrel of arrows." Elān assumed the barrels were stored near the tents, so he turned and walked back toward the camp. "Where you going?" growled the captain.

"Ach," Elān yelled. He turned and walked back the other way. He slouched his shoulders and plodded, dragging his feet along the ground, imitating a dejected slave guard. He came to the skid road, waited for a grunting giant pulling a massive rope attached to a tree to pass by, and then crossed the road and kept going. The giant wore thick clothes made of many ropes woven together and dyed grass green and a strange color Elān had seen only when red and blue were perfectly mixed. He could smell the giant's sweat even in the rain, but he didn't smell terrible. He had a hairless body, dark hair on his head, and massive legs. Elān could see his heartbeat pulsing in the thick veins in his neck, arm, and heel. A sadness lay about the giant that made it hard for Elān to hate him, even though the giants had killed his grandfather.

It had been drizzling all day and the road was muddy—a thick, clay-like mud. Runoff, no doubt, from the forest floor that no longer had its living trees to protect it. After a giant pulled a tree down to the beach, another giant would put it in the shallow water of the bay, where a Yahooni would tie it to other floating trees and then ferry it out to the Koosh ship. The Yahooni riding the logs would toss the end of the rope used to pull the tree along the skid road up to the giants in the ship, and they'd haul it aboard and stack it below deck and, so it looked to Elān, on the top deck as well. It pained Elān to see the damage the Koosh inflicted on the land. He could feel the terror of the trees in the thick, blood-like mud spilling into and fouling the bay.

Elān turned to see if the Yahooni captain still watched. The captain was busy yelling at another slave guard. Elān slouched away from the skid road and kept moving toward the end of the beach. He looked back again. Nobody was following him. He kept on moving. He felt a sense of relief as he crept away from the lantern light into deeper darkness. A shadow from the beach approached. "Hey, midnight guard is not over. Where you going?" It was a Yahooni guard. He'd been sitting on an upturned canoe down by the water.

"Ach," Elān gruffed. "Arrow barrels." He tried his best to pronounce it Yahooni-style.

"Oh," the man said. "Come on, then." Elān followed the man away from the beach up toward the forest. "Nothing worse than midnight guard, eh?" the man said to Elān.

"Ach," Elān said.

"What did you say?"

"Ach, too much ale."

"Where are you from?"

"Ale."

"Where?"

Elān didn't know what else to say, so he growled like Chetdyl.

"You ill?" the man asked.

Elān coughed hoarsely. "Ach," he said again.

"You're a talkative lout," the man said. They came to a level section of sandy beach. There were barrels and boxes of supplies spread out over the sand. The man grabbed a barrel by the top and tipped it over. "There you go. Now carry it back to your post or roll it back if you're too ill or weak. You young warriors are looking more like bookeaters these days."

"Ach," Elān said. He pushed the barrel toward the lights and skid road in the distance and kept rolling the barrel until the man disappeared back onto the shore. Elān stood up and looked around. It was dark on this side of the skid road, but he couldn't be sure people weren't watching. He kept rolling the barrel toward a platform next to the skid road. A group of Yahooni guards idled atop it. "Arrows," Elān called out. A few guards came down from the platform. One used his sword to open the barrel lid. They each grabbed a handful of arrows, loaded them into their quivers, and went back up the platform. "Thanks," one of them said to Elān.

"Ach." Elān made his way back to the supply beach. Nobody appeared to be around, but it was too dark to tell for sure. He crept through the boxes and barrels, walking as lightly as he did when hunting deer, heading toward the patch of beach grass he could see in the distance. At the edge of the supply beach, almost in the beach grass, he got caught again. "What are you doing here?" It was another Yahooni guard standing sentry at the edge of the supply beach.

"Ach," Elān said. He unslung his bow from his shoulder. "Arrows."

"R-O? What's that?" the man said. He walked toward Elān. "I'm tired of you midnight guards trying to get out of work. Who's your captain?"

"Ach. Goox."

"Who?"

"Goox."

"There's no captain named Goox. Who are you?" the man kept coming. Elān could see he wore no helmet, only a waterproof hat.

It's hard to do night watch in a helmet, Elān thought, *because you can't use your wide vision.*

The man stood in front of him. "I asked you a question."

"Goox." As fast and as hard as he could, Elān swung his bow across the man's temple. The sentry fell hard, letting out a loud oomph as he did. Blood sprayed from a slash along his cheek. He was stunned but not out. Elān hit him again on the back of the head with his bow. Now the sentry was out cold and snoring, or so it sounded.

Elān sprinted into the tall beach grass. He stopped to listen, but could barely hear over his own heavy breathing. He heard no alarm. The sentry would be awake soon, if he wasn't already. Hopefully, he wouldn't remember what had happened. Elān sprinted through the dark grass until he came to a rocky section of upland beach. Ahead of him, at last, lay the ledges.

CHAPTER 30

ELĀN CLIMBED UP the rain-slick ledges. He pulled himself to the top, crouched low, and looked back toward the camp and ships. There appeared to be no alarm. He crouch-walked along the ledges, away from the lights of the camp. Raven said the dzanti was near the far end, but in the dark it was hard to tell where the end was, and even harder to see the gaps between the ledges, where—if he misstepped—he'd fall twenty feet onto the rock or into the sea below. Slowly he made his way in the rainy dark, feeling for gaps or solid ground with an outstretched boot.

After a half hour of halting progress, Elān backed into the shadow of a ledge that blocked his view of the ships, kneeled down, and took the lantern from his belt. He had a hard time lighting the candle in the rain. When it finally caught flame, he put it in the lantern and, keeping the shutter closed, walked out to the edge of the ledge above the sea. He looked at the Koosh ships floating in the bay off to his right. Hopefully, nobody was watching. Elān turned the lantern toward the north end of the bay and opened the shutter. He closed, opened, and then closed the shutter. He opened and closed the shutter three more times and then huddled down atop the ledge to wait.

The rain fell heavier and still Elān waited. He flashed the lantern a few more times. And waited. He grew concerned when he saw lights flare up near the supply beach, but he was sure the guard he'd bowed wouldn't know the direction Elān had gone. Unless they saw his tracks... Of course they saw his tracks in the sand leading into the beach grass. He should have erased his tracks! Urgently, he flashed his lantern again and watched the lights moving around the supply beach. Elān had been a hunter. He knew the importance of tracks.

"Crapshack? Crapshack?" Raven cawed while gliding the air slowly along the ledges.

"Over here," Elān said.

"Is that you, Crapshack? What's the password?" raven asked.

"Stop it."

"That's not the password."

"Come, you stupid bird. We don't have time. Where is it?"

"Where is what, Crapshack?"

"There is no time," Elān hissed.

"Oh, Crappy, there's always time," raven replied. He flapped in the air beyond the ledge. "I have portside news and I have starboard side news. Which do you want first?" What the annoying bird meant is that he had good news and bad news.

"What do you mean, news?"

"Which do you want first? Portside or starboard?"

"Portside," Elān snapped.

"Okay, portside first. You're right above the dzanti. It glows below. Far, far below."

Elān crawled to the edge of the ledge and looked over.

"Don't you want the starboard side news, too?"

"Okay," Elān said, exasperated. "What is it?"

"I ran into that crap-buns of a sea eagle on the way over," raven said. "Same one, or at least a relative, that attacked me a few days back near that island of stupid bears. He was doing cloud-eyes duty for those Koosh canoes here in the bay. And 'stupid bears' is redundant. All one really needs to say is 'bears.' The stupid is implied, as it is with you."

"What?" Elān asked. "Where is he?"

"Where is who?"

Sea bond or not, Elān would have strangled raven if he could have gotten his hands around his neck. "Where is the stupid sea eagle?"

"'Stupid sea eagle' is redundant, too," raven replied.

"Tell me," Elān yelled. "Where's the bird?"

"Oh, off to warn the Koosh, I'm sure. I never liked that bird much and now I'm certainly not inviting him to my First Salmon Feast."

"Quick, go get *Waka*." It angered Elān the bird could be so relaxed. The Koosh were coming. "Go get *Waka*. Now. Go!"

"Enjoy your midnight cold bath, you fat turd," raven said, and then took off north into the night.

Elān looked at the ships and supply beach. Moving lights zigzagged in the beach grass headed toward the ledges. They searched for him. He looked over the edge down toward the ocean. It was too dark to determine how far down the sea was, or if there were rocks below. He unslung his bow and set it down, and then stripped off his helmet, gorget, and breastplate and dropped them on the ledge. He unfastened his sword belt and pulled off his boots and put them near his armor. Holding the handle of the lantern in his mouth, he lifted its shutter slightly so the light spread outward, away from him, then he lowered himself over the edge, and climbed down toward the sea. The rain blew cold on his back with the southern wind. When he reached a ledge down at sea level, he shuttered his lantern. The light had taken his night eyes away.

He couldn't wait any longer. They might be coming. He pushed himself off the ledge into the sea.

Eiiiiiii. The sea water was freezing. It's always cold in Éil', but on a rainy night it feels even colder.

He swam out a ways from the ledge and looked down

into the sea. He couldn't see anything. His eyes still blazed with the image of the shutter-cut light from the lantern. He swam further out and looked down into the sea. Nothing. He swam back close to the ledge and dove down underwater with his eyes open. Still nothing. Seawater stung his eyes. He shivered. He climbed back up on the ledge and closed his eyes. He took a deep breath, counting to five as he inhaled, and slowly let it out, counting to five as he exhaled. He breathed a dozen more times and then opened his eyes. The lantern light image in his vision had subsided a little.

He pushed himself back out into the sea away from the ledges. It was raining hard, and for a while, all he saw was the blurred water churned by the rain. Then he saw... a very dull glow—so faint, he couldn't be sure. He swam over it and looked down. Yes, there was a glow deep, deep down. He dove and kicked his way down until his ears hurt and then he opened his eyes. The glow was less dull but still far below. He came back to the surface and took several deep, calming breaths, and dove again. Down as far as he could, his ears nearly bursting, he opened his eyes. The dzanti was close, bright upon the blackness of the ocean floor. He reached out but couldn't grab it. His lungs hurt and he thrashed back to the surface. He dove down again, touched it, but had to come back up. The dzanti felt metallic, and for some reason didn't shock him when he touched it. Again and again he dove, and each time he came up without the dzanti.

He crawled out of the sea up onto the ledge exhausted, breathing hard. Suddenly, a large section of the ledge under his right hand moved. This gave him an idea. He grabbed its edge with both hands and rocked it back and forth until it came loose. It was large, flat, and sharp-edged. He scraped the broken chunk of ledge rock toward the sea and, gulping an extra large breath, he pushed the rock over the edge, holding on to both sides. Down he went with the ledge rock, holding tight, keeping his eyes open. A large pop sounded in his ears and the pressure eased. He saw the glowing dzanti coming closer. The ledge rock crashed into the sea floor next to the dzanti. The sharp edges of the rock slashed open both his hands as he let go of it. He grabbed the dzanti with his right hand. It grabbed him back. There was something metal inside he could hold on to, but it was cold and strange-feeling.

He kicked hard back to the surface, his lungs on fire, and gasped for breath as he broke through it. He swam toward the ledge and found he couldn't lift the dzanti out of the water. He grabbed the ledge with his left hand, but he couldn't lift the dzanti. The closer he brought it to the surface, the more it felt like holding on to a massive tree or carved pole underwater. He held tightly to the metal inside the dzanti and strained to get it above the water. It was impossible.

He clung to the ledge with his left hand and rested for a moment. He tried to lift the dzanti again by bringing his knee underneath. It came up to the surface of the sea, but not above. He cried out with rage at the futility. He let go of the ledge and thrashed in the sea. Useless. The dzanti glowed underwater. He let go of the handle inside and the dzanti slipped from his hand. He grabbed it again by the handle and tried with both hands to bring it above the water, but couldn't get enough leverage with only his frantic, kicking legs.

He swam back to the ledge and clung to it with his free hand to catch his breath. He pulled and pulled, but the dzanti would not break the surface. He thrashed and screamed in frustration and then fell limp. There was no use in fighting. He would wait, clenching the ledge, until *Waka* came. Maybe they could pull him out of the sea. Would he have to make the long journey back to Samish Island holding the dzanti underwater? The thought enraged Elān and he thrashed some more.

A soft plashing of paddles came from the bay. Over his shoulder he saw a red canoe. It was far out in the bay, though.

Was it looking for him? He let go of the ledge and swam out toward it. The dzanti dragged through the water, but he swam the best he could with one arm. He was tired and shivering. "Over here," he called out to the red canoe.

A light went on in the bow, and the canoe turned in Elān's direction. As the canoe approached, Elān saw a shadowed figure standing in the bow. At first, he thought it was the Choosh stone statue of his grandfather, which was strange. Why would a statue be captaining a canoe? But, as it came close, he could see that it was his real grandfather, alive. A vibration buzzed in his head. They had lied to him about his grandfather. His grandfather never died.

"Grandson," his grandfather said. "Why in Yéil's name are you swimming on such a night?"

"I'm cold, grandfather," Elān said.

His grandfather laughed. "Because the dark sea is cold, my grandson. Come here. I'll save you."

"They told me you died here in the land of cannibal giants before I was born."

"No, my grandson, I never died. I've been waiting for you."

"I've been waiting for you, too," Elān said. The canoe drew close. Elān grabbed its prow with his left hand. "I've always wanted to know you."

"I've missed you, grandson. Please, let me help. You're shivering." His grandfather grabbed Elān's left hand and brought him alongside the canoe until Elān was in the water below him. "The dark sea is so cold, grandson. Come, give me your other hand."

"I can't, grandfather."

"The dark sea is cold, grandson, and deep. You don't want to go to the depths, grandson. You'll never be reborn. Come. Give me your other hand."

"I can't lift it, grandfather."

"I can help, my grandson. I've been searching for you. Come. The dark sea is deep."

Elān tried to lift the dzanti out of the water, but it was still impossibly heavy. His grandfather smiled and reached down to grab Elān's right arm, below the dzanti, and lifted it out of the sea. The dzanti's heaviness fell away and it glowed in the night air. "Come into the canoe, my grandson." He pulled Elān up from the water.

A strangeness like cold fire spread over Elān's skull, below the skin, above the bone. Holes appeared in the fabric of the night, like the arrow holes in *Waka*'s sail. Where was he? He now saw it wasn't his grandfather who held his arms, but rather a strange being, smiling with ugly, carious teeth. Elān felt a pulling throughout his entire body.

When the first fire arrow ripped through the back of the strange being's skull and out its mouth, still aflame, Elān didn't understand. He felt the grip on his arms loosen and let go. Elān grasped the side of the canoe with his left hand; he hooked the dzanti over the gunwale and flail-kicked his legs to keep from sliding back into the dark sea.

The strange being toppled over him into the bay, grasping at the flames in its mouth. The second fire arrow, an instant later, slashed through the top of its skull as it was falling and spilled its brains, like blue-gray seaworms, into the rainy bay. A third arrow tore through its throat as it thrashed in the sea and sank into the depths.

Elān heard bows sing again and felt thuds against the floor of the canoe he was holding on to. He tried to pull himself into it, but he was too weak. He heard voices.

"Elān."

He was cold, shivering, and could not hold on to the canoe. He fell back into the dark sea.

"Grab him." He felt someone grabbing him from behind, pulling him up out of the sea.

"Got him. Caraiden, get us out of here. They're coming." Elān recognized, but didn't understand, the voice.

"Bring him up into the netting."

"He's freezing. We've got to get him warm. They're coming, Caraiden. Get us out of here."

"Ch'eet, Hoosa, get his wet clothes off and wrap him in blankets and bedrolls."

"Look. On his hand. Is that it?"

"Yes. Crapshack did it." The voice was full of mirth.

"Kwa, what are you doing? Get back in the canoe."

"I'm going to use it to destroy those Koosh ships."

"Back to the canoe. That's an order."

A massive jolt ripped through his body. His heart screamed and the left side of his body numbed. Somebody moaned.

"Kwa? Kwa? Are you okay?"

"Is she okay?"

"She's breathing. I think she knocked herself out."

"Hah. Stupid Old Sourbag thought she could grab a dzanti."

"Leave her there on the netting and get Elān's clothes off and wrap him in blankets and bedrolls." Elān felt hands removing his soaking sea clothes. He couldn't move from the shock. He shivered violently for a few moments, and then felt a sudden warmth as the hands returned and wrapped him tight. A hand felt his neck, another touched his chest.

"He's breathing and he has a pulse."

"Thank Yéil. Bring him into the canoe and lay him down. It'll be warmer in here." Elān felt himself being lifted and gently set down on hard wood.

"Caraiden, what about Kwa?"

"Looks like she's coming around. Leave her out in the netting till she wakes up."

"They're here. Let's go."

Elān grew warmer. His violent shivering calmed. He could feel the sea sliding underneath *Waka*. He lifted his right hand. A glowing dzanti was wrapped around it. It was made of a strange, clear metal. He could move his fingers freely inside it. He spread his fingers—what he had thought was a handle looked to be a figure eight piece of metal. It was multicolored like an abalone shell.

"They're lighting fire arrows!"

Elān looked up at the sky. The strange holes in the night were still there, blackness torn into darkness. Those holes, Elān knew, were connected to the dzanti. Elān tried to lift his head, but a wave of dizziness, a pleasant lightheadedness connected to the dzanti, spun him. He looked around and recognized where he was. He was aboard *Waka*. Caraiden was at the tiller, Ch'eet, Hoosa, and Chetdyl up front. Kwa was coming to her senses on the starboard netting. Raven was perched in his mast-nest and the night was full of holes. He pushed off the blankets and bedrolls and stood up, still dizzy and spinning. In the distance, he saw a Koosh ship following them. Yahooni warriors stood in the prow with flaming arrows on their bows, pointing up into the night.

The Koosh ship spun in Elān's vision. He held on to *Waka*'s mast and clenched the metal figure eight in the dzanti. He focused on the Koosh ship in his wide vision and thought, *I wish to destroy that ship.* The figure eight burned sharp-hot and what looked like a jagged shard of sun exploded from one of the holes in the night, followed by a shockwave that knocked Elān down and rattled *Waka*'s sail. The sun bolt blew the Koosh ship apart.

Elān pulled himself up from inside *Waka* and peered over the gunwale. Bits of Koosh ship smoldered and burned in living flame atop the dark, rain-pelted sea. Reddish fires leapt up into the night like spawning salmon from a dark stream.

"I know where the meanings are."

CHAPTER 31

ELĀN STARED AT the remains of the Koosh ship burning atop the sea. His legs wobbled as he stood and steadied his back against *Waka*'s mast in the easing rain. The lantern on the mast spilled an amber glow over the canoe and Elān held the dzanti up in the lantern light to examine it. A large grayish-white glob of foul crap spattered onto the dzanti.

"And now you know where the meanings aren't," raven cackled. Elān looked up. Raven's ass hung out from the mast-nest. "Wearing a silly mitten doesn't make you a philosopher, Crapshack."

Elān looked at raven, gripped the metal figure eight inside the dzanti, and thought, *I want to zap his feathery ass, not kill him, but sting and shut him up.* Nothing happened. No bolts of small sun came from the holes in the night.

"Ha! I know what you tried to do, Crapshack," raven crowed. "Wearing a stupid mitten doesn't make you a warrior, either."

Hoosa knocked the mast with his paddle. "No more talk."

Raven cackled.

"That Koosh canoe," Ch'eet said to Elān. "How did you do that?"

"I only had to think it," Elān murmured. "The dzanti did the rest."

"Can you do it again?" Caraiden asked. "We're not out of danger yet. There are two more Koosh canoes."

285

"Maybe," Elān said. The Koosh canoes floated far off in the bay, lit bright with lanterns. The one closest to *Waka* was unfurling sails. Elān wrapped his free arm tight around the mast and, keeping the closest Koosh ship in his wide vision, gripped hard the metal figure eight inside the dzanti and thought, *I want to sink that ship*. Again, the figure eight burned sharp and a jagged sun shard exploded from a hole in the night. The fiery shard ripped a massive hole into the side of the Koosh canoe, but the ship didn't explode like the last one. The gashed Koosh canoe was instead swallowed by the incoming ocean and rolled as it sank.

Elān collapsed to the floor of *Waka*. His body was ringing as though he were a Tas string plucked by a powerful finger. "Elān? Elān?" Caraiden said. Elān couldn't respond. "Ch'eet, put those blankets back on Elān. Hoosa, help Kwa back in the canoe. Let's not wait for that other Koosh ship."

The floor of *Waka* was cold and wet, but Elān didn't shiver. He felt heavy, wet blankets being draped atop him, and he could hear Hoosa struggling to drag Kwa off the netting into the canoe. Kwa's helmet banged into Elān's bare forehead. Kwa moaned but Elān didn't have enough energy to cry out in pain.

"Careful, Hoosa," Caraiden scolded. "Keep her away from that dzanti."

"Yes, no one touch Crapshack's special tool," raven cackled.

Elān raised himself on his elbow. "Caraiden, hand me that lockbox behind you. I need to keep the dzanti safe." It was difficult to speak. Caraiden grabbed the lockbox and handed it to Elān. Elān opened the lockbox with his free hand. He grabbed the key from inside the lockbox and then placed his dzanti hand inside, let go of the metal figure eight, and—with a surprising ease—removed the dzanti from his hand. The night returned to normal. The holes were gone. He closed the lid and locked the box and then hung the key around his neck. He looked at the last Koosh ship anchored far off in the bay. Its sails were still furled. "That other Koosh ship isn't following us," Elān said.

"No doubt it saw what happened to those other two Koosh ships when they got too close," Caraiden replied.

"I don't think I can use the dzanti again," Elān said. "I don't have the strength." With the dzanti off, Elān shivered against the cold. Both his hands had deep cuts in the palms from the sharp boulder he had used as an anchor to take him down to the ocean floor. "Ch'eet, I need clothes and bandages," Elān said. "I'm too cold to control the shivers."

"Stay there," Ch'eet said. "I'll get them." Ch'eet crawled out onto the netting and retrieved a waterproof bag with one of the medical kits from a hold in the starboard outrigger. He tossed it to Hoosa and then retrieved some spare clothes from the same outrigger and crawled across the netting back to Elān. "Get dry clothes on first and then we'll bandage your hands."

Ch'eet helped Elān put on the dry clothes and then smeared his palms with a salve made from Devil's Club and seagulls' eggs. He wrapped Elān's hands with bandages. "Wash your hands in the salt water and change the bandages and you'll be fine."

"Thank you," Elān said. The dry clothes slowed his shivering, but he was still cold and exhausted. "Caraiden, can you remain captain of *Waka*? I need to rest."

"Of course. Rest," said Caraiden. "I'll tack us out to sea and then back toward the mainland. We'll head up far north before turning homeward. There are too many dangers from the Koosh to risk going south."

Kwa moaned and pulled herself up on the side of the canoe.

"How are you, Kwa?" Caraiden asked.

"I'm okay," she said. "I'm dizzy and there's a terrible screech inside my head, but I'm fine."

"That's the first time there's been something inside your head," raven said.

"Kwa, when your captain gives an order, you must follow it," Caraiden said. "We can't afford to lose any warriors."

Kwa eased herself into her seat. "I apologize to the crew and to my mentor-uncle, whose name I dishonored this evening. It will never happen again." She looked at Elān. "How is it you can hold the dzanti without getting hurt?"

Elān looked at the lockbox lying next to him on *Waka*'s floor. "I don't know."

"How do you use it?" Kwa urged.

"I don't know," Elān replied. "There's a handle in it. I squeeze the handle and think something, and it happens. I don't know how."

"How do you put it on?" Kwa asked.

"My hand slid into it without trouble or resistance," Elān said. "It was deep underwater, so deep I needed a heavy stone to take me down to it. I was able put my hand into it without being hurt. Maybe it doesn't work underwater. When I surfaced, I couldn't lift it above the surface of the ocean, no matter how hard I tried. I thought I might drown because of it."

"It's above the ocean now," Kwa said. "How did you get it out?"

"The Koosh lifted it out for me," Elān replied. "It saved me from the sea and lifted the dzanti above the waves. It was yanking me into its canoe when you arrived."

"Even in rough seas, Kwa's arrows were true," Ch'eet said.

"It was an easy target in its flashing armor," Kwa replied. "And the fool wore no helmet."

"How does the dzanti feel when you're wearing it?" Caraiden asked Elān.

"Indescribable. Unlike anything," Elān replied. He was tired. No words came to mind.

"Try to describe it," Caraiden said. "You're a storycrafter."

Elān thought. "Like standing in the snow on top of Shaatlein Mountain when it's so cold and hard to breathe you feel faint. And it's also like being in a steam bath so hot your skin prickles and your head spins. And you feel full of energy yet drained of energy. It's all of that at the same time."

"Can others put it on and use it?" Kwa asked.

"I don't know," Elān replied. "I'm sorry, Kwa. I'm tired. I can't think."

Raven laughed.

"We now have the Koosh weapon," Kwa said. "We'll use it to destroy every Koosh in Éil'." She smiled at Elān. "You did well."

"Rest now, Elān," Caraiden said. "You should rest too, Kwa. Ch'eet and Chetdyl, stay alert."

Elān pulled the heavy blankets over him, leaned against the mast, and closed his eyes. He fell asleep to the sounds of *Waka* cutting through the waves.

EARLY IN THE still dark morning, Caraiden turned *Waka* back toward the mainland. Elān woke to the sail rippling as *Waka* turned. The rain had let up, but the clouds hung low in the night along the sea, and the crew couldn't see the stars. A mast-lantern sent out a weak, amber light in the mist. Kwa and Hoosa slept laying down along the center of *Waka*. Ch'eet kept watch as Chetdyl lay on the bow, every so often lifting his nose into the wind. Elān fell back asleep.

"ELĀN?"

Elān opened his eyes. The world was dark gray in a charcoal shroud.

"Elān?"

Then Elān understood: the fog had come. Caraiden was calling him. The fog was so thick Elān could see only a spectral shadow of Caraiden at the back of *Waka*. "Yes?"

"My time is up," Caraiden said. "Are you well enough to captain?"

"I think so," Elān said. He stood. There were strange, very small tremors within his arm, chest, and leg muscles, and he could feel his pulse throughout his entire body. He maneuvered his way to *Waka*'s stern. Caraiden let Elān sit at the tiller.

"The heavy wind died in the early morning," Caraiden said, "and is now a weak northerly, pushing the fog. I don't know where we are or how close to the mainland. I think we're heading northwest. Ch'eet and Kwa are asleep. Hoosa is on watch up front, but the fog is so bad he won't be able to see land. Chetdyl may be able to smell land. In fog like this, you must use your ears. You may be able to hear sounds of waves on a beach or echoes off the mainland."

Elān took the tiller. His hands hurt and his mind kept returning to the sight of his Koosh grandfather falling over him into the bay with a fire arrow through his skull. It was intimate and personal. The dzanti disturbed Elān. He couldn't recall any emotions except for euphoria while wearing it. Now, with the dzanti stored away, he recollected in tranquility the violence of the night: the thought of two Koosh ships burning, of drowning slaves and the horror they must have felt as the cold, dark sea flooded their world. It made Elān shudder. How could he have caused so much destruction? How many had he killed? As his crew slept, he wept without control.

Hours passed while *Waka* ran, blown by the weak wind, and morning turned the fog from dark to light gray. Elān struggled to captain the canoe, haunted by a flood of the night's image-memories. He found solace only in repeating to himself, songlike, in an inaudible voice, *I protected my crew, I protected my friends, as they would do for me*. He sang it until the morning arrived and he heard Chetdyl growl. The fog was still too thick for Elān, from his seat in the stern, to see Chetdyl up in the bow. The growl put him on edge. He listened to the sea around *Waka,* but couldn't hear anything but wind and sail.

Chetdyl growled again.

"Ch'eet," Elān whispered.

"Here," Ch'eet said.

"Can you tell what Chetdyl is growling at?"

Ch'eet scrambled up to the bow. Chetdyl growled louder. "He's looking toward the stern," Ch'eet said. "It's behind us, whatever it is, and I think he smells it on the wind."

"The Koosh ship?" Elān asked.

"I don't know," Ch'eet said.

Panic stung Elān. "Chetdyl, growl twice if the Koosh ship is nearing." Chetdyl remained silent. Elān took a few deep breaths. "Growl, Chetdyl, if something is behind us."

Chetdyl growled.

"Hey, bird, are you still here?"

From atop the mast, raven growled, imitating Chetdyl. Of course, as you know, a bird's thin growl is nothing like a wolf's deep growl.

"No time for your tricks, stupid bird," Elān said. "You're the only one who can speak the wolf language. Find out what Chetdyl is growling at."

"He's afraid," raven said.

"Afraid of what?" Elān asked. His panic surged.

"Afraid he may be pregnant," raven replied. "I think he had too much fun at Choosh."

Chetdyl howled.

"That would be the first contraction," raven said.

Chetdyl howled louder.

"I thought you were eating an extraordinary amount of deer crap for one wolf," raven said, peering down at Chetdyl, "and all along you were eating for two."

Chetdyl made three high-pitched yelps and woke the entire crew.

"Laters, fatheads," raven said. "I'm not getting bit again."
Raven flew off into the fog.

"What do you mean *bit?*" Elān yelled, but raven was gone.

"That dumbass bird," Ch'eet said. "I'll put an arrow through his throat if he returns."

"We may still need him," Elān said.

"Why?" Ch'eet asked. "He doesn't translate for us. If Hoosa hadn't been able to speak to the Xoots, we'd be dead. The stupid bird doesn't obey captain or crew. And he eats all our food and craps everywhere. We don't need him."

"He showed us where to find the dzanti," Elān replied.

"And now that we have it, we don't need him."

Chetdyl howled again, a long, agonizing baying that put the crew on a keener edge.

"I'm sorry, Chetdyl," Elān said. "We can't understand. If the shore or mainland is near growl twice."

Chetdyl remained silent.

"Growl twice if danger is nearby," Elān said.

Chetdyl growled only once.

"I don't understand," Elān said.

"Growl twice if something approaches but you don't know what it is," Caraiden said to Chetdyl.

Chetdyl growled twice.

"Everyone remain silent," Caraiden commanded. "An enemy may pass in the fog without spotting us. Chetdyl, thanks for raising the alarm. Now we're on alert. No need for further noise."

The crew remained quiet and listened. Elān could hear nothing except the outriggers cutting the sea and the sail straining against the wind. "Caraiden," Elān whispered, "should we take down the sail?" Caraiden shook his head and indicated with his hand to keep heading in the same direction.

"I hear something," Kwa said. "Listen." She stood up and cupped her ear with her hand, listening sternward. "A hum."

Elān cupped both hands around one ear and leaned out over the stern. He thought he heard something like a high-pitched hum. As you know, on the water sound can carry a long ways, but thick fog can deaden it. The wind gusted and Elān heard a faint humming. "I hear it," he told the crew. "Behind us."

Elān pushed the tiller and changed *Waka*'s direction. The sails flapped as they caught the wind. They traveled a short distance in the new direction and then Elān again cupped his ear and listened. The humming was closer. Elān looked at Caraiden. "We're being followed."

"Ch'eet, Kwa, retrieve all the blankets from the outriggers," Caraiden said. "Everyone put on sea coats and as many layers of clothes as you can wear." The crew paused and stared at him. "Now. Quick." The alarm in Caraiden's voice frightened Elān.

"Caraiden, what is it?" Elān asked.

"Mosquitoes."

CHAPTER 32

THE MOSQUITOES OF Éil' are not the mosquitoes you know. The mosquitoes of Éil' are bred by the cannibal giants. They are the size of small hummingbirds in your world. Vicious, they stab through clothes, blankets, and thin leather, and before they suck blood, they first inject a poison that in small amounts causes sickness, and in large amounts kills.

Elān maneuvered *Waka* in different directions, trying to escape the escalating hum from behind, but no matter the tack or change of course, the droning grew louder. The crew scrambled to grab blankets and put on extra clothes as Caraiden barked orders. "Ch'eet, cover Chetdyl in blankets. Hoosa, get air into the coals in the cooking box and get a fire going. When the fire gets going strong, throw one of those wet blankets on top of it. The smoke may keep the mosquitoes away. Elān, be ready to lock the tiller and take cover with Kwa. Everyone, use blankets for cover and hold down the edges as best you can."

The crew scrambled to put on extra clothes, grab blankets, and get the coals aflame. The high-pitched whine grew so loud Caraiden had to yell to be heard. "Let *Waka* fly where it may. Everybody take cover." Elān took one last long look around *Waka*, but the fog was still too thick to see much beyond the outriggers. He put the wind full into the mainsail, locked the tiller, and placed the lockbox containing the dzanti on the floor within reach. Elān crawled under the blankets with Kwa. She was holding down the edges of the blankets against the floor and sides of *Waka* with her hands, knees, legs, and back. "I prefer an enemy I can fight with bow or sword," she said to Elān while he pressed close. Elān smelled smoke. One of the heavy, rain-laden blankets was smoldering.

The whining grew to shrieking. In the dark, under several layers of thick hide blankets, Elān felt helpless. He could feel Kwa close. Her mouth was so close to his face he could feel the warmth of her breath. "I can hear your heart drumming fast," she whispered. "You need to calm. Take long breaths. Fill the bottom of your lungs. Count to ten as you inhale and ten as you exhale. Slow your heart and think 'klatseen.' That's our sacred word. It's a warrior word we don't share with bookeaters. It means envisioning yourself fighting through what is to come, and not panicking about it before it comes. That word is where your grandfather's name comes from. Klatseen, Elān."

Elān did as Kwa ordered. He took long-drawn breaths, counting ten in and ten out. After a dozen such breaths, a small calm descended upon him. He thought of himself grabbing the mosquitoes by their wings and slamming their long proboscises down into *Waka*'s gunwale. He pictured himself standing tall among thousands of mosquito corpses. The first crash impacted the blanket near his head with a loud thwack. "Here they come," Kwa whispered. "Hold tight to the edges. Klatseen, Elān."

If you want to know what the crew felt as they were swarmed by thousands of mosquitoes the size of small birds, and you shouldn't want to, take a blanket of elk or moose hide and wrap yourself in it. Have a group of friends surround you and hurl rocks the size of large pinecones at you. You will understand the explosion of mosquitoes against the crew's blankets and clothes. And you already understand the sting of the cannibal giants' mosquitoes' bites—you feel it whenever a doctor's needle plunges into your skin.

The crash of thousands of mosquitoes sounded to Elān like large hail hitting a tent during a storm. He had his thick sea coat on, and several thick blankets about him, and still the impacts hurt. Mosquitoes thunked against the armor Kwa wore under her sea coat. Chetdyl howled. Mosquitoes landed on the blankets surrounding Elān and Kwa, crushing them under their weight. *Waka* echoed with a whine so loud it hurt Elān's ears. Kwa whacked the blanket, trying to dislodge the mosquitoes' needles.

A needle popped through the blankets and stung Elān's cheek. It wasn't deep, but it hurt. He pulled the hood of his sea coat over his head. The second bite needled deep into his shoulder. He cried out involuntarily and flapped at the blanket above with his elbow, hoping to clear the mosquitoes. More needles ripped into his forearm.

Mosquitoes landed on the floor and sides of *Waka*. The canoe vibrated with their drone. Somehow, several mosquitoes squirmed under the blanket hiding Kwa and Elān. More needles plunged through Elān's leggings and hands. "They're getting in," he yelled out.

"Keep the edges sealed," Kwa yelled.

"I can't." His voice cracked. "I'm bit."

"So am I," Kwa yelled back. "Keep the edges sealed and protect your eyes. Klatseen."

Elān buried his head in the hood of his sea coat. He hadn't considered pierced eyes.

That wasn't fair. One massive mosquito needle could easily rupture his eyeball and permanently blind him. Screams erupted from the far end of the canoe. The oppressive weight of more mosquitoes bore down on Kwa and Elān. More needles stabbed through the blanket down to the bones of Elān's shoulder blades and into the fleshy back of his hands and muscles of his biceps. Elān screamed in frustration.

"Klatseen," Kwa urged. Her voice was weak but controlled.

A wave of nausea crashed over Elān. He vomited in the darkness.

"Klatseen."

Kwa collapsed backward and thudded her head on the side of *Waka*. Elān tried to lift her back up but was too feeble. His cheek, hands, arms, and shoulders were on fire. In the throes of nausea, he hadn't noticed the drone of mosquitoes grow faint. The needles were gone. Elān threw off the blankets and puked over *Waka*'s side, spraying the netting. He retched again. And again. His head spun and his stomach felt as though he'd been stabbed. Every heartbeat sent a searing fire through his veins.

"Elān."

Clinging to the gunwale, Elān turned and saw Hoosa standing just beyond the mast. Smoke pouring from the bentwood cooking box shrouded him. "Ch'eet got bit bad, so did Caraiden." Elān couldn't respond. He vomited again over the side of *Waka,* a thin stream of liquid. He let go of the gunwale and fell back to the floor of the canoe. He didn't have the strength to lift the blankets off Kwa to see if she was alive. The mosquitoes were gone.

Hoosa crawled out onto the netting and searched the outriggers until he found what he sought: a metal container filled with paste made from a tree that grew in profusion on the mainland and was much coveted and traded among the Aaní. You don't have it in your world, but it's related to your witch hazel. The Aaní call it *s'eil'aas.* You can remove one layer of bark without hurting the tree and grind that bark into a powder and combine that powder with the tree's sap for a sticky poultice the Aaní call *s'eil'aasneix̱*. A small spoonful of s'eil'aasneix̱ is powerful.

Hoosa scrabbled back over the netting and scooped a large glob of s'eil'aasneix̱ into a water skin, which he then shook violently. He went among the crew, forcing them to drink as much as they could. Elān could hardly swallow the bitter liquid. He took several large gulps and felt as though he would retch. Hoosa smeared a bit of the s'eil'aasneix̱ on Elān's cheek. Within a few dozen heartbeats, Elān's cheek stopped pulsing in pain.

Elān lay back against the stern seat and watched Hoosa administer the sticky s'eil'aasneix̱ paste and medicated water to the crew. Hoosa removed the blankets from atop Kwa and helped her drink. Her face was swollen and she looked blood-drained, but Elān saw her pulse in her neck and watched her struggle to swallow the water Hoosa poured in her mouth.

Ch'eet was by far the sickest. A mosquito needle had pierced his eyelid into his eyeball. He whimpered as Hoosa rinsed the eye with the medicated water. Hoosa then applied the s'eil'aasneix̱ salve to a bandage, tied the bandage around the eye, and eased Ch'eet, who was still whimpering, down onto the floor of *Waka*. Hoosa put a blanket over him.

After a short while, Elān felt well enough to sit on the stern seat. He took off his sea coat and a layer of clothes, and had Hoosa apply salve over the bites on his hands, arms, legs, and shoulders. He took more large drinks of the medicated water. "How could you withstand the mosquito venom?" he asked Hoosa.

"Smoke saved me," Hoosa replied. "The wind blew thick smoke from the cooking box into the blankets I was hiding under. I was bitten only twice."

"Thank Yéil, Hoosa, for smoke," Elān said.

"Thank Caraiden," Hoosa replied. "It was his idea."

"Ideas are great, so gunalchéesh to Caraiden," Elān said. "But ideas need to become actions, and your actions saved all of us, Hoosa. Gunalchéesh." Elān felt bad that he had wondered to himself why Hoosa was a part of the crew. The black bear human relative had saved the crew and proven his worth over and over again. The crew recovered in slow time with Hoosa's help. He was able to rouse Caraiden and Chetdyl so they could sit up. The floor of *Waka* was slick with vomit. Hoosa hovered over Ch'eet, checking his pulse, putting more salve on his angry bites, and rinsing and rebandaging his eye.

Elān slept for a while and in time felt well enough to take the tiller and guide *Waka* northward. The fog had thinned as they recovered, but was still so heavy Elān couldn't see the horizon. The sun appeared to be directly overhead, so he assumed it was midday, but the fog made it impossible to be certain.

"This fog should burn off soon," Elān said.

"We may not like what it has to reveal," Caraiden replied.

"What do you mean?" Elān asked.

"Mosquitoes are never far from cannibal giants," Caraiden replied.

"Do you think we're close to shore?"

"I don't know," Caraiden said. "Of all the dangers at sea, mosquitoes were the last I expected."

"Chetdyl would smell giants if they were nearby," Elān said.

"Chetdyl's nose got bit," Hoosa said. "I've covered it with medicine." Chetdyl lifted his head but he looked weak, drained. His head flopped down between his paws.

"The fog will keep us safe," Caraiden said, "as long as those mosquitoes don't come again or we don't run aground."

You WILL KNOW, if you are of the ocean, that sea fog can last long into the afternoon and hide horizons while the sky above clears. The fog that hid *Waka*'s journey north along the mainland thinned as the northerly wind grew but didn't release its grip on the ocean until a few hours before dusk, when it vanished from *Waka*'s path but clung low on the horizon, far off starboard.

"You think the fog is holding to the mainland over there?" Elān pointed with his lips.

"That would be my guess," Caraiden said.

Elān looked behind him. "I wanted the fog to burn off, but now I feel too out in the open. Perhaps we should head back into the fog to hide."

"It may also hide dangers near the shoreline," Caraiden replied.

"What do you think we should do?" Elān asked.

"You must decide as captain." Caraiden smiled. "Captaining is a heavy responsibility."

"Kwa, Hoosa, what do you think we should do?" Elān asked.

"It's as Caraiden said," Kwa replied. "You as captain must decide and take responsibility for what good and ill may come."

"Hoosa?"

"I am of no opinion on the matter," Hoosa said.

"Why should one person decide everything?" Elān asked. "Back home in Naasteidi we decide things by council. Why should it be different aboard a canoe?"

"Only a person from the Longhouse of Service and Trade would ask such a question," Kwa replied.

"At sea, this is how decisions have always been made," Caraiden said. "There's to be no questions. It's been Longhouse of War and Diplomacy tradition from time immemorial."

Tradition has to start somewhere, Elān thought to himself, *and if tradition has a beginning then changing tradition can be a new beginning. Tradition isn't a mind behind a mouth, telling us what to do. Tradition is an empty ear. Isn't the only thing that's traditional about tradition,* he wanted to ask his crew, *the fact that it changes?* But he didn't feel like arguing with them. Raven said Elān would pick at the threads of tradition until it unraveled. Elān desired to talk to raven. The stupid bird talked nonsense, but if one sifted through that nonsense, Elān realized, there was a strain of wisdom in his words.

Elān pulled the tiller toward himself. "I'll take us to the fog," he told the crew. "We'll hold just inside the edge. It'll be safer there. If the stars come out, we'll take a bearing and learn our location."

Waka ran eastward nearly perpendicular to the wind from the south. The fog covering what Elān thought would be the mainland looked a yaakw away. He had to hold the tiller tight to keep *Waka* sideways in the wind. Halfway to the fog, Ch'eet moaned and sat up. He lifted the bandage from his left eye, squinted and scrunched his face, and put the bandage back over his eye.

"Do you have your sight?" Caraiden asked.

"It's clouded," Ch'eet replied, "but light enters."

"Good," replied Caraiden. "The mosquito's needle didn't puncture deep to the back of your eye. Your sight should heal in time."

"Thanks, Hoosa, for helping me," Ch'eet said.

"We are crewmates," Hoosa replied.

Hoosa isn't one for speechifying, Elān thought, *unlike the stupid bird.* He looked around for raven. *He always leaves when trouble arrives*, Elān thought to himself, *but he returns when trouble is over. Why isn't he here now?* Elān was reluctant to note raven's absence to Kwa and Caraiden. He didn't want another lecture about his responsibility as captain. *Why can't a canoe be captained by council?*

Elān was happy to see Ch'eet sitting up. He still looked ill from the mosquito venom, and the bandage over his eye made him look vulnerable, but Elān had grown very fond of Ch'eet. He shivered to think of Ch'eet dying aboard *Waka*.

As they approached the fog bank, Chetdyl lifted his head and yelped a feeble warning. The prow of a Koosh ship broke from the fog. Its massive sails billowed as they pushed the ship into *Waka*'s path.

CHAPTER 33

ELĀN YANKED THE tiller and *Waka* veered north. Panicked, gaping at the massive Koosh ship, he didn't swing the boom in time with the tiller and the canoe stalled as its mainsail flapped. A whining cloud of mosquitoes emerged from the Koosh ship and swirled into the air. They moved in unison like a school of fish and droned as they sped wave-like toward *Waka*. The crew scrambled to don their heavy sea coats again and cover themselves as best they could with blankets.

Elān grabbed at a blanket on the floor of *Waka* and glimpsed the lockbox. He yanked the key from his neck, opened the lid, and paused as he saw the dzanti in daylight. It was the shape and size of a large mitten and translucent like a *taakwaanás*, which in your world you might know as a moon jellyfish, and it shimmered in what was left of the sun. It was made from a material so strange the only thing Elān could think of to describe it was *wobbly metal*. Inside the dzanti, the abalone-like figure eight handle shone multicolored. Elān was hesitant to touch it. He wasn't sure if he could put his hand inside it if the dzanti was out of the ocean. The droning wave of mosquitoes closed in on *Waka*. Elān ripped the bandage off his palm and shoved his hand into the dzanti. It was cold and his hand slid right through the wobbly, metal-like exterior. He grabbed the figure eight handle and held the dzanti aloft.

The tears in the sky looked different in the day. There were hundreds all around, out of reach. Clear-colored and wavy at the surface, like the shimmering air above a calm sea on a hot sunny day, they opened upon a hole of darkness as deep as the ocean's darkness at night. *I wonder if I can do it?* Elān thought to himself. He gripped the dzanti's handle tight and thought, *Burst the eyes of these cannibal giant mosquitoes.* The handle burned in his palm and the entire wave of the giant mosquitoes were sucked into a hole in the sky. There was silence for a moment, and then a cacophony of crazed, screeching mosquitoes tumbled floundering into the ocean from another hole on the other side of *Waka*.

A loud bellow came from the Koosh ship. Elān looked up and saw a cannibal giant bellering from the bow of the ship and gesturing at *Waka*. The sea next to *Waka* boiled with the mosquitoes' death. Their eyes leaked yellowish goo that turned the ocean mud-colored.

"Elān, destroy the ship," Kwa cried. The Koosh ship was close. Elān could see a group of Yahooni slaves, bows at the ready, standing along the sides. The cannibal giant continued screaming at *Waka*. "Elān. Now."

Elān gripped the handle of the dzanti, but he hesitated. He didn't want to kill the Yahooni slaves or the giant, who was also a slave.

"Elān, you must destroy the ship before it gets any closer," Kwa urged.

"I can't," Elān replied. He relaxed his grip on the dzanti's handle. The giant had disappeared from the bow.

"Elān," Caraiden barked, "you must protect your crew."

"I can't kill those slaves," Elān said. "They are innocent."

"The Koosh who controls them is not innocent," Caraiden yelled.

The giant returned to the bow with a large silver harpoon in his hand. Before Elān could bring a firebolt down upon him, the giant threw the harpoon at *Waka*. A gray chain fastened to the harpoon ribboned out in the air behind it. The harpoon slammed into *Waka*'s bow and shivered the canoe. Chetdyl had to jump into the canoe to avoid being speared through. The giant pulled on the massive chain and turned *Waka*'s bow toward the Koosh canoe. Hand over hand, the giant yanked them toward it. Elān gripped the dzanti's handle and thought, *Destroy that giant.* A tongue of fire shot from a hole above the giant and charred him where he stood.

A whistle—high low high—pierced the air. "Use that weapon again and our arrows will open hundreds of bloody holes in your crew."

The Koosh stood astride the cannibal giant's smoldering corpse in the bow of the ship. The air around it was blurry and pulsated. The Koosh wore glowing armor that changed colors from white to slate to blue and a white helmet. It kicked the giant's charred corpse over the edge of the ship into the sea below. Yahooni slaves picked up the harpoon chain and hauled *Waka* to the Koosh ship. The Koosh stared down at *Waka*'s crew from its perch on the bow. It opened its arms wide as they drew close. "Hello, my grandchildren."

"Grandmother," Kwa yelled up the Koosh. "Grandmother, it is I, your Kwaatk'wa."

"My dear granddaughter," the Koosh said. "I've missed you. Take down that sail and come to your grandmother."

Kwa loosed the mainsail until it flapped. Elān gripped the handle of the dzanti and thought, *Destroy that Koosh.* He waited, but nothing happened. No hotness to the handle, nothing from the rends in the sky. *I want to destroy that Koosh.* Nothing.

"My grandson," the Koosh said to Caraiden, "make him put that weapon away. Why does he wish to destroy your grandfather?"

Caraiden turned to Elān. "Put that away now." His voice had an edge.

"Elān, do as ordered," Kwa said. "Take off that weapon."

Waka's portside outrigger banged into the side of the Koosh ship.

"You're not safe with that weapon," Hoosa said to Elān. "Put it away or I'll kill you."

Kwa took a step toward him. "Do as we say." Chetdyl dashed through *Waka* and got between Elān and Kwa. He growled at Kwa and the rest of the crew behind her. He then growled up at the Koosh. The Koosh smiled down on them. "My grandchildren, take your knives and bows and kill that one with the weapon and his wolf."

Elān grabbed a shield. Caraiden, Hoosa, and Kwa made a frantic search around *Waka* for bows and knives. Ch'eet lay motionless under a thick pile of heavy blankets. Chetdyl growled at the crew as Elān tried to get his entire body behind the shield. Caraiden found a bow and was looking for an arrow, but Kwa had a sword unsheathed and looked as though she would run Chetdyl through with it. Caraiden grabbed an arrow and stepped outside the canoe, getting onto his knees in the outrigger netting to get a clearer shot at Elān. Elān gripped the dzanti handle and thought, *I want to stun but not kill Kwa, Caraiden, and Hoosa.* White bolts of a kind Elān had never seen before erupted from the shimmering sky-holes and crashed into the crew, buckling their knees. All three crumpled and writhed, moaning with pain.

The Koosh hissed and Elān looked up and realized the hiss was laughter. Elān gripped the handle tighter and thought, *I want to kill, burn, and destroy that Koosh.* Still nothing happened. The Koosh hiss-laughed again. *I want to the smash the bow in front of the Koosh,* Elān thought. A sun bolt erupted from a hole high above the Koosh ship and slammed into the ship's long prow, blowing it out toward sea and knocking the Koosh backward. Elān had to sit down on the stern seat. He shook with exhaustion. *The dzanti,* he thought to himself, *must use my body's energy in some way.*

After a time, the Koosh returned to what was left of the

ship's smoldering bow holding a large crossbow loaded with a thick, metal-tipped bolt. "You're going to get your crew killed," the Koosh said directly to Elān. "I raise my hand and thousands of arrows will open your veins. Give me that weapon and I'll let you and your crew depart unharmed." The air around the Koosh was no longer blurring.

Along the side of the Koosh ship stood a dozen or so Yahooni slaves with bows loaded and strings pulled taut. The crew of *Waka*, dazed and nearly immobile, would be easy to kill. With great effort, Elān stood and gripped the dzanti's handle tight and thought, *I want to kill the Yahooni who threaten the crew*. Firebolts burst from many holes above the Koosh ship, incinerating all the Yahooni archers who'd aimed their arrows at *Waka*'s crew.

The Koosh raised his crossbow and pulled the trigger. The bolt ripped through Caraiden's armor into his stomach. Caraiden's body lurched on the netting and blood bloomed around the wound.

"Stop!" Elān cried out, shaking so uncontrollably he had to hold the dzanti handle tight so it didn't fall off. He dropped his shield and collapsed onto the stern seat. The Koosh loaded another bolt and lifted his crossbow again and aimed it at the prone body of Kwa.

"Please stop," Elān murmured.

"Give me that weapon," the Koosh said, still aiming the crossbow at Kwa, "and I'll spare your crew."

Elān knew he'd be soul-dead if he took off the dzanti. The Koosh would trick him and take him and the crew as slaves. But the Koosh trickery didn't work on him if he wore the dzanti. "Don't hurt my crew."

"Your crew will live if you give me that weapon," the Koosh replied.

"Okay," Elān replied. "I'll come aboard your canoe and give it to you."

"Take the weapon off there."

"No, I'll come aboard your ship. Once my canoe is loosed from that chain and my crew safely away, I'll give you the dzanti." He held up his hand.

The Koosh hissed and Elān grew faint. He dropped his hand and the dzanti banged on the side of *Waka*.

"The names you people give things." The Koosh hiss-laughed.

"I'll come aboard if you free my canoe and crew."

"Simple language for a simple-minded people," the Koosh replied. It set the crossbow down on the deck. "I accept your bargain. Climb aboard and I'll let your crew live."

The crew recovered and sat up as Yahooni slaves pulled the harpoon chain and brought the side of *Waka* tight against the bow of the Koosh ship. Elān raised *Waka*'s mainsail, whispering to Ch'eet and Chetdyl as he pulled on the halyard. He was so frightened he couldn't keep his hands steady, and his voice tremored. "Chetdyl, let Ch'eet know when *Waka* is free from the Koosh ship. Ch'eet, stay hidden and don't move until Chetdyl lets you know it's safe to come out. Keep *Waka* clear but close until I use the dzanti to destroy the Koosh ship and then come back and pick me up. Caraiden is hurt bad. Get him in the canoe and get that arrow out of him and mend his wound."

Waka banged with the waves against the Koosh ship and a Yahooni slave tied the ends of a rope ladder to the remnants of the bow railing that Elān's firebolt had blasted. The slave tossed down the ladder, which was made of two strands of thick rope with wooden slats between them. Elān slung the shield over his shoulder and climbed onto the first wooden rung. He waited on the rope ladder looking up toward the deck of the Koosh canoe, ready to think destruction upon any Yahooni slave who peered down at him. "Let my crew go free," he yelled up to the Koosh in a high-pitched, tremoring voice. The silver chain clanked over the edge of the Koosh ship and splashed into the ocean below. *Waka* drifted off northward as the wind pushed the mainsail.

It was slow climbing the rope ladder with the dzanti on his right hand, a shield on his back, his body shaking, and his energy nearly drained, but Elān made it to the opening at the burned bow railing and peered into the Koosh ship.

"Come," the Koosh said. "You are welcome, grandson." The Koosh had a strong Yahooni accent, and its voice was thin with a slight buzz, as though it spoke through an injured nose.

Elān clung to the railing with his dzanti hand and spun the shield around his body with his left hand. He got his knees aboard the edge of the Koosh ship and hid behind the shield. The Koosh stood in front of him. It had removed its helmet and placed it on the deck next to him. Its armor glowed white in the fading light. Yahooni slaves stood behind the Koosh with bows notched and arrows pointed downward. "Have your slaves remove their arrows or I'll kill them all," Elān told the Koosh.

"Slaves?" the Koosh asked. "They are not my slaves. They are the saved, the enlightened."

"Have them remove their arrows," Elān yelled.

The Koosh raised its hand and the Yahooni removed the arrows from their bows. "Grandson, we have much to discuss," the Koosh said. "Come, we shall go below."

Keeping the shield in front of him, Elān shuffled on his knees several paces onto the ship's deck. He peered around the shield's edge and held the dzanti handle tight. "I'll stay here," he told the Koosh.

"You are a fool to come aboard this ship, grandson." The Koosh let out a long hiss-laugh. Elān felt the Koosh ship veering now to the southwest. Night was upon them.

"I saved my crew," Elān said.

The Koosh's hissing laughter echoed over the deck.

Elān glared at the Koosh from behind his shield and then at the Yahooni standing behind. The Koosh raised its hand and the Yahooni turned and walked off. Elān pointed with his lips at the retreating Yahooni. "They don't look saved or enlightened. They look like slaves."

"Come, grandson, let us go below and talk."

"I'm not giving you the dzanti," Elān replied.

"You've given it to me already, grandson." Elān shivered at the Koosh's words. "You should fear," it said. "You don't know what you have on your hand, do you?"

"I've killed one of you before," Elān boasted, "and I'll do it again."

"You didn't kill any of us," the Koosh replied. "And I killed the one of you who did kill one of us."

That took Elān aback. He tried to puzzle out the meaning. A wicked smile spread across the Koosh's face. Elān broke from the Koosh's gaze. Lanterns were being lit on the ship by the Yahooni slaves. Elān took a quick glance over his shoulder to see if he could spot *Waka* in the sea. He'd have to jump clear of the Koosh ship once he brought down a bolt to destroy it. He edged backward. The Koosh hissed with laughter. "Don't be a fool. I know you think you'll sink this ship with me on it, and somehow swim to your companions, but you'll drown, my dear grandson. You'll drown. And I know what that means for your people. Trust me, my grandson. Don't use that weapon here."

Elān took another look over his shoulder at the ocean below. "And you will not wish to jump into the sea with that weapon on your hand. That weapon does not belong underwater. You'll never lift it out of the ocean. Please, grandson, have some sense and don't use that weapon here." The Koosh laughed. "You have no idea how that weapon works, do you?"

"I've learned," Elān replied. "I've destroyed many of your ships with this weapon."

"You've learned nothing." The Koosh laughed. "You use it as a weapon to destroy what you fear. That's the extent of your nothing knowledge."

Elān hadn't considered the dzanti could be anything but a weapon. He tried not to show his hesitation as he forced a sneer. "I'm the only human in the world to have one."

"This isn't the real world, grandson," the Koosh said. "There's a far greater world. I can show it to you."

"Saaw Island?" Elān said.

"In our language we call it 'the Door,'" the Koosh replied. "And that's only the door to the real world, my grandson. I will show you the real world. Now, let us go below."

"I'm staying here," Elān said.

"It's a many-nights journey to the Door," the Koosh said. "You can stay where you are and death will take you as your body loses its heat, or you're welcome to come below deck and live to see the real world. Come. I have a room for you."

Like the Koosh Caraiden slew, this Koosh was grayish in color like the smoke from wet evergreen boughs. It had a craggy face with thin lips around a small mouth, very small nose, dark eyes, and what appeared to be very small ears. It wore the same multicolored body armor made of scales, identical to the other Koosh. Elān looked around the deck of the ship. It was new-built, the blond wood sanded smooth and covered with some sort of resin that formed a hard but not sticky shell over the wood. There were several small Yahooni-style canoes tied upside down near the stern of the Koosh ship. Elān could see a handful of rough-hewn logs through the opening to the hold below. He pointed to the logs with his lips.

"I saw your destruction of the mainland," Elān said. "You've enslaved the cannibal giants and have them destroy trees to build your canoes."

The Koosh laughed. "There are some from my world that say your simple form of language keeps your minds simple."

"I'm not simple."

"Those you call cannibal giants are nothing of the sort. Your name for them, your language, limits your understanding."

"They're giants and they are cannibals," Elān said. "Every Aaní knows this."

The Koosh hissed a long laugh from its small mouth. "They're not giant to their own eyes. And the one you destroyed on the very spot in which you now kneel, that one liked fish and berries," the Koosh said. "I never knew him or his people to eat one another, or Aaní flesh, or the flesh of any other human. But you make my point, grandson, and aren't clever enough to realize. You spout the ignorance of simple people."

"They are giants to my eyes," Elān said, "and they killed and ate my grandfather."

"And you witnessed this?" the Koosh asked. "You were there and saw your relative killed and eaten by these so-called cannibal giants?"

"No," Elān admitted. "I heard that is how my grandfather died."

"And the eating of your relative's flesh? Did you see that?"

"No."

"You simply assumed such a horrid thing because you call them the cannibal giants." The Koosh sneered. "Grandson, you should not assume they are cannibals, nor should you assume the saved are enslaved. One can discover much about you Aaní by discovering who your 'they' is," the Koosh said.

"What do you mean?" Elān asked.

"They whose extermination would, in the minds of such simple people as you Aaní, solve all problems," the Koosh replied. "The so-called cannibal giants are the Aaní's 'they.' So are the saved. So are all others who aren't Aaní. And that, my grandson, is why we must save you."

"No," Elān said. "You are my 'they.'"

The Koosh hissed with laughter so hard its body shook. "Simple and ignorant."

"How is it you speak my language?" Elān asked. "And have a Yahooni accent?"

"I am not simple nor ignorant," the Koosh replied.

Night had fallen completely now and the stars had emerged, but the lantern light on the Koosh ship dimmed them. The Koosh stood smiling in front of Elān.

"Is it not simple and ignorant to destroy living trees?" Elān asked.

"Why?" the Koosh hissed.

"They're alive," Elān said.

"Everything that lives must die," the Koosh replied.

"They live longer than most beings in Éil'," Elān replied. "Maybe they have a long intelligence you don't understand. Maybe many things you seek to destroy have an intelligence you don't or can't know about."

The Koosh paused. It smiled and stared straight into Elān's eyes. Elān gripped the dzanti. "Though poorly expressed because of your limited language, that is the only unsimple thought you've had this evening."

"Maybe you're too simple to understand the other thoughts I've expressed." The smile disappeared from the Koosh's face. "Maybe your language is limited and makes you foolish and causes you to seek the destruction of a world that you fear."

"This isn't the real world, grandson," the Koosh replied. "Take off that weapon and I can show you the real world."

"And become a slave," Elān said.

"Become saved, grandson," the Koosh replied. "Hand me that weapon and become enlightened."

"No," Elān said. "I'd prefer the weapon."

Raven, for some reason, popped into Elān's mind and Elān laughed aloud. Sparring words with the Koosh was like sparring words with raven. Their words were like a clear bay with an unseen roiling current along the murky sea floor below.

The Koosh laughed along with Elān, and then they both stared at each other in silence. After a long spell, the Koosh reached into its pocket and brought out a jishagoon identical to the one Elān took from the ransacked Koosh ship at Xoots Jin. The orb in the center of the jishagoon illuminated and the Koosh's body armor changed to a bluish glow. The Koosh turned the jishagoon around in its hand. "As I expected. Tell me, grandson, how did you find that weapon?"

"Aboard one of your ships after I killed one of you," Elān replied.

The Koosh hissed. "Don't lie to me, grandson. That very weapon belonged to my beloved friend. Together we went through the Door with it. So, tell me how that weapon came about finding you."

"I sneaked aboard your friend's ship and killed your friend and took the weapon."

"Come now, grandson, we both know you're lying."

"How do you know I'm lying?" Elān asked.

"I was with my friend when he died," the Koosh replied.

Elān stared at the Koosh. The jishagoon's orb lit the Koosh's face. "I also stole one of those," Elān said. "We call it a jishagoon. And I stole one of your musical instruments. We call it a Tas."

The Koosh acted unsurprised. "Jishagoon and Tas. Such strange names. I know you haven't any idea how to use this so-called jishagoon, nor do you have any idea of its capability." The Koosh held up the jishagoon toward Elān and its glow made him narrow his eyes. "Your vision is faulty at a distance. Tell me, grandson, do you have headaches, too?"

Elān was too astounded to speak. Fear compressed his chest and he felt faint.

The Koosh lowered the jishagoon and spoke softer. "Don't be afraid, grandson. Tell me. Do you have headaches, too, with your bad vision?"

Elān nodded, too frightened to speak.

"I can heal you," the Koosh said. "If I heal you, will you accompany me to Saaw Island and through the Door of your own free will?"

Elān remained silent.

"Would you like me to heal you, my grandson?" the Koosh asked.

Elān thought of Snaa<u>k</u>'s promise to find a cure for his headaches. "My teacher and mentor," Elān said, finding his voice, "is searching for a cure for my vision and headaches."

"He's no teacher and your world cannot heal you," the Koosh said. "Would you like me to heal you, grandson?"

Elān hesitated. The Koosh waited in silence. The thought of seeing distances clearly again appealed to Elān. And the thought of never having the blinding headaches again appealed even more.

"I can heal you, grandson," the Koosh said. "You know I speak the truth. You see that weapon on your hand and you must know my world has things it is not even possible for you to dream about. Amazing things, grandson. Medicines that can heal any ailment. Healing you of bad vision and headaches is easy for those from my world. I will heal you now if you agree to come with me to Saaw Island. You will find a world you could never imagine."

Elān remained silent. *I would give almost anything to be free of headaches*, he thought to himself, *and to see far distances like a true warrior.*

"Grandson? Shall I heal you?"

In his mind, Elān could hear the protests of his parents, of Íxt and Kwa and Caraiden, and of all his Aaní elders and relatives. The Koosh were his people's ever-enemy. But the pull of curiosity was too great. In a whisper, Elān said, "Yes."

The Koosh smiled and called to a nearby Yahooni slave. The slave jogged to the Koosh's side and the Koosh handed him the jishagoon. "Take this to the machine and bring me the medicine when it is ready." The slave ran below deck. "It will take a moment, grandson, to prepare the medicine that will heal you."

"How do you know these things?"

"Everyone in my world knows these things, grandson."

Elān stared at the Koosh. Silence fell between them.

"Is the sound from the Tas you stole pleasing to you?" the Koosh asked.

Elān relaxed. "It sounds nice," he said. "It's like an Aaní Tas except it has extra strings. And our carvers are better than yours."

"That Tas, as you call it, is made from things in this world. And like all things in this world, it's inferior. As you will learn, grandson, it is difficult to bring real world things through the Door." The Koosh inclined his head toward the dzanti on Elān's hand. "Except for that." The Koosh smiled. "And small things like the so-called jishagoon. So, we make do with the inferiority and limitations of this world for inconsequential things like the Tas. The Tas in our world is beautiful and has small strings made of beams of light instead of metal. And the music our Tas creates is heard far differently by each listener."

Elān laughed. "How can two people hear the same music differently?"

"It plays inside one's head, of course," the Koosh replied. "It's music not for ears, grandson, but for minds. Each person who listens hears different music and feels different emotions. I, too, play, my grandson. You cannot fathom what a real Tas sounds like."

"Why do you call me grandson? You are not my grandfather."

"Take that weapon off your hand and you'll see that I am your grandfather."

Elān looked at the dzanti on his hand. He thought about bringing a firebolt down onto the aft deck of the canoe, but his mind hesitated. No lightning came from the holes in the night. A horrifying thought came to him: *Do I really want to see the Koosh's world?* He looked at the dzanti and tried again to bring a firebolt down onto the deck. Again, his mind hesitated and no firebolt came. *Would I be the first Aaní to see the Koosh world?*

"Don't use that weapon here, grandson," the Koosh said. "Give it to me and come below. We can play the Tas. I have much to tell you before we reach the Door."

"If I go to Saaw Island," Elān replied, "this weapon will not leave my hand."

The slave returned and handed the Koosh his jishagoon. On the flat of his other palm, he held what looked to be a small, gray stone. "Give that to my grandson," the Koosh said.

The slave walked very cautiously to Elān, wary of the dzanti, and held out the small stone. "Take it, grandson," the Koosh said. "And put it in your mouth and swallow it, and your vision will be healed and your headaches gone."

Elān hesitated.

"I promise you, grandson, it will not kill you. It is medicine. It will heal your vision. You will have no more headaches."

Elān took the strange stone and popped it in his mouth and bit down. It wasn't bitter or hard. It was soft and strange and sweet like honey. He swallowed, waited a moment, and looked at the lantern-lit small sail at the far stern end of the ship. Blurry. "My sight is the same."

Mirth crept over the Koosh's face. "The healing will take time, grandson."

Elān gathered his confidence and faced the Koosh. "Why have you come here?" he asked. "Why are you in my world?"

The Koosh smiled. "You Aaní have a story about your emergence. The story of the Sun Father who lowers a canoe full of Aaní from the heavens down into this world. Think of that as how we come to your world, my grandson. We ride on the same story. Remember, in that story there's much fighting and killing before peace arrives. We are the peace foretold in your story. We are here to save you. What you call the dzanti is our protection against your violence. It isn't your weapon. No being in your world should have it."

"How many of you are here in my world?" Elān asked.

"There is only one of me, grandson."

"How many of your people are here?" Elān replied. "How many have come down into our world?"

"We, your 'they,' are many, my grandson."

CHAPTER 34

FIRE ARROWS STREAKED the night, trailing sparks behind. They sliced through sails and slammed into the deck of the Koosh ship. A Yahooui slave yelled an alarm up to the Koosh. The Koosh stood and looked out behind Elān. The Koosh's armor glowed and the air around it melted, but it shape didn't change. "Come, grandson!" the Koosh held out its hand to Elān. "Let's get below." Fire arrows slammed into the Koosh's body armor and fell, still aflame, to the deck. The Koosh retracted its hand, turned away from Elān, and reached out toward the white helmet that lay nearby. A fire arrow tore through the Koosh's chin, knocking it to its knees on the deck.

Roused from the trance-like eeriness of their conversation, Elān squeezed the dzanti handle and brought a firebolt smashing down through the deck just beyond the wounded Koosh. The Koosh toppled backward into a maw of burning wood. The entire deck under Elān shuddered with the impact. Elān squeezed the handle again and brought another bolt down into the hole he'd just made. He dropped his shield and scrambled for the ladder and lowered himself down the first few rungs. Flames appeared from the lower deck and Elān heard the cries of the Yahooni and the commotion of feet scrambling to get to the upper deck.

Elān clung to the ladder and looked out into the ocean. Flickering flame-light from the burning ship illumined dozens of large Yahooni war canoes floating in the dark sea. Elān saw the stunned visages of the warriors aboard those canoes gaping, uncomprehending, at the destruction. The Koosh ship listed, bringing Elān down toward the sea. He searched the ocean below, rising up to meet him. He doubted, if he jumped, he could keep the dzanti above water. He clung to the rope ladder with his arms and feet.

As he hung from the rope ladder, Elān heard cries toward the stern of the sinking ship. The Yahooni warriors in the large war canoes were loosing arrows at their enslaved cousins, who were crouching down behind shields on the deck of the Koosh ship. One of the slaves, stripped of armor and helmet, leapt into the ocean. He swam toward the closest war canoe. The warriors in the war canoe fired arrows at him as he swam. He reached the war canoe and tried to topple it by grabbing its gunnels and pulling down till the canoe took on water, but the vessel was too large and heavy. One of the warriors in the canoe ran a sword through his head. He fell back into the embrace of the dark sea.

It was strange to see Yahooni fighting each other. The war canoes paddled close to the sinking stern of the Koosh ship and fired arrows into the slaves hiding behind shields. The warriors in the war canoes were well trained. Half the crew hefted shields behind which the other half of the crew crouched as they reloaded bolts in the bows. They stood as a team, shield bearer and archer, and unleashed a volley of razor-tipped arrows into their Koosh-enslaved cousins.

Elān clung to the rope ladder until the ship rolled and spilled him into the cold sea. *Waka* was nowhere to be found. He held the dzanti above water and swam with his free hand. Only the masts and burning sail remnants of the Koosh ship were above water now. The world fell dark as the sea extinguished the fires. Elān swam from the chaos.

If you've ever tried to swim with one hand above water, you know it can be frustrating to the point of exhaustion. Elān struggled through the ocean in the darkness. The dzanti bumped into what Elān thought was debris from the ship and he grabbed onto it. It was smooth and pitchy. He realized it was one of the barkless logs from the mainland that the cannibal giants had loaded onto the Koosh ship. Elān hooked his elbows over the log and rested the dzanti against his chest. He had to kick his legs in constant motion to keep atop the log.

A ring of Yahooni war canoes lit bright mast-lanterns and formed a large perimeter around the battle site, while several other canoes maneuvered in and out of the wreckage with bow-lanterns looking for any surviving slaves. They found several clinging to flotsam from the Koosh ship. Archers in the war canoes pierced them with arrows or, if close enough, dispatched them with a sword or war club.

Elān kick-paddled harder to stay away from the war canoes on death duty. If he could stay hidden until the war canoes were gone, perhaps he could paddle to shore and make his way to the isolated Aaní Far Out Fort on the mainland, north of Latseen's Wall.

A war canoe glided not far away. Elān put his head down atop the log. He hoped his dark hair would hide him. A Yahooni warrior in full armor stood on the prow of the canoe with a large lantern. The canoe glided by and Elān lifted his head after it had passed. An archer toward the stern of the canoe yelled, "Movement. Over there." The archer pointed at Elān. The canoe swerved and the prow warrior lifted his lantern.

"Something's on that log," he said.

Three archers in the war canoe raised their bows, but before they could aim their arrows Elān brought down a firebolt that crackled as it descended and filled the bowl of the canoe with angry flame, incinerating the Yahooni aboard. Elān felt no remorse nor sadness. Rather, he was relieved he could use the dzanti while most of his body was submerged in water. And he noticed something odd in the night's darkness with the dzanti hitched atop the log next to his face: the edges of the dzanti took on a color, a faint shade like the hue of a fireweed flower, when it brought down fire from the sky. Afterward, it returned to being colorless.

Elān had no time to ponder the meaning. The war canoe's destruction raised the alarm. He waited as perimeter and death duty war canoes swarmed near to investigate the commotion. He counted them as they came closer. Fifteen. He was exhausted. The dzanti had drained his body's energy. Every bone ached. Warriors with lanterns were in the bows, scouring the debris for the cause of the explosion, archers stood behind them at the ready. Elān felt his will vanish. He needed to get out of the sea before he succumbed.

"Over here," he yelled.

The bow warriors lifted their lanterns at his words. Paddles flashed on the sides and pushed the huge war canoes toward him.

"Over here."

The lead canoe came close. The warrior standing on the prow looked down at Elān. "You're not Uyuuni. Where is Uyuuni and his crew?"

"Don't harm me and I won't harm you," Elān replied.

"You're Aaní," the bow warrior said. He lifted his lantern high. "Why is your hair cut in our fashion? Where is Uyuuni?"

Another large war canoe arrived. The two canoes held out paddles and pulled each other close until their sides banged together. "What happened to Uyuuni?" said the bow warrior in the second canoe. "I saw lightning, but the night is clear."

"I don't know," said the bow warrior in the first canoe. "There's another Aaní spy clinging to that log over there." He pointed at Elān. "This one has his hair cut in our fashion."

"What?" He held up his lantern and peered at Elān. "Who are you?"

"Don't harm me and I won't harm you," Elān said. "I have the Koosh weapon." He struggled to lift the dzanti off the log.

"Why is your hair cut in our fashion?" asked the bow warrior in the second canoe.

"Bring me aboard," Elān said, annoyed with the Yahooni's concern about his hair.

"Did you destroy Uyuuni and his crew with that weapon?" asked the bow warrior in the first canoe.

"Bring me aboard," Elān said, his tone sharp. "I have the Koosh weapon."

"How did you get that weapon?" asked the bow warrior in the second canoe.

"Bring me aboard," Elān replied.

"Give me that weapon," said the bow warrior in the first canoe.

"Quick. Bring me aboard but don't touch the weapon."

The bow warrior in the first canoe motioned his crew forward. The canoe glided next to Elān's log. Elān grabbed the side of the first canoe with his left hand, and then carefully hooked the dzanti over the gunwale. The bow warrior jumped from the prow into the canoe and grabbed the dzanti. The jolt dropped the warrior to the floor of the canoe with a thud, and the dzanti with Elān's hand inside flew off the gunwale. Elān gripped the dzanti handle tightly and strained to keep hold of the canoe with his left hand while keeping the dzanti out of the sea. "Don't touch the weapon," Elān yelled. He hooked the dzanti over the gunwale again. "Please, pull me aboard."

Two wide-eyed warriors grabbed Elān's arms, staying away from the dzanti, and pulled him into the war canoe. Elān slid down to the canoe floor with his back against the side. His will was drained. A dozen heavily armored and armed Yahooni warriors glared at him, the surprise in their faces turning to anger. "Give me that weapon," the warrior closest to him demanded.

Elān smiled and held up his dzanti hand. "Come take it." The warrior jumped back, clattering into the warrior behind him.

"You're aboard. What is it you want?" the warrior at the tiller asked. He was an elder and, if Yahooni tradition was like Aaní tradition, he would be the captain.

Elān bowed his head to the elder. "Take me to shore."

"Then what?"

"Drop me off," Elān said.

The elder laughed. "Give us the weapon first."

"This weapon doesn't leave my hand."

"Take off the weapon."

Elān held up his dzanti hand and nodded toward the dzanti-dazed bow warrior, who was moaning as he tried to pull himself up the side of the canoe. "This weapon can do far more damage than knock a warrior down. I destroyed that large Koosh canoe tonight. Take me to shore and I won't destroy your entire war party. This weapon doesn't leave my hand."

"Even if we kill your crew?" the elder replied.

Elān's chest tightened. "What crew? I have no crew."

The elder looked across the ocean to the second canoe. "Where is that foul-smelling Aaní crew we captured earlier?" he yelled.

The bow warrior in the second canoe waved his hand toward the horizon. "Dluuni is guarding them shoreward."

"Take me to Dluuni, then," the elder said. Both canoes turned. Elān's followed the other. "Soon you won't be so boastful," the elder said to Elān.

Elān's mind raced. Had they really captured *Waka*?

"Not so boastful anymore," said the elder at the tiller. "Don't talk to me about Aaní virtues. You stupid Aaní claim to be humble and abhor bragging and boasting, but in my long life I've never met a humble Aaní. I never met an Aaní who didn't love talking about himself."

A warrior nearby reached out and touched Elān's shoulder and then snapped his arm back when Elān turned to look at him. "Nothing happens when you touch him," the warrior said. "We could cut his arm off and take the weapon."

"Or throw him overboard with that stupid weapon and let him drown," another warrior said.

"He'll give up the weapon to save his crew," the elder said. "One is near dead and another half-blind." He glared at Elān

as he pulled the tiller. "We'll spare your crew, stupid Aaní, if
you give us that weapon."

"Dluuni," yelled the bow warrior in the second canoe.

"Ach," a voice in the distance replied.

Elān's canoe paddled toward the voice. *Waka* was
surrounded by a group of war canoes and chained fore and aft
to two Yahooni canoes. Elān could see Kwa, Hoosa, Chetdyl,
and Ch'eet, but not Caraiden. Three Yahooni warriors stood
aboard *Waka* with short swords unsheathed at the ready.

"Even with that weapon, I doubt he can kill us all," said the
elder. He looked at the warriors aboard *Waka*. "If anything
suspicious happens, kill the entire crew." He turned to Elān.
"Now, give us the weapon and save your crew."

"How's Caraiden?" Elān yelled to his crew.

"Alive," Kwa replied. "He needs help right away."

"I promise we'll do our best to save your crewmate if you
give us that weapon," the elder said.

"Is anyone else hurt?" Elān asked Kwa.

"Ch'eet's eye needs attention, but they won't let us access
our medical kits," Kwa replied. "Everyone else is okay. They
set upon us when you boarded the Koosh ship. They were
hidden in the fog. We couldn't outpace them." Elān had never
heard such a dejected tone in her voice before.

"Give us that weapon and your crew is free to use its
medicine," the elder said.

Elān took a long, deep breath. "Get me the lockbox from
my canoe," Elān told the elder. "I'll take off the weapon."

"Drop it on the canoe floor in front of you," the elder said.

"No," Elān replied. "Nobody can touch it and it can't go
underwater. Get my lockbox from under the stern seat in my
canoe. I'll put the weapon inside the lockbox."

The elder nodded at a Yahooni guard aboard *Waka* and
the guard searched under the stern seat until he found the
lockbox. He tossed it to the bow warrior on Elān's canoe,
who handed it to Elān. Elān took the key from around his

neck and opened it. He spoke directly to the elder. "We Aaní are going to use this weapon to kill the Koosh. Not to kill the Yahooni or any people in Éil'."

"Now it will be our weapon to do with as we please," the elder replied.

"The Koosh have entered our world in large numbers," Elān said. He lifted the Koosh map from the lockbox and held it up. "This is a Koosh map of all Éil'. All your inland villages are marked and named in the Koosh language. They've enslaved your island cousins and are coming to kill and enslave you. The large Koosh canoe you saw tonight, the one I destroyed with this weapon, is one ship of many, and the Koosh have many of these weapons. We Aaní have no interest in fighting you. Any enemy of the Koosh is a friend of the Aaní."

"That's a fine speech from a race of liars, thieves, and oppressors," the elder said. "Take off the weapon and save your friends."

"I ask that you use this weapon to destroy the Koosh and not the people of Éil'." Elān returned the map and then put his dzanti hand inside the lockbox, let go of the handle, and pulled his hand from the dzanti.

"Now give me that box." Elān handed the box the closest warrior, who passed it back to the elder. He took it with care and put it under his seat. "Hand me that key."

Elān tossed the lockbox key to the elder. "If you were to ally with the Aaní and the Deikeenaa, we could work together to destroy the Koosh and save Éil'."

The elder sneered and motioned to his warriors. "Bind him."

CHAPTER 35

THE YAHOONI WARRIORS paddled north through the night. Elān shivered against the side of the canoe. His hands and feet were bound tight with leather thongs. There was an old hide sail on the floor of the canoe, which Elān dug his feet and legs under for warmth as best he could. The elder glared at him but didn't say anything. The night was starry and moonless, the canoe lit by one somber mast-lamp, and if Elān turned his head away from the lamp's weak light, he could see the dark outlines of mountains to the starboard side of the canoe. They were near the mainland.

The elder pulled the tiller and the sea rippled as the canoe turned toward the mountains. It was hard to tell in the night, but Elān thought they had entered the mouth of a large bay. The warriors sang a quiet chant to synchronize their strokes as they pulled hard on their paddles. Elān drowsed to the drone of the warriors' chanting. Eventually, the sound of a paddle clanking against the canoe woke him. The bow warrior had laid his paddle horizontal across his lap and was thumping a beat against the sides of the canoe. The sound pulsed over the water and back in echoes, which puzzled Elān for a moment. But then he realized they were heading up a river, and though it was too dark to see, the mainland pressed close on both sides. The warriors were straining hard against the river's current, digging their paddles in deep to force the canoe upstream. The bow warrior's paddle-drumming set the stroke tempo. The bow warriors in the canoes behind and in front of Elān's were paddle-drumming in unison.

He heard drumming coming from far away upriver. The paddle-drummers matched the upriver drums until both river and mainland boomed and echoed. Elān heard singing. They were approaching the Yahooni village. The villagers were out in the night, singing a welcoming song, and a baying of dogs soon joined the human chorus. The river opened into a wide bay and the lights of a large village shimmered off starboard. Hundreds of villagers sang in full-throated joy at their relatives' return from sea.

As they approached the village, Elān could make out massive longhouses brightly lit with torches. People were sitting on roofs, pounding out their song with sticks and paddles on the wooden planks. When the bow of Elān's canoe ground across river rocks, the warriors jumped into the waist-high water and dragged the canoe up the beach. The elder stood, made his way through the canoe, yanked Elān up, and spun him around. The village erupted in cheers.

Numerous totem poles, some ancient, some new-carved, stood sentinel outside the longhouses, their figures too deep in shadows for Elān to read. He couldn't have read them in their entirety even in the day, of course, as one had to know the clan stories that went along with the poles. Were it daytime, though, he would have been able to read enough of the carved figures to get a general understanding of what they proclaimed. He guessed by the number of poles that there were several Yahooni clans present in the village. One large pole, ornate with story, stood in the village center and towered over all the longhouses, telling Elān that there was one especially powerful clan in the village.

The elder cut Elān's bindings and pushed him forward. Elān stepped over the wood spars that spanned the canoe and walked to the prow. The elder pushed him from behind and he leapt into the knee-deep water on the beach. The long, rocky beach sloped gently upward into the village, and slick beach grass and large drift logs marked the high tide line. Torches lit a cobblestone path from the beach into the village proper. The bow warrior grabbed Elān's left bicep and led him to the cobblestones.

The elder splashed into the water behind Elān, holding the lockbox, and followed them into the entrance of the village. There were hundreds of men, women, and children singing and laughing. They jeered Elān from the rooftops as he walked past the longhouses into the village center. A dozen Yahooni dogs, their skin drawn tight against their ribs, snarled at Elān's feet. Handfuls of wet seaweed flew from the crowd and slapped across Elān's face. Villagers erupted in laughter. More seaweed flew from the mob. As he neared the center of the village, Elān was pelted with what he first thought were rocks. They stung as they smacked his head. He caught a glimpse of one of the rocks on the cobblestones and realized the mob was throwing clams at him. The pelting slowed when the bow warrior barked at the mob to stop— they were hitting him, too.

Several rows of longhouses lay lengthwise, expanding out from the village center, which was lit up with lanterns hanging from tall poles and torches in ground holders. The massive totem pole—six men, Elān reckoned, could join hands and still not embrace its circumference towered above the village center inside a stone water fountain. Water sprayed out of the bottom of the totem pole into a shallow pool. Four ancient women sat on carved wooden thrones on raised stones around it. The elder approached the women.

"May I speak?" he asked.

All four women nodded.

The elder turned to face the villagers behind Elān. "Tonight, we destroyed the Yaabel's canoe and all his no-longer-our-relatives slaves." A roar went up from the crowd. They were alighting from the longhouse roofs and pressing close around the village center. "And we retrieved the Yaabel's weapon and map. I hold them in this box." The elder lifted up Elān's lockbox and the crowd gave a wild cheer. He took Elān's key from his pocket and opened the lockbox. "Snaanscaay," he said to the bow warrior who was still holding Elān, "present this weapon to our clan mothers."

The bow warrior let go of Elān and held out his hands to take the box from the elder. "Take it out of the box, Snaanscaay," the elder said.

Snaanscaay stepped back. "I'm not touching that thing again."

"Snaanscaay," the elder snapped. "Take the weapon from the box and present it to our clan mothers."

Snaanscaay peered into the lockbox. With hesitation, he tapped the dzanti with the tip of his pinky nail. Nothing happened. His eyes widened. The crowd hushed. Snaanscaay grazed the dzanti with the flesh of his pinky. Still nothing happened. He put all five fingertips on the weapon. The elder jerked the box upward and Snaanscaay's entire palm touched the dzanti. Nothing. Snaanscaay smiled and lifted the dzanti out of Elān's lockbox with two hands and held it aloft. The crowd roared in approval.

Snaanscaay studied the dzanti for a moment and then tried several times to put his hand through its clear metal, but couldn't penetrate it. "There's some sort of metal piece inside but I can't get at it," he said.

"Give it to our clan mothers," the elder scolded.

Snaanscaay set the dzanti on the stone base in front of one of the clan mothers' thrones and then returned to Elān and gripped his arm tight. The crowd behind Elān hissed. Elān turned and saw Kwa, Hoosa, and Ch'eet being led into the village center by a group of warriors. They were individually bound, with collars around their necks, which were chained to irons around their wrists. Chetdyl was leashed and muzzled and had to be dragged into the village center. Caraiden was carried on a stretcher held by four warriors. His eyes were closed but Elān could see his chest rise and fall. He kept his hand clamped on the wound. Tears streamed from Elān's eyes when he saw his companions. He tried to fight his way toward them, but was held tight. Seaweed and clams flew from the angry mob and pelted his crew.

The clan mother at whose feet sat the dzanti held up her hand and the mob fell silent. "Looks like you captured some sea debris on your journey this evening," she said to the elder.

"Yes," he replied. "We found a scout canoe full of Aaní trash out by the Yaabel's canoe." The crowd roared in disapproval.

"And this one?" the clan mother said, pointing at Elān. "Is he one of our no-longer-our-relatives?"

"No, Caskae," said the elder. "He's an Aaní disguised as one of our no-longer-our-relatives." The mob howled and pressed in. Elān was certain they would rip him apart, but the clan mother held up her hand again and the mob fell to an angry rumble.

"Continue," she said to the elder.

The elder pointed at Elān. "We found this one in the wreckage of the Yaabel canoe. He claims to have destroyed the Yaabel and the Yaabel's canoe with that weapon."

"He also killed Uyuuni and his crew," Snaanscaay interrupted.

Voices in the crowd erupted in a high, keening wail, and a Yahooni warrior with waves tattooed across his face broke from the mob and swung a wooden club at Elān's head. Elān leapt back out of the bow warrior's grasp and the club glanced off his flexed left bicep. The blow stung but didn't break bone. The tattooed warrior was about to strike again when the elder stepped between them and, in an angry voice, demanded the warrior yield.

The warrior stepped back.

"Bandeyaeni," the elder said and held out his hand.

The tattooed warrior handed the elder the ornately carved wooden club. The elder took the war club, motioned for the tattooed warrior to rejoin the mob, and turned back to the clan mother. "It is true that Uyuuni's canoe is lost. Some believe it was struck by lightning, but the night was clear. We have heard the Yaabel's weapon can imitate lightning and we found this one wearing the Yaabel's weapon."

The mob screamed for vengeance. Someone urged the clan mother to slice open Elān's neck vein. Another called for her to remove his head. The clan mother held up her hand again. When the mob was quiet, she said, "Are we certain this Aaní sea-trash who has cut his hair in our fashion killed Uyuuni and his crew?"

"I cannot say for certain, Caskae," the elder replied. "There were no witnesses. Some claim to have seen lightning bolts strike Uyuuni's canoe."

The clan mother nodded and addressed the villagers. "We are not savages like these Aaní. We don't make rash death-decisions, no matter how dreadful this news of Uyuuni and his crew. Their relatives will mourn their deaths as is customary. We will lock these Aaní trash in our forest stone-cells and determine their lives or deaths in the days to come. Tonight, we shall celebrate and rejoice in the destruction of the Yaabel and his ship, and the death of our no-longer-our-relatives." The mob thundered its approval.

In the commotion, Elān shrugged off the bow warrior and made his way to Caraiden. He grabbed Caraiden's hand before the guards holding his stretcher could react. "I'll find a way to free us."

Caraiden opened his eyes—there was surprise and then recognition in his gaze. "I thought you were your grandfather." Caraiden smiled and gripped Elān's hand. The bow warrior yanked Elān by the arm away from Caraiden. A small group of torch-wielding Yahooni warriors pushed and kicked Elān and his friends up the cobblestone path and out of the village.

CHAPTER 36

THE STONE CELLS were in the forest, a short distance from the edge of the village. It was too dark to tell how many cells there were, but in the torchlight the cells loomed fearsome. Made from thick, gray stone, the walls of the cells were straight and vertical, but their roofs were rounded in a stone imitation of a canoe turned upside down. The prow of the upside-down imitation canoe hung out over the cell door, which was made of solid wood and crisscrossed with thick metal bars. The only light source for the cell came from a small, square opening above the door too small for a human to squeeze through. The Yahooni guards shoved Hoosa, and then Ch'eet, into solitary cells and locked the doors with large metal padlocks.

"There aren't enough forest cells for all the prisoners," one of the Yahooni guards said.

"Put the wolf in the cell with the woman and the dying old man in with the young one," another guard replied. As they led Kwa to her cell, she turned to Elān and said, "Tell them nothing. Klatseen, Elān." A guard smacked her with the back of his hand and pushed her into the cell. Two guards dragged Chetdyl by a neck chain into the cell with Kwa.

The guards then led Elān and Caraiden to their cell. A guard with a torch opened the door and motioned for Elān to go inside. Elān hesitated. The cell was dark and smelled foul, as when animals are left to rot after being torn apart by a predator for just a few bites. A guard shoved him from behind. Elān turned to look at the bow warrior. "My crewmate here needs medicine and a healing doctor," he said. Before he could be pushed again, Elān walked into the cell. The guards carrying Caraiden's stretcher entered the cell, dumped Caraiden on the floor, and left with the stretcher. They slammed and locked the door. The light faded as the torchbearers walked back to the village.

Elān couldn't see in the darkness. He got down on his hands and knees and felt for Caraiden. The old warrior lay face down on the floor of the cold cell. Elān turned him onto his back and Caraiden groaned in pain. He pulled him to the corner of the cell and tried to prop him up, but Caraiden groaned louder. Elān felt along the floor for something soft to cradle Caraiden's head, but there was nothing but stone covered by a dank layer of dirt. He sat down in the corner next to Caraiden and shivered. His clothes were still damp from the sea.

"You were right, Caraiden. The biggest difference between warriors and bookeaters is that warriors are taught to ignore the cold. I have been frozen this entire journey." Caraiden didn't say anything. "You called the coldness of Éil' a *thick* cold. It's a thick, blood-freezing cold."

Caraiden didn't reply.

"Caraiden?"

Elān could hear the old warrior's shallow, almost-panting, breathing. He cradled his head off the cell floor. Caraiden's face was on fire. Elān stood, felt his way to the door and yelled for help into the little opening above it. His voice echoed through the forest. He could hear drumming and singing far off in the village. He yelled, screaming for help over and over until his throat was raw. The drumming and singing continued.

He felt his way in the dark back to the corner and kneeled above Caraiden. The old warrior was still breathing, but his face was burning and his shoulders shivering. "Caraiden?"

"Latseen?" Caraiden asked weakly.

"No, Caraiden, it is Elān."

"Elān?"

"Latseen's grandson."

"I shut my eyes for just a moment, Latseen," Caraiden said in a strange whisper.

"Go ahead and sleep," Elān said.

"At that forward lookout post on the edge of Kusaxakwáan territory," the old warrior whispered in a strange voice. "I rested my eyes a moment. It was so dark and cold that night on the mainland."

"We aren't in Kusaxakwáan territory, Caraiden. We are far north of there in Yahooni territory."

"You had us paddle upriver for two days straight, Latseen. We were all exhausted that night. Why didn't you set two warriors at watch?" Caraiden sighed. "When I woke you were gone. All our warriors were gone. I saw those giant footprints all around. They got past my lookout post. I never heard them. I don't know why they didn't grab me."

"Caraiden, you're delirious," Elān said. "I'm not Latseen. I'm his grandson Elān and we're in Yahooni territory on the mainland."

"I searched for you. I was alone but I searched deep into Kusaxakwáan territory." Caraiden's voice was almost a whimper. "I could never find bodies. I found your armor. I almost died a dozen times getting home, but I returned your flicker tail coin-mail to your daughter, Latseen. Shaa should still have it if you want it back."

Elān paused. "Caraiden, why were we in Kusaxakwáan territory?" he asked.

"Looking for Íxt's son," Caraiden replied. "Íxt held a healing ceremony for me when I got back, Latseen."

"Caraiden, Íxt's son was killed by the Koosh," Elān said.

"I understand why we had to go, Latseen, when we received the message from the Far Out Fort that said Íxt's boy had headed into K̲usax̲akwáan territory." Caraiden groaned loudly and writhed. "But why didn't you set two warriors at watch that night?" He yowled in pain. "I'm thirsty, Latseen."

Elān had so many questions, but Caraiden writhed and spasmed on the cell floor. "I'm dying, Latseen. I'm thirsty. Help me." Elān felt his way to the door and screamed again through the forest. He screamed until his voice was so hoarse it croaked. A breath of light appeared in the opening above the cell door and slowly grew brighter. He heard footsteps approach and then the padlock being keyed open.

The cell door sprung open and a guard with a torch stood before him. "Back of the cell," he ordered Elān. Two warriors with a stretcher stood in the torchlight behind the guard. "Bring the wounded man," the guard said to the stretcher-bearers.

Elān rushed to Caraiden's side and grabbed his hand. Blood had soaked through his thick leather tunic around his stomach. "Latseen?"

"No, Caraiden. I'm Elān. His grandson."

"Eesháan, Elān." Caraiden smiled weakly. His face was pale. "I thought you were your grandfather. Do you remember what I said about your grandfather while we stared at his statue in Choosh?"

"Aaá, Caraiden, I remember." Elān waited for Caraiden to say something more, but the old warrior just squeezed his hand and held his stare with that pale smile. The stretcher-bearers were rough in picking him up. They dropped him onto the stretcher and Caraiden howled in pain. Elān watched the old warrior leave. The guard slammed the door shut and locked the padlock. As the torchlight faded into darkness, Elān could hear the drumming and singing blown on the wind up into his forest cell.

CHAPTER 37

THE INSIDE OF the cell had grown dim, lit with the pre-dawn. Elān could see the faint outline of Caraiden's blood where it had soaked the dirty stones in the corner of the cell. He thought about what Caraiden had told him. Much made sense now: why Caraiden had grown angry when Elān had asked if he'd ever fallen asleep on watch, and why Íxt had grown angry with Caraiden and accused the old warrior of owing a debt to Latseen's family. But more had become unknown. Did Íxt know that Latseen died searching for his son? How did the Far Out Fort Aaní know Íxt's son was headed to the land of the cannibal giants? *I have so many questions I need answered*, Elān thought to himself, *but answers only uncover more questions*. Frustrated, he rested against the cold cell wall and closed his eyes.

Elān was unsure how long he slept, but he awoke at the sound of approaching footsteps. He heard a key being inserted into the lock. The door opened and torchlight flooded into the dawn-gray cell. Elān squinted and saw a group of Yahooni guards standing behind the one named Snaanscaay, the bow warrior who had tried to take the dzanti from him in the canoe. Snaanscaay held a burning torch in one hand and a short sword in the other. "Go to the back of the cell and sit down," he commanded Elān.

"Why?" Elān asked.

Snaanscaay raised his short sword so the tip pointed at Elān's head. "Back of the cell."

Elān walked backward until he banged into the back wall. It was dark there. He sat down. Snaanscaay nodded to the guards behind him. They ushered the elder from Snaanscaay's canoe through the door.

"For what purpose were you asea, spy?" the elder asked.

"How is my crewmate with the stomach wound?" he replied.

"Alive when last I saw him," the elder replied. "Now, why were you asea?"

Elān didn't reply. *Kwa said not to tell them anything. Have they interrogated the others?* Elān was too tired to think at any depth below the surface of things.

"Please, don't harm my crew. Let them live."

"Who sent you to spy on us?" the elder demanded.

"I am not a spy," Elān said.

"Your hair is cut in our fashion," the elder replied. "Unless you convince me otherwise, I must assume you've been sent here to spy on us. And, as you may know, the penalty for spying in our territory is death."

"Where are we?"

"You're in the village of Tsedi on the Atna'tuu River."

"Is that close to the Northern Wall?" Elān asked. He didn't want to upset the elder by calling it Latseen's Wall.

The elder laughed. "You think you can escape to your kinsmen in the north at the Far Out Fort? You think you can escape to the land you stole from us after the Great Oppressor's war? You're closer to our southern wall, separating us from the giants." Elān moaned and the elder laughed again. "Yes, your life is caught within enemy territory, and we will soon put you to death unless I can find a convincing reason not to do so. So again, I ask what you were doing asea?"

Elān exhaled in exhaustion. "I was trying to kill Koosh." The elder looked confused. "Those you call Yaabel, we Aaní call Koosh."

"Why is your hair cut in our fashion?" the elder asked.

"What does it matter how my hair is cut?" Elān asked with impatience. "The Koosh are here to kill or enslave you as they have your cousins from the islands and all you people care about is my hair. After the Koosh destroy your village with their dzanti, your skeletons will still ask me why my hair is cut in Yahooni fashion."

"What is your name?" the elder asked.

"Latseen," Elān replied.

The elder kicked Elān hard in the calf. Elān's leg needled with pain. "Say that name again and I will put you to death in this cell. That name is not welcome here. I'll ask again: What is your name?"

"Elān."

"So, Elān, as I see things, and I speak for my people, our watchtower on the Southern Wall raised the alarm at a Yaabel canoe running hard north, using the fog for cover. How strange then to find an Aaní scout canoe of the swiftest sort running alongside the Yaabel canoe. Even stranger to find you with your hair cut in our fashion, floating in the sea with a Yaabel weapon on your hand, just minutes after our warriors destroyed the Yaabel canoe and—even more suspicious—moments after Uyuuni's canoe is destroyed by lightning as comes from that Yaabel weapon. You see how thin and threadbare the net holding your life is, young Elān?"

Elān put his hands to his forehead. Tears pushed behind his eyes.

"I can draw no other conclusion than that you and your wretched crew are allied with the Yaabel and our no-longer-our-relatives from the islands to spy on us," the elder continued, "and the strange map, the strange object of strange metal, and the strange stringed instrument found in your canoe all support this conclusion."

Elān covered his eyes with his hands and shook his head. "I destroyed the Koosh canoe with the Koosh weapon," he said. "This is madness. You must join us in killing the Yaabel."

The elder laughed so loud it echoed in the stone cell. "We will be fine, Elān, without your help. Let the Yaabel kill off and enslave the Aaní and Deikeenaa just as they have our no-longer-our-relatives from the islands. When you're dead and gone, we will have no more trouble from the heirs of the Great Oppressor."

Tears ran down Elān's face.

"You should be embarrassed," the elder sneered. "You dishonor all Aaní warriors with your tears and in turn dishonor all your enemies, who, though we must hate you, once respected Aaní warriorship."

"I am no warrior," Elān replied. "I am in the Longhouse of Service and Trade."

The elder shook his head. "What?"

"I am still a student in Naasteidi's Longhouse of Service and Trade."

"A Naasteidi student? Is this another joke? Your canoe is a military scout canoe, not a trade canoe, and your crew are warriors."

"I was sent by our Aaní Islands Elders' Council to travel with the crew of warriors to help update our maps and scout the mainland for any Yaabel settlements."

The elder frowned at Snaanscaay. "They sent a bookeater to do warrior's work." He turned back to Elān. "How did you obtain this Yaabel weapon?"

"We Aaní are preparing for war against the Yaabel," Elān said.

"I've grown thin of patience," the elder said. "How did you come to have that Yaabel weapon when we pulled you from the sea?"

"I cut my hair in your fashion to pretend to be one of your no-longer-our-relatives. I sneaked aboard the Yaabel ship in Botson's Bay in the dark of night, and stole the Yaabel's weapon," Elān said. "My canoe was spotted during its escape and an alarm raised. I was hunted by many Yaabel canoes and attacked by the cannibal giants' mosquitoes. You can see the mosquito bites and bruises on my body. One Yaabel canoe cloaked itself in the fog and took me and my crew by surprise. I bargained with the Yaabel to save my crew. I agreed to come aboard the Yaabel canoe and return the Yaabel weapon if he let my crew go free. I was aboard the Yaabel canoe when you and your crew attacked. I used the weapon to destroy the Yaabel's ship."

Elān hoped the elder believed his story. As you know, there was much truth to the story Elān told. The elder squinted his eyes and glared at him. Elān stared back. The elder shook his head. "I find it hard to believe you simply sneaked aboard a Yaabel ship." He turned to Snaanscaay. "Yet, he did have the Yaabel weapon when we found him, and the Yaabel canoe may have been blown apart by what appeared to be a Yaabel weapon firebolt." Snaanscaay nodded in agreement. "Did you kill Uyuuni and his crew with the Yaabel weapon?" the elder asked Elān.

"No," Elān lied. "I destroyed only the Yaabel and his canoe."

The elder looked at Snaanscaay. "That's most likely a lie, but having Uyuuni and his ambitious clan brothers out of the way isn't entirely a bad thing." Snaanscaay snort-laughed. The elder turned back to Elān. "How did you get the Yaabel's weapon onto your hand?"

"I put my hand into it," Elān said. "The weapon let me in."

The elder raised his eyebrows. "Where do the firebolts come from?"

"When you wear the weapon, holes appear in our world, like a robe or blanket with rips in it. The firebolts come from those holes."

The elder shook his head and remained silent for a long time.

"I'm telling you the truth," Elān said.

"Let me see your hands," the elder said.

Elān held up his hands for the elder to examine.

"Snaanscaay, bring that torch here." Snaanscaay held the torch next to Elān's upturned hands. The elder smiled. "Do you see, Snaanscaay? His palms are cut. The Yaabel weapon must need blood to bring down the fire." The elder grabbed Elān's right hand and examined the palm. "How did you cut yourself?"

"I cut myself after I stole the Yaabel's weapon," Elān replied. "I was fighting the cannibal giants' mosquitoes. It was dark. I was hiding under a blanket. I grabbed a sword by the blade."

"That has the feel of a lie," the elder replied. "Snaanscaay, you will check if any of these Aaní prisoners' swords are sharp enough to cut flesh just by grabbing the blade." Snaanscaay nodded. The elder looked at Elān. "So much deception. I know you think you've fooled me, but I see through your deception to what little truth you've kept in your net. You deserve death." The elder closed his eyes. "Yet, you were indeed wearing the Yaabel weapon when we pulled you from the sea. Perhaps I can make this bargain with you, Elān: tell me how the Yaabel weapon works, and I'll spare your crew, and even let them leave our territory. You, however, will be held responsible for Uyuuni's death. As you know, that means you must die."

Elān's throat constricted.

"So, tell me how the Yaabel's weapon works," the elder said.

Elān remained silent. He could hear a note of interest and curiosity in the elder's tone. Then it dawned on him: the Yahooni didn't know how to work the dzanti. His tiredness had constricted his thinking, but now he realized he hadn't heard the explosions around the village he would hear if the Yahooni knew how to use it. If he alone could use the dzanti, the Yahooni would want him alive. His throat unclenched.

"Elān? Save your crew. Tell me how that Yaabel weapon works."

Elān composed himself. "Put your hand into it and grab the handle," he said. "All you need is your mind."

"Ach. All you need is your mind." The elder turned to go, and cast a final look at Elān. "Behold the mighty Aaní, Snaanscaay," he sneered. "The terror of the Éil', the fiercest warriors on the sea, the villains of stories that scare our children. But what are they really?" The elder frothed as he spoke. "They are a nation of thieves and liars. They are a people without honor. They are pitiful and pathetic. And they will always be our ever-enemy." The elder left the cell. Snaanscaay followed with the torch, stubbed it out in the ground, and locked the cell door.

Elān breathed deeply to calm himself. For some reason, the Koosh's words came to mind, about how one could discover much about people in this world by discovering who their 'they' is. The Aaní were the Yahooni's 'they,' just as the Yahooni had always been the Aaní's 'they.' The cannibal giants were also the Aaní's 'they.' And a dozen other nations were the Aaní's 'they' too, even though, Elān had to admit, all those nations had much in common with the Aaní. The Koosh said he and his foul brethren had come to this world to save the nations of Éil'. *Save us from whom?* Elān thought. *From ourselves? The Koosh think they're here to save us from ourselves?* Elān looked around the dark Yahooni cell. *Maybe the Koosh are right. We'd rather destroy each other than unite and destroy the Koosh.* Elān rested his head in the corner of the cell. *We're stuck in old stories.* He closed his eyes. *We're all stuck in ancient stories.*

CHAPTER 38

"Crappy? Oh, Crappy? Are you here?"

Raven's voice woke Elān as though it were a dzanti firebolt. He could hear raven's wings flapping around the cell next to his.

"Here!" Elān sprung from the floor and stumbled to the cell door. He'd slept disturbed by the faces of the dead Yahooni slaves floating disembodied through his dreams, as several nights had passed through dawn into morning and long days.

"So many stinking cells. Where are you, Crapshack?"

"Here." Elān's voice croaked.

Raven landed in the small square opening above the cell door and peered down at Elān. "What did I miss?"

Looking up at raven, anger, relief, joy, and panic swirled inside Elān. He was overcome, and words jumbled and blocked one another when he tried to speak. "Dláa."

Raven laughed. "A natural speechifier."

"Where's you been at?" Elan blurted, words stumbling into each other.

"*I been at* flying atop mountains to turn over even the littlest stone, you moron."

Elān stared at raven in disbelief.

"And I stopped by Choosh to crap on your grandfather's statue."

"We needed you," Elān said. Unblocked, words spilled out in a torrent. "Everything's come unraveled. The Yahooni have taken *Waka*. They said they would kill me. They've interrogated me. They're going to kill us. I know they are. They'll kill us, raven. All is lost. They may have killed the others already for all I know. The crew is locked in these forest cells."

"Yes, I saw Old Miss Sourbag in her cell," raven replied. "I saw Zero and Turds-for-Hair and that crap-eating wolf, but I didn't find Old Man Bellyache. What happened to him?"

"A Koosh's arrow pierced his stomach."

"Old Man Bellyache's nickname came true, then," raven said. Elān was surprised; raven sounded sympathetic.

"By the smell of things in this cell, your nickname has come true too. I'm famished. Where's the food?"

"They've been feeding me only salmon scraps."

"Scraps? I fly all the way here from Choosh and all you offer me is salmon scraps?" Raven looked around the cell. "Where's your stupid mitten?"

"The Yahooni took it and all my other possessions," Elān said. "They questioned me about how to use the dzanti."

Raven laughed. "Morons. You Aaní are stupid to be sure, but the Yahooni couldn't find their diapers to crap in without map and compass and jishagoon. How did they ever get that mitten off your hand?"

"They captured our crew," Elān said, "and would have executed them if I hadn't given them the dzanti. I was exhausted from being in the ocean after destroying the Koosh's canoe."

Raven's eyes widened. "You destroyed another Koosh canoe? That's good, Crappy. Very good."

"I tried to destroy the Koosh but the dzanti wouldn't work against him."

Raven talked to the cell's ceiling. "Crapshack thinks the dzanti works on beings from the otherworld." He looked at Elān, laughed, and then turned, bent his legs, and scrunched down on the ledge as though he would fly off. "Well, since things are going so swimmingly here with your steady hand on the tiller, I'm going to flap my ass back to Choosh for an evening of amorousness."

"Wait!" Elān yelled.

Still crouched, raven looked over his shoulder at Elān. "What?"

"I need you," Elān pleaded. "Caraiden and Ch'eet are hurt. The Yahooni say they're going to execute me. You must help us escape."

Raven turned, looked down at Elān, and in a slow, emphatic gesture lifted his left wing high in the air. He nodded with his beak at the uplifted wing. "This is the importance I place on an evening of amorousness." Raven outstretched his right wing and lowered it just off the ledge. He nodded at that wing. "And this is the importance I place on the lives of you and your stupid crew." Raven then pooped a small glob of gray crap on the ledge. "And that's what I think of the Yahooni," he laughed. "Now, convince me my priorities are wrong and I'll consider helping you escape."

"You promised Íxt"—Raven lifted his left wing higher at the mention of the old man's name—"that you would help me and our crew."

"I guided you to the dzanti. It's not my fault your crew of fatheads lost it."

"You were to guide and translate. You have never translated for us, nor are you finished as a guide until we set foot back on Samish Island."

Raven lifted his left wing higher.

Elān gave up. In frustration he kicked the cell door. The thud echoed in the forest. "Okay, leave! Abandon us in your selfishness. I don't need your nothing-help to make my decisions. I'll save the crew on my own."

Raven lowered his left wing and raised his right. Elān's eyes widened. "Because I don't need your help? That's why you lowered your wing?" he asked.

"No," raven replied. "I enjoyed seeing you kick the door. Why don't you smash your head into this stone wall? Come. Do some more fatheaded crap. You might make me stay."

"Shut your stupid beak." Elān punched the door. His hand rang with pain, which he tried to hide from raven. Raven lowered his left wing further and raised his right again. "I'm serious," Elān said to raven. "Go. Fly. I don't need you anymore. The Yahooni don't know how to use the dzanti, so they need me alive. They will have to bring the dzanti to me, or me to the dzanti, and then I'll use it to save my crew. I don't need you. From here forward, I make my own decisions."

Raven lifted high his right wing and lowered his left to the ledge and broke out in a screech of laughter. "Okay, I'll help you."

"Go ahead and mock my words, you stupid bird. I don't need your help."

"I'm not laughing at your fatheaded speech," raven replied. "I'm laughing that you think you're free to make your own decisions."

Elān stopped. "What do you mean?"

"How do you know some other being isn't making your choices for you?" raven asked.

"What other being?"

"There's many other beings besides you, Crapshack."

"Who cares? I need to escape. It doesn't matter right now whether it's me or some other being making decisions for me."

"Or both," raven replied. "Maybe you *and* another being are making your decisions."

"What do you mean both?" Elān asked. "It can't be both."

"Why not?" raven replied.

"Because that doesn't make sense," Elān said. "It's a contradiction."

"Ha, you're too stupid to see that contradictions are the natural order of things in this world. The answer to everything in this world is both, Crappy."

"Are you going to help me?"

"Not until you admit the answer is both."

Elān looked at a dark stone in the wall of his cell. The stupid bird was as annoying to talk to as the Koosh. "Things can't be both. This stone here is a brick in my cell. It can't be an axe, a statue, a grinding stone, or anything else if it remains a brick in my cell."

"It is all those things and more," raven replied. "Admit it. Smash your head into it and admit it."

"Okay, I admit it," Elān said in exasperation.

"To what are you admitting, my dear Crapshack?" raven asked.

"This is a world of contradictions and the answer can be both."

"Both what, Crappy?"

"Both yes and no. Both I am making decisions and another being is making my decisions. Everything in this world is a contradiction."

"Good. I'll be back soon." Raven leapt off the ledge into the air. His wingbeats faded off toward the village. Elān thought about what raven said about contradictions being the natural order of things in this world. *Yes, raven,* Elān said in his mind, *our world is full of contradictions, and we create tradition to solve them. But tradition itself is a contradiction. Some of us refuse to understand that; some of us understand but ignore the contradiction; and some of us unravel it.*

RAVEN RETURNED AS dusk fell into darkness. He landed in the opening above the cell door and fluffed his wings. "I spent the day in the village, and I've found a way to get you out of here. Like all stupid humans, the clans in this village don't get along. Your silly little mitten has caused quite a commotion. Every crapsack in the village has tried to put the thing on. Morons. One idiot even cut his hand and bled on it, thinking that would work. None have succeeded. Now some old bag of bones clan mother has it locked up in her longhouse and is refusing to let anyone near it. She's set a guard outside her longhouse."

Elān sighed. "How does that help me?"

"First, don't be a dumbass," raven replied. "Second, quit being a dumbass. Know your stories. I've convinced a dumberass-than-you Yahooni warrior from a jealous clan to help you steal the box from the old clan mother's longhouse. Just open the box and let out the light, so to speak."

Elān nodded. "Yes," he said. "That could work. What's his name?"

"I didn't ask his stupid name," raven said.

"Why will he help?" Elān asked. "What does he want in return?"

"He wants to be leader of this village when you destroy the clan mother's council."

"Destroy the clan mothers? I don't want to do that."

"Then don't. Or do. Or both. You must get that dzanti back on your hand and get back to destroying Koosh. We've wasted too much time as it is because of your little vacation here."

"When do we escape?" Elān asked.

"I don't know," raven said in exasperation. "This Yahooni is a special variety of dumbass. Planning, thinking, and breathing are not his strengths. Just be ready when he comes. Now, any more stupid questions before I go?"

"You're leaving?"

"Apparently you are full of stupid questions."

"Why do you always leave when I need you most?" Elān asked.

Raven shook his head. "Of the massive crapsack of despicable traits you humans carry around on your backs, clinginess is the reekiest."

"At least tell me where you're going and where you'll be."

"I'm off to Choosh for a feast of real salmon," raven said. "And afterward all the passion these wings can hold." Raven leapt off the ledge and took flight through the forest. "Laters, Fathead."

CHAPTER 39

TWO NIGHTS LATER, with the forest cloaked in that deep darkness just before dusk, Elān heard his cell door open. He crawled to the back. "Hello?" Elān couldn't see anything in the thick darkness of the cell. The intruder bore no torch or light.

"Elān?" The voice came in a whisper across the dark cell.

"Yes."

"Your ancestors," the voice whispered.

"And yours," Elān whispered back.

"I'm here to help."

"Did raven send you?" Elān asked.

"What?"

"Raven. Did raven send you?"

There was a pause. "Yes. I'm raven-sent."

"What's your name?" Elān asked.

"It's best for your safety that you do not know," the voice replied in an Aaní accent. "Call me Raven-sent."

"Your accent," Elān said. "It's Aaní."

"Yes. I'm mainland Aaní from the Far Out Fort. I'm spying for our people. I'm here to help you escape."

"Raven didn't say you were Aaní."

"What?"

"Raven didn't say you were Aaní."

There was another pause. "I didn't tell him."

"Raven said you were a Yahooni warrior."

"I am an Aaní spy pretending to be a Yahooni warrior."

"If you're Aaní, why do you want to become leader of this lousy Yahooni village?"

"What?"

Elān was suspicious. "If you're Aaní, what are the Houses of Naasteidi?"

"There's no time for stupid tests, Elān," Raven-sent urged. "You must listen to me."

"Answer my question," Elān demanded. "What are the Houses of Naasteidi?"

"How dare you test me?" Raven-sent growled. "You're the one locked in a cell in enemy territory and I'm here to help."

"Name for me the Houses of Naasteidi or I'll inform every guard sent here that they have a spy in their midst."

"You'd betray a fellow Aaní?" Raven-sent asked.

"What are the Houses of Naasteidi?"

Raven-sent exhaled aloud. "On the eagle side, you have the Flicker House of the famous Latseen, the Murrelet House, the Heron House, and of course the Dreamer's Vision House. There's also the Star House, Puffin House, and Medicine Bow House."

"Is that all of them?" Elān asked.

"That's all from the Stomach Tribe, but I would never omit the raven houses of the Tribe From Across The Water: the Man's Foot House, the Sea Monster House, the Owl House, Brown Bear House, Marten House, Whale House, Raven's House—which is home to my clan relatives—and, of course, the famous House Drifted Ashore." Elān relaxed. It was unlikely a Yahooni would know all the houses specific to Naasteidi. Raven-sent was indeed a fellow Aaní. Elān smiled in the darkness. There was security in knowing he was in the presence of another tribesman.

"Which house are you?" Raven-sent asked.

"Flicker House," Elān replied.

"Ah, just like the great Latseen," Raven-sent replied. "One of your relatives, perhaps?"

"He was my grandfather."

Raven-sent laughed. "Ei haaw! The grandson of the great Latseen. Trapped in a stinking Yahooni cell." Laughter echoed off the stones.

Elān didn't like the depth of the laughter. "How long have you been a spy?"

Raven-sent controlled his laughter. "An entire winter and I've one more winter to go," he replied. "I pretend to be an Island Yahooni who escaped the Koosh onslaught. The Yahooni here attached me to a small outsiders' house of disenfranchised and distant cousins. They have me doing warrior duties. Now, if you trust me, let's get you out of here."

Elān wished raven were here so he could verify for certain Raven-sent's trustworthiness, but that stupid bird was always gone when needed. Elān nodded into the darkness. *I must make my own decisions.*

"Elān?"

"I trust you," Elān said. "Get me out of here. I've got to save my crew and get aboard my canoe. We need to get the dzanti first, though. We'll need it to fight the Koosh. I also need the maps and other things these lousy Yahooni stole from me."

"I will help you," Raven-sent said. "Tell me, how does the dzanti work?"

"I don't know," Elān said. "I put my hand inside it, grab the handle, and use my mind to call down firebolts through holes in the sky."

"Can others use it?"

"I don't know."

"Where did you find the dzanti and how did you first put it on?"

Elān felt he needed to guard his answer, unsure where the feeling came from. "I snuck aboard a Koosh ship and stole it. It was sitting in an opened lockbox. I was able to put my hand inside, but I don't know how."

"Where did this happen? Where was the Koosh ship?"

"In Botson's Bay down south," Elān replied.

There was a long pause in the darkness. "Yahooni rumor says your palms are cut," Raven-sent said. "Does blood have anything to do with using the dzanti?"

"That elder asked the same question," Elān said. "I told him I cut my palms after I got the dzanti, but that was a lie. I was bleeding when I grabbed it. I think it's powered by my blood in some way. I can feel it diminishing my energy. It's exhausting. The flames are not as powerful when I'm exhausted."

"Hmmm. What about that strange glass and metal object that the Yahooni took from you?"

"I stole it from the Koosh ship, too. I was told by a dying Yahooni slave that the Koosh use it like our jishagoon for navigation, but I don't know how it works."

"Does it have anything to do with the dzanti?" Raven-sent asked. "Did you need to hold it to put on the dzanti? Do you think it powers the dzanti?"

The question gave Elān an odd feeling. "I don't know," he replied. "I don't need to hold it or have it with me to use the dzanti, but I've always had it close by when I've worn the dzanti. Maybe it does have something to do with it."

"Is there any more you can tell me about how the dzanti works?" Raven-sent asked. "The Yahooni have bled on it but not been able to use it."

"Maybe I need to bleed on it first before others can use it," Elān said. "I don't know for sure. All I know for certain is when I put it on, my thoughts become reality."

"There's nothing else you can tell me?" Raven-sent asked.

"No. Get me out of here. Raven said the dzanti is with the head clan mother. Take me there. Once I get the dzanti, I can free the crew."

Dusk had arrived. "Okay," Raven-sent said. "Let's go now while they all sleep. Follow me and I'll lead you into the village." Raven-sent grabbed Elān and ran out of the cell through the gray forest. Elān could see that Raven-sent had his long black hair cut Yahooni fashion. He wore thin leather Yahooni armor but carried no weapons. Elān wondered for a quick moment why he wasn't armed if he were pretending to be a Yahooni warrior.

Raven-sent stopped on the edge of the forest, let go of Elān, and nodded toward the path to the village. "Come. We must go." Elān hesitated for a moment and then ran after Raven-sent. The clean, cool air of the forest hit him, and he felt a sense of relief at being free of the close, rancid air of his cell.

Elān caught up with Raven-sent. "Should we free my crew first?"

"There's no time," Raven-sent hissed. "We must get you to the dzanti."

Elān saw the logic. Without the dzanti, he could do nothing. His crew would have to remain in their cells a while longer. Still, Elān felt suspicious of Raven-sent's eagerness.

He ran behind Raven-sent out of the forest toward the outskirts of Tsedi. Elān could see the massive totem pole rising in the distance. They approached Tsedi from the forest road behind the village, and Elān noted there were no sentries guarding it from this side. Naasteidi always had a cordon of warriors on guard around the entire village throughout the day and night, but perhaps the Yahooni trained their sentries in different tactics. Raven-sent sprinted down the forest road and hid behind a longhouse on the edge of the village. Elān caught up and crouched down next to Raven-sent. They both peered around the edge of the longhouse toward the village center. The streets looked empty.

Raven-sent pointed with his lips toward the center of the village and took off running. Elān followed. Whenever Raven-sent ducked behind a longhouse, Elān did the same. The village of Tsedi was much larger than Elān recalled. They made their way toward the center, weaving in and out of streets, ducking and hiding as they went.

When they reached the massive pole in the fountain, Raven-sent nodded toward a large, stone-walled longhouse set off behind it. He led Elān toward the stone longhouse. They then hid among blankets and clothes hanging from a long drying rack off the corner of the large stone building.

Most longhouses in Tsedi, as in Naasteidi, were built with split cedar planking. Stone longhouses were rare. Up close, Elān could see the roof of the longhouse also appeared to be made of long, thin overlapping slats of stone. He'd never seen a stone roof on a longhouse before. The main entrance on the front was made of two wooden canoes—one right side up, one upside down—that looked like a protruding bird's beak. The top canoe could be lowered down onto the bottom canoe to close the door. The canoe-door was painted in the thunderbird design of Yahooni fashion.

Raven-sent gestured toward the canoe-door. "That's the entrance," he whispered. "I'll go first. Wait here. If it's safe, I'll signal you."

Elān grabbed Raven-sent's arm. "We can't go through the front," Elān said. "We'll get caught."

"Trust me," Raven-sent said. "They're all asleep. It's the only way in."

"There has to be another entrance in the back," Elān whispered. Longhouses always had back entrances.

"No," Raven-sent whispered. "Wait here." Raven-sent sprinted from the drying racks. He peered into the canoe-door and then ducked inside and disappeared. A moment later he popped his head back out and signaled for Elān to come.

Elān ran from his hiding spot behind the blankets on the drying rack to the canoe-door. He looked inside. Raven-sent stood by a thick leather curtain that hung before the opening leading into the longhouse. Raven-sent lifted the curtain and motioned Elān forward. Elān walked through the canoe-door. He could smell cookfire smoke. He thought he heard whispers. Elān hesitated. Raven-sent grabbed Elān's arm and dragged him through the curtain. Once inside, two Yahooni warriors grabbed Elān by the arms and clapped a heavy metal collar around his neck.

Raven-sent stepped back and smiled. "Sorry, cousin."

THE LONGHOUSE WAS filled with Yahooni. Warriors lined the perimeter. Carved, thick wooden posts reached from floor to ceiling across the open space inside, and a large firepit in the center held glowing coals. On a high platform above the firepit sat the clan mother, Caskae. Hers was the largest chair. A few Yahooni, weighed down by the heavy blankets they wore, sat on pillows around her. "Where are the other Aaní sea-trash?"

"They're coming, Caskae," replied a warrior standing toward the back of the longhouse.

Caskae glowered at Elān. "He looks even more meager than he did the other night."

"Yes, Caskae."

"I would have run my sword through him with ease in my younger days."

"Certainly, Caskae."

Rage and confusion wove themselves through Elān's mind. His entire body trembled. *Why did you send a betrayer, raven?* he mind-pleaded. *Why send a betrayer?*

"Did you get the information I requested?" Caskae asked Raven-sent.

"Yes, Caskae," Raven-sent replied.

"Well? How do we use the Yaabel's weapon?"

"You agreed to free me," Raven-sent replied. "Is that still our agreement? I would have it proclaimed in front of all Tsedi."

"Yes," Caskae replied. "You are free once you tell me the secret to the Yaabel's weapon."

Raven-sent pointed at Elān. "He thinks it runs on his blood, Caskae. He also thinks he must first bleed on it before you can use it."

"He thinks? You don't know?" Caskae asked.

"I'm certain it is his blood, Caskae."

"Why his blood?" Caskae asked. "What is so important about *his* blood?"

"He's the grandson of Latseen, Caskae." The longhouse roared in anger, with Yahooni of all ages screaming for vengeance against Elān.

Caskae held up her hand to silence the crowd and glared at Elān. "The Great Oppressor's grandson." A slow smile played across her face. "The grandson of the Great Oppressor stands before me." She turned to Raven-sent. "It's his blood, then? His blood will allow us to use this weapon?"

"Yes, Caskae."

"You may go. You are no longer a slave." Raven-sent ran from the longhouse. "Bring me the grandson of the Great Oppressor," Caskae said. Two Yahooni guards grabbed Elān by the arms and collar chain and forced him to stand before Caskae's raised platform. She looked down at Elān and shook her head. "So much trouble from one so meager." She looked to a blanketed Yahooni on the platform next to her. "Who could imagine the blood of the Great Oppressor runs through the veins of one so meager?" Caskae turned back to Elān. "This morning a headless corpse drapes a shame pole at the entrance to Atna'tuu Bay. Your headless corpse will soon accompany it."

Elān's legs buckled. Caraiden. The Yahooni warriors on either side of him grumbled and yanked him to his feet. A commotion broke out from the back of the longhouse as Kwa, Ch'eet, Hoosa, and Chetdyl were ushered in chains into the center of the longhouse. Elān's eyes welled when he didn't see Caraiden with the rest of the crew. Caraiden was indeed dead—murdered in the most dishonorable fashion.

Yahooni warriors forced Elān's crew to their knees in front of the coals. Chetdyl growled when a warrior kicked him, but he relented and lay down next to the others. Ch'eet wore a bandage over his eye, but the bandage looked clean. The crew looked tired but healthy considering their long, cold confinement. Elān held each of the crew with his gaze as long as he could bare it. Tears ran from his eyes.

"We heard you were a dishonoring sort," Caskae said. "You dishonor everyone here with your tears. We shall redeem this dishonor with your death." She turned again to a blanketed Yahooni next to her and motioned with her lips. The blanketed Yahooni picked up a box laying nearby and handed it to Caskae. Elān recognized the lockbox. Caskae placed the lockbox on her lap and pulled the key— Elān's key—from around her neck to open it. She glared at Elān. "Four more shame poles are being readied right now. They will hold the bodies of the rest of your Aaní sea-trash friends unless you show me, straightforward and simple, how to use this weapon." She tilted the lockbox toward Elān.

"Your head we'll throw to the ocean," the blanketed Yahooni said.

Caskae held up her hand to silence the other Yahooni. "The grandson of the Great Oppressor dishonoring his memory and his enemies. Whatever could be said of your grandfather, and a lot could and should be said about his evil, he would not stand in dishonor crying like a child."

Elān hung his head. *Poor Caraiden*, he thought to himself. *Beheaded far from home. I'm sorry, Caraiden.* Tears dripped from his eyes.

"Well?" Caskae barked. "Have you no honor? Speak."

"I don't care about honor or dishonor. I don't care about my grandfather, or you or your stupid village," Elān said. "I care about my friends." He reached out to Caraiden in his mind. *I'm sorry.*

"Spoken like one without honor," Caskae replied. "Look at me." Elān looked up at the clan mother. She lifted the box off her lap. "Show me how to use this weapon or I'll kill the rest of your friends." With her lips, she motioned at the guard next to Elān. "Unsheath your sword and put it against the neck of young one-eye there. On my command, I want you to slice through his neck. Not chop, not hack. Slice. Slow and painful."

The guard dropped Elān's arm and neck-collar chain and strode behind Ch'eet. He bared his sword and lay the edge against Ch'eet's neck. Caskae nodded at the guard and looked down at Elān. "Show me."

Elān heard raven's laughter. The laughter was so clear and close Elān looked around the posts and rafters of the longhouse thinking raven may be perched or flitting about nearby. Raven wasn't there. Raven was in Elān's mind. His voice was bright and playful. *Who's making your decisions now, dumbass?*

"Show me how to use this weapon," Caskae demanded.

As usual, it falls to me to get you out of this, Crapshack. Raven's voice was loud in Elān's head. *Repeat every word I say to that decrepit pile of crap sitting in her fancy chair.*

"Show me!"

Shut your fat crap sack, you moldy pile of bones.

Through raven, Elān found his voice. "Shut your fat crap sack, you moldy pile of bones," he yelled up to Caskae. The mob in the longhouse gasped in unison.

Raven kept going. *Pry your stinking butt cheeks from that stupid fancy chair of yours and hand me that lousy lockbox that has all you dumbass Yahooni crapping your diapers. Give me a knife so I can cut myself and I'll show you how to use this horrible weapon.*

Elān yelled the words up at Caskae as fast as raven put them in his head. "Pry your stinking butt cheeks from that stupid fancy chair of yours and hand me that lousy lockbox that has all you dumbass Yahooni crapping your diapers. Give me a knife so I can cut myself and I'll show you how to use this horrible weapon."

Sure, you'll become the most powerful clan mother in the history of Éil', but that's like being the brightest berry in a furry pile of grizzly turds.

"Sure, you'll become the most powerful clan mother in the history of Éil', but that's like being the brightest berry in a furry pile of grizzly turds."

You'll still be a stupid, fatheaded log of crap, no matter what silly mitten you wipe your ass with.

"You'll still be a stupid, fatheaded log of crap, no matter what silly mitten you wipe your ass with."

Raven's laughter faded in echoes from Elān's mind. Elān turned and looked at the Yahooni crowding the longhouse—all eyes shocked, all mouths opened or palmed behind trembling hands. He looked at Ch'eet and saw the fear in his exposed eye. Kwa had her eyes closed and was shaking her hung head in a slow arc. Elān listened but heard no more words from raven. *Where are you?* his mind yelled out. No answer.

Elān looked up at Caskae. He expected to see a scalding rage and hear the command that would bring the razor's edge of the Yahooni sword biting into Ch'eet's neck. Instead, the wrinkles in Caskae's forehead and cheeks creased in a wry smile. The longhouse remained silent. All eyes turned to her. Her smile widened.

"You do have some honor, then," she said to Elān. "So, it is your blood after all?"

Elān remained silent, waiting for raven's words.

"Answer me," Caskae demanded.

"Yes, yes," Elān stammered. He wasn't sure what to say. "My blood will open the dzanti and then you can put your hand into it, clan mother, and the Yaabel's weapon will be yours." Caskae held Elān's eyes for a long time, smiled again, and then turned to the blanketed Yahooni next to her and held out the open lockbox. "Take this to that crap-brained, turd-from-the-Great-Oppressor's-ass-cheeks, Aaní sea-trash down there, but don't let him touch it. Give it to Saghani."

The blanketed Yahooni took the lockbox and disappeared from the platform. Caskae looked down at the guard next to Elān. "Saghani, do you have a knife with you?"

"Yes, Caskae," the guard replied.

"Give it to this Aaní sea-trash," Caskae replied. "Hold the lockbox with the Yaabel's weapon beneath his hand as he cuts himself. Let him bleed on the Yaabel weapon, but do not let him touch it."

The blanketed Yahooni came out from behind the platform bearing the lockbox. Saghani drew a small-bladed knife from his belt and handed it to Elān. Elān took the knife. It had an ornately carved handle in the form of a raven's beak.

"Eldaan'ne and C'aats'ne," Caskae said to two Yahooni warriors standing nearby, "grab hold of this Aaní sea-trash and make sure he doesn't use that knife on anything but himself." The two warriors nodded and made their way across the longhouse to Elān. They grabbed him tight by the arms. The one on Elān's left also grabbed hold of his collar chain.

"Nalbaey," Caskae called to the guard whose sword lay against Ch'eet's neck, "any sign of trouble, slash that man's head from his body."

"Yes, Caskae," the guard replied.

Elān trembled with panic. The clan mother would soon realize Elān didn't know how to let others use the dzanti. *Where are you, raven?* No answer.

"Take the lockbox, Saghani, and hold it under this Aaní coward so he may bleed onto the weapon."

Saghani took the lockbox from the blanketed Yahooni and crouched down next to Elān. He held the lockbox below Elān's hands. The dzanti rested inside it. This was his only chance. He jerked his arms hard and lowered his hands down toward the dzanti, but the guards were ready, and they yanked him back up and held him firm.

"Try that again and your friends all die," Caskae said to Elān. She stood from her chair and looked around the longhouse. "Many winters ago, the Great Oppressor came to our land bringing death and destruction with every footstep. I was here when he and his allied Aaní and Deikeenaa army attacked Tsedi and killed our warriors. I stood among my warrior ranks with my hands bound as I watched him burn our bows and take our weapons. I warned him he should not leave me alive, for I would smolder for revenge. 'I would you had that same passion for peace,' he said to me." Caskae spat without looking onto the fine blanket of a young woman sitting below her. "He should have never left me alive, because today his dishonorable, coward grandson will give me the very weapon that will bring about the undoing of all Deikeenaa and Aaní people."

The longhouse burst out in cheers. Yahooni warriors banged their swords on the stone walls. Caskae waited until the crowd calmed. She sneered down at Elān. "Now, bleed, coward."

With his guards holding him tight, Elān used his left hand to push the raven blade into the fleshy part of the bottom of his right palm. Blood spilled from around the blade. He clenched his hand into a fist and blood dripped and oozed over the top of the dzanti.

"Now, Saghani, bring the weapon here."

"Yes, Caskae." Saghani, still crouched, looked up at Elān and paused. The ghost of a smile appeared in Saghani's eyes. In a slow, exaggerated movement, Saghani stood, his knees cracking as he rose. Instead of turning away, he brought the lockbox straight up to Elān's hands. Elān slid his bleeding right hand into the dzanti. The crowding Yahooni gasped.

How did raven put it? Elān thought to himself as he felt

the familiar oddness of the dzanti on his hand. *Open the box and let out the light?* He squeezed the figure eight handle and thought, *No, raven, I will open the box and let in the light.* The floor of the longhouse rumbled. The Yahooni warrior to his left tried to grab the dzanti. His fingers smoked and he collapsed with a shriek. The floor heaved. The guards holding Elān's arms fell away. *Now*, thought Elān, *bring the fire.*

A flash brighter than anything Elān had ever seen from the dzanti erupted above the heads of all gathered in the longhouse, and the entire roof exploded outward.

CHAPTER 40

SUNLIGHT STREAMED INTO the longhouse. The sky around Tsedi was torn full of holes. Broken roof slats clattered down over the village. The Yahooni inside the now roofless building covered their ears after the explosion and gaped in shock. Elān looked at the warrior whose blade had been on Ch'eet's neck. He'd fallen to the ground with the sword still in hand. Elān squeezed the dzanti handle. *Never again will he threaten my friend.* A firebolt roasted him to cinders as quick as Elān had had the thought. He looked up at the raised platform. Caskae's lackeys had surrounded her—as though their feeble arms and heavy blankets could protect her. A bolt vaporized them where they huddled and set the platform afire.

Some of the Yahooni warriors in the now open longhouse had recovered from their panic and were drawing weapons. *I want to destroy them all and save my friends.* The sky-holes responded. Angry firebolts erupted from dozens of holes and seared through the bodies of the Yahooni warriors where they stood.

Elān lifted the dzanti from the lockbox still in Saghani's hands. The ghost smile was gone and only terror shone on Saghani's face. "Your ancestors," Elān said. Saghani dropped the lockbox. Elān handed him the raven knife and nodded to his friends still kneeling by the firepit, whose coals had sprung into small flames. "Free them," he said. Saghani took the knife and cut the binding cords of the crew.

Most of the Yahooni men in the longhouse had been charred to death, but the remaining Yahooni villagers—old men and women and children—clogged the entrance to the longhouse in a mass of bodies as they tried to get out in a panic. Some were scaling the crumbled stone walls. Soon, the longhouse was empty of Yahooni except for Saghani. Elān felt a hand on his shoulder and turned to see Kwa. Overwhelmed, Elān embraced her in a firm hug.

"Careful," Kwa protested. "That dzanti almost killed me last time I touched it."

"Sorry," Elān said. He lifted his right hand up and away from her.

Ch'eet and Hoosa came over and he embraced them both, though Hoosa didn't seem interested in a reunion requiring human touch. His embrace was quick and stiff. Elān knelt, grabbed the back of Chetdyl's head with his left hand, and put his nose to Chetdyl's nose. They breathed each other's exhales several times. "Thank you, my friend," Elān said.

He stood. Tears streaked down his face. "Kwa, can you be in charge, please?" Elān pleaded. "This is a battle situation and Caraiden..."

"I hear you, Elān," Kwa said. "First, we need weapons and armor. Swords and shields. Bows if possible. This longhouse should have them. We move as a unit outside this longhouse. We keep Elān behind our shield wall. There's no escape without the dzanti. Do not linger in the open streets, shields up always for archer attack, eliminate any resistance, and let's make our way to *Waka*. Elān, be ready to use that dzanti. We'll bring this entire village down on top of these lousy Yahooni if we must. Quick, now. Gather weapons, shields, and armor and then we go."

Ch'eet, Hoosa, and Kwa went in different directions in a frantic search of the longhouse. "Over here," Ch'eet yelled. "There's a small armory under the platform." Kwa and Hoosa ran to join Ch'eet. Chetdyl stayed at Elān's side. Saghani, the

Yahooni guard, stood off by the firepit. He kept his head low and looked at Elān sideways.

"Don't worry, we won't harm you," Elān told him.

"Don't destroy the village. My family lives here. I have children."

"I won't harm anyone who doesn't threaten me or my friends." Elān held up the dzanti. "I don't like using this."

"I didn't understand that weapon," Saghani replied. He looked at the longhouse and then up at the sky. "I didn't want this."

"You've never seen the Yaabel use one?"

"No."

Chetdyl left Elān's side and went to Saghani. Saghani scratched Chetdyl behind his ears. Chetdyl inclined his head, enjoying the feeling. Elān felt a warmth, a brotherhood, with both wolf and human. He tapped his metal collar with the dzanti. "Can you take this off me?" he asked Saghani.

Saghani nodded. He left Chetdyl and came next to Elān, retrieved a key ring from his belt, and clicked through several keys until he found the one he sought. He unlocked Elān's collar and tossed it, clanking, to the floor.

"Why did you do it?" Elān asked Saghani.

"Caskae and her clan are unbearable to live under," Saghani replied. "I wanted to end Caskae's tyranny over our village. But I didn't want this." He waved his arm across the corpse-strewn longhouse.

Kwa, Ch'eet, and Hoosa returned wearing ill-fitting Yahooni armor and helmets, and bearing swords, shields, and bows with full quivers. Elān could see through Ch'eet's helmet that he had fastened a leather patch over his wounded eye. Kwa set down a leather cuirass and metal helmet at Elān's feet. "They might not fit well," she said, "but they'll provide some protection. Ch'eet, scout the front entrance. See if any Yahooni are stupid enough to stand against us. Hoosa, search the back of this longhouse for another entrance. Make sure we're not taken by surprise from behind." Ch'eet and Hoosa ran off as instructed. Kwa pointed with her lips to Saghani. "Do we kill him?

"No," Elān said. "We let him live."

"What do we do with him?"

"He doesn't want us to destroy Tsedi." Elān turned to the Yahooni. "Can you convince your people to let us go?"

Saghani thought for a moment. "I don't know. Many will be happy that Caskae no longer keeps our village in her tight net. But, after seeing this…" He waved his arm again over the burnt corpses. "You killed our relatives." He pointed to the charred corpse that minutes earlier had been the Yahooni guard whose sword lay along Ch'eet's neck. "He was my brother from the opposite clan," Saghani said. "He was a good warrior. He was a good man." Tears welled up in his eyes. "Yaahl, help me."

"Tell your people to let us go," Elān said. "We'll walk through your village, get in our canoe, and leave. We won't harm your people if they leave us alone and let us go."

Saghani stood silent. Tears fell down his face.

Kwa lifted her sword toward Saghani. "I won't leave you here alive to attack us from behind while we make our escape. Stay and die, or go and talk to your people."

Saghani looked to be in shock. He didn't speak. Kwa lifted her sword to his neck. "Go and talk to your people, or you die."

The touch of metal against his skin appeared to waken him. "I will ask them," he said, "but I don't know if they will listen."

"You must convince them," Elān said. He bent down and picked up the cuirass and put it on. It was loose, but the thick, hard leather would provide some protection. He put on the metal Yahooni helmet and looked at Kwa. "Ready?"

Kwa nodded. "Hoosa!" she yelled toward the back of the longhouse. "We're moving out. Protect our rear." A moment later, Hoosa jogged out in full armor from behind the platform. Kwa motioned the crew forward. As they approached the entryway, she motioned the crew to halt and lifted the edge of the leather curtain. "Ch'eet?"

Ch'eet poked his head under the curtain. "Yahooni warriors block all the streets out of the village center, Kwa. They're waiting for us. Come. Look."

The crew went through the thick leather curtain and stood in the canoe-door. The top canoe had collapsed down into the bottom one, but there was enough space on both sides between the canoes to see the streets around the longhouse. Yahooni warriors formed a shield wall in an arc, forty paces from the entrance.

Elān motioned Saghani into the canoe-door and held up the dzanti. "Go. Convince them to let us pass unharmed." Ch'eet walked to the front of the canoe-door and pushed up on the top canoe, opening the door enough to let Saghani exit.

"Give me time," Saghani said.

"Go," Elān replied.

Saghani stepped through the small gap in the canoe-door and held up his hands as he sprinted toward the shield wall. The shield wall opened to let him through. Elān crouched in the bottom of the canoe-door and peered out of the gap at the wall of Yahooni shields and the helmeted heads behind those shields. Their way out was through the village center, past the massive totem pole. Several rows of Yahooni warriors stood in front of the pole, blocking Elān's view. "How long should we wait?" he asked Kwa.

"Not long," she replied.

"I don't want to kill those warriors out there," Elān said.

"You may have to help us escape," Kwa replied. "Hoosa, what do you see?"

Hoosa was guarding their rear. "Nothing," he replied.

"Is anyone entering over the walls?"

"No."

Kwa looked at Elān. "Never more than a word or two in any Hoosa sentence."

The crew waited, anxious for some sign from Saghani. The sun was still on its morning climb in the cloudless sky. With the dzanti on his hand, Elān could see the rips in the world shimmering above him. A wobbly darkness wavered inside them.

"Movement out front," Ch'eet said. He opened a small gap in the canoe-door so the crew could get a better view. In front of the large totem pole, the warriors in the shield wall had stepped aside to form a corridor. A young man walked through the shield wall and approached the longhouse.

"Someone's coming," Ch'eet said.

The young man stopped twenty paces from the canoe-door. "Elān," the young man yelled out. "Elān, cousin, I have a message."

"Who is he?" Kwa asked. "And why does he have an Aaní accent?"

"He's the one who betrayed me," Elān replied. He crept to the front of the canoe-door next to Ch'eet.

"Elān. Listen to me."

"You're lucky to be alive, Raven-sent," Elān yelled. "Did Saghani convince the Yahooni to let us go?"

"What?" Raven-sent looked confused. "Saghani?"

"Did he convince the Yahooni?"

"Convince them to do what?" Raven-sent said in an amused tone.

"To let us pass through the village unharmed and leave in our canoe."

"The last we saw of Saghani, he was running with his family into the forest behind the village."

Kwa laughed. Elān glared at her in annoyance.

"Did he not say anything to the Yahooni leaders?" Elān asked.

"Not that I know of," Raven-sent replied. "Listen, Elān, I've got a message for you. The three remaining Yahooni clan mothers demand—" A jagged, electric bolt flashed from a rip in the sky and knocked Raven-sent to the ground. His entire body spasmed and his arms and legs flailed on the flagstones.

"Did you kill him?" Ch'eet asked.

"I don't think so," Elān replied. "I wanted to shut him up." He held up the dzanti.

"Shouldn't we at least have listened to his message?" Ch'eet asked.

"We can't trust anything that traitor says," Elān replied.

Raven-sent's body was spasming on the street. The shield wall had reformed behind him. "Archers!" Ch'eet yelled. "On top of the longhouses." Elān peered through the canoe-door opening and saw a long line of archers gathering on the roofs of longhouses on both sides of the village center. They were lighting arrows. Ch'eet closed the top of the canoe-door.

"Shields to the sides," Kwa ordered. She and Ch'eet held up their shields to the gaps in the canoe-door. "Now, Elān."

"I can't kill them," Elān said.

"Elān, they will kill us."

"Elān, we need you now," Ch'eet said.

"I can't kill them."

"Then stop them without killing. When we were at sea, how did you get the dzanti to make those mosquitoes disappear?" Kwa asked. "When they reappeared, they were blinded."

"They didn't disappear," Elān replied. "They went into those holes in the sky."

"What holes?" Kwa asked.

Elān forgot that he alone could see the rips in the world.

Fire arrows thwocked into the canoe-door, their burning metal tips ripping through the wood. The reverberations made Elān's ears ring. Chetdyl howled. Flames licked up the insides of the door. Ch'eet broke off an arrow in his shield.

"Elān," Kwa yelled.

371

He looked at Ch'eet's bandage and thought about the mosquitoes and their bleeding eyes. Elān closed his eyes and grabbed the dzanti handle. *I want to blind but not kill these Yahooni warriors.* Elān waited. The handle didn't grow hot. He heard no sounds outside the canoe-door.

"Elān," Kwa pleaded. "Klatseen."

"I think I have to see my enemy," Elān said. "Ch'eet, lift the door."

"Are you insane?" Ch'eet cried.

Another round of fire arrows ripped into the canoes. Elān felt as though his eardrums had burst. Chetdyl lay on the floor with his paws over his ears.

"Elān."

"Now, Ch'eet. Lift the door."

Ch'eet put his shield in front of him and lifted the top canoe on the canoe-door. Elān could see entire the angry ring of shields and helmeted heads. He gripped the dzanti handle and thought, *Yéil, take the eyes and ears of all these Yahooni warriors.* The words flashed in Elān's mind as he thought them. Jagged bolts exploded from scores of holes in the sky, rippling down into the warriors in the shield wall, the archers on the rooftops, and the warriors crowding the village center. Elān collapsed. The dzanti had taken all his adrenaline and energy. He felt life-emptied.

A wave of dreadful wailing, louder than the fire arrows against the canoe-door, filled Tsedi. Ch'eet lifted the canoe-door high. "Come on." Kwa helped Elān to his feet and called for Hoosa to join them. The crew emerged from the canoe-door into the wailing, writhing mass of Yahooni. Kwa and Ch'eet shielded Elān in the front, while Hoosa, bow in hand, and Chetdyl, his massive head turning side to side, guarded from behind. The scene in the village center was awful. Yahooni warriors screamed for help. Blood gushed from their ears, spilling through their helmets onto the flagstones. A thick, bloody, brown ooze trickled from their eye sockets. The flesh around their eyes had been scorched to blackened bone.

Kwa drove her sword under the chinstrap of any blinded warrior who grasped at the legs of the crew as they stepped through the undulating bodies that had formed the shield wall. Elān shuddered at the cool, calm manner in which Kwa walked among the moaning bodies, driving her sword into the throats of the wounded. *The distance between warrior and bookeater is too vast for me to span,* Elān thought. *Yet, I've done more damage with this weapon than any warrior can do with their sword or any writer with their pen.* He tried as best he could to push the questions and confusion from his mind, but each scream, writhing body, and corpse was an accusation he couldn't ignore.

They made it to the fountain at the base of the massive totem pole. "That's the road to the riverbank," Kwa said, pointing to a road off to her left. "We need to stay out of the open. Keep under the awnings of the longhouses on the left side of the street." Kwa crouch-ran down past the fountain. Ch'eet was right behind her, his shield held above his head. Elān couldn't run. He was exhausted and his legs were wobbly. He walked, unsteady, down the steps to the side of the fountain after Kwa.

Hoosa hefted Elān's left arm and supported his body. "Come," he said. "And don't touch me with that weapon." Elān shifted his weight to Hoosa and they made their way across the village center, around the writhing bodies. Many Yahooni warriors were on their knees and crying for help. A few had made it to their feet and were wandering, unsteady, with their arms out as though drunk, falling over other Yahooni, plunging back down to the flagstones. The sickening sound of skulls cracking on stone echoed among the moans.

Chaos and pain, Elān thought as he and Hoosa weaved their way through the trauma to the longhouse where Kwa and Ch'eet waited. Chetdyl trotted behind.

Kwa nodded at Elān. "We make our way along these longhouses. The river is just a short ways down this road. If *Waka* isn't there, we take whatever canoe can hold us all. Let's go." She turned and ran off, holding her shield high. The crew followed her lead as she sprinted across roads and ducked around the corners of longhouses. Elān could see the river's beach in the distance. Kwa sprinted down the cobblestone path onto the beach, threw off her shield, pulled the bow from her shoulder and with amazing speed, fit and loosed an arrow at something in the river outside Elān's view. Ch'eet joined her and together they fired a half dozen arrows each from the beach. Ch'eet stood and Kwa ripped off her chest armor and helmet, sprinted to the river, and dove in.

Elān and Hoosa struggled forward. Kwa swam in smooth, long strokes out to *Waka*, which was floating away in the wide river's current. Ch'eet followed her on the beach, an arrow ready in his bow. Someone moved aboard *Waka*. An unarmored man sat hunched in the canoe stern. Arrows pricked through his chest from the back and out the front. Ch'eet's bow sang and his arrow tore through the man's throat and he fell back to the canoe's floor. *Waka*'s mainsail was half untied—the man had been trying to hoist sail.

Ch'eet raced down to a Yahooni canoe pulled up along the river beach, looked inside, and yanked out a thick coil of rope. "Chetdyl!" he yelled up the beach. "Take an end of this to Kwa." The wolf leapt down onto the beach and grabbed the end of the rope in his mouth and crashed into the river. The rope spooled out of Ch'eet's hand as Chetdyl swam with the current.

Elān couldn't believe how fast Chetdyl could swim. His powerful paws pushed through the river. He reached *Waka* just as the spool of rope came to an end in Ch'eet's hand. Ch'eet held tight the end of the rope and raced downriver alongside the canoe. Chetdyl reached the port outrigger and lifted his head up high, the rope still in his mouth. Kwa had pulled herself onto the netting of *Waka*. She leaned over the outrigger and grabbed the rope, and then lay back down in the netting with her feet against the outrigger. Ch'eet couldn't find purchase in the riverbank sand against the weight of *Waka* and the strength of the current, and he got dragged into the river, still hanging on to the rope.

"Guard our rear," Hoosa said to Elān. He sprinted down the beach and grabbed Ch'eet. And together they hauled on the rope holding *Waka*. Elān turned to the village. He could see no movement down the cobblestone road. He looked back at the river. Far down the beach he could see Ch'eet and Hoosa working together to pull *Waka* ashore. Kwa had lashed the rope around the portside outrigger bow spar and had *Waka*'s prow turned against the current.

Elān sat down on the end of the cobblestone path and watched his crew struggling. He heard the wailing warriors far off in village. *Chaos and pain* came again to his mind. He closed his eyes and saw in vivid color the oozing eye sockets, burned out and sightless. He opened his eyes. *Waka* was closer to shore. Ch'eet and Hoosa were on the riverbank, leaning backward against the force of the rope.

Elān stood and walked the cobblestones into the village. He felt sick. Nobody lingered in the street, no faces appeared in the longhouse doorways, but he had the feeling he was being watched. He could see the top half of the massive totem pole rising above the village. He stopped in the street and examined it. Elān could see the figures on the pole clear and hard-lined even at such a great distance, but he wanted to see the pole in its entirety. He walked past the first row of longhouses and peered up at it. At the very top of the pole, a human, hair cut in Yahooni fashion, held on to the wings of a thunderbird as though in control of and riding the beast. Lower on the pole, the thunderbird held in his claws a human whose tongue was out, and on whose breastplate was a figure

Elān recognized: the Flicker. Elān squeezed the dzanti handle. *Burn*. A tongue of flame crackled from a sky-tear and set the pole afire.

The Yahooni called his grandfather "the Great Oppressor" and crafted a story about their own innocence. They invaded Aaní territory and crafted a story about being the victims of the invading Aaní. They were forced into a peace treaty because they lost the war, and yet they crafted a story about how they killed the Great Oppressor and had the gall to commemorate that lie on the most prominent pole in the village! And they'd beheaded his friend and stuck his head on a shame pole. Contradictions burned inside him as he watched the pole burn: anger mixed with sadness, elation mixed with relief, and, above all, confusion. Elān turned his back to the burning pole and walked back to his crew.

Hoosa and Ch'eet ran up the beach to meet him. "Trouble?" Ch'eet asked.

"No." Elān said. "I corrected the story that pole was proclaiming."

Ch'eet chuckled. "Good. Kwa is with *Waka* down the beach. Chetdyl's gone to look for Caraiden. Hoosa and I are going to scavenge for food and water and anything else we can find in the Yahooni boats over there on the riverbank. Can you watch our backs? Any sign of trouble, we retreat to *Waka*."

Elān wandered around the edge of the village and riverbank, alternating between watching the main street and surrounding longhouses, the beach, and Hoosa and Ch'eet rummaging through the Yahooni canoes. They tossed waterproof bags and bentwood boxes of all sizes out of the canoes into a pile on the beach. They leapt from canoe to canoe and hauled boxes and bags over to *Waka*. As they lifted the last bentwood box, a large box that looked to Elān like a cooking box, Elān noticed a solitary figure, arms loaded, walking down the village street toward the river. Elān gripped the dzanti handle and waited. "Stop there." The figure halted fifty paces from Elān. "What do you hold in your arms, Raven-sent?"

"Your things," Raven-sent replied. "They were in Caskae's clan house." He lifted the Koosh Tas case, and then held up Elān's lockbox. "I put the map and tináa and the Koosh jishagoon inside. All I ask in return is that you take me back home." Raven-sent hugged the lockbox and Tas case tight. "If you torch me, you also torch these."

Elān stared at him in silence for a moment.

The pole burned high above Raven-sent. Elān motioned to it with his lips. "Truthful, now. Did you know about that pole and the story it proclaimed?"

"Yes," Raven-sent replied.

"I remember your laughter when I told you I was Latseen's grandson," Elān said. "What do you think my grandfather would do to you if he were in my place?" He lifted the dzanti. "And had such a weapon as this?"

Without hesitation Raven-sent replied, "I would be fried like Caskae right now."

Elān nodded. He turned the dzanti over, examining the strange, clear substance it was made of. *Like a metal jellyfish*, Elān thought. *Like everything, this dzanti is a contradiction. And how do we make sense of contradictions?* He thought of Caraiden, of his grandfather he never knew, and of raven. *We change the old stories.* He looked back at Raven-sent. "I never knew my grandfather. I'm not him. I'll take you aboard *Waka*." Raven-sent's entire body relaxed in relief. "Come." Elān turned and walked to the beach.

Waka was pulled up downriver on the sandy bank, loaded and ready to sail, when Elān arrived with Raven-sent. Kwa stood on the riverbank, still in Yahooni armor, leaning against the bow of *Waka*. Her sword was out and her bow slung over her shoulder. "We're waiting for Chetdyl to return. Hoosa and Ch'eet are up in the tree line keeping watch," she said. "Why don't you kill that traitor?"

"I've decided to take him with us," Elān replied.

"We don't need captives," Kwa said.

"I'm not a captive," Raven-sent replied. "He's taking me home."

Elān took the lockbox from Raven-sent. "Leave the Tas there on the sand and get in the canoe. Sit against the mast facing the bow." Raven-sent climbed into *Waka* and did as ordered. Once he was seated at the mast, Elān said to Kwa, "Bind him to the mast."

Raven-sent protested but stopped when Kwa vaulted into the canoe with her sword still drawn. She forced Raven-sent to put his hands behind his back around the mast and she bound his wrists together, ran the rope through mast hoops, circled his neck twice, and then tied off the end of the rope on a mast hook above his head. She leveled her sword at his eyes. "Don't make me bind your feet." She kept the sword an inch from his face before turning and jumping over the side of *Waka* to the sandy riverbank. "He won't escape," she told Elān. "You don't intend to take him home, do you?"

"Of course not," Elān replied.

"What will you do with him?" she asked.

"I don't know," Elān said. "I made an unpredictable decision I haven't thought through."

Kwa shook her head. "I don't like unpredictable. Unpredictable leads to impossible situations. But we can always throw him overboard if he grows too burdensome."

CHETDYL, HOOSA, AND Ch'eet jogged out of the woods together down to *Waka*. "Chetdyl found Caraiden's body, I think," Ch'eet said, "on a shame pole where the river meets the bay. But, if I understand what Chetdyl is indicating, he couldn't find Caraiden's head."

Elān peered over the edge of the canoe at Raven-sent. "Do you know what they did with the head of our crewmate they put on the shame pole?"

"Fed to the sea, I would guess," Raven-sent said, "at the bottom of Atna'tuu Bay."

"Poor Caraiden," Elān said.

"Poor Caraiden. We'll need his ashes to do the necessary ceremony when we get home," Kwa said.

"Yes," Elān replied. "Let's retrieve his body."

"Everyone aboard. Hoosa push us off," Kwa said. She pointed her sword at Raven-sent. "Any trouble from you, traitor, and we'll feed your head to the sea."

"Who's this?" Ch'eet asked when saw Raven-sent. "A captive?"

"Something like that," Kwa replied.

Ch'eet took his place in the front seat of *Waka* and grabbed a paddle. Chetdyl leapt onto the bow. Elān tossed the Tas into *Waka* and hooked the dzanti over the side, and with Kwa's help pulled himself into the canoe.

"The lousy Yahooni stole most of the things we had in *Waka* and in the outrigger holds," Kwa told Elān. "But Hoosa and Ch'eet were able to outfit us for the voyage home. Our main need will be food and water. I've filled the skins and the outrigger holds, but we'll need to plan frequent water stops on our voyage home."

"I can't captain *Waka* with this thing on," Elān said, lifting the dzanti. "But I should keep it on in case of danger until we're out in the ocean. Kwa, can you remain captain until we're safe asea? Then I'll take off the dzanti and we can spread the map and figure out the quickest route home. A route far north and away from the Koosh would be ideal."

Kwa nodded and worked her way past Raven-sent to the stern seat. She unlocked the tiller. "Now, Hoosa." Hoosa shoved *Waka* off the riverbank into the current. Kwa pulled the tiller and turned the bow downriver. The current ran swift. Elān turned and saw smoke rising from the burning pole in the center of Tsedi. He thought he could hear a faint wailing on the wind.

CHAPTER 41

THE CREW SAW the shame pole as *Waka* left the river into Atna'tuu Bay. The pole stood at the southern end of the bay, just beyond the river mouth. Kwa maneuvered *Waka* onto the beach nearby. Caraiden's body was recognizable by his Aaní armor. Kwa and Ch'eet cut him down. Elān cleaned out a small bentwood in which to put his ashes. The crew lifted the body atop a large pyre that Hoosa made of dry driftwood, which Elān set alight with a flame from the dzanti.

As Caraiden burned, Elān, Ch'eet, and Kwa stretched their arms around each other and sang four times the Aaní death song.

> *Death's a widening way that countless feet have walked before,*
> *Our lives a path through trees to shadows on a river's shore.*
> *Haa Shúka is all we were, all we are, all we'll be.*
> *Until we meet again, dancing on the edge of this world once more.*

Chetdyl and Hoosa wandered the edge of the woods during the burning, watching, and guarding the crew as they cremated Caraiden. Ch'eet, Kwa, and Elān sat on the sand before the pyre as it burned. The blue waters of Atna'tuu Bay rippled with wind and shimmered as the wave tops reflected the bright sun.

It was late afternoon before Elān could collect Caraiden's ashes. He stored the bentwood-box-turned-urn in one of the waterproof holds in *Waka*'s starboard outrigger. As he sealed the hold, he felt a hand on his shoulder.

"Are you okay?" Kwa asked.

"All my emotions have been wrung from me," Elān replied. "I'm gray driftwood now."

Kwa nodded. "Caraiden wasn't the only one burned on this beach today."

The crew climbed aboard *Waka* and shoved off into Atna'tuu Bay with Kwa at the tiller. Elān unrolled the mainsail and spread it along the boom. Ch'eet unfurled the jib, and *Waka* bucked as it caught the wind. Kwa turned the bow westward—the direction of home.

CHAPTER 42

ONCE OUT OF Atna'tuu Bay, Elān took off the dzanti and stored it in the lockbox. He then spread the Koosh map out over the bentwood cooking box and with Kwa's help plotted a path homeward. They decided to run that night north up the Yahooni coast and turn northwest at dawn to make for the south end of Kasaan Island in Aaní waters, where—with a bit of luck and a lot of wind—they'd shelter the following night.

From Kasaan they'd navigate north toward East Shanaax and into Deception Pass—a narrow cliff passage between East Shanaax and Sukkwaan Island—and shelter in Naukati Bay, which, because of the treacherous current swirling from Deception Pass, was the only uninhabited bay on Sukkwaan. They thought it best to avoid all villages, Aaní or Deikeenaa. From Sukkwaan, it would be a long day's journey to Kéet Island and another long day's journey to Quintus on the south of Samish. They could be home in five, six days if the wind held. They would bypass Kwa's home village of Yelm—Kwa insisted her duty was to protect Elān until he was safe back at home—and head straight for Naasteidi to get the dzanti into Íxt's hands.

As you may know if you, like the crew, are of the ocean, in the great northwestern waters of Éil' the winds almost always blow from east to west. When the summer dawns over Éil', the wonderful warm winds come hard from the southeast and push westward off the mainland. The tacking struggle that *Waka* had on its journey east fell away on its voyage back home.

Kwa stayed at the tiller throughout the afternoon after Caraiden's cremation and late into that night. Hoosa and Chetdyl kept watch for Kwa while Elān and Ch'eet rested. The moon came out full and bright, lit up *Waka*'s sails, and illumined the dark outline of the mainland off starboard. Once, in the middle of the night, a canoe to the northeast ran from the mainland to intercept *Waka*. Kwa woke Elān, who opened the dzanti lockbox as he watched the mast-lantern of the unknown canoe approach. But *Waka* flew and, seeing that it would reach the intercept point too late, the unknown canoe turned and headed back toward the mainland.

In the morning, as the sun crested the mountains on the mainland to the east, Kwa handed the tiller over to Elān. She was exhausted and needed to sleep. They maneuvered around each other to trade places. "We're approaching Latseen's Line," she said to Elān. "Latseen's Wall is visible from the ocean, but we might be spotted if we remain close to the mainland. I think we should turn northwest now out into the open ocean."

Elān placed the Koosh map atop the bentwood in the stern behind his seat, looked it over, and then pushed the tiller, which sent *Waka* heading northwest away from the mainland.

Raven-sent, feeling the canoe shift direction, protested. "You were to take me home."

"I never promised to take you home," Elān said. "I said you could come aboard *Waka*."

"My village isn't far if we're near Latseen's Wall," Raven-sent replied. "I live in the Far Out Fort just beyond the wall."

"We're not taking you home."

"This isn't how Aaní treat each other," Raven-sent said. "You can't exile me."

"You exiled yourself when you betrayed our people," Elān said.

"I had no choice," Raven-sent yelled. "I was a captive."

Kwa yanked Raven-sent's neck ropes, choking him against the mast. "I'm trying to sleep," she said. "Don't make me kill you just so I can sleep." She held the ropes another moment, then let go, and Raven-sent gasped.

Sometime during the late morning or early afternoon, they crossed Latseen's Line. The detailed Koosh map didn't demarcate the line, but Elān knew from memory where in approximation it lay. There were no human-made lines on the sea or in the sky and they were far out in the open ocean with no Aaní island or any other land in sight to get a bearing. Other than the wind straining the sails and outriggers sizzling through the sea, there was no sound. Elān looked around. Sea and sky covered the entire world. Kwa and Ch'eet were asleep, and Chetdyl rested in the sun on *Waka*'s bow.

As a child, he believed Latseen's Line was a tangible property, something he could see and touch since it was real on every map he'd seen. Sitting in the stern of *Waka*, he realized Latseen's Line was an illusion. Its meaning was something humans agreed upon even to the point of death. *How many other illusions have meanings just because humans agree upon them?* Elān thought to himself. *And what happens when we stop agreeing on the meaning of an illusion? Does the world unravel, or do we become free?* Elān wished Íxt were here to talk to. He heard the voice of raven in his mind: *Wearing a silly mitten doesn't make you a philosopher, Crapshack.*

Elān laughed. "It's both, raven," he said aloud. "Latseen's Line is both illusion and reality."

Ch'eet and Hoosa stirred and looked back at Elān.

"Trouble?" Ch'eet asked.

"Nothing to be alarmed about," Elān replied. *But trouble nonetheless.*

*   *   *

LATER IN THE afternoon, Ch'eet stood from his seat in front of the mast, made his way to the back of *Waka*, and sat down in front of Elān with his back against the side of the canoe. Elān was surprised. He could see Ch'eet struggling to say something. For once, his smile was gone, and his face wore a heavy seriousness. His punctured eye was covered by a thin, black leather patch, but his good eye struggled to meet Elān's. Elān looked away at the open ocean in front of *Waka* to allow Ch'eet to feel less scrutinized.

"I know my brother Ch'aal' hurt you somehow," Ch'eet said in a whisper. "I know it in the way he talked about you and how he still talks about you. And I know it in the way you looked at me in the first days of our voyage. Fearful, as though I had stabbed you. I am not my brother, Elān. Ch'aal' is a boy pretending to be a warrior. You were a boy bookeater pretending to be a warrior. Now, I'm not sure what you are, but you are no boy. Maybe a bookeater warrior. That's what Caraiden always said your grandfather Latseen was. Whatever you are, you deserve better from my family and clan."

Elān tried hard not to cry. "Gunalchéesh. Your ancestors."

"And yours," Ch'eet replied. "I would like to repay the dishonor my brother caused you and your clan. What repayment would you have?"

Elān was shocked. In your world, no doubt, you have many ways of repaying a dishonorable act, but in the Aaní world such repayment often meant the taking of a life. Elān blurted, "Nothing. Coming on this voyage was more than enough to repay any insult your brother gave me. And your poor eye…"

"This voyage was my duty as an Aaní warrior and my poor eye will heal," Ch'eet replied. "What repayment would you have for the insult my brother gave you?"

"Just your friendship," Elān said. "And nothing else."

Ch'eet's smile returned. "You're a strange young man, Elān. I'm honored to be your friend. You have my forever friendship. I won't forget that my family and clan owe you a debt."

Elān and Ch'eet shared the silence of the ocean as a wind from the southeast filled *Waka*'s sails throughout the rest of the day into night. The moon came out full and bright as they approached the south end of Kasaan Island. Elān relaxed, knowing they were once again in Aaní waters. With the moon and Ch'eet's help, Elān navigated into a shallow, rocky bay at the south end of Kasaan without having to light the mast- or bow-lanterns. He beached *Waka* without camouflage and the crew made a small camp above the high tide line. Kwa untied Raven-sent so he could bathe and then tied him back to the mast for the night. She took the first watch. "I'll wake you when it's your watch," she told Ch'eet as she walked up to the trees. Elān fell asleep almost the moment he lay his head down on the blanket he'd spread over the sand.

He woke with the sun. He recalled waking several times in the night with a chill, but he'd slept better than he had in days. Kwa and Ch'eet lay in blankets beside him. Elān stood and walked down the beach to *Waka*. He looked at Raven-sent. He was slouched over, asleep. Kwa had bound his hands behind the mast but did not bind his neck, so he could sleep without suffocating. Raven-sent's hair was streaked white and gray and it took Elān a moment to realize the streaks were bird droppings.

"Where did you get that stupid leather shirt, Crapshack?"

Raven. Elān looked at his leather Yahooni cuirass and then up at the keen-eyed bird peering out over the mast-nest. "I'm too wrung out to argue with you," Elān said.

"Did you get your stupid mitten back?" raven asked.

"Yes," Elān replied. "Caraiden's dead."

Raven fell silent for a moment. "I would have wished to insult Sleepy Old Man Bellyache once more before he left this world." Elān took it as a compliment to Caraiden. "At least he helped you retrieve that stupid mitten of yours."

"He helped me more than you," Elān said. "This worthless Yahooni you sent to help me escape turned out to be a traitorous Aaní slave."

"Slave? What slave?"

"The one chained to the mast here that you crapped on all night."

Raven looked down at Raven-sent. "I've never seen this dumbass in my life."

"He came to my cell right after you did," Elān replied, "and told me you sent him. He told me to call him Raven-sent."

"I've never clapped eyes on this fathead, and calling somebody by a dumbass nickname doesn't mean that somebody is that name. Of course, Crapshack, there are exceptions."

"You didn't send Raven-sent?"

"Of course not," raven replied. "Look at him. His hair is full of crap. You think I'd send one craphead to help another craphead?"

"Yes. That is something you would do. And I heard your voice in my head," Elān said. "I repeated everything you told me to say."

"What?" raven asked.

"In Caskae's longhouse. I heard your voice in my head. I repeated every word you said."

"I heard you the first time," raven said, "but find less sense the second time. I've spent the past days in the wings of a paramour in Choosh, Crapshack, not inhabiting your unstable mind."

"I'm done with your trickery, stupid bird," Elān said. "I'm too drained to carry a conversation with you." He turned and walked up the beach toward the others.

Raven laughed. "Oh, Crapshack, that moldy old man has no idea what he set in motion when he asked you and Miss Sour Bag Traditional to go on this journey."

CHAPTER 43

THE CREW REFILLED their waterskins and after a quick breakfast of mussels, oysters, and clams, they left Kasaan on the strong western wind. Kwa, Ch'eet, and Elān took turns at *Waka*'s tiller throughout the day. Raven-sent stayed quiet except to protest whenever raven stuck his feathery ass out over the mast-nest to crap on him. They neared Deception Pass at dusk and risked lighting lanterns so they could see the treacherous cliffs as they approached. Kwa took the tiller when they entered—she'd been through the pass several times and was familiar with its currents—while Elān sat on *Waka*'s portside outrigger and Ch'eet sat on the starboard outrigger, lanterns and paddles at hand to protect *Waka* from any damage posed by the cliffs.

Kwa maneuvered *Waka* through the pass and beached the canoe in Naukati Bay. The crew hadn't seen another canoe the entire day or evening. Elān didn't think it too strange to be alone around the southern part of Sukkwaan Island. The island was home to many Aaní villages, but most lay in the north. Not many Aaní canoes attempted Deception Pass. He grew suspicious, however, about the emptiness of the ocean the next day as they made their way north of Kéet Island. The day arrived sunny and warm and the wind blew strong west by northwest as *Waka* flew across Aaní waters toward home, but still no other canoes were to be seen. Sailing season had come, and it was not like the Aaní to stay ashore when the sea beckoned.

They stopped on Kéet Island long enough to fill their waterskins and scavenge enough shore crabs and beach food to ease their hunger. They spent the night aboard *Waka* taking turns at the tiller and sleeping, and sailed through the next day toward Samish Island. Elān took the tiller when the sun was straight above *Waka*. He was excited at being so close to home, but worried about the emptiness of the sea. He kept a close eye on Chetdyl, whose nose would raise the alarm if Koosh or other enemies were nearby, but Chetdyl lay quiet on the bow the entire afternoon. As evening fell, Elān could see Samish Island rising in the west. The island couldn't come soon enough. The sun had fallen behind Samish, leaving the eastern side of the island in shadows as the horizon behind glowed red.

The moon was high when Elān pulled *Waka* onto the beach at the southern end of Samish Island just south of Quintus Kwáan. Chetdyl, Hoosa, and Ch'eet jumped into the surf and yanked *Waka* ashore. Elān locked the tiller, helped Kwa put up the mainsail, and then vaulted over the side of *Waka* into knee-deep sea on Samish's shore. He cupped his hands and pulled the sea of his homeland over his head and through his hair. The hair on the right side of his head had grown since he'd cut it all those days ago at Botson's Bay, but was still much shorter than the hair on the left side. He stood and walked to Chetdyl and Hoosa.

"You don't have to stay with us this evening if you're anxious to return home," Elān told them. "We'll be safe on Samish Island."

"We will stay with our crew through the night," Hoosa replied. "In the morning we will return home."

Elān fetched his blanket from an outrigger hold. Kwa had untied Raven-sent to let him stretch his legs and wash the raven crap from his hair and off his clothes. Elān lit two lanterns and handed one to Kwa. She held up the lantern and they watched Raven-sent cleanse himself.

"What will you do with him?" she asked Elān.

"I don't know yet," Elān replied. "I thought Íxt could use an apprentice."

"Does the old man want an apprentice?" Kwa asked.

"Doubtful, but maybe Íxt can fix Raven-sent's mind."

"Someone should fix your mind, dumbass," raven yelled down from his mast-nest.

Elān ignored the annoying bird. "I am trying to understand why someone would betray their own people. He doesn't seem like a bad-hearted person."

Raven laughed.

"Perhaps that's why you are becoming a teacher," Kwa said. "As a warrior I don't have to understand betrayal. I need only kill it."

"How about as a human instead of a warrior?" Elān asked. "Do the motives behind betrayal interest you?"

Kwa paused in thought. "Not if I don't know the person," she replied. "If a friend or relative betrayed me, though, or betrayed our people, then perhaps I would be interested in the reasons behind the betrayal."

"Are we not all related, though?"

"All the Aaní? I guess so," Kwa said. "But we're not all friends."

"I meant all of Éil'," Elān said. "Aren't we taught that all humans are related?"

Kwa frowned. "Maybe you're taught that in the bookeater longhouse, but that's not what we're taught in the warrior longhouse."

Elān paused. "Can I ask something of you, Kwa?"

"Of course," she replied.

"Would you become my mentor-aunt and train me to be a warrior?"

Kwa looked as though she were about to laugh, but when she spoke her voice was full of compassion. "You know I can't do that, Elān. It's not how things are done."

Elān was stung. "Caraiden was willing to be my mentor-uncle. At least I think he was willing."

"Whatever he may have promised you while at sea, he wouldn't have been allowed to be your mentor-uncle when you returned to Naasteidi, just as I can't be a mentor-aunt to you since you're not in the Longhouse of War and Diplomacy." She put her arm around Elān. "But be encouraged. Maybe whatever path you take in the future, whatever stories you craft, will become new Aaní tradition in the *looong* ago that comes after us." She ordered Raven-sent back to the canoe. He splashed some final handfuls of seawater over his body but seemed reluctant to leave the ocean. Kwa walked into the surf to fetch him. "I have this strange feeling that our stories will be ever-entwined after this journey, Elān, yours and mine."

"It makes me happy to hear that, Kwa," Elān said and, in verbalizing it, he realized that he had grown incredibly close to and fond of Kwa after all they'd been through.

Kwa laughed. "I'm not sure having our stories entwined is such a good thing, though." She grabbed Raven-sent by the arm and yanked him from the sea. Once she had secured Raven-sent to *Waka*'s mast, she leapt over the side of the canoe, grabbed her blanket from the outrigger, and walked up the beach with her lantern. "Sleep now," she said over her shoulder to Elān. "We're home."

In the morning, Chetdyl and Hoosa took their leave of *Waka* and the rest of the crew. It was a simple ceremony: a song sung in harmony, a final embrace, and a round of mutual "Your ancestors," and together Hoosa and the wolf walked up the beach and into the forest toward their villages. Elān had noticed bear tracks and wolf prints across the beach. Hoosa and Chetdyl's clans had come in the night to watch over their relatives.

Kwa and Ch'eet pushed *Waka* out to sea as Elān took the tiller. They only had a short distance to cover that day—around the south end of Samish and a short sail north to Naasteidi. An intense nervousness and excitement gripped Elān, and as the morning spun away and he pulled the tiller portside to turn *Waka* north around the end of Samish, he couldn't contain his excitement or his anxiety. No other canoes paddled the ocean surrounding Naasteidi.

"Almost home," he yelled up to Ch'eet. Ch'eet turned and smiled back. The bandage on his eye was fresh-changed and tied with new leather around his head. *Waka* ran crosswind north as the afternoon came and then Elān saw it: the long, tree-covered peninsula reaching out into the sea at the south of Naasteidi Bay. "Ei haaw!" he yelled.

Ch'eet stood in the bow and scanned the peninsula. "No canoes, no smoke from the longhouses."

"There might be a ban on travel with the Koosh canoes around." Elān didn't quite believe his words. His throat clenched with anxiety.

"No smoke, though," Ch'eet said. "Surely there'd be cookfires from Gooch's Dad and Raven's Tail."

"Maybe they're closed today," Elān said. *Waka* ripped through the sea northward. There was no human movement at all along the peninsula. Elān's heart thudded and sweat ran down his face. As *Waka* came around the end of the peninsula, Elān held his breath, and when *Waka* turned into Naasteidi Bay, he exhaled in relief. The longhouses stood intact. He could see his own clan house, the Flicker House, unmarred far down the beach.

"Thank Yéil!" Ch'eet yelled. "Naasteidi is unharmed." He pointed with his paddle at the Longhouse of War and Diplomacy set back along the peninsula. "They've boarded up the Longhouse and my barracks."

"There are no canoes on the shore," Kwa said.

Elān had to tack in a crooked path to the beach in front of the Flicker House. The large flicker pole, black-headed with blue eyes, red beak and wings, and red spots on a white body, high over the house looking out to sea, moved back and forth from port to starboard in Elān's view as he tacked *Waka* back through Naasteidi Bay.

There was no movement in the village. All the longhouses and clan houses were boarded up. The sea floor, sandy and seaweedy with Dungeness crabs scuttling from *Waka*'s shadow, came into clarity as they gained the beach. *Waka* scraped ashore and Ch'eet jumped into the surf. He unsheathed his sword and waited.

Kwa loosed the mainsail on the boom so it flapped in the wind. Elān locked the tiller. Still no movement in the village. Elān cut the bonds holding Raven-sent to the mast. A day's worth of fresh crap covered Raven-sent's hair and clothes. "We are in the village of Naasteidi," Elān said to Raven-sent. "At my family's clan house. You can wash here in the sea. You're unbound. You're free now."

Raven-sent stood, stretched, and climbed over the side of *Waka* into Naasteidi Bay. Elān picked up the unlocked lockbox, walked to the bow, and jumped down onto the beach. Home. Kwa jumped next to him and they walked over to Ch'eet. "The village looks abandoned," Ch'eet said.

The crew heard a door on the side of the Flicker House open. Kwa drew her sword. Elān opened the lockbox. The sight of the dzanti comforted him. He held his right hand over the weapon. A woman with long black hair now streaked with gray peered around the corner post of the Flicker House.

"Tláa."

"Elān."

"Your ancestors."

"And yours." Shaa sprinted seaward from the Flicker House to embrace her son, Skaan ran right behind her. Even old Íxt jogged down to the beach. The reunion, as you may know if you've ever returned from a moon at sea away from loved ones, was tearful, both joyous and bittersweet. Shaa, Skaan, and Íxt couldn't fathom the death of Caraiden. And, deep inside where words do not touch, Shaa mourned the change in her son and the loss of something that was with him when he'd left just a moon before.

"We did it." Elān handed the opened lockbox to Íxt. "But I lost my key."

Íxt pulled a key from a leather strap around his neck. "I still have mine," he said. He looked inside for a moment, smiled, and then closed the lid and locked it.

"Inside is also a Koosh map and Koosh jishagoon and a forever-welcome tináa from the Aankaawu of Choosh," Elān said.

"And many tales accompany them, no doubt." Old Íxt smiled. "Study much on the journey, did you, for your upcoming exams?"

"Not once," Elān laughed. "And I lost my books."

"I'm sure you learned much more than you ever could from a book," Íxt replied. He turned to Ch'eet. "Good to see you again, Ch'eet. I hope whatever happened to your eye isn't permanent."

"No, Mr. Íxt," Ch'eet replied. He tapped the leather patch over his eye. "This is just temporary. My sight is returning."

"Glad to hear it," Íxt replied.

"This is Kwa," Elān said, introducing the warrior to Íxt and his parents. "She's the warrior from Yelm. Without her, we would have all died. I owe her my life."

"You have my gratitude, Kwa," Íxt said. "What you've done may have saved the Aaní and all of Éil'."

"Gunalchéesh," Kwa said. "I began this voyage by stating to the crew and the ocean that I was displeased to go on this journey. I apologize to you Íxt, the Flicker clan, and especially you, Elān. I was wrong. I would travel the seas again with you as captain whenever you ask. Especially if it means we can kill more Koosh." She turned to Shaa and Skaan. "Your son brought honor to the Flicker clan on this voyage. He is the indeed the grandson of the great Latseen."

"Your ancestors, Kwa," Shaa said.

"And yours."

Íxt addressed the crew. "You have many questions no doubt, and many stories, as do we. Most questions will have to wait but these few perhaps I can answer. Koosh canoes are attacking villages on Samish Island and other Aaní islands across northwest Éil'. Naasteidi villagers retreated days ago to their strongholds in the mountains. Yelm also abandoned its village, Kwa, and took refuge in the mountains. They are safe, last we heard. Your parents, Elān, refused to leave without you and have been hiding in the Flicker House awaiting your return. I too stayed. But now we should make our way to the mountains. Is that lousy raven still with you?"

"You dung-filled seal's stomach. You owe me a winter and three moons of salmon, plus five regular-sized bentwoods of the finest smoked sockeye," raven replied from within his mast-nest. "I'll never forget your little joke with those tiny boxes, you moldy skeleton."

"Come," Íxt said to raven. "You'll get all the salmon you can eat in the mountains."

Skaan pointed to Raven-sent. "Son, who's this one in the sea?"

"His name is Raven-sent," Elān said. "He's one of our cousins from the Far Out Fort on the mainland near Latseen's Wall. But he's a traitor and a betrayer for the Yahooni."

"Why is he here?" Shaa asked.

"I thought Íxt might know the answer to that," Elān said.

Íxt smiled. "Perhaps. But now hurry and make haste into the mountains. Grab your belongings. We must go. You, Raven-sent, come with us."

The crew retrieved their weapons and belongings and Caraiden's ashes from *Waka*. Elān grabbed the Koosh-made Tas. They tied up the sails and pulled *Waka* far up the beach, almost to the Flicker House, and tied the canoe off bow and stern to the house. The crew covered the body and outriggers in heavy canvas to keep it from cracking in the sun. Elān ran his hand along *Waka*'s outrigger. "Thanks for bringing us home safe," he whispered to the canoe.

Kwa and Ch'eet stood with Íxt and Raven-sent on the cobbled street that would take them through the village center and out onto the forest road. Shaa and Skaan were gathering things in the Flicker House and were about to lock up as Elān came up from the beach. "Wait," he said to his parents. "Let me change clothes and get a warm coat. Take this." He handed his father the Tas. "It's Koosh-made." His father hesitated for a moment, then grabbed the Tas.

"We'll meet you behind the village on the forest road," Íxt warned. "Do not tarry. Your people await you in the mountains. This weapon will bring them hope."

Skaan gave Elān the key to the Flicker House kitchen door. "Be quick."

Elān walked into the dark clan house. The windows were boarded, and no light seeped into the house except through the open kitchen door. Elan walked through every room. Memories of childhood flooded his mind. He stopped in his room, changed clothes, and loaded a few shirts and pants and an oiled waterproof sea coat into a pack. He looked at his small room. A bed with a heavy wool blanket woven with a now faded flicker design sat low in the corner. On the floor and windowsills lay seashells and rocks, arrowheads and fishhooks, and a few antlers from his youthful hunting trips with Ch'aal'. Overwhelmed, he left his room and followed the weak light toward the kitchen door.

"Elān."

Elān stopped. Raven stood in the shadows on the counter, under the cupboard where Elān had once trapped him in darkness. Raven's tail feather, the one that Elān had bitten in what now seemed a time *looong* ago, lay on the counter.

"Elān."

Raven had never called him by his real name.

"Raven?"

"You know where you have to take that weapon," raven said, "and it isn't to any stupid stronghold in the mountains."

"I gave the dzanti to Íxt," Elān said. "He knows what to do with it."

"That drooling sack of bear crap will have no more idea how to use that weapon than those lousy Yahooni at Tsedi."

"I brought the dzanti back. I've done what was asked," Elān protested. "I'm done."

Raven peered unblinking into Elān's eyes. "You know who I am, and you know the truth of what I say."

Elān didn't reply.

"Elān. You know where you must take that weapon," raven said again.

Elān stayed silent.

"Elān." Raven's dark eyes reflected sunlight into Elān's.

"Saaw Island," Elān said. "To the place the Koosh call the Door."

"Yes," raven replied. He leapt off the counter and flew out the open door into the sun. "Laters, Fathead."

ACKNOWLEDGMENTS

I MUST FIRST say gunalchéesh (thank you) to my sons Chet and Aiden—this novel began as a way to help them overcome their homesickness when we moved to Aotearoa in 2013. I would write a page or so a day and read it to them every night for their feedback. (This is for you, boys. Sorry for what happens to your character, Aiden. Wait until you see what I do to Chet's character in the next book!) Gunalchéesh to my supportive and very patient wife Kristen. Gunalchéesh to my family: Amelia/Teew, Francis, Carl, Ray, Mary, Skip, Jon, Pat, Mike, and my many cousins, nieces, and nephews. And gunalchéesh to the Russell, Caskey, Klaphake, and Bernard families. And, of course, a gunalchéesh to Jose Chaves.

A bittersweet gunalchéesh to my grandmother Teew—who walked into the forest in 1997—for gifting stories of the kóoshdakáa and of her life in Klawock and helping me with the Tlingit language. Always my inspiration. Gunalchéesh to the Peratrovich clan and an aatlein gunalchéesh to Stanley and Evelyn Peratrovich for being our family's historians and for all the support and knowledge. A special gunalchéesh to Evelyn Edenso for gifting stories of the Kooyu Kwáan and stories of my grandmothers going back three greats all the way to Kaat'eich.

A massive gunalchéesh to Lauren Bajek at the Liza Dawson Agency. This wouldn't have been possible without you, Lauren. I am grateful for all the work you've done. And a huge gunalchéesh to Amy Borsuk and the incredible team at Solaris Press. It has been a joy to watch this novel come to fruition.

FIND US ONLINE!

www.rebellionpublishing.com

/solarisbooks   /solarisbks

/solarisbooks   /solarisbooks.
bsky.social

SIGN UP TO OUR NEWSLETTER!

rebellionpublishing.com/newsletter

YOUR REVIEWS MATTER!

Enjoy this book? Got something to say?

Leave a review on Amazon, GoodReads or with your
favourite bookseller and let the world know!